A CLASH OF CARNIVORES

ALSO BY LISELLE SAMBURY

A Mastery of Monsters
Tender Beasts
Delicious Monsters
Blood Like Fate
Blood Like Magic

A Clash of Carnivores

LISELLE SAMBURY

Margaret K. McElderry Books

New York Amsterdam/Antwerp London
Toronto Sydney/Melbourne New Delhi

MARGARET K. McELDERRY BOOKS
An imprint of Simon & Schuster Children's Publishing Division
1230 Avenue of the Americas, New York, New York 10020

Jacket design by Greg Stadnyk

Interior design by Irene Metaxatos
The text for this book was set in LTC Metropolitan Pro.
Manufactured in the United States of America
First Edition
10 9 8 7 6 5 4 3 2 1
Library of Congress Cataloging-in-Publication Data
Names: Sambury, Liselle author
Title: A clash of carnivores / Liselle Sambury.
Description: First edition. | New York : Margaret K. McElderry Books, 2026. | Audience: Ages 14 up | Audience: Grades 10–12 | Summary: Seeking vengeance for her mother's murder, eighteen-year-old August searches for answers within the secret society of Monsters by competing in a dangerous tournament with her bonded partner, Virgil.
Identifiers: LCCN 2025033629 (print) | LCCN 2025033630 (ebook) |
ISBN 9781665957397 hardcover | ISBN 9781665957403 ebook
Subjects: CYAC: Secret societies | Monsters | Revenge | Contests | Fantasy | BISAC: YOUNG ADULT FICTION / Fantasy / Contemporary | YOUNG ADULT FICTION / Fantasy / Dark Fantasy | LCGFT: Fantasy fiction | Novels
Classification: LCC PZ7.1.S2545 Cl 2026 (print) | LCC PZ7.1.S2545 (ebook)
LC record available at https://lccn.loc.gov/2025033629
LC ebook record available at https://lccn.loc.gov/2025033630

AUTHOR'S NOTE & CONTENT WARNING

While this is a work of fiction, some of the topics discussed do exist in our real world. I've compiled a list of content warnings to help those who may need them. I've done my best to address everything here, but I keep an updated list on my website in case I am later informed of triggers that I may have missed. Please visit that site for the most updated information.

While these subjects are important to the story, if at any point you find the material distressing or triggering, you are encouraged to stop reading and return only if you feel ready. Your well-being matters.

Death of a parent, child death, discussions of fatphobia, mentions of disordered eating (restriction, overexercising), drug and alcohol use, violence/gore, mention of suicide

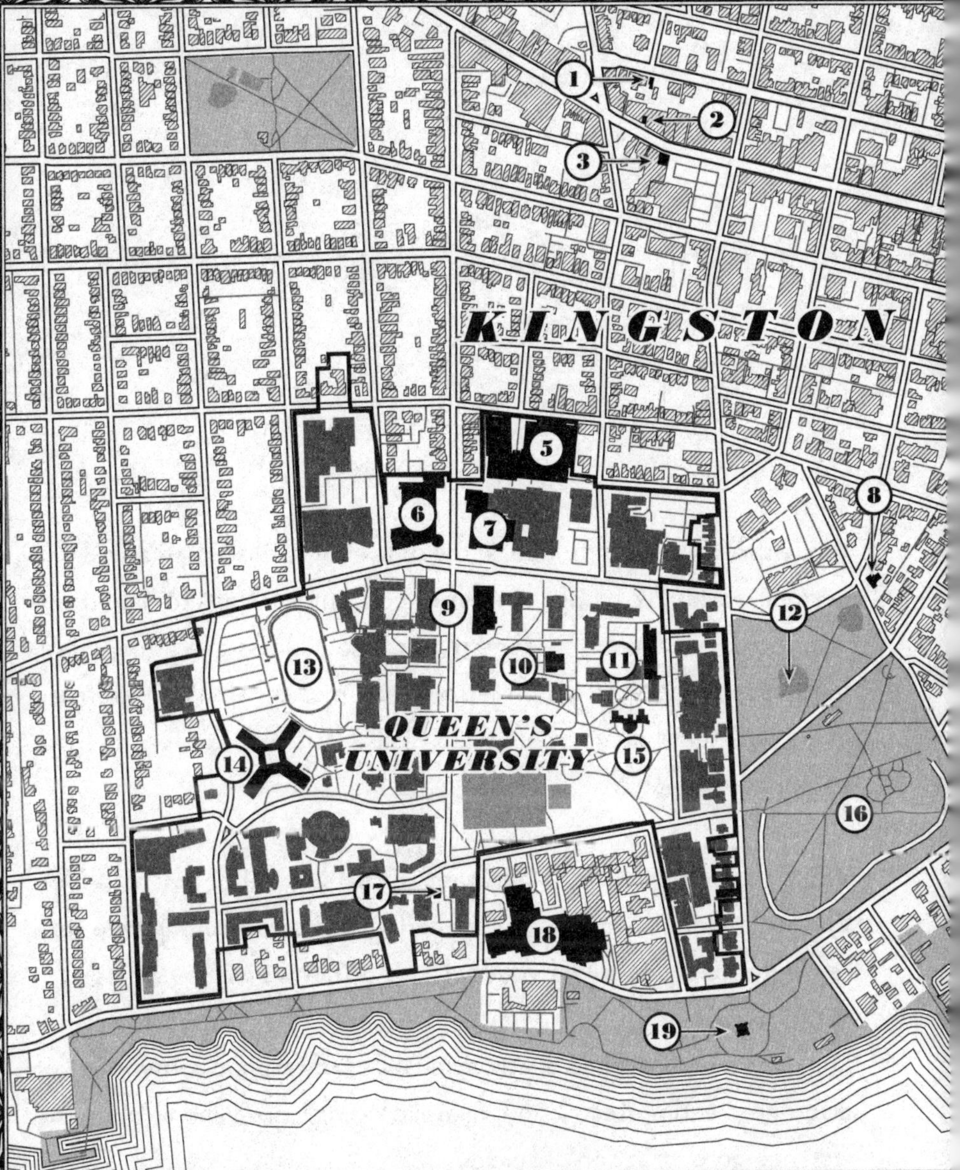

1. Yang Family Dojang
2. Bubba's Pizzeria
3. Stages Nightclub
4. Ferry to Wolfe Island
5. Queen's Athletics & Recreation Centre (ARC)
6. Joseph S. Stauffer Library
7. John Deutsch University Centre
8. McIntosh Castle
9. Douglas Library
10. The Campus Bookstore
11. Humphrey Hall
12. Cricket Field
13. Tindall Field
14. Victoria Hall
15. Summerhill
16. City Park
17. Yellow House Student Centre for Equity and Inclusion
18. Kingston General Hospital
19. Murney Tower Museu National Historic Site of Canada

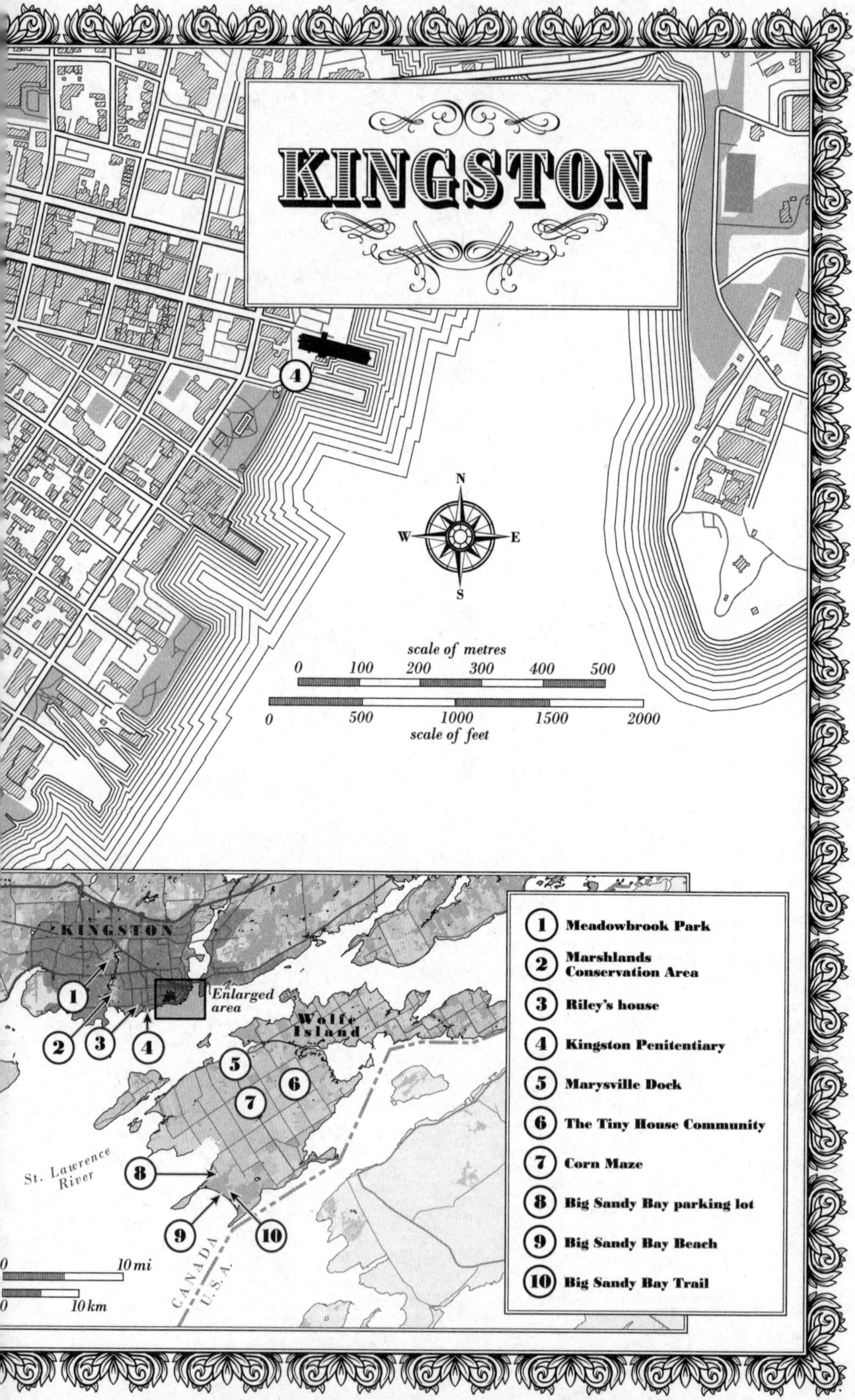

KINGSTON
N
W
E
S
scale of metres
0 100 200 300 400 500
0 500 1000 1500 2000
scale of feet
KINGSTON
Enlarged area
Wolfe Island
St. Lawrence River
CANADA
U.S.A.
0 10 mi
0 10 km
1 Meadowbrook Park
2 Marshlands Conservation Area
3 Riley's house
4 Kingston Penitentiary
5 Marysville Dock
6 The Tiny House Community
7 Corn Maze
8 Big Sandy Bay parking lot
9 Big Sandy Bay Beach
10 Big Sandy Bay Trail

A CLASH OF CARNIVORES

CHAPTER ONE

Riley

This is supposed to be the best day of my university career. My official acknowledgment as the president of the Queen's University Black Student Society. The first Townsend to hold that title in over sixty years. Achieving what both Dad and Grandma failed to acquire during their tenure. A title that I was sure I would have to wait until I was a senior to even attempt to seize.

Doing it as a sophomore was unimaginable. But I did.

At no point in the process of working toward this goal did I expect to find myself standing before the elder council while they stare down their noses at me, my peers lining both sides of the room, not for the official acknowledgment of my status as president, but a meeting held explicitly to challenge it.

The ballroom of the new clubhouse is empty of any adornment besides the four crystal chandeliers and the dais raised at least six feet off the ground. The podium's desktop is lined with oak trim

interrupted by shiny metal labels featuring the names of the five elder council members who occupy the leather chairs behind the mounted mics: the speaker, secretary, and three sitting members.

People who I was raised to respect and revere. People who now seek to rip from me the one thing I've wanted most in the world.

I think briefly of Sammie, standing next to me, beaming and alive. Instead of the way I last saw her, eyes wide and empty, back torn open and bloody.

I chew the inside of my cheek and stand straight, chest out, meeting the gazes of the esteemed alumni.

Dr. Michaels sits in the middle place as the speaker, operating as the voice for all alumni. Salt-and-pepper curls cover his shaved head, and he folds his fingers together as he regards me. "We'll be opening this gathering of the elder council and enlightened members now. Today we'll address the events of the fall semester, which included a confrontation with the Society for the Pursuit of the Fundamentals of Learning and an early shift in the presidency. Would you like to explain how you came to ascend from treasurer to president, Ms. Townsend?"

It's a small consolation that my parents retired from the council last year and are now happy to concentrate fully on their real estate empire. I couldn't handle it if they had to participate in this. I've been lectured and berated enough by them already.

I say, "There was an internal vote among the enlightened members, and a decision was made. I assume that I was chosen because I was addressing a threat that my predecessor was not."

On either side of the ballroom, my peers are still. They represent the chosen few among the larger student society, those aware of the true origin of our organization dating back to our founder Joseph

Lawrence's original purpose set in 1864: to gather his own under one banner to protect each other from the threat of Monsters. And from the society who claims to govern them. Only a select few enlightened members wield artifacts, and even fewer hold a student council title, but we all are aligned in this mandate.

"And who authorized the calling of this vote?" Ms. Howard asks, adjusting the braids that lie across her shoulders.

"I did. As per the QBSS handbook section 8, article 6, in times of peril when the president fails to sufficiently protect our organization, there may be a vote called to reassign any student council member to take over as the new acting president."

I have to thank Grandma for forcing me to memorize that little notebook from cover to cover as though it was equivalent to the Bible she kept dog-eared and tabbed on her nightstand. The handbook was written by Joseph Lawrence himself, and it's the be-all and end-all of most things in QBSS. Knowing how to make it work for me is a good skill for law school in the future too, after I get my business degree.

"That takeover is meant to be temporary," Ms. Howard says. What she's not saying is that Malachi is her nephew and she wants him to keep his position despite the fact that two members died under his watch.

Two . . . or three, including Sammie.

I need to stop thinking about her.

I say, "There's no note in the text that this change in presidency is temporary."

"It's *implied.*"

"With all due respect, ma'am, the handbook is a document meant to be followed in a legal sense, not a biblical sense. If implications

were considered, then much of it would become irrelevant."

Her lip curls.

"Ms. Townsend is correct," Ms. Nelson says. As secretary, it's her duty to be up-to-date with the handbook and record minutes. "That matter is closed. If the debate is whether she is suitable to preside as president, that remains open." She turns to me. "And we, as the elder council, have the authority to deem you unfit and call a new vote. One in which you are no longer on the ballot."

A bead of sweat rolls down my back. "To help assuage the concerns of the council, I will note that I have performed well in my duties as treasurer, I am a Historic member of this society, and I was instrumental in bringing the man who murdered our members to justice."

If instrumental meant that I was bait to lure out Bernie Mathers. Though, bless her soul, August isn't anywhere near crafty enough to think of using me to get what she wants. She brought me to give me a chance to avenge Sammie. Her innocence is almost charming.

There are murmurs among the elders as they consider what I've said. The other two sitting members, men I'm not as familiar with, have been quiet thus far, but that doesn't mean they don't have opinions. I slide my eyes to the right, where the current student council stands. Darius, our secretary, who honestly takes appalling notes, stands with his shoulders slouched. Meanwhile Jackson, my now ex-boyfriend and our social chair, is alert but avoids looking at me. Which is difficult, I imagine, because *everyone* is looking at me.

He and Malachi should have reported that I took off with August and her group to confront Mathers. I can guess why Jackson wouldn't. Stay in my good books, maybe try to get back together, which will *not* be happening. But Malachi . . . he should have tattled

right away. He would be in a better position to contest my presidency that way. I don't understand his endgame.

The last member of the student council, Inaya, is staring at me so hard that I couldn't ignore her if I wanted to. Her hair is freshly twisted with perfect parts and edges, and she has a full face done impeccably. She always looks like she's heading to an event and has the sort of grades others abuse medication to get. She was vice president last semester and should have become president when Malachi graduated at the end of this year. Instead, I became president, and Malachi dropped to VP, which pushed her into the treasurer spot. Furthermore, I'm a year below her. She'll never get a chance to become president as long as I hold the position.

"The girl can't even wield the sickle," Ms. Howard sneers. "All this talk about protecting the members, and the weapon is dull in her hands. Not to mention she lost the chain in battle so she can't even fall back on that. Denying it to our current treasurer as well, I might add."

It takes everything in me not to swallow. August better not make me regret giving that necklace to her. I saw her activate it. She has some connection to QBSS, and *I* need to maintain that connection to *her*. Especially now that the Doctorate candidate who already favored her has become the leader of their society. There is a long game to be played.

I unchain the pendant around my neck and grip it within my fist. Golden light blooms from between my fingers as the weapon grows from a tiny metal charm into a full sickle the length of my forearm. "Respectfully, I have to disagree. I have no problem with the sickle."

When Ms. Howard grins, I falter for the first time, my grasp on the weapon loosening. "So you don't mind a little challenge, then?" she asks.

I look at the other members of the council, but none of them are speaking against her. It's not enough that I was a good treasurer and a Historic, and I helped put a murderer in the ground. They want more.

They always do.

The crowd parts, and Malachi steps forward. He slips his necklace free of its clasp and clenches it in his right hand.

I grit my teeth. If I ask why this is necessary, it'll make me look weak. If I back down, it'll be even worse.

I bend my knees and bring the sickle in front of my face.

Malachi's pendant thickens and lengthens into a golden staff that's somehow taller than his already more than six-foot frame. He holds it with an ease that I lack with my own weapon.

He charges with a shout, and I only just manage to bring the sickle up to block before he's moving again. He sweeps out at my feet, and I jump in time to evade, but as I land, he shoves the end into my stomach, and I gasp.

I slump onto my knees and drop the sickle, struggling for air that won't come. I bite down on my lip hard enough that it bleeds, the copper taste running along my tongue. When I look up, Malachi stares at me with a wide grin, canines flashing gold. He steps aside and reveals the frowns of the elder council.

With the chain, I could have taken him. But the president does not wield the chain. They wield the sickle. The only artifact with the power to transform further and increase in power. The goal isn't the sickle, but the scythe. Except it won't transform. It's useless.

Just like me.

Dr. Michaels taps his nails on the table. "What shall we do about this Ms. Townsend? The members have chosen you, but it's clear to

us that your skill is lacking. And Bernard Mathers is dead. What reason do we have to allow you to continue in this position when we could reinstate Mr. Jones?"

If they take this title from me, where will I be? How could I come back from that sort of shame? I'm a Historic. A direct descendant of Joseph Lawrence. I should be better than this. I need to make myself invaluable to the board. Give them a reason to keep me on long enough to prove that I should be here.

I think of Mathers. Of what made me worthwhile to him.

"The weapon," I say. "Mathers was looking for an artifact. He believed it had the power to kill Gods." Some of the council scoff, but I keep going. "Obviously metaphorical. Still, the society has no record of it, nor do we, but it must exist. A weapon of that degree of power could give us an edge over the society. We have lived in 'peace' with them this whole time under *their* terms. This could allow us to make our own terms."

"How do you plan to find this weapon?" Dr. Michaels asks. "Of course if we have an artifact of that magnitude, it would be valuable to study it, especially as we lost members in Mathers's pursuit of it. Yet, if no one before you has managed, then how will you?"

This is the moment when I could lose them. But nothing ventured, nothing gained. "I have a society contact. She's a Bachelor paired with the ward of Henry Scott, and she was nominated by Adam Shaw himself for that candidacy. I believe she has the resources to assist in this search."

The board is silent for a moment as they stare at me. This, I know, is what they want more than anything. It's what we all want. To no longer be under the thumb of the Learners. Ms. Howard opens her mouth, but Dr. Michaels silences her with a hand. "The

new Doctorate nominated her?" I nod. He shares looks with some of the other board members. "Why would she help you?"

"Because someone in her family was one of us. Before it was lost, she happened to touch the chain and was able to activate it. Someone's given her bones to us. There's a connection there." What I don't say is that this connection can be exploited. It doesn't need to be said. I can see it in the way the council members trade glances.

Dr. Michaels straightens in his seat. "You have until the end of the semester. If you cannot hand over the weapon by then, you will give the sickle to him instead." This with a tilt of his head toward Malachi.

"Yes, sir," I say.

Not that Malachi has proven himself as any more adept with the sickle than I am. He can't call forth the scythe, either. But they would still rather the weapon be in his hands than in mine.

Even if he could wield the scythe, only I would have the stomach to draw blood.

He hid behind his title while our members were slaughtered. While Sammie was carved up and left to bleed out. *Alone.* He had no business calling himself president. And now I know that the board doesn't think I have any more right to the title than him.

They don't now, anyway. But come the end of the semester, they will.

CHAPTER TWO

August

I first understood death in Mom's arms. I was eight years old, and Grandma was dead. That was why I had to wear my black dress and stockings and the tight formal shoes that cut into my ankles. After the service, we came home, and I went to the fridge to get a drink and paused at the sight of the calendar there. Two weeks from that day, Grandma was supposed to come stay with us. I turned and asked Mom if Grandma would sleep in my room when she came.

Mom folded me into her arms. She said that Grandma wouldn't be coming over. She was gone. She wasn't going to announce her arrival and give me a kiss that was too wet, or make macaroni pie and stewed chicken for dinner, or snuggle with me in my tiny bed, where she'd snore too loud.

That was when I cried.

At first, I cried because of Grandma. But as it went on, I cried because Mom was holding me now, but what would I do when she couldn't? When she was gone too?

In that moment, her death became my worst fear.

Now I know there's something worse than the death of a parent.

The *preventable* death of a parent.

If I had answered her phone call, if I had been there as I am now, with Virgil at my side, power running through my veins, I could have torn her murderer apart and spat on the corpse.

I flex my hand around the paper cup of hot chocolate. Ever since Jules told me what really happened, that Mom was dead and not missing, that bit of monstrousness inside me that reared its head during the initiation has been growing. I've had a little over two weeks to let the knowledge fester. It's alive now. Flexing its claws, its hackles raised.

Waiting for the chance to feed.

I stare at the marshmallow floating in my hot chocolate, which I'm told is in the likeness of Dr. Weiss, the first ever Doctorate of the society, whose graduation to the title, and creation of it, happened on January 11, 1865. I could have done without knowing the exact year, but Corey insisted on adding it when she explained the holiday. The celebration is why we're in the Marshlands this Saturday, nearly a month after fighting Bernie and his once-presumed-missing-and-now-dead son in this same place.

They've set up the area like a winter carnival with stalls serving food and drinks, and games where you can win stuffed animal prizes. The baskets you throw balls into are shaped like the maw of a lionlike Monster. I've also seen kids running around with other Monster-themed masks and merchandise. It's a good way to celebrate without giving any of the secrets of the society away.

I pull my toque lower on my head to cover my ears more. It's an obnoxiously spirited one, mostly navy with a tricolor pom-pom that

declares QUEEN'S, and if that wasn't enough, there's also a big *Q* on the brim. I wouldn't be caught dead in it except Bailey sewed in a satin lining for me so my braids wouldn't get messed up. So here I am, wearing my aunt's Christmas gift despite myself.

Now I get why most winter festivities happen in November and December, because I always forget how January is somehow the coldest month of the year. I slurp my drink and wince as the liquid, hotter than I expected, burns my tongue.

"The Monster that was partnered with McCray, his sister, had a lionlike form," Corey says, catching me looking at the ball-throwing game. Wilden McCray, the first Master.

"I guess this whole day is about celebrating firsts," I say.

For some of us, anyway. While the Progressive faction of the society is happy that Adam became the seventh Doctorate, I doubt the Traditionalists are. They wanted his brother James to win. To continue a history of oppressing Monsters and elevating Masters under the guise of sticking to the traditional values that Dr. Weiss set out when he created the Learners' Society. As opposed to Adam, who plans to lead with Progressive ideals, giving Monsters more autonomy and striving for equality.

"This is a great first for Adam too. The first Progressive Doctorate," Virgil says. When I turn to him, his eyes shift to look around the festival grounds.

It's only been three weeks since me and Virgil bonded, Master and Monster, linking ourselves together to save his humanity. It's been even less time since we kissed for the first and last time. Agreeing not to cross that line again and actually following through, however, are two different things. We both know it's a bad idea to couple up with someone who you're bound to for life regardless of how your romantic

relationship turns out. I just didn't expect his solution to our situation would be to act like the feelings never existed in the first place.

I was on board with not moving closer. I didn't agree to pull back.

I glance at Virgil's cup of hot chocolate, eyes narrowing. "I feel like you got a bigger marshmallow."

He rolls his eyes. "They're the same size."

"Are they?"

Sighing, he lifts his marshmallow out of his cup with two fingers and plops it into mine. "There, happy?"

I glance up, and he's close enough for me to see his eyelashes behind his glasses and smell the chocolate on his breath. It's the longest he's made eye contact with me since the break ended. "Very," I say.

He swallows and steps away, taking a big gulp of his drink that I'm sure must burn.

I scan the crowd of people moving through the space as if the milk on my tongue doesn't suddenly taste sour. "Isn't Carrigan supposed to be here?"

Corey says, "Technically, yes. But Carrigan doesn't tend to make a habit of being where he's supposed to be."

The middle Shaw brother, and also apparently Mom's old university friend, has recently made my shit list. Partially because Carrigan was supposed to help Jules when my brother started showing signs of turning and instead did nothing, but mostly because now that I know Mom was murdered, he's become suspect number one. I don't care if she was the one who jumped off that cliff—she was forced to do it. And jilted lover is a motive that never gets old.

Jules is less warm to this theory. Even I can admit that it's not

enough evidence. I want nothing more than to make Mom's murderer pay in blood, but I need something concrete. I have Virgil to consider. My missteps can land him a permanent spot in the Kingston Penitentiary with the rest of the imprisoned Monsters. Assuming they let him live at all.

I need to figure out whether Carrigan has an alibi for November 25, the day Mom disappeared the year before last. And, if he doesn't, connect him to the Monster who attacked her and Jules. With that sort of evidence, Adam will have to consider punishing his brother. Ideally, he'll let me do it.

I was hoping to strategize with Jules today, but apparently his new partner, Natalie, doesn't "do" Doctorate Day. Natalie is her own question mark. As the unofficial leader of the Pro-Liberation Coalition, the faction that wants to see Monsters set free, she led a rebellion with the Wilds for that purpose and failed. She came out of it pretty well in comparison to the Wilds, who despite not needing Master partners to keep control in their monstrous forms, became chained in another way, by the agreement between them and Cyrus Shaw, the sixth Doctorate. Last semester, the Wilds seemed to be waiting to see how the election would shake out, but they haven't made any moves since.

I, for one, intend to keep a close eye on Natalie. I won't let her use Jules. Especially since people around her tend to end up dead. It'll help to keep Jules focused on finding our mom's killer and away from anything Natalie might get him involved in.

"We should head over to Adam's tent now," Virgil says. "Our time's in ten minutes."

I groan. "The tent is like two minutes away. How early do you want to be?"

"Early. Because when you're early, you're always on time."

"Jesus Christ, what's that from, the Goody Two-shoes handbook?"

"You're not going to like . . . do anything, right?" Corey asks. "About Carrigan. I know you have your reasons for suspecting his involvement in your mom's death, but he's still the Doctorate's brother."

"I want to keep an eye on him, that's all." I chug the rest of my drink and crush the cup, dumping it in a nearby recycling bin. "Fine, let's go to Adam's tent."

Virgil beams and leads the way. I give Corey a look behind his back, and she just smiles. Given that they've been best friends for years, she's used to the way he is. As we walk through the field, she pauses and shakes out her left leg—the one she lost in her attempt at the Bachelor candidacy and now uses with the addition of a prosthesis below her knee.

"You good?" I ask.

She grimaces. "The cold sometimes makes my little leg shrink and then my prosthesis doesn't fit right, so it's uncomfortable."

Virgil turns back. "You don't have to wait with us. You can hang out by the heaters, and we can meet you after." The society, ever prepared, set up a seating area with a dozen portable heaters to help attendees stay warm during the celebration.

"Good idea," she says. "I saw Margot and Isaac over there too. Text me when you're done."

We wave to her and continue to Adam's tent. It's an off-white structure with its own indoor heating, I'm sure, set up in the center of the festival. It's giving VIP Coachella camping experience with the small patio in front with decorative plants on either side. As part

of Doctorate Day, every student, Master, and Monster is allowed to sign up for a five-minute time slot to chat with him. Formerly, Monsters weren't allowed for some vague safety reason, a rule Adam has already changed.

To my immense joy, Henry signed me and Virgil up for a joint five minutes so we can kiss the ring. Though Henry didn't much care for me phrasing it that way. Essentially, I'm to say thank you to Adam for nominating me last semester so that I could have a chance to become a Bachelor. And also for vouching for us and Virgil with the whole Bernie thing so Virgil wouldn't be murdered for technically having tried to run away.

"How do you say thanks for having our backs to the leader of a secret society?" I ask.

Virgil sighs. "Just be normal and say thank you. Adam did us several solids last semester. We're incredibly fortunate to have this connection to him. We owe him and Henry *everything*."

"Everything? We did a lot of work too. I, for one, am very proud of how I avoided dying." I shake my head. "Also, why would you think I wouldn't be normal?"

"Just don't, like, make it into a joke and bow or something."

I press a hand to my chest. "I would never, *never*, jest in front of the king."

Virgil is about to say something else when a booming laugh from across the way draws our attention. James is cackling and waving around a paper cup that's been layered onto several other cups. Like he's drunk multiples and just keeps stacking them. His wife's smile is tight, and their two kids are talking to her about something. They look like they're heading to Adam's tent, but James is struggling with walking in a straight line.

I beam. "Oh, he's fucked up."

Virgil winces. "Just look away. He's clearly not dealing well with his first Doctorate Day after losing the election."

"Um, no, I will not look away. Holy shit, what if he falls?"

My partner, meanwhile, tugs on the sleeve of a random white guy who seems to be our age. The guy turns and narrows his eyes at Virgil. He's a redhead, slim, and only wearing a light jacket for weather that demands something warmer. On his right bicep, he's got a forest green circular patch of a pair of sharp-toothed jaws clamped around a sword. I've seen the odd person with that patch today and keep forgetting to ask about it.

"Shouldn't you handle that?" Virgil asks the guy.

The redhead only narrows his eyes further. "How is that my job?"

"You're a proctor. . . ."

My eyes widen. That must be what that patch means. Proctors are Wilds who are bound by the agreement to oversee the Monster's Ball. Not that I understand what that means. I haven't even been briefed on the competition itself yet despite the fact that I'm meant to compete in it to become a Master in less than a month.

"Yes," he says. "I proctor. I don't deal with drunk Doctorate candidates. Especially not at the demand of a guy who was just arguing like a married couple with his partner."

Virgil splutters, and I throw a cool look at the redhead. The group in line with us are glancing at him in a way I'm familiar with from last semester, curled lips and barely concealed disdain. We got more than our fair share of those with me being an outsider and Virgil being hated because of his parents' attempt to kill the Doctorate. But since we've become an official Bachelor-Monster pair, attitudes have changed toward us for the better.

Their derision is 100 percent focused on the proctor.

I look back at James, who has tripped and whose family is now trying to keep him upright. Honestly, this event needed the entertainment. I dig out my phone and start recording.

"*August!*" Virgil hisses.

"What? He was such a dick to us last year. This is gold."

"Stop recording!"

With a sigh, I'm about to hit the stop button when something glows from within the shadow of the trees. I squint, zooming in on it. "What is th—"

Two Monsters burst out of the foliage. It happens in seconds. I'm frozen, my phone gripped in my hand.

The first Monster has full heavy jowls and oversized teeth that remind me of a sort of ape or baboon. It snaps its maw around James's head and bites down. Blood sprays onto his wife's face, and she doesn't even get a chance to scream before it crushes her in its massive fist. The crack of her ribs breaking is sharp and cutting. The other Monster, a rhinoesque beast with twin horns, spears the two children through their stomachs before they can run away. Their bodies hang limp as their mouths open, gasping without sound.

At some point, the phone dropped from my hand. I don't know when.

Part of me is recoiling. Shrinking. Retreating.

Another part of me smells the sharp tang of the blood and wants to lick its lips. Sends my heart racing at the sight of the viscera splattered across the frosted grass. Shivers at the promise of more violence.

There's screaming and stamping feet and running. Virgil pulls me to his chest as people surge around us. I should be afraid, probably,

but instead, my hands flex at my sides and my muscles tense, readying themselves as the Monsters shake off the bodies.

The apelike Monster turns its head toward us as Adam steps out of the tent, its gaze focusing.

Adam.

I turn and meet Virgil's eyes, and we don't need to say a single word. I jump away from him, and in that moment his body transforms, limbs bending and cracking, fur exploding from his body, and teeth and claws forming. It's fast. Faster than I think it's supposed to be. But this is Virgil. If I learned anything last year, it's that Virgil is not a normal Monster.

I look to my left, where the redhead is still standing, eyes glued to the carnage. "Are you planning to do anything?" I ask him.

He grits his teeth. "Still not my job."

Figures.

Virgil bounds in front of Adam, triangular ears perked, claws flexing with their sharp points—the dark color of the metal gleaming like carbon steel. The spikes jut out all over his wolflike body. He bares his teeth at the other Monster. I leave the redhead and position myself beside Virgil, slipping two throwing knives into my hands from my pockets. Something I learned last semester: always carry knives. I'm already picturing the euphoria of that first cut of the blade, trembling.

"James, Cate," Adam mutters, eyes glassy. "The girls . . ." His voice chokes on that one.

The apelike Monster keeps coming, screeching, teeth bared, with the Rhino one on its heels.

That is, until Adam looks up.

I see the exact moment he moves from grief to action, eyes narrowing.

The apelike Monster stops in its tracks, then it turns and darts into the trees, the other Monster following.

Adam blinks several times, looking at the place where they disappeared.

I clench my jaw. They're gone. The fight is over before I could draw even a bead of blood. "Where are you sending them?" I snap, eyes darting from him to the trees. Doctorates have a unique mutation that allows them to control any Monster without being bound like me and Virgil. So I assume that's what he did.

Adam shakes his head and licks his lips. "I'm not sending them anywhere. They weren't listening to me."

"Isn't that, like, your one power?"

Virgil spins around and cuts me a look of abject horror so palpable that I'm shocked he could manage it in Monster form. Adam, on the other hand, is unfazed. "Wilds are more difficult. I wasn't fully prepared, and they used that moment to flee." He pauses and gnaws his lip.

Virgil remains transformed, his hackles raised.

"Should we go after them?" I ask. *Say yes.*

Adam nods to the sky, where a giant bird-thing is skimming the trees. "Leave it to the senior Masters."

I'm unprepared for the surge of heat through my body. The urge to bare my teeth at Adam. To defy him. By the time I wrestle it down, I'm breathing hard. Everything else has come into focus. The fact that we're only a couple of feet away from four corpses. The screaming and chaos of everyone else still running away or sobbing in place, clinging to one another. Only now are some people inching toward us, curious despite themselves.

I look up at Virgil, who stares at me, something incomprehensible in his monstrous gaze.

"Wait," I say, my mind finally catching up. I jerk toward Adam. "Did you say Wilds? *Wilds* attacked?"

"So it would seem."

In the corner of my eye, the redhead is finally moved to action, turning and speed walking away from us. Not suspicious at all . . .

Turns out, the Wilds aren't going to passively accept Adam as their new Doctorate. Not when last year Garrett Murphy, their leader, made it clear that the agreement was with Cyrus, not his sons.

I swallow, staring at the corpses as their blood pools in the snow.

A thought occurs to me while I watch their broken bodies.

Where the fuck is Carrigan?

CHAPTER THREE

Two days ago, I thought if I'd been there when Mom and Jules were attacked, with the power I have now, I could have saved her. That same day, I stood frozen while an entire family was slaughtered. By the time I was focused enough to do something, it was too late. I clench my hands into fists in my pockets as we file into Summerhill in a wave of black. Monday evenings are usually reserved for lectures—which I make a point to skip—but this evening will host the public funeral of James, his wife, and their two daughters.

As we enter, we're given a lit black candle. I take mine after Virgil and follow him and Corey inside. Usually the chandeliers are sparkling and bright, the tables and chairs covered with white linens. Now the only light in the room comes from the candles, and the tables and chairs are bare wood. Stripped.

On the stage at the front of the room is a long table with photos of the deceased surrounded by dozens of black candles, unlit and

waiting. Below that is a shallow wooden box the same length as the table.

There are also cameras set up around the room, I assume to broadcast the funeral to the wider society across the country. James wasn't their leader, but he's still the son of a Doctorate.

Virgil whispers, "Did you bring pages?"

"Yeah." I was instructed to cut out pages from books with passages that I want to send to the dead.

Corey gestures to the stage. "After Adam's speech, we'll line up, and you light a candle on the table, burn a corner of the paper, and then put it in the wooden trough. They'll burn them fully at the end."

"And in the meantime?"

Virgil shrugs. "Just mingle around." He points across the room. "There's Margot, Isaac, and Laira."

We join the Bouchard siblings and Henry's Monster partner, who stand off to the side with their candles. Margot gives us a grim smile while Isaac keeps his gaze on the ground. Laira smells like weed, and the redness in her eyes reflects how baked she is. Not good with funerals, I guess.

"Strong start to the semester," I say.

Everyone cringes except for Laira, who chuckles. "For fuck's sake," Virgil says, looking around as if he expects someone to throw us out. But there are more than enough people talking to drown me out. They mill around the space, their pages held loosely in their hands, leaning against the wood-paneled walls or sitting in small groups on the bare furniture.

Margot crosses her arms over her chest. "You saw everything? At Doctorate Day?"

"Yeah," I say, scuffing the toe of my Docs on the ground. "And did fuck all."

"Not even Adam was fast enough to do anything," Corey says.

I thought I was stronger. Better. Hell, I even thought I could take Carrigan on. A Doctorate candidate. Instead, I watched someone else dispatch one. What would have happened if they hadn't retreated? If we'd actually gotten to fight?

Something in me paces, back and forth, back and forth. Carving a tread into the ground.

The only thing worse than death is preventable death.

A hand lands on my shoulder, and I jump, spinning around to find Henry behind me. "Come with me." I let him steer me into the hallway.

Without the other people and their candles, the hall feels narrowed to the two of us, standing with our single flames. For all that Henry has done for me and Virgil, he also has his own game. The only thing that keeps my trust in him is knowing that I'm a valuable part of his strategy. In fact, I feel confident that he's the one who put me in this game in the first place, even if I don't know why.

Henry leans against the wall, staring into his flame. "You gave the senior Masters the descriptions of the Monsters?"

"I told them everything." I gave them my phone video too. Deleted it right after. Don't much care to have a snuff film in the palm of my hand.

"And Adam?"

"What about him?"

"He couldn't control them?"

I shake my head. "He said it's hard with Wilds. And I guess he was struggling on account of watching his family be slaughtered."

Henry looks up abruptly, and I swallow, averting my eyes. "Yes," he says. "That would make it difficult." He would know, considering that his own family died from a Monster attack.

It should have been hard for me, too, seeing that massacre. In the moment, the only way I could push myself to act was to sink into the part of me more concerned with drawing blood than processing the carnage.

Henry waves a hand at the door to the main room. "We had a funeral just like this for my family. I chose a page from a history textbook for my father, who was also a professor. For my mother, a page from a book of poetry she'd loved. And for my sister, one from Peter Pan with the quote 'Never say goodbye, because goodbye means going away and going away means forgetting.'"

Henry has never forgotten his family. And here he is, clinging tightly to the new one that he's built. To Adam, Virgil, Margot, Isaac, and Laira. I question the man's motives when it comes to me but not them.

"In the end, I never lit a single one," Henry says. "I hid in a side room with Adam. Cyrus had to come and drag me onto the stage to deliver my speech. Which I did. Flawlessly. People were complimenting me even weeks later. One of those being a man who later invited me to his Mastery group and became my mentor." He smiles at me. "Death is worth nothing if you cannot use it."

Maybe to someone else, the phrase would be callous. But I get it. Mom is dead. She doesn't care if I avenge her. There's nothing that can come from her death except for me to motivate myself to do what I need to do.

"Can you make me stronger?" I ask him. "In the Mastery group?"

"I can't make you anything. I can only guide you. You have to

make something of yourself." I nod, shoving my free hand into my pocket. Henry gestures to the door. "Let's get back."

I follow him, rejoining the others just as there's a commotion at the entryway.

I make out Garrett Murphy squeezing through the crowd, followed by Jacques. My eyes go wide, seeing Mia's dad outside of the context of the tiny house community. Following behind the two of them is the redhead from Doctorate Day who was even more useless than I was, and a host of other people, many with that same patch on the right shoulder of their jackets.

"Wilds," Henry says. "Double-edged sword. They come to the service and society members despise them for it, but if they stayed away, they would be despised nonetheless."

"So everyone suspects that they planned this," I say.

Laira nods. "Even though it was against their will, the Wilds specialized in assassinations. They were specifically trained to use any advantage to get around Master-Monster bonds and were always more equipped for these sorts of takedowns. It's why they did so well with the rebellion. It looks especially bad when two guys who were vicious during rebellion days take out a Doctorate candidate. No one has ever succeeded at killing a Doctorate, period. Even worse that it was done on the day meant to celebrate the title. It feels like a message."

"Bad time to be a Wild," Isaac mutters.

"There hasn't been a good time to be a Wild for years," Margot says.

The door to the left of the stage opens, and Adam strides out. His expression is flat, his cheeks dry, and his eyes clear. He looks like a leader, not a grieving family member. He approaches the podium, and the room goes silent. "It is an honor to learn with you," he says.

"And us with you," the room intones. Even I make the effort of mumbling the words.

Adam says, "It is a tragedy that on the day we come together to learn, we must now mourn. My brother was a cherished member of this society, as were his wife, Cate, and children, Gwen and Jenni. I am so appreciative of you all who have joined me here today to bring words and light in a time of loss." He swallows and shifts in place. "I would also like to say that I have met with Garrett Murphy, who speaks for many of the community of Wilds, and he has assured me that this was not a coordinated effort on their part." Adam motions to Garrett. The man stands tall, surrounded by the people he brought along. "This was an act of individuals. The culprits were found dead the same day. We are investigating and—" He cuts himself off as a group pushes near the stage, the crowd of mourners spreading for them.

"What's happening?" I look to the others, but they're just staring at the stage.

"Yes?" Adam asks through gritted teeth.

The group rearranges themselves so that one man can be seen at the helm. He's an older white man in maybe his forties or fifties with dark hair shot through with gray and silver. There's something familiar about him. Instead of facing Adam, he turns toward us in the room.

"I don't mean to interrupt, but I, Thomas Mosser, senior Master, and some of my peers have joined together to create what we believe will be a solution to this issue."

Mosser . . . I jerk my head toward Virgil. "As in . . . ?"

"Caden's father," Virgil says, biting his lip.

That shit stain who did everything within his power to get us

kicked out of the Bachelor candidacy only to end up dying in the initiation. Caden's trainer was his dad, Thomas. He was at the initiation, which is where I recognize him from.

Thomas continues, "It's come to our attention that the agreement that governs Wilds has proven insufficient. And while, as our esteemed Doctorate has shared, they do not claim responsibility for this attack, that does not change the fact that two of their number were responsible. We would like to present a proposal for a new set of terms. I would invite you all to consider signing on with your support so that we can protect what is most precious to us: each other, and our Doctorate, who will become our savior in the apocalypse." He turns and gestures to Adam. "We already have twenty-five signatures from senior Masters who agree. I hope that our Doctorate will consider our pleas should we garner enough support."

"Is this really the time and place for this?" Corey says, frowning.

"It is exactly the time and place," Henry says. "They have put Adam on the spot when he is already in a vulnerable position. If he strikes down their effort now, he will be seen as emotional. Furthermore, they've presented this to the entire society when *they* are at their most emotional. Students are afraid, and Mosser has played into it."

"Traditionalist, isn't he?" Margot asks.

"They all are," Henry replies.

Corey adds, "But you don't have to be a Traditionalist to believe in restricting Wilds."

"No, you don't," Henry says. "That's the problem."

Adam smiles tightly. "Thank you for your proposed solution. Should you gather enough support, I'll be happy to hear your presentation of it."

Thomas beams and steps back, he and his group blending into the audience. Meanwhile, Garrett looks like he's forcing his face to stay still, the wrinkles around his eyes trembling, while some of the other Wilds with him are openly furious.

They're already under so many restrictions. What exactly are these additional ones going to be?

Adam says, "I will invite you now to share your words and light. Thank you." He moves to the photos, lighting a candle for each and burning the corner of a page in turn. When he's finished, he exits the stage, and everyone lines up.

Henry excuses himself to go check on his friend. As I move to follow the others, someone stumbles into me from behind and apologizes. I turn. "It's oka—" The words die in my throat as I face Eleanor Mathers, Bernie's widow.

"A tragedy, truly," she says, her voice mild, though she must recognize me. She did hold me at gunpoint. A fake gun, but still. She looks haggard, hair stringy, with dark circles under her eyes, but there's also a brightness to her expression. "It's horrible to lose your entire family."

"He still has Carrigan."

"Does he?" she asks, gesturing to the room. "I haven't seen him."

I noticed. Carrigan wasn't at Doctorate Day when he should have been, and he's not here at his own brother's funeral. If Adam had been killed too, Carrigan would be the Doctorate right now.

"It's funny, isn't it?" she says. "These same people who voted with glee to kill my husband and child are here crying over another husband and his children. Lucky for the wife, she died with them." She straightens her blouse. "Would you like to see the pages I've prepared?"

I wouldn't, but I also don't think she's giving me a choice.

Three of the pages are normal, but the fourth is handwritten—*burn in hell* scrawled in tiny script over and over again. She smiles and tucks the pages away. "I may not know who, but one of the Shaws entrapped my family. I'm too weak to make anything happen myself, but I will celebrate the downfall of each and every one. They're cannibalizing each other, and I'm happy to watch them eat." She pats me on the arm. "I'd be careful if I were you. In this society, there's always someone waiting to stab you in the back. It's why I've left Kingston, personally. Among other reasons. But I'll always make time for their funerals." With that, she proceeds to the line with that same serene smile on her face.

The puppet master who Bernie blamed for his misfortune wanted a weapon that could kill Gods, but I guess in the end, they didn't need it. They killed James fine.

The Wilds didn't act on their own. I would bet anything that they were controlled. There are only three people in the world who can command Monsters without a bond.

One is missing. One is dead. And one is next.

CHAPTER FOUR

Mastery group meetings are usually held in the study room at the Grad Club. The building is on the edge of campus, opposite the baseball field—cricket field, according to Virgil. It's a brick house that was definitely someone's residence in a previous life, three stories tall with dormers and bay windows.

Virgil fidgets beside me as we walk, adjusting his peacoat like Henry might kick us out of the group because the collar isn't lying perfectly straight. I give Corey an exasperated look, and she only shakes her head and pats Virgil on the arm.

"What are you researching for Henry?" I ask her.

She tilts her head. "Some data on Monster abilities to share with the Mastery group. He also wants to see what I can find about the apocalypse. I assume because Carrigan is now MIA, and the spontaneous birth rate has been rising since last semester. Adam doesn't have the headspace for it, and Henry doesn't trust the

Scientist faction, so I'm his personal fact checker."

Right, the supposed Monster apocalypse that Dr. Weiss predicted more than a century ago. I continue to feel that I'll believe it when I see it, but I don't want to undermine Corey's research when she fought for this recognition. "As long as you're excited about it."

Corey beams. "I am! It's a lot with my course load and librarian duties, but Henry's paying me by the hour, which is nice."

"He should be! You deserve it."

She ducks her head but doesn't deny that she earned this.

We walk into the Grad Club, which also operates as a restaurant and bar. The Victorian theme extends to the interior, with arches and columns between the bar and dining rooms, and an antique fireplace.

The server, a white guy with side-swept blond hair, says, "Sit wherever you like."

"We're supposed to be in the study room, actually," Corey says.

"Upstairs." He points out the staircase to us, and we head up.

I sigh. "I wish I could get paid."

Virgil says, "You wouldn't need to if you hadn't abused the credit card."

"Oh my God, it was one time."

"A single infraction is enough."

I roll my eyes at him as we reach the second-floor landing. "Do you ever get tired of being a walking, talking rulebook?"

"Do you ever get tired of breaking rules?"

"Some are worth it," I say without thinking. When his eyes drop to my mouth, I splutter, "I mean, yeah, some, not all, or whatever."

Virgil swallows and turns away from me, heading toward the open door at the end of the hall only to nearly crash into Margot as she's coming out. Her jaw is tight. "You're early."

"You know what they say," I chirp. "If you're early, you're on time." Margot hits me with a flat, unamused expression that I find I've really missed. "Doesn't your cohort meet on a different day?"

"We do," she says. "I came to have a conversation with my mentor."

"About?"

Margot stares at me for a beat before saying, "Things are going to change. The successful assassination of a Doctorate candidate isn't something to take lightly. If Adam is in danger, every Progressive should be on alert. All of us benefit from his support, so a threat to him is a threat to us."

"I doubt it'll be that easy to take him out."

Margot presses her lips into a line. "We'll see. I have to go."

As she leaves, she passes by Violet and Bryce and their respective partners, Frankie and Mitch, as they come up the stairs. We fill the already cramped second-floor hallway.

"That looked serious," Violet says.

I shake my head. "Just the potential impending doom of our Doctorate getting murdered."

"Hopefully not," Virgil says, grimacing.

Together, we enter the study room, immediately having to sidestep the large piano beside the door with a massive TV mounted on top of it. The walls are half covered in wallpaper featuring cartoon owls staring out, with white wainscoting on the bottom. There are multiple tables and chairs, and a few sets of leather couches on the other side of the room by the bay window.

"Didn't Dr. Scott used to do these in his house?" Violet asks, taking a seat on one of the couches.

Virgil nods. "A long time ago, yeah, but it's been at the Grad

Club for the last few years. I think there's a society member on staff who makes sure the room is secure."

"Wait, why don't you live with Henry, then, instead of at McIntosh Castle?" I ask, collapsing on one of the other couches. It's so squishy that I sink right into it. "I didn't realize he had a whole house." I assumed that Henry just lived in a place too small for Virgil.

"Henry felt the castle would be a better environment, since Dr. Liu was around all the time as both company and a tutor. Henry has a more packed schedule and isn't home that much." He hesitates for a moment before adding, "And I think it would have been hard for him. He's been alone for a long time. Even when the Shaws took him in, it was more figurative. He still lived in his family home."

I raise a brow. "By himself?"

"Yes. Since he was fifteen."

The man himself comes into the room, dressed in a peacoat over a pair of tan slacks and a maroon sweater, followed by Laira, who's wearing a pair of joggers and a sweatshirt under her coat, her locs pulled into a ponytail, completely ruining the ambience that Henry is creating, and I love it.

"Welcome," Henry says. "Take a seat. The others should be here soon."

Virgil settles beside me on the couch, careful to make sure our thighs don't touch. For fuck's sake, he's acting as if liking me is some sort of disease. As if there isn't a difference between our legs touching and his tongue down my throat. I lean back and spread my legs, so he's forced to squish into the armrest. He glares at me, and I grin.

Corey heads to the front of the room, where Henry stands while Laira dumps her backpack onto a chair.

Five minutes later, two more pairs enter the room. I guess they're the last members, because Henry closes the door and has us do introductions as soon as they sit.

A couple of the Mastery group members throw brief looks at Corey's left leg. It's not like they can tell she's using a prosthesis with the clothes she's wearing, but as the youngest Bachelor candidate in decades, they must know her story. Corey shifts a bit in place but keeps her back straight, smiling at the group.

There are ten of us in the cohort. The two unfamiliar pairs are sophomores. One is a girl named Kare, who looks biracial with some Black features, and her Bachelor partner, Harmon, a Black boy with short curls dyed blond. The other pair are siblings—twins, actually. Yufei, an East Asian–looking boy with the same sort of severe facial structure that Jules has, and his sister, Jasmine, the Bachelor of the pair, who I'm pleased to see is plus-sized. It's nice to not be the only big girl in the room. But if they're here as sophomores, it means they weren't able to become Masters-in-training during last year's Monster's Ball and have to try again. If you fail a third time, then they break your bond, and your partner gets sent to the Pen. The society never gets tired of holding the threat of bond breaking over everyone.

Once the introductions are done, Henry says, "Over the course of this semester, I hope you'll come to think of this group as your extended family."

My God, he loves being Daddy. I attempt to make eye contact with Virgil to communicate this, but he ignores me, concentrating on Henry.

The professor continues, "This group is meant to help you advance within the society and also serves as a means of support,

protection, and community. Your cohort will meet biweekly on Wednesday afternoons, and you'll also be assigned a mentor from the Master-in-training cohort, who you will meet with monthly. Each group session will begin with a short lecture and a progress report from members. After, there will be a practical component, followed by a homework assignment. I expect both Bachelor and Monster to attend every meeting *on time.*" He gestures to both Laira and Corey. "I will be assisted by my partner, Laira, and my research assistant, Corey. Corey is also the interim librarian at McIntosh Castle, training under Dr. Liu, and has great knowledge of society history. She's prepared packages for each pair based on observed Monster types and skills, the reading of which is mandatory. Understood?"

Everyone in the room nods, and I grin at the way Corey holds herself straighter. This really is the perfect role for her. Henry waves for her and Laira to take their seats at the table beside him while he remains standing.

"As you are all aware, a Doctorate candidate was murdered by a pair of Wilds, who have since been found dead, we believe by suicide. Garrett Murphy has spoken for the Wild families in Ontario to deny any involvement, and a Traditionalist-led group has come forward to present a document requesting restrictions on Wilds nationwide. I've seen the terms, which include banning Wilds from attending a post-secondary institution since, as you may or may not know, when Wilds acquire degrees, they are released from proctor duties. The rationale for the ban being that this results in too much unrestricted movement. They plan to mitigate any issues with ability to gain meaningful employment by assigning Wilds to private security details unclaimed by Master-Monster pairs. They also propose constant surveillance and limits on where Wilds can live, travel, and

gather. This new agreement will also reverse the ban on Wild experimentation, allowing it if Wilds agree to the study."

What the actual fuck? They basically want to strip everything from the Wilds. If they can't get degrees and can't set work schedules because of proctoring, they'll have no choice but to take the unwanted missions or submit to experimentation. From the way the others in the room scowl, they understand the subtext too.

Henry says, "I hope it's obvious to you that this is unreasonable, and yet, they are acquiring signatures. It was Dr. Weiss's wish that our society exist in equality, not oppression. As Progressives, we must protect that intent. However, if this group gains traction, it may force the Doctorate's hand. I encourage you to think critically about these sorts of propositions, especially when they undermine our Doctorate's authority." He looks at each of us in turn as if to lock in our promise.

"But Adam's the Doctorate," I say. "Doesn't that mean he has the ultimate authority to strike anything down?"

Virgil whispers, "You should raise your hand."

I roll my eyes and raise my hand. "Adam's the Doctorate—"

"*Doctorate Shaw,*" Henry says, leveling me with a hard stare. "And yes, the Doctorate has the ultimate authority, but we cannot be naive. Transitions of power are uncertain times, and the society technically has options for their Doctorate. We must be prepared for anything."

It's not that different from what Margot said at the door. As if she and Henry are expecting a civil war, which is wild. These people practically salivate at the Doctorate's feet. But then again, Adam rules in a different way than his dad did. Maybe that's enough for people to take advantage of.

"Moving on," Henry says. "Our focus this semester will be the

Monster's Ball." Everyone in the room becomes more alert at the mention. "The competition will begin in three weeks. The format is two-on-two matches where you'll compete against other bonded pairs. In the initial rounds with the Bachelor league, you need to be the first Bachelor to grab both flags from the other to win. But from semifinals on, it's until yield or knockout. Fatalities are not encouraged and will be punished but will not result in disqualification, so stay vigilant."

Finally, someone gives me some details about what this thing is actually going to be. I prefer the idea of duking it out to dealing with mazes or riddles.

Henry continues, "The preparation time is purposely tight to help push you. It is a double elimination bracket, so you have one chance—and one chance only—to fail. Out of the fifty to sixty pairs competing, only the top twenty-five percent of you will graduate to the title. I hope that everyone will make it through this time around." He gives a pointed look to the pairs who failed last year. To their credit, they take the jibe in stride. "I will tell you right now that if you cannot reach monstrous evolution two before the competition begins, you will lose. August, remind the group of the first two levels of monstrous evolution."

Of course he calls on me. "Monstrous evolution one is basic control, meaning that the Monster can shift their form at will. Required for attaining the title of Bachelor. Monstrous evolution two is transfer of power, where the Master shares the enhanced physical abilities of their Monster partner. Things like increased speed, strength, and stamina."

Henry adds, "In addition to senses such as smell, sight, and hearing." This guy can't even give me a "Good job, August"? The professor moves on. "You must reach monstrous evolution three in order to

be given the title of Master-in-training. Even if you somehow came in first in the Bachelor league, if you cannot demonstrate third-evolution mastery, you will still fail. Who can recap the third evolution for us?"

"I was voluntold, but other people get to volunteer?" I ask.

"August, thank you so much for volunteering."

I grind my teeth. "Monstrous evolution three is the transfer of abilities, where the Master can share in the special skills of their partner. Such as healing or Margot's sparky fists."

"And one cannot take advantage of these abilities unless the Monster has mastered them. This is a joint effort. You both take responsibility for your win, even if only one of you is getting a title. Some of you may have multiple third-evolution abilities, and some may only have one." He spreads his arms out. "There are also benefits to doing well in the Monster's Ball beyond attaining the title. The first-place Bachelor will be granted a request by the Doctorate in addition to a private tour of the Doctorate's cottage conducted by the Doctorate during the celebration banquet. The request can be large or small, within reason. In the past, winners have asked for many things from prize money to new cars and other such frivolities, but I would encourage you to think bigger. You can make requests for introductions to prominent people both in and outside of society, job placements, internships, and more."

I peer around the room, wide-eyed, but I'm apparently the only one who didn't know this competition had a prize. Though I don't know what I'd ask for. I doubt Adam would be cool with me requesting permission to take out his brother.

Henry claps his hands. "Since this is our first meeting, we'll skip the progress report and go straight into a test of which level you're at."

Frankie throws a frazzled look at Violet, whose gaze remains

steely. This is the one thing I'm confident about. In initiation, me and Virgil did that roar. Which means we must already be at level three. I took advantage of his healing, too.

Henry says, "First, Monsters will do a partial shift. This is a useful skill that you should practice, since there may be times when it isn't appropriate to transform fully. Second, a strength test for Bachelors." He gestures to Laira, and she opens her backpack and pulls out a literal gold bar, setting it on one of the empty tables. "This is a Good Delivery bar. Its standard weight sits around twenty-seven pounds. You should be able to lift this using only the strength of two fingers. However, if your partner cannot do the partial shift, then there's no point in an attempt. Let's begin."

One by one, Henry calls up pairs to do the tests. Yufei can't manage the partial shift, earning a long, hard look from the professor. The other sophomore, Kare, can do the shift, but Harmon can't pick up the bar with two fingers. Mitch does the partial shift without any visible effort, his right hand growing white fur and thick, gorilla-like fingers. Bryce almost seems like he's going to manage the bar, but can only get one corner off the table. Still, Henry nods at him. It's the best anyone has done thus far. I expect better results from Violet and Frankie—after all, they ranked higher in the candidacy—but Violet doesn't even get to try the gold bar. Frankie screws up her face, her nose scrunching and brow furrowing, but her russet-skinned hand doesn't change.

"Just give me a second," she says, gripping her fist.

Henry says, "Please take your seat."

"I can—"

"Let's just sit," Violet says, avoiding Frankie's eyes as she returns to the couch. After a moment, Frankie follows her, keeping her gaze on the ground.

Virgil swallows when we get up for our turn. His hand shakes as he sticks it out, but then sharp metal claws grow from the nails at his command. Henry nods, a hint of a smile on his lips. I reach for the gold bar, expecting to heft it without any effort, but I can't even get the corner up. I squeeze harder, focusing and grinding my teeth. Henry is opening his mouth to stop me just as something inside me shifts. Strength surges to my fingers, and several group members scream as my arm whips up and the bar goes flying out of my hand. Twenty-seven pounds of gold puncture the drywall of the room, a dull thud echoing when it lands.

I whip around to Henry, whose lips pull down, but for a second . . . I swear it almost looked like a smile.

The door opens to reveal the same server who let us in, his eyes wide as he looks from the group to the hole in the wall. After Laira leaves the room to smooth things over, Henry sighs. "I think we have just learned a valuable lesson in control, don't you?" He levels a stern look at me.

"I mean, I did it," I mutter.

Virgil lets out a sound somewhere between a groan and a whimper, dragging his hand over his face.

Henry dismisses us to our seats before saying, "You may have experienced some of second or even third evolution during the initiation because the serum allows for a stronger connection that, in turn, leads to you presenting more advanced skills than you ordinarily would. And it stays in the Bachelor's body much longer than your partner's. However, now that the serum has fully metabolized, just as you noticed a decreased mental connection, it is the same for abilities. You will have to train them up from ground zero."

Henry can say what he likes, but I did the thing. Bryce is the only

other Bachelor who made any progress, and Virgil and Mitch the only successful partial shifters.

"If you're disappointed with your progress, train to improve," Henry says. "For your homework, continue to work on your partial shift and find something weighted to lift, working your way up to thirty pounds. And be careful." This with a pointed look at me. "Be sure to collect the research packages from Corey on your way out. Laira will send an email with your Master-in-training mentor's contact details later today." Henry takes a deep breath before saying, "As a final note, and I do hate to mention this, but it comes up at least once every year: these bonds, especially as you work to strengthen them, can at times become confused with . . . hormonal urges."

"Oh my God, he's giving us a sex talk," I mutter.

"There is a reason that intimate relationships between Master and Monster are forbidden. For one, there is a power imbalance. Any way you slice it, the Monster is reliant on your partnership to retain their humanity and could be coerced into submitting to a relationship."

It's not dissimilar to the conversation we had last year about the struggle a Monster may have trying to escape an abusive partnership. They stay and suffer, or they leave and lose their partner and therefore their humanity. It's also something I never really gave that much thought to when it came to me and Virgil. I mean, he initiated the kiss. And I understand why we can't do it again on a practical level. But I hadn't considered that he might feel pressured to give into what I want just because he needs me.

On his end, he focuses on Henry, ignoring me as much as possible. I didn't manspread again when we sat down, but he's still squished to one side of the couch.

Henry continues, "And for another, you are bound to each other for life. This becomes ever more complicated if children are involved, which has created volatile situations in the past, hence it being forbidden now. Not only will an infraction result in your expulsion from this year's competition, if there is reasonable proof of repeated offenses, your bond will be broken." I swear Henry looks at me for a second longer than he does everyone else. Virgil is so tense beside me that he might tip over if I poked him. "Doctorate Shaw is kind, but he will not risk looking soft by sparing anyone a punishment that has been carried out for decades. Be sensible and seek outlets for your hormonal desires outside of your partnerships. That's all. You may leave. Virgil and August, stay back."

I can't help but feel that making us stay back right after he says that shit is a move.

Corey steps into the hallway with the others to give them their research packages and Laira slips back into the room. Me and Virgil stay in our spots.

"Daddy's not happy with us," I whisper to Virgil.

He sighs. "Please stop calling him that."

"I think he likes it."

"I do not," Henry says from across the room. "Also, as you may remember since you explained it, second-evolution mastery comes with enhanced senses. Meaning I can hear when you whisper."

"I didn't think you'd have it turned on all the time," I mumble.

"There is no 'turning on or off.' When you understand your partner's skills to be your own, they become second nature. Now, as I mentioned last semester, you two will also be privately training with me. And you'll be pleased to know that I've assigned Margot to be your MiT mentor. However, my methods will not be the same as

hers. They may be, at times, extreme, but they are for your benefit." He looks at me. "You said you wanted to get stronger, yes? Then work for it."

I nod while Virgil says, "We will, sir."

"Good. The pair of you have the potential to do very well, not only in this arena but in the society in general. Your performance last semester made that clear. Do you understand what I'm saying?"

"You want us to win?" I try.

"I want you to perform well. Winning would be a bonus."

"We'll do our best to repay your efforts," Virgil says.

Henry doesn't even look at him. He stares at me. "How did you feel as you watched James and his family slaughtered?" Laira makes a noise in the back of her throat and Henry ignores her.

I swallow. "Not great." I lick my lips. "Frozen, I guess."

"Powerless," Henry says.

That's the word, isn't it? The exact description for how it felt to watch children speared through their guts while their mom's corpse lay on the ground. A more macabre version of how it was when Jules told me that Mom wasn't missing. That she was dead. All I could do was curl up in the snow.

Henry would have seen the same scene once upon a time. His own family, a mess of muscle and blood on the ground.

Henry says, "If you don't want to feel that way again, work hard."

I nod. I want this. Even if it means submitting to whatever training Henry has in mind. I'm going to get stronger. I have to.

That's the thing about power—you don't crave it until you've experienced being without it.

CHAPTER FIVE

I trudge back to Victoria Hall on Monday after my last class, slouched under the weight of my backpack. It's only the third week into the semester, and I'm already sick of this shit. All my courses are full credits, spanning both semesters, so I can still coast in the easy ones, but I did shit on my PSYC100 midterm. Probably because during the study period, I was dealing with the knowledge that Virgil would be going underground for the rest of his life. You can volunteer for research studies to get extra credit, except I won't have the time for them between training, Mastery group, and trying to find evidence that Carrigan killed Mom.

And that's not even getting into how I'm supposed to find him. However much he pretended not to want to be Doctorate, that has to be his goal. Using Bernie as a means of pitting his brothers against each other, maybe hoping to use that weapon to kill them while they were distracted. I just have no idea how Mom plays into everything.

When I reach my dorm, Jules is waiting for me outside like he

said he would. This used to be *his* dorm, and now he's living with Natalie at her house with her dog, which he posts about incessantly. I have to admit he looks much better, standing straight in his navy blue jacket with a matching knit hat.

"Cool hat," I say.

"Thanks. Nat made it."

My eyebrows shoot up. "I'm sorry, the woman who led a rebellion knit you a hat?"

"*Allegedly* led. And she crocheted it, actually."

"Wow, she's got you trained."

Jules shakes his head. "Let's go up."

I lead the way to my room, chatting with my brother about how my classes are going. He's in Commerce with an aim to do consulting like Mom. I continue to not understand what consulting is and can't be bothered to learn. Jules is, of course, worried about my psychology midterm. Meanwhile, he's busy catching up on what he had to drop last semester due to being held captive by Bernie, and already has a comprehensive plan involving taking courses during the summer alongside an internship.

We get to my room, and Jules wrinkles his nose at the piles of clothes strewn around. I make a show of shoving them in my closet and do a ta-da pose when I close the door. He sighs.

"Okay," I say, sitting on my bed. "I know you're not warm on the Carrigan theory when it comes to Mom, but I hope that recent events have shown you just how sus he is. I think he controlled the Wilds who murdered James and his family, and I suspect that's how he attacked Mom, too. We'll need solid evidence, and so we can plan how to get that."

Jules drops onto the chair at my desk and scrubs his face. "This

is what I wanted to talk about." He takes a deep breath before saying, "I think you should leave this to Nat and me."

"Uh, what the fuck?" I narrow my eyes at him. "No."

"You need to concentrate on everything else you have going on. This is your first Monster's Ball— "

"Yours too!"

"Yes, but I'm paired with Nat, who is a senior Master. We're already at monstrous evolution three. How is that going for you?"

I swallow. How did they reach three so fast?! We're not even a month into the semester!

Jules continues, "Your schoolwork has already suffered. I'm here now, like I should have always been, so I can handle it for you. If anything comes up that requires your help, I'll let you know."

I shake my head. "During the break, you said you needed me. Needed my connections to Henry and Adam and all that. We were going to find Mom's killer *together.*"

"Why does it matter who finds the person responsible as long as they get found?"

I gape at him, my mouth opening and closing. "Because she's *our* mom!"

"Nat has connections of her own, and she's agreed to use them to figure this out."

"Has agreed to help in exchange for what?" There's no way Natalie is doing this out of the goodness of her heart.

Jules's jaw tenses and then relaxes. "She has a vested interest in discovering who's behind James's assassination. Like you said, she doesn't believe this was a coordinated effort by the Wilds. She feels confident that they've been manipulated and framed."

"Yeah! By Carrigan."

"Carrigan doesn't have any motive to kill his brothers. He didn't even try to win the Doctorate position when he could have done it legitimately. Nat will explore all possible options. You concentrate on your own stuff."

"I want to find Mom's killer just as much as—"

"Stop putting yourself in unnecessary danger!" Jules shouts, shooting up from the chair. I jerk back. "People *die* in the Monster's Ball. You are going to be up against Bachelors who are more experienced than you. You were in the kiddie pool before, and now you're in the sandbox with the big kids. And tracking down a murderer is an even higher level for which you are unprepared. For once, *for fucking once,* trust me on this."

"Unprepared or weak? You think you're better than me now because you're paired with a senior Master? Did you forget who saved your ass last semester?"

"No, I didn't," he says. "Because if memory serves, *Isaac and Virgil* were the ones who stopped Bernie, while by some miracle you survived almost being beheaded *by me*!" Jules is breathing so hard that his chest is heaving. "I almost killed you. That's what happened the last time you went after a murderer. Look at your hands, August!"

I drop my eyes to my fingers. At some point I started clutching my comforter. Now it's shredded, cloth and bits of feather down in a pile on my lap.

"You can't control your abilities yet," Jules says. "I'm not putting another thing on your plate. It's not about being weak; it's about being safe. I owe that to you as your older brother."

"You don't owe me anything." Jules stares me down, saying nothing. "Does she even have any leads? Anything concrete?"

"Yes! The Wilds keep documents in a hidden vault in a forest

near their compound in Sydenham, just north of Kingston. They used to do assassinations, and clearly someone is taking advantage of those skills. It's possible that whoever went after Mom was tasked to do so by someone else. Not controlled necessarily, just incentivized. Nat has a plan to use her connections to access the files subtly and securely. At which point, I'll share with you what I can. I don't intend to leave you in the dark. I just want you to avoid direct involvement."

Jules wants to take getting justice for Mom away from me and once again leave me watching someone else do what I should.

"I have to get to training," I say.

"Are you going to stay out of this?"

I open the door to my room and gesture. He gives me one last long look before he leaves.

For once, I'm glad for the chill as I stomp south of Victoria Hall to Henry's house, following the directions on my phone to the address Virgil texted me. I need to cool off. I can't believe Jules. Not only that he had the audacity to tell me to take a back seat in finding our mom's murderer, but that he'd act like I'm not good for anything other than getting in the way because I *"can't even control my abilities yet."*

When I slam my fist on the door, Laira lets me inside. "You do know that traditionally you knock on the door, you don't punch it?"

"Not in the mood," I say, kicking off my boots in the entryway.

Laira hums. "We're in the parlor." I follow after her, looking around the space as I do. The interior of the home is what I would expect of Henry's style. Like his office in Humphrey Hall, it gives off the vibe of a gothic Victorian mansion—high ceilings and textured green walls so dark they veer on black, thick patterned

curtains draped just so, and an abundance of ornate rugs.

When I reach the parlor, Virgil is already there with his nose in a book. I stand in the doorway. He must know I'm here, given his hearing, but he keeps his gaze on the pages. My breathing slows, and the stinging cold on my cheeks dulls.

The curtains are drawn, making the already dark space feel dim and moody, further enhanced by the half-lit wall sconces and burning logs in the fireplace. The room is big enough to hold a fair number of people, with several couches and armchairs. It fits Virgil's aesthetic perfectly. Like he's a feature of the room itself in his soft plum sweater and black slacks.

Laira mutters something that I barely hear about going to get Henry.

Virgil is right there, but he's also miles away. It's probably better like this. If I give it a few weeks, everything that makes me want to kiss him so badly will disappear. We can be platonic partners. The way we have to be if we don't want him to end up in the Pen.

Virgil isn't the sort of boy who takes risks. And yet, he took a risk on me. But it was one thing to put it all on the line when his prospects were nonexistent, and another to tempt fate now that we have so much to lose. I understand why he's pushing aside the feelings that led to our kiss in the first place.

Still, there's something in me that aches at the fact that he can do it so easily.

Virgil looks up and grins. "There's some good stuff in here. I can lend it to you after." He waves me over, and I sit next to him. "This is about enhancing connections between Monster and Master. Corris suggested it to me. It even talks about blood bonds, which is a bond that Monsters can have with each other and only

requires a significant exchange of blood and mental connection. After, those Monsters can share abilities." He's positively giddy, and a tiny smile peels onto my face despite myself.

"Have we met anyone like that?" I ask.

He shakes his head. "No. It was more common among Wilds and used heavily during the rebellion, which created a negative connotation around it. Wilds were banned from blood bonds in the agreement with Cyrus as well. He broke them all as soon as the ink had dried." Virgil furrows his brow. "The author also talks about bonds being more flexible than they seem. Like they're their own animal. He says that bonds between Master and Monster are the same in that they're formed in a limited number of ways, but the bonds themselves are unique to each pair." Virgil smiles at me, pushing his glasses into place. "Cool, right?"

"Yeah." I swallow, aware of the fact that to look at his book, I ended up closer to him. Our thighs touching. I wait for him to move away, because I'm not strong enough for it. But he doesn't.

He licks his lips. "August—"

"Sorry for the delay," Henry says, walking into the room with Laira behind him. Virgil shoots to his feet like something shocked him. Henry waves him back down. "You can sit. I want to take some time to explain a bit of theory to you. Though I see you've already been reading up."

Virgil shoves the book into his bag and retakes his seat, farther away from me this time. "Just some extracurricular reading. I went over Corey's notes last week."

"I assume you haven't had a chance yet?" Henry asks me.

"Still have to fit it into my busy schedule." I planned to read it on Wednesday right before the Mastery group meeting.

"Of course." He adjusts the sleeves of his sweater and sits in the armchair across from us. "Our first goal for you two is to master the second stage. It will be ideal to manage this before the competition starts. Third stage, on the other hand, we'll train for, but you'll also benefit from the fights in the Monster's Ball. That is why this competition exists, after all—to help push you to reach those higher evolutions." He crosses one leg over the other. "Mastery of the second stage requires two things: first, a strong understanding of your Monster partner's abilities, and second, tapping into that mental connection like you did in the initiation. Like a muscle, the more you do it, the easier it will become. Understood thus far?" Me and Virgil nod. "Good. I find it best to be practical with these things. So, Virgil, your task today will be working on isolated transformations. Start with each limb. Then work on smaller edits, such as growing claws from each fingernail one at a time. Then increase speed. The more control you have over this, the more control you'll have over your body when transformed."

"Yes, sir," Virgil says.

Henry turns to me as he rises from his chair. "You'll join me over here. Bring a knife." I stand and grab one of my knives from my backpack before following Henry to a table. He holds out his hand for the knife, and I give it to him. He places his hand on the table, palm down, and stabs the knife between each finger. Slowly at first. Then faster, and faster, and then at a speed where his fingers blur and my eyes cross. He stops and regards me coolly, extending the knife. I take it.

"I'm guessing you want me to do that?" I ask.

"Yes. Keep in mind all the times that you have seen Virgil move quickly. Consider his speed as your own, because it is."

I press my hand on the table and bring the knife down between the fingers, working through one at a time.

"Faster," Henry commands.

I attempt to move the knife at a quicker pace.

"Faster," he says again.

I gnaw on my lip.

"Faster!"

The knife comes down and slices the side of my index finger. "Fuck!" I snarl, whipping my hand away, sticking the digit into my mouth.

"She's fine," Henry says, his tone bored as Virgil looks over at us. I glare at Henry. "When you reach level three, you can simply heal. You could throw a gold bar into a wall, but you can't manage this simple task. Do you know why?"

"Enlighten me."

"You have the power, but you lack control." I grind my teeth, and Henry leans forward, coming close. "You have something inside you, a simmering rage that could make you one of the strongest Bachelors in the running. What has always been your problem is that you let your emotions run wild. One moment you're a flickering flame, and the next you're a wildfire. Learn to mold your anger to your will and use it. Because if you cannot harness it, then it's useless."

Before I can process what's happening, my blade is flying toward my face, and then it's between my fingers. I'm breathing heavy, the knife pinned between my pointer and index finger, the blade millimeters away from my nose.

"Did you just throw my own fucking knife at me?" I spit.

Henry shrugs. "And you caught it. At a speed that is beyond your abilities with a strength that is beyond your abilities with enough

precision to avoid bending the metal. You said you wanted to be stronger, so prove it." He gestures to the knife. "Keep doing the exercise."

I clench my jaw, and the feeling rises in me again. Like the initiation. When I wanted to taste my enemies' entrails and crush whoever annoyed me. Like Doctorate Day, when I wanted to chase down those Wilds and slice into their flesh. To make them pay. To make *someone* pay.

I'm so fucking tired of being told to control myself. This thing building inside me is giving me the power I need to avenge Mom. If I push it down, I'll be too weak to go after Carrigan.

And why should I push it down?

Does a wolf hold itself back on a hunt?

No, it doesn't.

It goes for the kill.

CHAPTER SIX

Virgil falters as he steps out of Watson Hall with a flood of students to find me waiting. The building is a flat beige-gray hybrid in an uninspired blocky assortment of rectangles. It has none of the romance of the other brick buildings that line University Avenue. Makes me wonder if that's why it's tucked in close to Victoria Hall.

Virgil slips his hands into the pockets of his peacoat, wary as he approaches me. It's not that I memorized his class schedule, necessarily. That would be sad and desperate. It's just common knowledge that the ENGL100 course is Wednesday and Friday afternoons. A lot of people take the class.

"Were we supposed to meet up?" he asks. As if he's ever forgotten scheduled plans. The only thing we had happening this week was Mastery group on Wednesday, where I almost bludgeoned Mitch with a gold bar. Though I did do Corey's reading outlining potential applications of healing and roar skills—useless to me because those are

third-evolution abilities, and I can't even manage second-level ones.

I straighten. "You promised me that this bond was forever. That if I needed you, you would help me. Do you still mean that?"

Virgil stares, catching me in the dark molten amber of his eyes. Things aren't the same between us. There's no point in ignoring it. But I would hope that hasn't changed the fact that he cares about me. I'm overheating under the weight of what's inside me. I need someone who, if only for a moment, will let me burn the way I need to.

"If you need me, I'm here. Always." He hesitates for a moment before reaching his hand out to me. I raise my own, clasping our hands and pulling us together, our forearms resting against each other's. His breath is warm on my face, the chill making it visible.

I lick my lips. "I need you."

The town of Sydenham is about an hour north of Kingston. Somewhere I couldn't get by myself because I can't drive and don't have money to take an Uber. Unlike Virgil, who *can* drive and is trustworthy enough for Margot to lend him her SUV. I would say no questions asked, but she definitely had questions. Virgil fielded them smoothly, stating that we wanted to drive to a secluded area on Wolfe Island to train and didn't want to ask Bailey for a ride and deal with *her* questions.

Now Virgil glances at me in the passenger seat as we wind our way down the road. We pass by multiple churches and cemeteries. Enough that it starts to feel a little concerning—like, how many people are dying out here?—until we hit more farmland. I expect modest houses on the side of the road, and there are some, but there are also luxury mini mansions with four-car garages and massive plots of land.

"Jules didn't say anything about where the documents might

be besides a forest?" Virgil asks. He cuts down a side road that I wouldn't have even realized was a road. The SUV bumps and shakes on the uneven terrain, and he winces at the sound of rocks plinking against the sides of the vehicle.

"Can't you sniff it out? Should be paper smells or something."

"I feel like you have a mistaken impression that I'm some sort of hound."

I throw my hands up. "I don't know!"

"There's a strong scent of metal over this way. It's close enough to their property that it might be the place we're looking for."

"I'm sorry, so you *can* sniff it out?"

He scowls. "Yes. But I don't want to be relied on to use my nose for everything. I do have a brain and other senses."

"Can we circle back to the part where I asked something reasonable and you tried to act like it wasn't reasonable?"

Virgil turns off the ignition. "We'll go on foot from here."

I huff but follow him as we trek through the forest. From what I can tell, Sydenham is rural but in a suburb way. The houses are on neat little plots, but there's only a handful of stores. Though this area is more rustic than what we passed by earlier.

Finally, we come to a clearing where a rusted metal door sits nestled in foliage on a hill. It has a rounded shape behind it and reminds me of a bomb shelter.

"Can I compliment you on your scent-based skills, or is that offensive?" I ask.

Virgil walks to the door, which is chained and padlocked. "It's going to be obvious if we break it."

"How would they know it was us? I thought people didn't have distinctive smells or whatever."

"That's not what I said."

"You literally said that last semester!"

"No," Virgil says, crossing his arms. "I said people generally smell the same, and they do. There's no special unique smell that you're born with. Rather, people have subtleties in their scents, and the combination of those creates something novel. But it's not like I could smell your possessions and know that it's you if I had never met you. I have to catalogue the handful of scents as belonging to you."

I groan. "I didn't want a lecture. Are we going to get caught or not?"

"We have to hope that whoever investigates the break-in doesn't come into contact with us again. There's a small chance that they might match the smells. But it's unlikely that we'll be caught, yes."

"Amazing, then let's break it."

My fingers twitch at my sides. I could break it myself if I tried. I can't wait around and hope that Natalie manages something. Besides, the chains look untouched. She hasn't even bothered with it.

Virgil sighs. "Fine. I'll break them. Hopefully we'll be gone before anyone notices." He holds the chains and flexes, his muscles bulging under his jacket, and his nails turning black and sharp as he breaks the links apart.

Of course Virgil can control *his* strength.

He cranks the handle wheel on the door and opens it. I head in first, pulling out a knife just in case. It's dark inside, but I have some awareness of where I'm going.

"It's interesting," he says. "The society should have the same records, and Wilds can access them unless they're stored in the vault. I don't know why they'd need their own separate storage."

"What's 'the vault'?" I make sure that it sounds as ridiculously ominous when I say it as he made it seem.

"It's on the Doctorate's island in the cottage. The cottage is actually a really interesting historical building. That's why the prize includes a tour. There are—"

"No more lectures!" Virgil throws me an annoyed look but shuts up. "Maybe the Wilds don't trust society record keeping? I mean, could you blame them?" I ask.

"That's true. They might have information that the society doesn't too. Shouldn't be possible, as I'm sure they've been raided before, but you never know."

I walk down the stairs until reaching a room at the bottom, where I flip the light switch. Fluorescents flicker to life, illuminating a bunch of file cabinets. "We're looking for anything from November twenty-fifth, two years ago," I say.

We spread out and work in silence, digging through the cabinets and files as fast as possible. It's not like an alarm went off, but you never know.

"Here," I breathe as I find a cabinet with dates and pull out a folder, flipping through it. "On November twenty-fifth, a Wild named Kendrick Durand was dispatched to Scarborough from Kingston to investigate a sighting of a reptilian Monster. He returned to Kingston on the twenty-sixth to report that the sighting could not be validated, and the case was closed." This confirms that there was a Monster who could have attacked Mom—Kendrick and this supposed reptilian Monster. I sag against the file cabinet. "That's it. . . ."

"Who dispatched it?"

"Um . . . Hailey Jenkins."

"Are there dispatch notes attached? Sometimes they do follow-ups."

I look through and find the dispatch report. It shows that Hailey Jenkins authorized the send-out based on police reports from that night of a wild animal described as reptilian. Naturally, the police never followed up, but the society did. "There's an update from the twenty-eighth saying that a guy who lived nearby had security cameras. The society hoped that the footage on them might show the Monster. They sent Durand to seize the physical memory cards from the cameras and bring them to the office to be verified. It's noted that he brought in the video, but there's nothing about whether that Monster was in it or not. Why wouldn't they put that in?"

"Maybe they didn't verify it for some reason. That or the Wilds never got a copy of the most up-to-date information?"

"Or the whole dispatch was just an excuse for Durand to get to the area, so the video doesn't matter."

"Either way, the society has that video. If we can get a look at it, there may be some clue about what happened. If it's a dud, then Kendrick is the main suspect, and if the other Monster is on there, then we have two suspects."

It's something, which is better than nothing. I take pictures of the file and start rooting through more of the documents.

"Someone's coming," Virgil says, his eyes going wide. "We have to go. *Now.*"

I clench my fists. "But what if there's something else here?"

"August!"

"Okay, fine, fine!" I put the files away and sprint up the stairs after Virgil.

When we come out of the hatch, a Wild is waiting for us.

Something in the pit of my stomach roils. The last time I saw a fully transformed Monster, they were slaughtering children. The high-pitched screams play back in my mind and mingle with the imagined cries of Mom. Of her tossing herself over a cliff to protect Jules from a Monster who'd come to kill her.

The Monster in front of us is in the form of a fox, on all fours, with thick orange fur and two pairs of narrow eyes set deep into its face. There are patches missing on the sides of its body, exposing bits of bone and muscle where mist seeps out. It's built thinner and wirier than most Monsters I've seen. Though it has no lack of claws and teeth.

The fox leaps at us, and I dive to the right while Virgil goes left, an explosion of fur and spikes. His transformation is almost faster than before, and it was already fast. The fox ignores me while Virgil evades it and manages to get into his full wolf form.

The two of them smash against each other, locking claws and shoving, the muscles of their legs flexing.

I pant, chest heaving, looking between the two of them. My knives clenched in my fists. I mean to step forward, but pause.

Anything I do will just be getting in the way.

If it had been me with Mom instead of Jules, the result would have been the same. I wouldn't have been able to save her. Hell, I can't even do anything useful with my second-evolution powers.

What am I even good for? Why am I even here?

The fox bashes its head against Virgil, sending him reeling backward. He tries to regain his footing but can't. The fox catches him, ripping into Virgil's fur. My partner's howls fill the air, striking me like I'm the one who was bitten.

I need to do something, or he'll die.

I'll lose him.

Just like I lost Mom.

Virgil promised to help me, but I made a promise to him too. That we were a team. We fight together.

Something in the back of my mind unfurls, stretching its legs and back, claws extending. It's too volatile. Too dangerous.

But right now, dangerous is what I need to be.

The spark lights, the flame blooming.

I rush toward the fox, knives out, and stab it in the back. It howls and throws me off. I fly toward a tree, but somehow I get my legs under me and hit the bark with my heels, using it to propel me back toward the fox. I slash at it with my blades. It raises its claws and maybe it cuts me. I don't know. All I care about is digging the metal into its flesh as much as I can.

I think I laugh. I'm not sure.

My hands blur, going faster than I can keep track of. The fox kicks me in the stomach; something cracks. I'm pushed away, and it rushes toward the trees, trying to escape.

No. That won't do at all.

I smile, twirling my blades in my hands, strength flooding through my body.

I'm not weak. Not helpless. I'm better than I've ever been.

Virgil snaps his jaws around the fox's tail, tossing it into the trees. It hits a trunk and goes down, the soft flesh of its belly exposed. Before it can recover, I'm there, slashing with my knives. Shallow cut after shallow cut, because I want this to last.

Why would I ever need control when I have power?

"August, you need to stop! Stop! Fucking stop!"

I come to myself drenched in blood. The fox isn't a fox anymore.

It's a boy I've seen before, heaving and struggling to breathe, ginger hair plastered to his forehead. His clothes are tatters on his pale white skin, soaked through with blood. Muscle and bone exposed.

"Fuck, fuck, fuck," Virgil is saying over and over. "He's going to die. Fuck, I think he's going to die."

What? No. I . . . I . . .

I'm looking at the boy, and I know he's my age, but now I'm seeing the kids. The girls with their stomachs ripped open and their mouths agape. Jules on the hill crying for our mom. The Monster is there.

And the Monster . . .

The Monster is me.

"I . . . I . . ." My hands are trembling. I want to kill Carrigan. *Carrigan.* Someone who deserves it. Not some random guy my age. "We can heal him, right? Or he can heal himself? Monsters are tough."

"*No.* This is . . . this is beyond. Monsters are tough; we aren't immortal. And he, he doesn't seem like he has a regeneration ability. My regeneration only extends to you because we're bonded. I'm nothing to him."

"So then we make you something to him," I say. Virgil looks at me, slack-jawed. The boy beneath us has wet breaths. Like he's drowning. "That blood bond you told me about. Monsters can do it. You bond with him, and we can save him, and then . . . and then Adam will undo it after, okay?"

Virgil shakes his head. "I've never done it—"

"You've read about it. You know the theory."

He licks his lips and cringes—there's blood on them. On his face and shirt. All of us covered in crimson. "Okay, okay."

"No . . . ," the boy mumbles.

"The choice is this or death," I say.

He stares at me, his eyes a watery sort of green. Like a pond. Growing duller by the minute, as if covered with scum or oil.

My lip trembles. "We know the Doctorate. He'll undo it after. Everything will be fine. Just let us help you. *Please.*" I can't be the reason he dies. I can't.

Finally, he nods.

Virgil transforms only his arm into a monstrous form and splits it open with a nail, parting the flesh. He raises the cut over the boy's mouth, letting the blood pour in. It's so much. Enough that it spills over the edges of the boy's lips.

"Your turn," Virgil says to him.

The redhead winces as he transforms his own arm into the orange fur of the fox. It's already bleeding, so all Virgil has to do is lap up what's there, wincing as he sucks at the fur, which I know now is surprisingly soft. Soft and sticky. I stare at his wounds, willing them to knit up and heal.

Come on, come on, come on.

He can't die. I wanted power, but not like this. I suck back a sob. I should have known. Jules and Henry told me that I didn't have control, and I didn't think I needed it, but now . . . I've fucked up so bad, and I've dragged Virgil down with me.

"I'm sorry," I choke out, looking at the boy and then Virgil. "I—"

Virgil's cheeks are wet with tears, and his hands are shaking. He's not looking at me. "It's not working. I don't know. I . . . I'm trying."

"Do you want to live or not?!" I scream at the boy on the ground, those eyes like still water. "If you want to live, then fight. Fight

because you're fighting for your life!" Only then does something ripple in those eyes.

I double over as a torrent of voices and images explodes in my mind. This isn't like initiation. It's painful. Punishing, even. And I can't say that it's not what I deserve.

He doesn't want this. This boy. Doesn't want to be bound to us. Is disgusted by the link even as he fights for it to form. He wants to live, and that's what I grip onto. He wants to keep going, and me and Virgil don't want to be the reason he can't.

And it's enough.

The wounds on his chest and stomach, the gaping holes that I slashed open, start to close.

A dry sob pulls itself from my body, and I cry out from sheer relief.

"August?!" I whip my head to the side, and of all people, Mia is standing there. Mia Levesque from the tiny house community. "What are you doing here?"

I'm about to ask her the same when suddenly it feels like every ounce of energy in my body is tugged away, and my vision goes black.

Though as my own eyes close, something inside me opens its eyes for the first time.

CHAPTER SEVEN

I wake to Corey peering at me, her brow furrowed. But the creases clear as I blink awake, and she disappears from my field of vision, shouting for someone. I sigh against the sheets and scan the room. It's the guest bedroom in McIntosh Castle but transformed to hold three single hospital beds and associated equipment: the one I'm on, Virgil to my right, and the boy to my left. *Nolan.* My brain supplies the name as if it's something I've always known. Both of them are already awake.

"How are you doing?" Virgil asks. His glasses, which he doesn't actually need, are on the bedside table, and he's in a gown like me.

I roll my shoulders back. "Tired. How long have I been out?"

"A day. It's Saturday afternoon. We only woke up a few minutes ago."

I press the button on the side of the bed to lift myself into a sitting position and address Nolan. "You alive over there?"

"Apparently," he says. "No thanks to you."

For once, I don't have a comeback. We may have saved him, but he wouldn't have needed saving if not for me. Defending Virgil is one thing, almost killing someone is another. And at some point, I wasn't even thinking about Virgil. I don't know when it transformed from a fight to a slaughter.

The worst part was that I was enjoying it.

The door opens and an older East Asian–looking man with wisps of gray hair covering a balding patch enters the room. "Well, not how I imagined our first meeting, Ms. Black, but given what I've heard about you, this somehow seems appropriate." He comes to my bedside with Corey and a Black woman I don't know behind him. He extends a hand to me. "Dr. Liu."

"Oh shit," I say, numbly shaking his hand. "You're back."

"I am. It seems my ward has been through quite an ordeal in the last little while." That with a glance at Virgil, who hunches. "A blood bond," he says humming to himself, looking from Virgil to Nolan. "Exceptional. Simply exceptional."

"I thought people used to do them a lot," I say.

Dr. Liu adjusts the spectacles on his nose, ones that look suspiciously similar to Virgil's pair. "Wilds did, yes. But the bonds were made between close friends and family. Making one with a stranger is rare. I would love to study the effects with your permission, but alas, the Doctorate is here to sever the tie."

"Good," I say. I'd made that promise to Nolan on the assumption Adam would break it for us.

Minutes later, Henry pushes open the door and enters with Adam and Margot.

Adam seems almost as tired as I assume I look. Understandable, given the state of his family life.

The woman who came in with Dr. Liu mumbles something about getting out of the way and ducks out of the room, but not before locking eyes with me for a moment too long. I squint at her. According to Dr. Liu, this is unprecedented, so I guess we're something of a spectacle.

Corey settles on a chair between me and Virgil. Judging by the side table with her phone and multiple notebooks, this has been her perch for a while.

Henry narrows his eyes at us. "We'll spare Adam the conversation of what you thought you were doing trespassing on the Murphy compound and skip straight to the bond breaking. But rest assured, we will be discussing the multiple ways in which you've embarrassed us all and endangered yourselves."

"Also, why you thought it was smart to go alone," Corey mutters, acid in her voice.

Margot adds, "With someone else's vehicle."

I cringe and glance at Virgil, who's sinking lower and lower into the bed. Henry will never be happy with me, but I do feel like shit about leaving Corey out and lying to Margot. I just didn't think getting more people involved in my already flimsy plan was the right move.

"I'm sure they had their reasons," Adam says, offering a small smile.

"No reason could be good enough," Henry grumbles. "Please proceed."

"Pushy," I mutter, and Henry shoots me a look that could melt ice caps.

Adam squares his shoulders. "This should be quick. I'm going to take a look at the bonds first. It's a mental thing, so don't mind as I close my eyes for a minute."

"Hold out your hands," Henry says to us.

Adam shakes his head. "Not necessary."

Henry stares at him. "No?"

"No. Uh, since my graduation to the title, I can manage it like Dad could without contact."

"I didn't realize you get special powers when you become Doctorate," I say.

Adam smiles. "Not as such. I've just been enlightened about the extent of what I can do based on what my dad left for me to inherit." What does that even mean? Like Cyrus gave him instructions or something? Whatever it is, Henry didn't know about it either, because he's acting like this is new information. "I'll look at Virgil and Nolan's blood bond now."

"You know my name?" Nolan asks.

Adam nods. "You're the second son, yes?"

For some reason this makes Nolan's jaw clench. Who are Nolan's parents that Adam would casually know his name? Nolan turns to the wall and stares at it like it's the most interesting thing in the room.

Adam closes his eyes, and we watch in silence as he stands there. His fingers twitch at his sides, and his nose scrunches.

After five minutes, Henry starts to shift in place, and he and Margot share a short look. Even Dr. Liu has a furrowed brow.

Finally, Adam opens his eyes and sighs.

"What?" Henry asks.

"Uh . . . I can't break it."

That makes Nolan turn away from the wall, eyes wide. "What do you mean you can't break it?"

Adam licks his lips. "August and Virgil have one bond. Now,

Virgil made a blood bond to heal you, that's two bonds. Even in a case where a Master bonds with a second Monster, those bonds would be separate. In order for those Monsters to share abilities, they would need an independent blood bond. In all those cases, the bonds are one-to-one. But yours . . . they're all tangled up. Partner bonds are unique. August, yours and Virgil's, to my eyes, is more intertwined than most. The only theory I can come up with is that when Virgil connected with Nolan, his bond with August came along instead of staying separate. Now the three of them are in a knot. When I try to pull on any of the bonds, they resist."

Back at the compound, I could tell when the bond snapped into place. It hadn't occurred to me that I shouldn't have felt anything. I thought I was just experiencing sensations through Virgil somehow.

I swallow, not sure how to feel about the revelation that my connection to Virgil is that strong.

"Bonds cannot *resist,*" Henry snaps.

"These ones can," Adam says. "I did try to see the potential of creating a partial break, but they won't even let me do that much."

"What do you mean a partial break?" I ask.

"They're also called temporary breaks," Adam says. "Back in my grandfather's time, it was used as a punishment. If you break a bond halfway, the Monster loses control of their body, killing and maiming as they would without a partner, but they are conscious during the experience and their partner bond remains. This means that the Doctorate can repair the connection between the two, pulling the bond back together."

My jaw drops. "That's so fucked up."

"Language," Henry says. "Besides, it was a punishment preferable to death."

Adam shakes his head. "She's right. It was cruel. Still, I thought maybe the bonds would allow a partial break instead of a full one, but it's not happening. The tangling is odd, though at least explainable, but the resistance . . . I don't know if it's the unusual circumstances of having a Wild mixed up in this or what. With some time to research—"

"We don't have time!" I say. "The Monster's Ball is next week."

Adam crosses his arms over his chest. "You could forfeit."

"No!"

I need to get stronger if I want to have a chance at going up against Carrigan. I almost took out Nolan on my own. Out of control, yes, but there's power in me. I just need to learn to manage it like Henry said. Fighting in the Monster's Ball is the only way I'm going to be able to practice and level up. I can't do that if I'm put on ice for a year. And what if Carrigan kills Adam and becomes the Doctorate during that time? It'll make it even harder to get to him.

Henry nods. "I agree with August. She and Virgil will lose opportunities for advancement in society if they can't secure the two consecutive wins in the Monster's Ball. Starting with a forfeit will ruin that."

"Can't we just participate anyway?" I ask. "I mean, don't you make the rules?"

Adam says, "Yes, and I cannot continue to break them for you. I will remind you that what you two have done is an illegal bonding. Virgil and Nolan are *both* August's partners now. That may not have been the intention, but that is the result. I cannot break the bond myself, and according to the rules of society, that would mean I have to break them via death."

I swallow, and Virgil and Nolan stiffen on either side of me.

"But I will not. As I said, this wasn't your intention; however, this means I have already bent the rules in your favor. Either you forfeit this year, or you fight following the rules for Masters with multiple partners. Meaning you compete with both Virgil and Nolan, alternating between matches. If you place within the cutoff, you'll graduate to the next title."

"So we'll compete, then," I say.

Nolan drawls, "Do I get a choice in this?"

I shut my mouth with a snap.

"What's your price?" Henry asks, turning to Nolan.

Nolan sizes him up. "You know, you are just how everyone says you are. You have every resource at your fingertips, don't you?" Henry says nothing in response. "This is in violation of the agreement. Wilds are not to be bonded."

"I think that agreement became null and void when Wilds slaughtered my brother and his family," Adam says. His tone is neutral, but the look in his eyes is cool to the touch.

Nolan doesn't back down. "That wasn't us. You made a big show of acting like you were on our side with that, but then you let those bigots parade their oppressive proposal in the public eye. Someone is trying to frame us, which is why my dad had me guarding our files in the first place."

"Wait, who's your dad?" I ask.

"Garrett Murphy."

My eyes go wide. "Garrett?! Isn't he, like . . . old?" Though this explains why Adam knew Nolan's name. Garrett is the closest thing to a leader the Wilds have—in Ontario, at least. And he led the rebellion. *Second son.* The first I assume being Jacques, Mia's dad.

Nolan gives me a flat look before turning back to Adam and

Henry. "You asked what I wanted. Here's my demand: strike down the proposal."

Adam scrubs at his face. "It's not that easy."

"Isn't it? It's oppressive and you know it. Not to mention we've already been suffering compensatory violence even with your grand declaration that it wasn't a coordinated effort by us. Anti-Wild sentiment is building, and you need to stop it."

I look between them. "What compensatory violence?"

"Some Masters and their partners have been taking it upon themselves to intimidate and threaten Wilds as a result of what happened. Including an attack on another family recently where two small children were severely injured."

Adam cringes. "I have condemned—"

"You haven't done enough!" Nolan snarls.

"Is that what you thought we were doing at the compound? Launching an attack?" I ask.

Nolan shrugs. "I didn't know what you were doing. But you were trespassing, and the Wilds are not in a secure position right now. My dad lost everything in that rebellion. Sacrificed it all just so we could get an agreement not much better than what we had before. I refuse to lose everything for the sake of my legacy like he did. The Wilds are not a monolith. I, for one, don't want to be punished for the choices of others."

Adam shakes his head. "I cannot strike it down out of turn. It's not that simple to dismiss it, not now that it has support."

Nolan crosses his arms over his chest and grits his teeth.

"There's another more immediate matter to consider," Margot says, and everyone turns to her. "We saw what being bonded to multiple Monsters did to Bernie last year. How is it going to

affect August? Even if they want to compete, if her body and mind are breaking down under the stress of the bonds, then it doesn't matter."

Automatically, I touch my chest as if expecting my heart to suddenly seize. I feel normal. Tired, sure, but Bernie was struggling to stand and breathe. Beside me, Corey grips the sheets of my bed, eyes roving over me.

"I don't feel sick," I say.

Margot presses her lips into a thin line. "You don't feel sick *now*. Bernie's deterioration took time. I'm just saying that we need to keep an eye on you. I know you want to fight, but the more you exercise the bonds, the more pressure it'll put on you. Most Masters have years of training to take on a second partner, and you're still only a Bachelor."

"I don't know that that will be an issue," Adam says, tilting his head. "In normal circumstances, August would be shouldering the load of both bonds. But that's not the case here. The way they're tangled, they're all bearing the burden. I've never seen this happen before, so it's possible there will be other side effects, but the pressure of this bond isn't centered on August. If anything, I would say Virgil is the center of it. Besides that, as a Wild, Nolan doesn't need the support of a Master to maintain his facilities like Virgil does. Still, ideally I'll find a way to break the bond before we see any adverse effects." He steps back. "I'll give you some time to think through whether you'll compete. Henry can let me know what you decide." With a final nod, he leaves the room.

I think of how Virgil bent those Monster-proof bars to escape back when we fought Bernie. How he resisted turning longer than should have been possible. Even how fast he can transform. I know

Virgil is a legacy Monster and therefore stronger than normal, but the amount of exceptional circumstances surrounding him are starting to stack up. I can't help but wonder if this weird bond resistance is something to add to the list.

Dr. Liu claps his hands. "That's enough for today. I think the patients could use the rest." Henry protests, but Dr. Liu ignores him, shooing the man out of the room with vicious effectiveness. Margot leaves along with him, casting one last lingering look at me. Even Corey stands with a sigh, gathering her things and giving Virgil's and my hands a quick squeeze before she goes.

Meanwhile, Jules slips into the room. I balk. "How did you—"

"I was waiting downstairs, but it was taking a while," he says.

Dr. Liu sighs. "I am attempting to close up visiting hours."

"That's my sister," Jules says and attempts a smile. But on his face, it ends up looking more like he's baring his teeth. "I'll be quick."

"Fine."

Dr. Liu leaves the room, and now I'm the one sinking low in my bed.

Jules says nothing for a moment, just stares at me. It's a technique that Mom would use when we'd messed up. "I hope you know what you did wrong."

Even those words are hers. "You're not Mom."

"I can't trust you. I told you one thing, and you blew it up. You don't consider your own safety or the safety of others. I can't bring you in on anything. Leave it to me and Nat. I don't want any more blood on my hands."

"It's not on *your* hands."

"It is! It is because I enable you. I'm not going to do it anymore! Concentrate on your schoolwork and the Monster's Ball, and try, for

fuck's sake, *try* not to get yourself or anyone else killed." With that, Jules storms out of the room.

The door shutting almost seems to echo. Leaving me, Virgil, and Nolan alone.

"So," Nolan says to me. "Shitting the bed kind of seems to be a regular occurrence for you, eh?"

I grit my teeth.

"It's not a bad idea," Virgil says. "Leaving things to Jules and Natalie while we concentrate on this."

"They haven't even done anything!"

"I just . . . Have you . . . I mean, have you given yourself time to process everything with your mom? I know we're not the same, but it took me years to properly grieve losing my parents. You've barely had a couple weeks, and—"

"You're right," I snap. "We're not the same." Virgil sighs and looks away.

Time to grieve. What does that even mean? I'm never going to stop missing Mom. If I put my life on pause now, I'll never press start again. I have no choice but to keep going.

I say, "Did you do the blood bond because you wanted to, or because you thought you owed it to me?"

"*We* owed it to *him*," Virgil says, looking at Nolan.

"I was the one who lost control."

"You weren't the only one," Nolan says.

I whip my head from him to Virgil, who keeps his gaze down.

"Bonds go both ways," Nolan continues. "One of you loses control, both of you lose control." He tucks his knees up to his chin. "I didn't ask to be born a Wild, didn't ask to be forced into being a proctor by the agreements, and I certainly didn't fucking

ask to be chained to you two. All I wanted was to live. So I had to say yes to all those things. But I'm telling you right now, I'm not a part of your bullshit. Your forfeit doesn't affect me." He motors his bed down and pulls the covers up to his chin, turning away from us.

CHAPTER EIGHT

Riley

I take a deep breath before stepping up to the wrought iron door of McIntosh Castle in the chill of the evening. It's as grand as expected, but in an understated way. It's not like the building is a mansion. Certainly not when compared to the new QBSS clubhouse only a few blocks away. I do wonder if the council chose to do that on purpose. This isn't the hub of the Learners' Society, just their library. But Henry Scott has a vested interest in the people who reside here, and perhaps that's enough.

That's why I'm here, after all. Though I've set my own sights higher.

I can do it all. Even now, I'm managing my student council duties despite Inaya questioning me at every turn. She's still acting like she's VP even though that's no longer her title. Meanwhile, my actual VP, Malachi, is constantly MIA when I need him. Only Jackson is performing his duties as usual, though now he communicates primarily via text instead of in person. Which is fine by me.

I need to concentrate on achieving what I promised the elder council. I ignore the churning in my gut. This will benefit August, too.

The door opens, and Corey beams at me from the entryway. She's using a pair of crutches to stay upright, wearing a set of copper satin pajamas, the left leg on the bottoms loose and empty below the knee. Her hair is tied up when I'm used to seeing it down. She's always struck me as feminine with a hard edge, but that updo softens her.

Heat rises at the back of my neck, and I rub it as if that will dispel the feeling.

"You're here to see August?" Corey asks.

"Yeah, uh, are you okay?"

She tilts her head.

"Just . . . the crutches?"

"Oh!" She laughs. "My little leg felt swollen, so I took off my prosthesis, and crutches are my backup."

"Oh, okay, cool." Embarrassing. I'm usually more eloquent than this. I take off my shoes and put on a pair of black slides at Corey's instruction and follow her to the stairs.

She sets the crutches against the wall. "Um, you should go up first. . . ."

"Sure . . ." I start up the steps. When I glance back, Corey is facing away from me, sitting on the stairs and slowly scooting her way up. I turn away to give her privacy, only making eye contact once she's at the top of the landing, her breath coming a bit faster.

"Sorry," I say. "You didn't have to bring me all the way up the stairs."

She stands and grabs the second set of crutches leaning against the wall. "This is just how I get around. Not much I can do about it

if I'm dealing with swelling. Going up the stairs on my butt is kind of embarrassing, but it's dangerous to go up with crutches, so . . ."

"It's not embarrassing. Do what you have to do."

Corey bites her lip. "Anyway, if you were going to make me go up and down the stairs repetitively, then yeah, I'd be annoyed. Anyone would."

I nod several times. "Of course. I just wanted to make sure I wasn't making you overextend yourself."

She looks down, nudging her toe into the carpet on the landing. "I'm not a porcelain vase. I won't break with a little pressure."

"I've seen you kick a Monster in the face. I know you're not fragile. Just, sometimes when people know you're strong, you end up pushing yourself more than you ought to because they figure you can take it."

Corey jerks her head up, her mouth the slightest bit ajar. Her lips are shiny and pink, like she just swiped the gloss on.

I swallow and look away, motioning down the hall. "Uh . . . what room are they in?"

She leads me to a door at the end of the hallway, which she knocks on. "Riley's here!"

A voice I don't recognize from inside says, "Is this your hot friend?"

Corey's entire face flushes red.

I grimace. Why is August calling me her hot friend? Jesus, she turns everything into a joke.

"Come in!" August says.

Corey opens the door and releases a hand from one of her crutches to gesture for me to go in. I enter the room, where August and Virgil are on hospital beds. I expected that but I didn't expect

to see the random guy in the other bed. He's pale even for a white guy, with a slim build, a narrow face, and ginger hair that falls loose on his shoulders. He's not bad to look at in a folksy musician sort of way.

His eyes trail up and down my body. "I see it," he says.

It takes me a moment to catch up with what he's referring to before I scowl. I turn to August. "Don't describe me to people as your hot friend."

She has the audacity to look scandalized. "It wasn't me!"

"I'm sure." She starts to protest more, and I wave it away. "Did you want to get into what's going on here?"

"Not particularly."

I glance at Corey, who's settled on a chair between Virgil and August. "They did something exceptionally ill-advised and got in a fight with and almost killed Nolan." She pauses to point at the redhead. "That's Nolan. Anyway, to save him with Virgil's healing, he and Virgil did a blood bond, but now they're all bonded somehow, and Doctorate Shaw says he can't undo it."

"I guess we are getting into it," August mutters, slouching in her bed.

I cannot understate how ridiculous this girl's life is. First, she gets caught up with the society and this whole Bernie thing trying to save her brother. Then she saves him but still does the initiation to save Virgil. Now she's doing something else that almost made her a murderer, only to ultimately save yet another stranger.

"Do you have the chain?" I ask.

August says, "So you're just going to ignore all that or . . . ?"

"Do you?"

"It's in my dorm room."

I sigh. "If you carried it with you, you could have used it to bind Nolan instead of fighting."

"I'm sorry that it's not my first instinct to carry around something that I don't know anything about!"

I hunch my shoulders. I can't blame her. I meant to take some time to teach her more about QBSS and how to use the chain, but I got caught up in my own stuff and neglected that responsibility.

"Did you come here for a reason?" August asks. "Or just to lecture me?"

I tilt my head toward Nolan. "And he's what? Just going to listen in?"

"I couldn't give less of a shit," he says, turning away.

It's not ideal, but the guy is bound to August and Virgil. He's going to be attached to this group, and so I doubt they could help me without him noticing. He'll find out eventually, so I may as well make my pitch while I have a captive audience.

"I've been spending the semester thus far attempting to figure out why you're able to use the chain at all. I took off one of the links before I gave it to you and have been waiting for lab results. They just came in." The whole process had taken a century, it felt like. I'd suspected the answer but had needed confirmation to be sure. "And your bones are in the artifact."

"Um . . . gross?" August wrinkles her nose. "How do you put bones in a necklace?"

"That's proprietary information," I say.

Corey says, "I assume you melt the metal and combine it with ground-up bone, and then re-mold it into the existing shape. That's why the necklace is so chunky, because over time the continued additions of bone would alter the amount of material."

I bite the inside of my cheek, because that is, in fact, exactly how we do it.

"Just a guess," Corey mumbles, seeing my expression.

I ask, "Did your mom keep your baby teeth?"

"Uh, no, because that's creepy as fuck." August pauses, perhaps remembering that Historics' parents keep their baby teeth. "Like, I mean, if you don't have a reason to."

"Well, someone did. That's the only way they could access your bones and put them in an artifact without you realizing. They wanted you to have a connection to QBSS. And whoever helped them—because someone must have—isn't sharing, because no one in QBSS is aware of how this happened."

"Am I supposed to know who did that? Because I don't."

Virgil says, "Her mom."

"Thank you!" I say, throwing my hands up. "Glad someone is thinking critically." I cannot believe I have to walk this girl through everything.

August scowls at me. "Care to share with the class how you came to that conclusion?"

"You said your mom sent your brother to QBSS because she felt he would be protected by us. But there's no record of her. However, in QBSS when we have spies who operate within the Learners' Society, we don't keep records of them, since it's dangerous. They have a single point person, a handler. And again, whoever they were is not coming forward. But it's suspicious that in the same year that Bernie goes looking for this weapon, your mom was targeted. She must have known something. If she was in danger, that would also explain why her QBSS handler is staying silent. Maybe they're scared."

"If she knew something, she would be alive." August stares at her

sheets. "Just like Bernie wouldn't kill you because he needed what he thought you knew."

"Who says the person who targeted her wanted to use the weapon? What if it was the opposite?"

She looks up. "You think the person who killed her did it to *stop* information about the weapon from getting out? Like, to make sure no one else could get it?"

"Yes. I mean, Bernie said it was powerful enough to kill a God. Who else in the society could he mean but a Doctorate?"

"The Doctorates aren't Gods," Corey says.

"No, but you can't pretend they aren't revered as if they are. If I were a Doctorate, I sure as shit wouldn't want someone getting a hold of something that could kill me."

I swear that Nolan's face twitches in my periphery. He's definitely listening even though he tries to pretend otherwise.

"Doctorates can die from anything," Virgil says. "They're hard to kill, but they aren't invulnerable."

"Fine," I say. "But you have to admit that someone is either afraid of this artifact or they want it. When it was hidden within QBSS, it was one thing, but if August's mom knew something and that person realized it . . ."

"It could risk the weapon being found," August says. "So what's your angle here?"

I pull myself straight. "We combine our resources, and *we* find it."

"And then QBSS uses it?"

"And then QBSS safeguards an artifact that already belongs to us. I will remind you that we were targeted last semester, and we lost people. So excuse us for wanting a bit of security." I cross my arms over my chest. "We see that the Wilds are moving and—"

"Not the Wilds," Nolan interrupts. "*Some* Wilds. Some *individuals*."

Corey mouths, "He's a Wild."

Well, that's an intriguing tidbit. Now I'm even more baffled as to how August found herself in this situation. Wilds keep to themselves, generally. How did she even get the opportunity to— Actually, I don't want to know.

I say, "*Someone* is making a move. You want to find out what happened to your mom, and I want to get this weapon. We can pool our resources."

"Does QBSS know you're pooling resources?" Virgil asks. I don't like him without his glasses. His eyes are more penetrating like this. Uncanny, almost.

"This time, yes. They're on board if we get the weapon."

It's not like I want to be here begging for a team-up. But it would be ridiculous to act like I don't need help. It's been weeks, and I still can't get the sickle to the second stage. I can't even think about the third. Finding this mysterious weapon is all I have right now.

August collapses on the bed like she's already exhausted, and we haven't even started.

"I can help," Corey says, and I whip toward her. "August, Virgil, and Nolan are going to be busy with the Monster's Ball—"

"I didn't consent to that," Nolan says.

"—and I don't know how much time they'll have for research, but it's my specialty. I'm already looking through society sources for Henry, and I'm sure there's some overlap in the material. Then we can bring August in if we find anything specific to her family."

"Does that work?" Virgil asks. "Corey's right. We have trainings with Henry plus Mastery group, meetings with Margot, and classes, and August's grades are already suffering."

"Why does everyone know about my grades?!" August says, looking around the room.

Corey smiles at me. "What do you think?" Teaming up would mean uninterrupted alone time with her. Despite myself, I think of late nights studying with Sammie, where she'd always fall asleep with her nose scrunched and her mouth open. And I'd watch, smiling. Once, Jackson came by to surprise me while I was doing it. Just staring at her sleeping.

He looked at me like I'd done something wrong, but I hadn't *done* anything.

"I can only meet during the day," I say.

Corey beams. "That works."

As long as it gets me closer to my goal, that's all that matters. I'll prove that I'm where I'm meant to be. I'm a Historic. I was built for this. Not destiny, but an inevitability. I was born to do nothing less than succeed, and I intend to keep to that birthright.

CHAPTER NINE

Corey yawns for what feels like the tenth time in the last twenty minutes. Since Riley left, she's set herself up between me and Virgil, making notes while consulting several different leather tomes—the same books she had in the room before we woke up. Nolan is still determined to ignore us, apparently.

"Did we put too much on you?" I ask Corey, and she jerks her head up. "You have a lot going on too."

"I wouldn't have said yes if I couldn't handle it."

"And it definitely has nothing to do with the opportunity to spend time alone with Riley?"

She flushes. "Okay, fine, my motives aren't entirely altruistic, but I'm good."

"How's the research for Henry going?" Virgil asks. His gown has slipped a bit, so I catch a glimpse of the dark curly hairs on his chest. For fuck's sake, I need to get laid. Maybe that's the problem.

I haven't been with anyone since hooking up with the guy I had a crush on at that party the night Mom died. I was obsessed with going to Rachel's place that night specifically because I wanted to see him. Now I haven't so much as liked an Instagram post from him in over a year.

Corey says, "I've got a good basis of background information. The first recorded spontaneous Monster birth happened in 1900. A seventeen-year-old transformed in his parents' kitchen. There were incidents across the country and beyond, but the highest concentrations are in southern Ontario. In 1901, Dr. Weiss predicted the apocalypse. Then there are all these rises and dips."

"What causes the spikes?" I ask.

"No one knows. So far, the only thing that stands out is a plateau in 1950 that picked up again in 1968."

"What happened in 1950?"

Virgil says, "Meredith Grant graduated to the Doctorate title. She was the fifth Doctorate, Cyrus's mother."

"Yes," Corey says. "But she died in 1966, so if there were some effect based on Doctorates, I would expect it to rise again in 1966, not two years later. Still, I feel like there's something there with Meredith. I want to look more into—" Corey is forced to pause as she yawns again.

I shake my head. "Go to bed. You're clearly exhausted, and it's already past midnight."

"Fine," she says. "I'm leaving my research stuff here. You should sleep too."

"We will," Virgil says. "Grab the light on your way out?"

Corey nods, gathers her crutches, and flips the light switch off as she leaves.

I settle into the cushions and lower my bed, closing my eyes and attempting to sleep, but hours later, I'm still awake.

In the darkness, the only sound is the short, punctured grunts that come from Virgil's open mouth. I add this to the unattractive things I use to stop myself from feeling the way I do. But as usual, it's wasted, because there's something refreshing about the fact that even though he holds himself so tight, he lets go like this at night.

Though I'm sure with a couple more hours of sleep deprivation, I'll feel less generous.

On my other side, Nolan has his knees up to his chest, staring out the open window. A society doctor—a medical one, not more liberal arts PhDs—came earlier and checked him out, giving him a clean bill of health. Me too, despite Margot's concerns. However, the doctor also said Nolan would be fatigued and ordered him to stay overnight. Nolan had tried to get up but almost fell over, so he'd submitted to staying the night.

Not that he seems to be getting any rest either.

We need to participate in the Monster's Ball this year. We have a wave to ride. If we stop now, everything stops.

But Nolan, I've observed, isn't like Virgil. He's not going to help us just because we saved his life. There doesn't seem to be a single part of him that thinks he owes us. Which, I guess, is fair considering that I'm the reason he needed saving in the first place. Or rather, *we're* the reason he needed saving. According to Nolan, Virgil was just as out of control.

"How bad are the Wilds doing?" I ask.

There's no answer for a few minutes. I scowl. Is he really going to ignore me?

"Bad," Nolan says finally, not looking at me. "It'll be worse once

the Monster's Ball starts. Proctors always get some level of abuse, but this year it'll be more hate-fueled. This proposal is doing more than adding fuel to the fire. It's like dropping a nuclear bomb on the whole mess."

I lick my lips. "You know about Virgil's parents?"

"Everyone knows."

"So then you know he's one of the least popular people in this society, and yet students still cheered when I came first in the Bachelor candidacy. At our graduation, Masters and Monsters of higher ranks came to congratulate us. We have the backing of both Henry and Adam."

I can feel Nolan rolling his eyes even if he's not looking at me. "Good for you."

"Listen to what I'm saying," I hiss. Virgil stirs, and I pause, but he just rolls over. "No one liked us. In fact, some people fucking hated us, but when we did well in their little competition, that changed."

Now, Nolan turns to me.

I keep going. "One semester, that's all. I bet they won't make you proctor either. You want to change how people perceive the Wilds, then do well in their games. When was the last time a Wild competed, if ever? They can't cheer for you and vote to restrict you in the same breath. You change the way they see Wilds, they'll change what they support."

"It'll reinforce reductionist ideas that Wilds should be paired. Should be controlled by a partner. *Civilized* by them." He turns away again, hugging his knees closer to his chest. "Not interested."

Shit, shit, shit. I *need* him on board.

"I'll give you my prize," I blurt out. Nolan stiffens. "The

Doctorate has to grant a request for the winner, right? I'll tell him to strike down the proposal. Adam doesn't even want to approve the agreement. Making it my winning request will give him an excuse to say his hand was forced."

He turns back toward me. "That'll only happen if you win."

"Didn't you hear me? We came first in the Bachelor candidacy. Hell, we nearly killed you, and you're Garrett's son, so I bet you're not a pushover. Plus, we have the advantage of being a trio. Not to mention Henry and Adam's backing plus personal training from Henry. Since when has a Wild had that much going for them?"

"You sound like her," Nolan says, so quiet I have to strain to hear.

"Who?"

"Natalie Soer."

My lip curls.

He says, "The many times she's come to see my dad and do her spiel to try to lure him back in. That's what she sounds like." He pauses, then says, "But she's never been able to promise anything concrete." He rests his head on his knees. "I'll compete, but know that I'm not here to help you; I'm here to use you. If at any point I think there's no chance of winning, I'm out."

I slip out of bed, walk over to Nolan, and hold out my hand, pinkie extended. "We'll win. I promise."

He looks from my wiggling finger to my face. "What are you, five years old?"

I roll my eyes. "Fine." I'm in the process of lowering my hand when he sticks out his. I grin, and we lock pinkies.

Nolan releases my hand and lowers his bed, curling away from me on his side.

I return to my own bed and lean back, trying not to think about what it means to be compared to someone like Natalie. One by one, people drop like flies around her, but she always survives.

I check my phone, staring at the unanswered calls and texts from Mia about what I was doing on her granddad's property with her uncle, all of us covered in blood. It takes me a moment to catch up. Right. Nolan and Jacques are brothers, making Mia his niece.

I think for a moment, and then text, *I was helping a friend.*

I glance at Nolan in the dark. This partnership won't be like the one I have with Virgil. Nolan is looking out for number one. If we aren't useful to him, he'll leave. So we'll just have to make sure that doesn't happen.

Henry peers at the three of us, looking from me, to Virgil, to Nolan and back again. After taking the weekend to rest, he demanded we meet on Monday to make the most of what little time we have before the Monster's Ball. We're back in the Marshlands, which I can't help but hate a little. It makes me think of Jules almost biting my head off, and Davy Mathers screaming as his flesh burned. This time we're in more of an open field. The chill in the air is biting and feels almost unfair when it should be on its way to spring next month. It never feels like it when February is so ridiculously cold.

Behind the professor, Laira hefts a machine from the trunk of his Lincoln SUV, a huge black vehicle with gleaming rims that Laira drives while Henry sits shotgun. He didn't appreciate when I said that I, too, was a passenger princess.

Henry waits until Laira has set down the machine beside him. "Today, we're going to work on your coordination. Even though

you'll fight in the matches as pairs, the bond will affect all three of you. The benefit of being in a triumvirate is that Virgil will have access to Mr. Murphy's abilities and vice versa, as will August. If you train properly, you'll have a huge advantage in these fights."

"I'm sorry, a tri-what now?" I ask.

Henry takes a deep breath. "A triumvirate. A group of three powerful or notable people, originating in Ancient Rome for three men of power. Which I am making more inclusive."

"What's the difference between that and a threesome—"

"Whether you *are* powerful is a fact that remains to be seen. So perhaps the more diminutive trio is a better descriptor. Thank you for that, Ms. Black."

Nolan glances at Virgil. "Is she always like this?"

"Yes," Virgil says with a sigh.

"And you're into that?"

Virgil splutters, "What does that—"

"Children!" Henry snaps. "We're going to be doing three-legged races, though in this case, it will be five legs." He nods to Laira, who delivers a set of ropes to us with a sparkle in her eyes that's too joyful for my tastes. "Tie yourselves together."

Virgil immediately coordinates the tying of our legs. I'm in the middle, which seems to now be my permanent position, with Virgil and Nolan on either side.

Henry says, "You'll run from one side of the field to the other. If you fall, you'll restart. If your pace drops to walking speed, you'll restart. We'll continue like this until you can run to the other side of the field and back. Begin."

"Okay," Virgil says. "So maybe on the count of—"

But me and Nolan are already moving, and Virgil's attempt to

catch up with us means we all fall to the ground. Nolan swears on my left, the bun he's tied his hair into is askew.

Virgil straightens his glasses. "We should do a count to coordinate this."

"You don't need a count," Nolan says. "Just feel it through the bond. That's obviously the trick to this exercise."

"Because that worked so well just now," I grumble.

"It didn't work because you wanted to go, but then you saw your boyfriend was lagging and decided to compensate for him."

"Wow, name calling? Are we in kindergarten?"

"I'm calling it like I see it."

"Let's just reset and do it," Virgil says.

We drag ourselves back to the starting line. I expected Henry to interrupt our argument, but the man didn't say a thing as he watched us struggle.

The second run, we make it maybe a foot before falling. The third, we fall right away. At a certain point, I lose count of how many times we've fallen onto frost-tipped grass. Henry only speaks to tell us if our pace is too slow, and that we therefore need to restart. At some point Laira sits on the ground and puts in earbuds, watching something on her phone.

After we manage about half the field before our next fall, Henry raises a hand. "That's enough."

"Thank fuck," Nolan says, wiping sweat from his brow. We've all shed our coats, warm enough from the sprints. He rips the rope off our legs and walks a few feet away.

I let Virgil handle the one binding us. He's been grinding his teeth steadily for the last few runs. His dentist is going to cry at his next appointment. And I know it'll hurt Virgil, because getting a

good grade in being a patient is something he really believes in.

Henry says, "Well, that was pathetic, to say the least."

"Thanks for the encouragement, Coach," I say.

He gestures to the machine beside him. "For the next exercise, I'm going to shoot three tennis balls out of this machine. You each need to catch one."

The three of us spread out in the field, and Henry launches the first three balls. I glance at Virgil and Nolan and shift to the ball that's farthest away from them, catching it. When I hear twin grunts, I turn to see they've both crashed into each other going for the same ball.

"You should be very concerned that Ms. Black was the only one who thought logically about this exercise and succeeded," Henry says.

"Wow, okay," I mutter.

Virgil and Nolan recover and the second time the balls get released, it's clear that we're thinking more about where we are in space. Each of us catches a ball.

"Good," Henry says. "Go again."

This time, roughly ten balls shoot out of the machine instead of the three, making it harder to know who's going for which ball. Nolan nearly smacks into me, which is only avoided by Virgil jumping between us to block me from the hit.

"Maybe be careful?" Virgil snipes at him. "You're a Monster, remember? You could seriously injure her."

Nolan says, "She's not made of glass. I'll remind you that this is the girl who almost killed me."

"You do know the point of this exercise is that we *don't* collide with each other?"

"No, the point of it is that you be aware of your surroundings and get out of the way if you see someone is there."

I used to think that *I* riled Virgil up. I say, "Having Nolan here is amazing because now it's like I'm not even the worst anymore."

Nolan glares at me. "Oh, you're still the worst. I watched you jump just now. When you came at me in the compound, you jumped like six feet in the air. Now you can't even clear one. You two are so obsessed with each other, and you still can't manage second-evolution skills?"

"Listen, you don't—"

"Mr. Murphy is correct," Henry says, stepping toward us. "This is a test of your coordination, but it was also a test of Ms. Black's ability to use second-evolution skills. Which she failed at. You're too reliant on Virgil making up for your shortcomings, and you, Virgil, are too willing to do so. You need to work together, yes, but you cannot encourage each other's weaknesses."

I open my mouth but can't think of anything to say.

Henry steps into my personal space, and I straighten my back. "What were you thinking at the compound? Taking down a Monster by yourself, I'd say that's the strongest you've been all year. You should remember that moment, call that feeling back to you, and use it. Maybe if you'd been that capable before, your mother wouldn't have died."

I reel back from him, and Virgil makes a choking sound behind me. "Henry—" he starts.

"Tell me you haven't had the same thought," Henry says to me, stepping closer.

My lower lip trembles, and I catch it between my teeth, biting hard enough to hurt. At the compound, I was thinking that Virgil was going to die, and I wanted to save him. My heart beats faster, remembering the blood, and the way my body moved, and how *good* it felt.

In the back of my mind, something shifts, and I have to stop myself from crying out. What was just a sensation before now feels . . . tangible. Amber eyes and a maw full of sharp teeth. This was what I gave in to. Not a person with a Monster title. Something else. A monster in the purest sense of the word.

It's in my head. Has been since the initiation. It just never felt this . . . *alive.*

Henry is right. It was the most powerful I had ever felt. I lost myself in the monster. That version of me could have saved Mom.

But that version of me also almost killed Nolan.

If I let myself go like that again . . . No. I can't. I need to be in control of it. Whatever this is, it can't be set loose.

Henry says, "You told me you wanted to get stronger, so do it. Because from my point of view, you've gotten worse, not better." I fight a wince and Henry shifts his gaze to the boys. "Work on your syncing with one another and your second-evolution skills. Remember that you all chose each other." Nolan opens his mouth to protest, and Henry stops him. "If you didn't, the bond wouldn't have taken, and you would have died. Find whatever works between the three of you and use that understanding to strengthen the bond. Dismissed."

A moment passes, and Nolan says, "Does that mean we leave or—"

"Dismissed!"

The three of us trudge away from the field. Nolan bypasses the bus stop, choosing to walk back to campus while me and Virgil wait, since I guess we haven't earned a ride back with Henry and Laira.

"He shouldn't have said that," Virgil mumbles.

I shrug. "What were you thinking back then, at the compound

with Nolan? I didn't even realize you'd lost control too."

Virgil clenches his hands into fists. "It was terrible. Like being in the initiation again. Just . . . fueled by this . . . this anger that came out of nowhere. Hurting someone . . ."

Back in the initiation, Virgil said his greatest fear was that he would hurt me and not care. He hated it. Hated the monster inside him. The monster I'm now sure is inside me, too. Whether I suddenly feel it this viscerally because of my new bond with Nolan or some other reason, my promise to Virgil hasn't changed. I said I would take it on. I would hold the burden of it for him, because I wanted to use it. Even now, I still do. "We won't lose control again," I say. "I'll master the monster. I promised you that. The rage, and the pain, and the hatred."

"You shouldn't have to. I should be able to do it." Virgil's voice cracks. "I should be better—"

"You *are* better," I say. "You always have been. That's why the monster isn't for you. It's for me. This is what *I* bring to the table. And you . . . you stop me when I need to be stopped."

That was the difference between us. Virgil had been terrified of who the monster made him, and I had been delighted. Without him there, I would have killed Nolan.

Me and Virgil bring the scales to balance. And now that we have a new partner to accommodate, I need his help more than ever.

CHAPTER TEN

The dojang feels different on an actual class day. Me and Corey aren't the only people in the changing room now, and it's filled with chatter and slamming lockers as everyone gets ready. My phone rings for the thousandth time that day, and I groan, tilting my head back as Mia's name lights up the screen.

"Just answer the phone," Corey says. "She's not going to give up."

I sigh and accept the call, putting the phone to my ear. "What?"

"Hey, remember me, your supposed friend whose calls you've been ignoring?"

"I've been busy. As I am busy now."

"Nolan won't say anything. Are you going to pull the same bullshit, or do you have even a small amount of respect for me, if not as a friend then as the girl who showed you how to sharpen your knives?"

I lean my head against the lockers, watching as students file out.

I would love to tell Mia the truth, but it's complicated when her parents are obviously trying to keep her out of this. If I spill, who's to say that Jacques won't try to get me into shit in retaliation. If even Nolan is keeping his mouth shut, I won't be the one to fuck up, yet again. "Nolan was injured, we happened to be there, and we tried to help."

"Injured *how*?"

"I don't know! He wouldn't tell us what happened either."

"Why were you there at all?"

I look at Corey, who rapidly taps on her phone and then shows it to me. She's written, *Murphys have police connections, your mom.*

I say, "I've been looking into stuff with my mom, and apparently the Murphys have some police connections. I convinced Virgil to sneak onto their property with me to search their documents. I know, bad idea. We got there, and someone had already broken in, and Nolan was hurt."

There's a long moment of silence on the phone. Corey looks at me expectantly while I bite my lip. *Please, please, buy it.*

"You should have just asked me," Mia says. "Also, Royce is, like, the only Murphy cop related to us, and he's an asshole with an inflated ego."

"Yeah," I say. "We learned that from Nolan. Also, I only just learned you were related to one Murphy—how was I supposed to know that extended to Nolan and the cop guy?"

Mia says, "Well, you know now."

"Are you going to stop calling me incessantly?"

"If you acted less suspicious, I wouldn't have had to call you so much!"

"Bye, Mia," I say, and hang up before she can add anything else.

Corey hands me my belt, white like the rest of my uniform. I

glance at her matching white outfit and the belt around her middle. "Okay, black belt."

She shakes her head with a smile. "There are ten levels of black belt, you'll learn. I'm only a third Dan."

"Still! You don't have to put yourself through a beginner's class with me." I did agree to do some classes so I could learn proper taekwondo foundations instead of the piecemeal that Corey had to teach me last year to make it through the candidacy. But she doesn't need to suffer through exercises way below her level.

"I don't mind. It's good to remind myself of the basics."

In the main room, Mr. Yang stands at the front. Me and Corey join the rest of the class on the mats. After some warming up, we bow and begin to learn the movements. I appreciate that Mr. Yang goes through it slowly, coming around the room to double check each of us. He beams at Corey, whose form is perfect.

Though the counting is in Korean, I get used to the rhythm and the sound of Mr. Yang's steady voice as he repeats them and we cycle through the block and punch movements, following the count in my head and doing my kihap with the rest of the class. My kihap is the one thing I'm most confident about, having learned to do the shout when Corey taught me, and Mr. Yang seems pleased with my ability. When we add in kicks, mine are level with Corey's beside me. Her balance, which she struggled with last year because of the shift with the weight of her prosthesis, seems pretty damn perfect now. She's been practicing.

I get why she wanted me to come to an actual class. Most of Corey's instruction worked with knowledge I already had, and she just showed me necessary movements. Now, I'm learning the proper names of stances and the building blocks that go into them.

At the end of the class, we bow, and the group makes their way to the changing rooms, though me and Corey hang back as Mr. Yang comes over to us. Up close, I can see Corey's features in her dad's face. The fluff of their eyebrows and curve of their noses. "Did you enjoy the class?" he asks me.

"Yeah," I say. "It's helpful to learn the foundations."

"Good, good. You have great form already, thanks to Corey." He looks at his daughter and then behind her at Ms. Yang, who's hovering in the entryway.

Corey looks between them. "Everything okay?"

"Yes!" Mr. Yang says, grimacing a bit. "Um, just, would you maybe want to come by the condo for a snack? Mom can put together something."

"Oh, we have plans." Corey rubs the back of her neck. "Maybe another time?"

Mr. Yang is fighting to keep a smile on his face. "Yes, of course. Another time."

As we walk away, Ms. Yang races over to her husband, and they start speaking in hushed tones.

"What was that about?" I ask Corey once we're inside the changing room.

She shrugs, pulling her regular-use prosthesis out of her gym bag to exchange for her taekwondo leg—it's not specific to the sport, but she said it's more responsive than her everyday one, and she prefers it for athletic activities. "It's still awkward. I did visit them over the holidays. I think they wanted me to stay over, but sleeping in my old bedroom would just remind me of everything, you know?"

"Yeah." However sweet Mr. and Ms. Yang are to me, once upon a time they pressured Corey into competing in the Bachelor candidacy

to save her older brother from being sent to the Kingston Penitentiary. Specifically brought her into the world to be his savior. In the end, he was sent underground anyway, and Corey lost a leg and two fingers. She also cut ties with them and moved to McIntosh Castle. Since their apology last year, she's made efforts to repair the relationship, but it's not going to happen overnight. "Don't let them rush you."

"I won't. It feels like they want me to move on, but I can't help clinging to the past. They took something from me that they can't ever give back. I can't just forget that."

"Who says you have to forget it? Have they?"

She shakes her head. "No, but it feels like they want to go back to the way things were."

"Have you asked if that's what they want?"

Corey is silent for a moment, staring at her feet. "No."

"Not yet, you mean."

That gets a grin out of her. "Yeah, not yet. Now, what's on this video we're looking for?"

"Something worthwhile." Hopefully.

Summerhill is apparently not just a place for the weekly lectures but also houses the society's more bureaucratic operations. Corey leads me and Virgil through the main doors and to the right down a hallway and up a set of stairs. The place still looks like someone's home, albeit one that has the feel of a museum. Something preserved in time with the ornate hall rugs and ceramic busts. Though they don't have any names, I recognize some of the statues as Masters and Doctorates from the few photos I saw when Corey was quizzing me for the candidacy.

We stop in front of a door with a plaque that reads DOCUMENTS

AND FILES. I raise an eyebrow at Corey, who says, "This is where dispatch operates. They also have the records of dispatches and how the missions went, et cetera. They communicate by phone with Masters about their various jobs and store the records here securely."

"So we can just ask for stuff?" I say.

Virgil replies, "Yes, unless it's classified. But we have to view them here."

I step into the room. It's jarring how much like a normal office it looks. There's a desk set up at the back of the room, and some armchairs by a rack of magazines. There's a Black woman with her hair in twists sitting at the desk, typing something into the computer. Her skin's so smooth and dewy that it's hard to guess how old she is. She could be our age or Bailey's age. She looks up as we enter. "Can I help you?"

"Yes," Virgil says, stepping forward. "I'm Virgil Hawthorne—"

"I know."

He falters for a moment. "Uh, yes, well, we're doing some research for McIntosh Castle and wanted to pull a dispatch record, number 6589."

She raises an eyebrow. "McIntosh Castle authorization is limited to Dr. Harold Liu and Ms. Cordelia Yang."

I whip around to the stranger who I've been calling my friend. "Cordelia?!"

Cordelia, apparently, shrugs. "Corey is a nickname."

"And who are you?" I ask Virgil. "Virginington the third?"

He rolls his eyes. "Just Virgil."

The woman puts out her hand and clears her throat. "Does Corey or Cordelia have ID?" Corey digs her student ID out of her pocket and hands it over. "Government-issued ID is preferred, but

this is fine." She hands back the card and types something into her computer. "What are you researching?"

"Oh," Corey says. "Is that . . . like, you need to know for the records?"

The woman looks between us. "No, just curious."

"Some cataloging is all."

"Cataloging isn't research."

Corey lets out a high-pitched giggle, and I fight the urge to cringe. She says, "I mean, what isn't research? It's all research."

"Mm-hmm." The woman glances at me. It's one of those times when I figure it's best to keep my mouth shut, so I just give her a tight smile. She returns her gaze to the computer. "This is one of my dispatches."

"Wait," I say. "You're Hailey Jenkins?"

"Correct. Is there something specific that you need to know, or do you just want the file pulled?"

"We're interested in the video footage that was attached for verification."

"We don't have it."

My jaw drops. "What do you mean you don't have it?"

She looks at Corey. "Are you doing the cataloging or is she doing it?"

"They're helping me," Corey says.

Hailey looks at each of us in turn before saying, "The footage was sent to the office for verification, but then the Wild who was dispatched came in and requested it. Said that he would do the verification himself."

Virgil furrows his brow. "I thought you couldn't take material or records out of this office."

She shrugs. "He had a signed order from the sixth Doctorate."

What the fuck was on that footage that Cyrus Shaw would have okayed? "Sorry, Cyrus signed off on it in November?"

"The late Doctorate Shaw, yes. Order was dated November twenty-seventh."

Last year Adam told me that his dad died in November, and they kept it secret from the rest of the society. So Cyrus was either dead or seriously ill when he gave that order. Meaning he might not have given it at all. But it would have been easy for one of his sons—say, Carrigan—to manage. Maybe Carrigan even put it together and asked his dad to sign it. The man was probably sick enough to not realize what he was authorizing.

Virgil says, "But the Wild should have brought the footage back after authorization."

"Should have," Hailey says. "But he died. Heart attack, apparently. You'd be surprised how many young people get them. Even Monsters."

I swallow. Kendrick Durand is dead. Just like the Wilds who attacked Adam. Sure, the cause of death is different, but it's still the death of someone who may have been tied up in Carrigan's puppet strings. "You never found the video?"

"No. We tried to recover it from his home, but it wasn't there. It's easy to lose those tiny things."

"What do you mean?" Virgil asks. "Like it's a USB key or something?"

Hailey opens the drawer of her desk and pulls out a tiny fluorescent green metal square on a string. "USB-C, actually. Handy because they can be stored in a small space. I order these neon ones because they're easier to see, but they still get lost. Which is exactly

why records aren't supposed to leave this office, but if the Doctorate orders it, there's nothing I can do." She looks straight at me. "Maybe ask the current Doctorate if he knows what happened to it?"

I say, "I'll do that." Like hell I will. The last thing I need is for Adam to get any inkling that I'm looking into his brother before I have enough evidence to legitimize my claims. "Actually, do you know who the Wild was living with at the time? Maybe we can ask them?"

"That's personal data."

I lean on the desk. "I'm sure he won't mind. On account of being dead."

"*I* mind." She pins on a smile. "If that's all . . . ?"

I look at Virgil and Corey, but there's not anything else we can do here. I can't ask Adam, but there might be a way to find someone Kendrick knew while he was working the job. Someone he might have said something to who kept quiet. And luckily for me, we've recently acquired a partner who knows a lot about Wilds.

CHAPTER ELEVEN

The operation of the Monster's Ball is a well-oiled machine. On Wednesday evening, we're expected at the Kingston Penitentiary at four p.m. sharp for the opening parade. Upheld by the micromanaging of Corey, Henry, and Margot. As if Virgil texting to remind me of the time every half hour since this morning wasn't enough. Upon entry, we're separated into spectators and competitors, and then further separated by leagues. Those who already have a Master-in-training title and are defending this year like Margot, and untested Monsters who are paired with senior Masters like Jules will compete in the MiT league, while we'll be in the Bachelor league.

This time we won't just be competing against people at Queen's but pairs from universities across Ontario. All of them have their own chapters of the society presided over by the Doctorate, the same as the rest of the chapters across the country and clustered around the US-Canadian border. There are Monsters around the world, but

apparently the Doctorate and the society's jurisdiction only spreads so far.

We're shoved into a room with a table of beverages and snacks, where we've been left for the last half hour. It's like a strange costume party. All of us in this dimly lit underground chamber with the Bachelors dressed up to the nines in sleek suits and evening gowns while the Monsters are in casual clothes. They have to walk in the parade in their Monster forms, so there's no point in wearing nice outfits. Those have been saved and put on racks in a chamber at the end so they can change before the banquet, where both leagues will get to mingle with senior Master-Monster pairs.

"He does know that we have to walk in together, right?" Virgil says, looking at Nolan, who is across the room, as far away from us as he can get. It would be an understatement to say our teamwork hasn't improved since that last training session.

Virgil attempted to organize several meetups with no-shows from our new partner.

"He'll get it together when it counts," I say. I hope, anyway. He has a stake in this too. He wouldn't have agreed to participate if he didn't.

Virgil turns away from Nolan to me. But only for a second before averting his eyes. "You look nice. I don't think I've said."

With Henry's approved release of funds, me and Corey were able to browse a few websites and pick out a dress for the occasion. Black, of course. The dress has a nude underlay, and black appliqué vines cover the bodice, the ankle-length A-line skirt, and the sleeves. The whole thing is adorned with Swarovski crystals that sparkle even in the dim light of the space. And my tits look just awesome in it. I styled my braids in an updo with the assistance of an exceedingly

large claw clip and about a dozen bobby pins, finishing the look with a smoky eye and plum lipstick.

I ask, "Are you allowed to compliment me?"

Virgil shakes his head. "There's no society rule against compliments."

"Then can you at least look at me when you say it?"

He swallows and returns his gaze to me.

"Once, and never again," I say, and he shifts uncomfortably. "I get it. But we are never going to be able to manage this if you can't even look me in the eye. Not to mention the avoidance comes off as suspicious. Like we have something to hide."

That, and I want him to be able to look at me. To be near me without pulling away. This is the most we're ever going to get, and yeah, I want it. I want *something*.

Virgil nods. "Okay. Yeah. You're right."

"I always am."

He rolls his eyes. "Hardly."

"Queen's University competitors!" A man shouts from the front of the room. "Please line up now! Queen's University competitors!"

We walk over and are arranged in order of our Bachelor ranking. Meaning me, Virgil, and Nolan will be the first to be seen in the parade. But no pressure.

"August . . . what's going on?" Violet says behind us, looking from me to Nolan.

I sigh. "It's a long story."

"It's not," Nolan says. "They almost killed me, I did a blood bond with Wonder Boy to heal me, and somehow now we're inextricably linked to one another."

"You are just so helpful," I say with a thin smile.

He grins. "Thank you."

Frankie eyes Nolan, brushing her bangs out of her face. Her usually warm brown skin looks pale tonight. Last year she had this totally comfortable and confident air about her. Now she frequently looks like she's two seconds away from a panic attack. "You're a Wild. I've seen you proctor before."

"Ding-ding."

"That's quite the advantage." Violet keeps her voice mild, but there's an edge to it. Something strained.

I shrug. "Yeah, assuming you don't get sick and die from having two bonds, sure."

It's a joke, but she doesn't laugh. She only turns to talk to Bryce.

There are eyes all around the room watching us now. When Nolan was avoiding us, we didn't stand out, but now that we're here—the three of us, a confirmed trio—Violet isn't the only one noticing our supposed advantage. Even if it's a double-edged sword. Though it isn't, actually. I still feel fine, meaning Adam was probably right about me avoiding side effects, but *they* don't know that.

I face the front and roll my shoulders back, saying nothing as we're led into a secondary room where the Monsters shed their clothes behind privacy screens and don thin, paperlike robes.

We're brought down a long hall into yet another room, but this one has ceilings high enough to accommodate Monster heights and a grand entrance door.

A woman comes over to us with a headset. "Queen's University competitors! Please listen up. Okay, see above the entrance?" She points to a light above the fancy door that's currently red. "Red means stop, amber means Monsters transform, green means go. Easy, right? It will turn red again between each Bachelor-Monster set. Monsters

on the right, and Bachelors on the left . . ." She pauses and looks at us. "Um, Monsters on either side for you. It's a straight shot from one chamber to the other. Monsters, please be mindful of the space when you transform. Thank you."

Beside me, Virgil takes a long, deep breath.

"It's just a parade," I say.

"Just a parade in front of hundreds of people ready to judge you." He stares at me for a moment before picking a stray piece of hair off my sleeve. "The dress really does suit you," he murmurs, and this time, he doesn't look away when he says it.

A flush spreads across my face, and I bite my lip.

"If you think she looks hot, just say so," Nolan drawls. "It's not illegal to notice."

Virgil splutters something, but the light has turned amber, Nolan is already transforming, and I'm trying to figure out if he was calling me hot in a roundabout way. Virgil clears his throat before also shifting into his Monster form. Once they're finished, I stand between them. You would think that being sandwiched between two six-foot-tall Monsters would make me feel small, but it almost has the opposite effect. I stand taller, my shoulders back.

Triumvirate. I could get used to that title.

The light turns green, and the instant we clear the doors, there's a moment of utter silence. They must have announced our names already, but people still look stunned as we enter the stretch of walkway. It's about the length of two city blocks, flanked on either side by raised spectator stands. How they crammed this underground is a goddamn marvel.

I keep my head high, and the silence is broken by Corey wooing in the stands. I jerk around to see her, where she's waving her hands

and clapping. That starts an eruption of cheers from the rest of the spectators.

I could live a thousand lifetimes and not deserve that girl as a friend.

We walk together, me at a faster clip, given that Virgil and Nolan get much farther with a single step. Before I know it, it's over, and we're in the second chamber.

Someone shouts at Virgil and Nolan to transform back quickly and ushers them over to a privacy screen in the corner of the room where their dress clothes wait. With the encouragement—aka the rushing—of the staff, they get changed into their suits, and we're told to wait in the room until they're ready for us to enter the banquet.

Virgil has gone for a tweed suit in a muted brown that makes him look, as usual, like he's straight out of a period drama, while Nolan opted for a pair of black slacks and an olive dress shirt with the top two buttons left undone, his long hair loose and falling on his shoulders.

Nolan doesn't bother saying anything to the two of us as he skulks away to make himself a coffee.

I peer around the room. "It's wild how much there is down here."

Virgil says, "A lot of the underground levels of the Pen were modeled after fallout shelters and bunkers. Not surprising, perhaps, when you remember that this infrastructure was created because of the threat of the apocalypse. It's just that we could manage more with the assistance of Monsters and Masters. Increased strength and speed, plus special abilities, made all this possible."

I have to admit that it's impressive. But after a while of looking at it, the splendor wears off, and half an hour in, I'm bored and in the

process of eating a third mini cheesecake when Virgil gasps, looking at his phone.

"What?" I ask.

"I . . . Ellis . . . *Ellis* is here. Corey is freaking out." He paces in a circle, looking around like he expects someone to come help.

"Ellis? Who's Ellis?"

"Shit, shit, shit. We can't leave right now."

"Hello?? Virgil? Who is Ellis?"

Virgil looks at the door and swallows as it opens to reveal the next pair. "You'll see in a second."

Through the door walks the most Polly Pocket–coded girl I've ever seen in real life. She looks East Asian, with blond hair pulled in a ponytail that ends in a perfect ringlet adorned with a satin bow, and her dress is a poufy peach gown with a sweetheart neckline that ends just above her knees. When she walks into the room, people turn to her, drawn like moths to a pretty pink flame.

But Virgil is looking at the Monster beside her, a sleek black panther who literally looks like they're coated in oil, with blinking eyes not only where you expect, but also on the back of their head and different parts of their body. They transform and disappear behind the privacy screen and the boy who comes out is immediately familiar. Even now, older, with a chiseled jaw and dark hair that hangs in front of his eyes, shaved neatly on the left side, where he's tucked the strands behind an ear covered in piercings. I've seen that face in a family photo in the Yang Dojang.

"That's . . . that's Corey's brother," I say.

Virgil nods. "Ellis."

I jerk toward him. "But he—"

"I know."

He's supposed to be in the Pen. But here he is, with Polly Pocket, the two of them looking like a model couple on the runway. The girl catches us staring and grins, throwing us a little wave. Ellis doesn't even look our way.

"The girl?" I ask.

"Barbara Hu," Virgil says. "They call her Killer Barbie at Ottawa University. Came first in the Bachelor candidacy there and absolutely brutalized anyone who got in her way, and finished the initiation in half an hour. She's a favorite to win in our league. Her parents became friends with Corey's after they joined the society. That's how she, Barbie, and Ellis ended up being close. It was before Corey and I knew each other. She and Corey dated for a bit, actually. But after Ellis went underground, they fell out, and her family moved to Ottawa. But Barbie had a different partner in the candidacy. I *know* she did. So how is she with Ellis now?"

I picture Corey in the stands, seeing the Monster who ripped off and ate half her left leg and multiple fingers strolling down that catwalk like nothing. With her fucking ex, no less. "Can we go out to Corey?"

"Henry says no. Dr. Liu is here, and he's taking care of her. We can see her after the banquet."

Me and Virgil are the first people at the door when they say they're ready to let us into the ballroom. The sooner we can get in there, do the minimum amount of mingling, and then leave to go see Corey, the better.

The banquet hall looks like every other antechamber we've been in, except in this one they've made a greater attempt with the aesthetics, the floor decked out in an intricate tile pattern, and tables with neat ivory linens and tall floral centerpieces.

Everyone we speak to wants to know how we ended up as a trio. Henry concocted a more palatable lie, which is that we found a Wild injured, and Virgil did the blood bond to save him, thinking it could be easily reversed, only to find out that it was more complicated than that. Given that Nolan refuses to talk to anyone, how he became injured remains a mystery. No one seems to care about that, though. They're more enthralled by the idea of us being bonded to Garrett's second son. They call Nolan that, just like Adam did, as if it's a title, "Second Son."

"Is it that big of a deal to be his youngest son?" I ask a Master as he once again refers to Nolan that way.

The Master shrugs. "Jacques was always meant to be the next Wild leader, but he took off during the rebellion, and so Garrett went and plucked his bastard out of obscurity and started parading him around. Like a do-over. Second son."

"Gross," I say.

Virgil chokes on his drink, while the Master makes a face. "Sorry, what?"

"Would you excuse me?" I move, dragging Virgil with me, trying to get as far away from that guy as possible. I would like to think that wasn't how Adam meant it when he called Nolan that.

I almost sag in relief when Professor Chen slides over to us in a form-fitting black sweater dress. I can't talk to another annoying Master. "So lovely to see the two of you in today's parade," she says, beaming. "Though I was shocked by the addition of a second partner."

"Yeah," I say. "I think everyone was."

Chen looks me over. "Are you feeling well? Dealing with side effects?"

"I mean, I feel normal? Adam suspects I'll be fine since Nolan is a Wild."

"Doctorate Shaw," Virgil says under his breath.

Our professor is unfazed by my failure to use the proper title. "That's positive. And honestly, Bernie was forcing your brother into that partnership, which may have been at least partially to blame for why he became so ill. He wasn't equipped for it as a Bachelor in general, but he might have been okay otherwise. It even took a while for the effects to get bad. Still, I would hate to see anything happen to you. So please take care of yourself."

Virgil's eyes are almost boring a hole into me. He's been incessant in texting to see how I feel day to day. Like I'm going to suddenly drop dead. "I really do feel fine."

"That's good. But remember, physical illness is not the only kind that exists." Chen waves her hand. "All right, enough doom and gloom. It's a beautiful banquet, don't you think? I haven't been to something this nice since the Doctorate's Ball. Not last year's, mind you, it was canceled, but the year before."

"The one in 2023?" Virgil asks, nudging me with his hand where Chen can't see. "That was in November, right?"

"Yes, the twenty-third . . . or no, the twenty-fifth! I remember because my uncle's birthday was the next day."

November 25? My heart skips a beat. "What's the Doctorate's Ball?"

Chen says, "It's a fancy to-do that the sixth Doctorate used to put on every year at the end of November. It's more a networking opportunity than anything, but I'm pretty sure that's how I got the position as a presiding professor in the Bachelor candidacy. Made some good connections."

"Were all his sons there?" I ask, sweat beading on my upper lip.

Chen tilts her head. "James definitely was. I spoke with him. And I feel like I remember someone saying that our current Doctorate wasn't feeling well. I think he was upstairs, because Henry went to check on him. I didn't see him all night either. Oh! I did see Carrigan on my way out."

"You saw him?!"

"Yes . . . Everything okay?"

"Of course," Virgil says, covering for me.

Chen lifts her eyes. "Oh, speaking of the Shaws . . ."

I turn around to see Adam approaching us. He nods to Chen. "Kaitlyn, lovely to see you. Would you mind if I spoke to Ms. Black and Mr. Hawthorne privately for a moment?"

"Not at all." Chen gives us a final smile before she strides away to another group.

Adam says, "How are you two holding up? Where is . . . Ah, I see Mr. Murphy over there in the corner. Well, how are you two doing?" He's asking both of us, but he looks at me.

I say, "Fine. Even better if we win our first match."

"I'm sure." Adam regards me for a moment. "You seem . . . tense."

"Just nervous."

Carrigan has an alibi. I'm fucking peachy.

Still, this doesn't let him off the hook. It's possible that he blackmailed or forced that Monster to go after Mom without using direct control. After all, he didn't need his abilities to manipulate Bernie and those Masters on the Bachelor panel who voted to disqualify me.

I barely pay attention to whatever Adam says to us, and at the first opportunity, I make my way over to Nolan. My new partner is

less than thrilled to see me. “What?” he asks, looking from me to Virgil and back.

“There’s a Wild named Kendrick Durand who died in November of 2023 of a heart attack. Do you know who he was living with at the time? Family or a partner?”

“Girlfriend.” Nolan narrows his eyes at me. “How do you know Kendrick?”

“Could you set up a meeting between us and her? We want to ask some questions about him.”

“Why would I do that?”

I open my mouth, then close it. I have nothing else to bargain with. “Because you’re a kind person?”

Nolan grins. “Wrong.” He turns and walks away from us.

“I’m going to call it,” Virgil says under his breath, his hands flexing. “I can’t stand him.”

“You’ll have to learn to tolerate him. He’s our partner now.”

For better or for worse, the three of us are in this together.

CHAPTER TWELVE

We find Corey in one of the sitting rooms in McIntosh Castle staring into the fire. She must have showered, because her hair is wet and hanging limp around her face, and she's changed into a set of pajamas. Dr. Liu is beside her, though neither is speaking. There are two cups of tea, but only the one in front of him shows any signs of having been drunk.

Me and Virgil are still in our full formal clothes.

Corey looks up when we enter, her eyes bloodshot.

Dr. Liu pats her knee. "I'll take my leave, then. We can have breakfast with Georgia tomorrow."

She nods without saying anything, and Dr. Liu gives us a tight smile on his way out. I thought he lived in McIntosh Castle too. I figured after the Nolan thing that he was staying elsewhere because the three of us had commandeered his bedroom, but it would be empty now.

I let Virgil take the spot on the couch next to Corey while I settle in the chair across from her.

"What was he like?" Corey asks. "You saw him, didn't you? Up close."

Me and Virgil look at each other before he speaks. "I never knew him in the first place, so I don't know that I can discern what normal would be like. He seemed fine."

Corey sighs and grips her left thigh, compressing the fingers into the silken pajamas. "I'm going to call them," she says, already pulling out her phone.

I throw a wide-eyed look at Virgil. "Right now?" he asks. "You don't want to sleep on it or—"

Corey puts the speakerphone on, and the call makes it through two rings before someone picks up. "Did you know?" she asks before they can even say hello. There's silence on the other line. "Did you—"

"Lydia called us." Ms. Yang's voice comes through soft on the other end. "She said that Barbie had arranged things so Ellis could get out. That she found a senior Master to take over the bond with her own partner and had been approved to bond with Ellis since she did so well in the candidacy. Dad and I . . . we didn't want to hope too much. We didn't believe it until a couple of weeks ago when he called and said he would be coming for the Monster's Ball. We wanted to tell you in person. . . ."

Corey stares at the screen as her mom trails off. In the background, Mr. Yang requests that the call be put on speaker.

I'm still stuck on how the hell Barbie managed to pull a partner switch. From what I remember, Corey said it was hard even for full-fledged Masters to get approval for that sort of thing. Never mind a new Bachelor.

"Corey?" Mr. Yang says. "Are you still there?"

"Yes."

"Your brother is going to come by tomorrow night for dinner. If you're free, maybe you could come too? To see you both together again would be—"

Corey presses the end call button. She tosses her phone aside and buries her head in her hands. Virgil puts his arms around his best friend. He doesn't say anything, and I don't know what there is to say.

Last semester in her family's dojang, Corey said how all she wanted was to live her life as though her brother had never existed. Even if she knew that was unfair to him. It's not like he chose to be a Monster. But still, the fear was there, and as long as the fear existed, she wanted to avoid it. He was her big bad wolf. And he'd appeared without warning.

There was something smug about the way Barbie had greeted us too. That little wave. Like she had wanted this undoing of Corey.

I couldn't wait to get in the ring with that bitch.

Corey mumbles, "I thought I was done being afraid. I didn't think I was this . . . this pathetic and weak and . . ." A sob breaks through, and Virgil pulls her closer, resting his head on top of hers.

"You aren't any of those things," he says. "Maybe we should stay here with you tomorrow."

"No!" Corey shakes her head. "You have to go watch the matches. You should use the time to learn before your fights." She takes a deep breath. "I'm going too."

I say, "You don't—"

"I'm going too," she repeats, lifting her head. Her tone leaves no room for disagreement.

I nod. "We'll go together."

She doesn't smile, but there's a relief there, and that's more than enough. My girl is no pushover. She'll be okay. I have to believe that.

Nothing could have prepared me for the sheer number of people filing into the underground tunnels of the Pen for the first day of the Monster's Ball. Objectively, I know that there can't be an audience of more than five hundred people, about the amount that a decent concert venue could handle. But the concrete hallways are dark and narrow, and so it feels more packed with both the spectators and the various volunteers helping direct people toward different fights.

There's a hum in the air that reminds me of the few times our family went to Blue Jays games in Toronto. There are even vendors set up in side rooms with mobile carts and fryers selling snacks and drinks. I can't stay I'm surprised to see posters hung around the food stalls calling for people to sign the proposal to put more restrictions on Wilds.

I trail behind Virgil and Isaac, who have been leading the way and discussing which of the matches will be best to watch. In this case, despite being younger, Isaac is the veteran Monster of the two. It's kind of endearing watching Virgil learn from someone who he usually treats like his younger brother. Margot walks behind the two of them, scrolling on her phone.

There's no sign of Jules. I'm still pissed at him, but I did text to double-check that he had also been seeded higher based on Natalie's status. He won't be fighting until tomorrow.

On my left side, Corey's eyes dart around the space. It's like she both does and doesn't want to see her brother. I ask, "Are your parents coming?"

"Probably not until tomorrow. Ellis and Barbie would have been seeded higher too, so they won't compete until day two like you guys," she says. "They sent me the time of dinner."

"Are you going to go?"

She sighs. "No. I'm not mad at them for being happy that he's back. But it's a lot for me. I don't even know that I can see them for a while, let alone him. I'm sorry, I know we were supposed to be dojang buddies, but I don't think I can do classes either."

"It's cool. I'm a big girl. I can go by myself if I want to."

Virgil and Isaac head to a door with a sign above it that reads LING ARENA.

"How many arenas are there?" I ask Corey. I'm sure she would appreciate a conversation topic change.

She says, "Eight. Four for each league. They're named after prominent Masters."

"Of course they are."

We enter the arena space, which reminds me of a Greek colosseum if the shape were rectangular instead of rounded. The seating dips down and then stops, leaving a pit in the middle big enough for Monsters to move around. The pit itself must be at least ten feet below the spectator seats, but there are still glass shields around the lower levels. I assume it's a specialty barrier, like what they have for hockey matches. There's also glass embedded up high in the wall, sunken in, though I can't see inside. I imagine that's where the announcer sits. On the walls there are giant screens that will likely show close-ups of the match, but right now they simply say LING ARENA.

Isaac points, leading us lower. "This is the reserved seating for the Scott family. Henry lets everyone in the Mastery group use them." We take our seats, and Virgil glances at Corey, who's

fiddling with her phone, and then at me, eyebrow raised.

I shrug, and he sighs.

Even with Virgil's explanation from last night, I'm still in awe of how much they've fit underground in the same space where they already hold uncontrolled Monsters.

"Don't people notice a bunch of out-of-towners suddenly flooding into the Pen?" I ask.

Margot says, "People use multiple entrances. And there are enough society folks who house out-of-town people so the hotels aren't suspiciously full. The society has been holding this competition for a long time. They're efficient."

"Look who showed up," Virgil says.

I glance at where he's looking to see Nolan strolling toward us with his hands in his pockets. He stops briefly to speak to a guy wearing a proctor patch—the same thing Nolan had on when we first met.

I ask, "What do the proctors actually do?"

"They monitor whether any rules are broken," Corey says. "They also step in if someone goes too far. Sometimes competitors have tried to go in for the kill when someone is already unconscious. And so they jump in to defend."

"Getting attacked themselves in the process," Margot mutters.

Finally, Nolan makes his way over to us, sitting heavily at the end beside Margot and not bothering with a greeting.

"Well, since the three of you are here now, I'll do the rundown," Margot says. "Which I suppose is really just for August. As you already know, because you guys just did the Bachelor candidacy, you get seeded based on your standing there. If you're a Master-in-training like me, you get seeded based on your standing in the

Monster's Ball last year. Which is why I'm also not competing today. Or you can be seeded based on the Master's standing if they already have a senior title. So who we're seeing today in the Bachelor league are people who either weren't seeded high enough or who failed to get the Master title last year or any previous year."

"So these matches are going to be pretty uneventful?"

"Don't assume. These people are hungrier for the win, and in the case of those on their last chance, they are desperate. That combination can lead to a Monster evolving at an unprecedented rate."

There's a chime, and a voice sounds from the loudspeaker. "The match will begin in five minutes. This will be the Price-Kumara pair vs. the Barlowe-Torres pair."

"Barlowe . . . ," I say; it sparks something in my memory. "Wait, *Hudson*?! That shit stain who followed Caden around like a puppy last semester?"

A quick look in the program confirms that it's him. The program lists all the competitors, including their names, pronouns, league, the university they attend, and a couple of tidbits about them, but they conceal who's fighting where until you're sitting in the arena.

Isaac says, "It's good to go to a match for someone in your candidacy cohort so you can see how they've improved or not. Helps you mark your own progress."

"Exactly," Margot says, not hiding the pride in her voice.

Even I smile a bit. Isaac has obviously built up some level of confidence from having done this before.

The announcer comes back on and says, "Welcome, everyone, to the first Bachelor league match of the day at this year's Monster's Ball in the Ling Arena!" He pauses to let the cheers of the crowd ring out. "Before we get started, I'd like to remind you of the fabulous

prizes that await our competitors beyond the honor of a title. The first-place Bachelor will get one special request from the Doctorate, plus a VIP tour led by the Doctorate of the historic cottage where Dr. Weiss himself lived for many years. The Master-in-training league winner gets twenty-five thousand dollars!"

"The Bachelor prize seems better because you could ask for more money," I say. Minus the boring historic tour. Could do without that.

Isaac shakes his head. "You can't ask for more than 10k. There's, like, 'invisible limits' on it."

"It would be a waste of the Bachelor prize to ask for money," Margot says. "Ask for the right positioning in society, and you could be set up to make much more."

Nolan mutters, "Said like someone who's never needed money."

"I'm sorry, do I know you?"

"We've literally met before."

Margot tilts her head. "Did we meet? Because who I remember is some boy my students beat the shit out of sulking because they saved his life. I don't remember meeting the author of my biography."

Nolan grinds his teeth hard enough that his jaw cracks, turning away from her.

Sure, okay, he's my partner and all, but fuck does it feel good to see him shoved off his high horse. Me and Virgil shit the bed, okay, but he came hot out of the gate too. He could have killed Virgil. Now we're stuck together, and we each have something we're going to get out of it. There's only so long it's cool to be miserable to everyone.

The announcer says, "I'll now introduce the competitors." One of the giant doors at the end of the arena opens. "First up, Hudson Barlowe and his partner, Remington Torres, from Queen's

University. Barlowe came in fifth in the most recent Bachelor candidacy but was one of only four candidates who succeeded in graduating to the title."

Hudson walks out, his sledgehammer clutched in his right hand, and his light bronze skin gleaming in the arena lights. His brunette curls are shaved close to his scalp, the wavy shoulder-length hair gone. It gives him a harder look. He's wearing a belt with two red ties dangling down like flag football. These must be the flags that Henry said we have to grab from the other Bachelor to win.

Remington's Monster form has the vague appearance of a badger, with a white strip running from forehead to tail, scuttling on all fours. Where the comparison falls apart are the several appendages coming out from his back. They look like scorpion pincers, shifting and moving as he walks.

Corey consults the program. They apparently very strictly collect them when you leave. I guess they don't want the paper trail. "Remington, who goes by Remy, is from a legacy Monster family. He may be a tough competitor."

"But if they lose, they're not out, right?" I say. "Because of the double elimination bracket or whatever."

Margot nods. "If you lose one match, you go to the repechage."

"The what now?"

"*Repechage.* It's your second chance, essentially. If you win enough matches there, you can still rank higher in the end. You have to be within the top twenty-five percent to be given the title or to have successfully defended your title. Just win your match within half an hour and you're good."

"What if you take longer?"

"You get pushed into sudden death."

"And that's where people die?"

Virgil side-eyes me. "Sudden death is a turn of phrase. Remember what Henry said—you get penalties for killing. It's a fine balance between pushing Monsters to evolve and not losing valuable pairs. Sudden death is where the Bachelor or Master has to fight on their own without weapons."

The announcer cuts in as the door on the other side of the arena opens. "Challenging is Xavier Price and his partner, Deni Kumara, from the University of Toronto. This is Price's second Monster's Ball, and he previously came in third in his Bachelor candidacy."

From the other side Xavier enters the arena wielding a short sword. He's a white guy with cropped dark brown hair, thick eyebrows, and a scar across his chin. I peer over Corey's shoulder at the program. Deni doesn't have any notes about her. Her form is deer-like but with two extra hind legs, ribs on the outside, and an oddly humanlike face covered in fur. She's smaller than most Monsters too, maybe five feet tall.

"She's gonna get crushed," I mutter. No wonder Xavier ranked high in his Bachelor candidacy but failed in the Monster's Ball. I understand why Virgil said this competition is more a test of the Monster.

"Just watch." Margot leans toward the glass barrier. We're not at the very bottom of the arena, but we're close enough to have a good view.

A whistle blows, and Deni darts out faster than I can follow and returns to Xavier's side with a red flag in her mouth that she spits onto the ground. A horn sounds, and the screen mounted on the wall shows their headshots with a point. It also shows a slowed-down replay of Deni getting the flag.

Margot grins at me. "That's called using your strengths to your advantage." Hudson stumbles back, his mouth wide, but then catches himself and runs behind Remy, putting space between him and his competitors. "You don't learn who your opponents are until you see them in the arena, but you can count on a few things. For example, most Monsters are large and therefore slower. Deni knows she's on the smaller side, but she's quick. She went for the flag right out of the gate, and now they have an advantage. Making the first move is a good strategy to start. Especially when you have experience. Remember, this is Barlowe's first Ball."

Remy goes on the attack, scrambling forward, pincers snapping toward the opponents while Hudson hangs back. For a guy who spent most of the candidacy hiding behind his friend, it's so him to now hide behind his partner.

But it's also the right move. Xavier and Deni are forced to dart around Remy. I almost miss the moment when Hudson rushes out, grabbing one of the flags and then backtracking. Xavier tries to kick him, but Hudson is already safely behind Remy again.

"Why wouldn't he try to grab both flags at once?" I ask.

I'm surprised when Nolan answers, "You need to have a thirty-second delay between grabbing one flag and the next. Otherwise it would be too easy. Grab it beforehand, and it's a foul, and you're forced to reset. Two fouls in a match, and you lose automatically." He gives me a look. "Why are you only learning this now?"

Margot says, "I've found that with August, it's easier to teach using visuals—mainly because this is the only way she'll pay attention."

"I resent that," I grumble, though it's true. This is a much better way to understand how the Monster's Ball works than when Henry was droning on about it.

Margot crosses her arms. "It's over."

I jerk my head back to the match. "What do you—"

Deni cries out as one of Remy's pincers spears her through the side. The blood splatters onto Xavier's face, and while he's scrambling to both wipe it away and attend to her, Hudson dashes forward and tugs away the last flag. The horn sounds again.

It's a nasty wound, but Monsters and bonded Bachelors and Masters heal a lot faster than the average human. Not as fast as a pair with regeneration abilities, but enough to be ready to go for a match the next day. Assuming you don't get hurt too bad.

I turn to Margot. "How did you know they were about to lose?"

"Deni started to slow down. Her stamina is bad. She couldn't manage to keep dodging like that, and you could tell that Xavier was trying to keep his opponents' focus on him. He knows his partner is more fragile than most Monsters. Remy picked up on that and went to injure her because it would distract Xavier, and it worked." Margot looks at me and then Virgil. "Do you understand? Anything you give away to your opponent is something they can exploit." She tosses her head toward Nolan. "He may be an ass, but he gets it. You and Virgil, on the other hand, give much more away than you think."

Virgil looks at the ground, and I stiffen.

Anything you give them, they can exploit. The way that me and Virgil are is detrimental to our progress in every way. All the more reason to suffocate the feelings. To bury them six feet under and piss on the grave. We need to get stronger. That has to matter more than anything else.

CHAPTER THIRTEEN

Riley

August trudges into my foyer with a sigh, kicking off her Doc Marten boots and flinging her toque and mittens onto the side table. Never mind that I have a neatly arranged shoe cubby and a row of hooks where my own hats reside.

"Where do I put my jacket?" she asks.

Shaking my head, I say, "Wherever." I walk toward the living room and August follows me into the space, collapsing on one of the couches and kicking her feet up like this is her personal hangout. I sit on the couch across from her, noting the furrow between her brows. "First day of the Monster's Ball," I say.

"Wow, you guys really do keep tabs on the society."

"Wouldn't you also keep tabs on the people who are supposed to be stopping bloodthirsty Monsters from murdering people and yet seem to be rather inept at their one job?" August wrinkles her nose but doesn't comment further. "Not you getting offended on their behalf."

"I'm not."

I lean forward. "You are. You're buying into their shit."

"No. I'm *not.* I just need them right now. I'll remind you that you're the one who wants to use my connections to them to help you. You can't deny that they have their uses."

Fair, but still. Indoctrination is a slow process. Insidious. And the society are experts at it. "You used to act like they had nothing to do with you."

"Because they didn't. But now I'm bonded to Virgil. I'm a part of it whether I like it or not. I can't bail on him." She shakes her head. "It's not that serious." She pulls the chain out of her pocket, tossing it onto the coffee table. "This is what I'm here for, right?"

"I'll ask you to not handle a centuries-old artifact that casually. But yes."

August regards the necklace as I lift it, rolling the links between my fingers, power pulsing with every move. "How many bones are in that thing if it's been around that long?"

"A lot. The contributed bones increase the power, and thus far, we haven't had any issues with continually adding to the stock."

I mastered the chain in only a week. After all, Dad had wielded it before me, and Grandma before him. The problem was that, despite being Joseph Lawrence's descendants, none of us had been named president in two decades. It was embarrassing.

Holding out the chain to August, I say, "Grab the other end." After a moment of hesitation, she grips the necklace so we're holding it together. "The first step to mastery of an artifact is to recognize the feel of your bones inside."

"Okay, but what does that mean, the feel of your bones?"

"Recognize the part of you that is part of the artifact. Accept

that it's yours. Someone in your family added your bones. They can't be stolen. Which means you gave them to this person willingly. Even if you were a child. You trusted them. And in turn, they entrusted this artifact to safeguard you. That means something."

August looks from me to the chain and then closes her eyes, fingers flexing. "I think . . . I think I'm doing it?"

"Good enough. Now, call the power. It's actually best to be unspecific. My grandma said to think of it like waking yourself up from a nap." The moment I feel a pulse from August's side of the chain, I release it slowly, letting her work on it. It's got a faint glow. It could be better, but it could also be worse. "There are exercises. The first is to warm each link, one at a time. You'll feel it. Then once you've mastered that, enlarge one link at a time. Once you've done that—"

She drops the chain and opens her eyes. "How many exercises are there?"

"I'm sorry, do you want to occasionally succeed at using this, or do you want to master it?"

August barks out a laugh and leans back into the couch. "Maybe I'm tired of having to master everything."

For someone so outwardly blasé about so much, this girl overthinks a lot more than the average person. Yet neither is an act. August is very much what you see is what you get. Too much, really. She shares herself without realizing. It's the sort of thing that people take advantage of. Making the society the worst possible place for her. "You're worried about the Monster's Ball."

She quirks the corner of her mouth up. "Virgil told me that I was going to have to fight over and over, and I'm only now understanding what he meant. Everything is a fucking uphill battle."

"Welcome to being a Black woman."

August laughs again, but this time it has actual mirth behind it. "Yeah, right?" She tilts her head. "Why are you helping me with this, anyway?"

I straighten my back. "Don't be sappy. I'm not that altruistic. I need you to buy into this."

"Into QBSS?"

"Yes. Do you know how long we've lived in a reactionary bubble when it comes to the society? Then you come along out of nowhere, your bones in our artifact, and with the favor of two prominent people in society. You have Adam Shaw's ear, and I don't think you realize how valuable that is." This is what makes me different from the society. I'll be as honest and up-front about my intentions as possible. I owe August that much, at least.

"He's not as all powerful as you think."

"Isn't he? Any change you see him make, even the small ones, is him defying over a *century* of tradition. The society, no matter what allusions to democracy they make, is ultimately a dictatorship. If he's listening to people to keep the peace, know that he doesn't have to. His father certainly did whatever he wanted. After all, your founder said to have one child, and he said, fuck it, I'll have three."

August snorts. "Yeah, that didn't work out well for him."

"I'm sure someone told him that—many someones—and he did it anyway because he's the Doctorate. You have tremendous power here."

She lifts the chain, fingering the links. "Doesn't feel like it."

"If self-esteem is the issue, try a therapist."

"You first." I scowl, and August grins. She always has to remind me how incredibly annoying she can be. She says, "What's your ideal

scenario, then? In a situation where I care about QBSS, and I make Adam care too."

I steeple my fingers. "The society recants the designation of Joseph Lawrence as a traitor and instead shares the legitimate history in which he disagreed with Edward Weiss and made his split. The crimes against us committed by Bernie and others over the years are acknowledged, and whoever in the society pointed Bernie our way is punished, with their crimes against us noted. Plus, access to society documentation should we want to do our own historical investigations."

"If you think I can manage all that, why do you need the weapon?"

"It's good insurance."

Which is to say that the weapon will give QBSS something that we desire from the society that can't be given, even by a Doctorate.

The weapon will, for the first time, make us the ones to be feared. And against an organization that, despite their flaws, can still bring Monsters to their knees, it's a must-have.

CHAPTER FOURTEEN

Me, Virgil, and Corey enter the McCray Arena in the morning with paper cups of coffee. Henry suggested getting a good night's sleep before our match today, and yet when I texted Virgil at seven a.m., he was up too. And Corey is just naturally up that early. I didn't expect her to skip class, but I guess our first match is too important. The society organizes official absences for all competitors. Though ultimately, I'm glad we're up so we can see Margot and Isaac's match before ours in the afternoon.

This arena looks exactly like the previous one—the only difference is the name—and as before, there are two proctors at the ready. I glance at Virgil as we descend the stairs to Henry's section. His eyes are half-lidded and barely focused. He's not even fighting today. Nolan is. Corey must notice it too, because she takes the time to link their arms and ask a bunch of questions about how his reading of Beowulf for class is going.

I falter as I spot Nolan already sitting in Henry's section along with Violet and Frankie.

"Is he actually having a normal conversation with someone?" Virgil mutters.

"Apparently."

"Morning!" Violet says as we approach the group. Any of the awkwardness from the parade seems to have dissipated. Though she also looks like she got about as much sleep as we did. I can't think of any time during the Bachelor candidacy when she seemed nervous. She was always focused and confident. I couldn't apply either descriptor to her now. Frankie looks worse. She's forgone any makeup and shoved her hair into something vaguely resembling a ponytail, and she sits hunched over like she's expecting to throw up at any second.

"Couldn't manage to sleep in either?" I ask as we take our seats.

Violet throws me a tight smile, her signature black lipstick absent. "No. But Margot is Henry's protégé, right? Should be an interesting match."

I look around. "No Bryce or Mitch?"

"Those fuckers are sleeping like babies," Frankie mutters.

"Must be nice," Virgil says.

"We were having a great chat with your new partner," Violet says, gesturing to Nolan. We haven't trained together once since that session with Henry. But here Nolan is, with his hair pulled back in a bun, slouching in a jean jacket with a breakfast sandwich. Like he hasn't been ignoring all our text messages. "We were talking about the Wilds stuff."

Corey frowns. "Did something happen?"

Nolan says, "We've been setting up protest stations in the Pen

to combat the people trying to push the proposition. They even gave Thomas Mosser a full five-minute interview spot. But of course we can't get airtime."

I assume he's talking about the interview clips that play on the jumbo screens between matches.

I ask, "Can we help somehow?"

Nolan stares at me for a moment. "I . . . Yeah, I guess, if we got any airtime as competitors."

"I can make signs too," Corey says. She already made one for me and Nolan for today's match. She has another one for me and Virgil too.

Nolan ducks his head. "Thanks."

Lights flash in the arena, and the announcer comes on the loudspeaker. "Welcome to this MiT league match for the morning session in the McCray Arena. It's time to introduce our competitors!" The first door at the end of the arena opens. "We have Emerson Patel and his partner, Alexandra Noble, from the University of Waterloo. Emerson was fourth in his debut Bachelor league Monster's Ball, and then due to a knee injury was forced to postpone defending until this year."

Must have been a hell of an injury to affect him participating, given how fast bonded people heal.

Frankie makes a face. "Way to reveal a weakness as a fun tidbit."

Emerson is a big, beefy South Asian–looking guy with wraps on his hands. His partner is a good match for that. Her form is a massive hippopotamus with horns all over her face and seemingly no eyes, packed with muscle and six feet tall.

The announcer continues as the second door opens. "The challengers will be Margot Bouchard and her partner, Isaac Bouchard,

from Queen's University. That's right, we have a sibling duo here! And what a team they are. Margot came first in last year's Bachelor league Monster's Ball and also first in her Bachelor candidacy cohort. Mentored by Henry Scott, she was a dark horse last year and now is a favorite to win it all! Can she defend, or will this be where we see the new queen fall?"

"What the fuck?" I blurt out, looking at Virgil and then Corey. "Did you know that she came first in *both*?!"

Virgil nods. "Yeah. She's really good. That's why she's Henry's protégé. Isaac holds his own too."

Fuck me. No wonder she was so annoyed to be stuck mentoring me. Now it's extra embarrassing how much Isaac took it easy on me in training.

"They said so much stuff about her," Frankie says, leaning forward to rest her elbows on her knees. "And not that many people get the MiT title, so it's not like the other guy is a pushover."

According to Margot, the Bachelor league tends to have more participants. Around fifty to seventy. Because the top 25 percent get the title, that's only twelve or fifteen people. Once you get into the Master-in-training league, it's harder because they usually have thirty to forty participants, meaning only seven or eight will graduate to the title. You get three chances to pass the first time and three to defend, but still, it's not easy.

Margot walks out, her brass knuckles already on. She seems relaxed but ready. Isaac comes out from behind her, looking more menacing than I've seen him since we fought Bernie. It's easy to forget that there's a fifteen-year-old boy in there as he steps forward on huge paws, saliva dripping and sizzling on the concrete.

They don't have the flags either, since it's the MiT league. The match will end by knockout, yield, or death.

The horn sounds.

The instant it goes off, Margot moves. Really fucking fast. *Virgil* fast. She slams her fist into Emerson's face, and he goes flying into the wall. Without even checking to see if she got him, she pivots on her heel toward his partner and decks the Monster on her biggest horn. Flames bloom, and Alexandra screeches and falls back, and in the corner of my eye, Isaac steps back too. I glance at him, but there's nothing happening over there. Margot speeds toward Emerson, who is attempting to recover, and hits him again before he can get his block up, smashing him into the wall a second time.

"Jesus," I mutter.

I look to Isaac, expecting him to get involved, but he just stands there, muzzle wrinkled, half looking away.

Emerson falls and doesn't get back up. The horn blows.

Margot jumps several feet back, landing softly in front of Isaac, breathing hard.

Meanwhile, Alexandra is wobbling around on her feet like she doesn't know what just happened.

"The match goes to Margot Bouchard!" the announcer cries. "Folks, that was a two-minute match! The society record is one minute and thirty-three seconds, and she came pretty close."

Margot rolls her neck back and walks out of the arena like nothing even happened, Isaac following her.

"Why didn't he do anything?" I ask.

Virgil says, "It's a strategy. They did the same thing last year so competitors wouldn't know everything Isaac could do."

But Isaac didn't just look like he was standing back. He seemed almost . . . wary. The last time he fought, he burned Davy badly. I'll never forget the scent of charred human flesh. And I was several feet away. What was it like for Isaac up close?

The antechamber where we're sent to wait before our match is dimly lit. They have water dispensers and bathrooms handy, which is nice, because I'm starting to think I might throw up and all I've had today is coffee and a banana. I stretch for what feels like the millionth time since we got here thirty minutes ago. I decided to wear a black T-shirt bodysuit with a pair of leggings overtop, and pulled my braids into a ponytail. I have on my knife holsters: the leather around my thighs and across my chest, two under my arms, the single strap on my back, and the wrist guards Margot gave me last year. The only new addition is the waist belt with two red ties.

I grip the chain around my neck, and it warms to my touch. Obviously, I can't use it in the match, but I've started wearing it at Riley's insistence. I've been doing her little exercises, too. But what's stuck in my mind the most is that someone put my bones in this because they wanted me to have the protection. I can't think of anyone it would be other than Mom.

"You asked about Kendrick," Nolan says. "Does that have anything to do with why you were looking through our files?" He leans against the wall drinking from a paper cup of water. He hasn't stretched once.

"Is this really the best time?"

"You're the one who wants my help. So convince me."

I sigh, crossing my arms over my chest. "Someone in the society killed my mom on November twenty-fifth, the year before last.

They used a Monster to do it. One that didn't seem to have a partner nearby. It reminded me of the Wild attack. So I wanted to see if there may have been a Wild in the Toronto area that day, and Kendrick was the only one confirmed. Now he's suspiciously dead, just like the Wilds who killed James."

"They died by suicide. Kendrick died of a heart attack."

I throw my arms up. "It's still suspicious. And he checked out a video from the official record, and it's also missing. I just want to talk to someone who knew him to see if he mentioned anything about the assignment."

"So your mom is an on-par assassination target with a Doctorate candidate?"

I blow a breath out of my nose. "I don't know why they tried to kill her. I just know a Monster did it, and she recognized them. My brother was there too, and he was spared."

"Would you not be better served finding out which Monsters she could have known personally?"

"No, because she hid that entire part of her life from us. She's not even in any society records. So Kendrick is the only lead I have."

"A dead man isn't much of a lead."

"Yeah, well, can we concentrate on the match we're supposed to win despite only practicing together once?"

"Do you want to win?"

"Obviously!"

"Then let's win," he says with a shrug.

"Because it's so easy."

"You almost killed me *by yourself*. Trust me when I say that's not easy to do. Today, your only task is to steal a couple of flags. It's not that deep."

The light above the door flashes amber, and Nolan rolls his shoulders back and starts to take off his clothes. I jerk away, attempting to give him privacy that he didn't care to have. The shadow on the floor grows, and I turn back to come face-to-face with the fox.

Something in the back of my mind stirs. Remembers the heady scent of his blood, and the way our claws dug in. It stretches, yawning and flexing, ready for more. But I can't let it out. Not again. I grip the chain around my neck, letting its warmth ground me. I need to stay in control.

The light turns green, and the doors open.

I swallow and walk out, keeping my head held high. The screams and claps become white noise. It's like all I can hear are Nolan's steps behind me. Nolan and the monster inside me, dragging the tip of a metal claw down my spine.

I recognize the team in front of us—or rather, I recognize their names on the big screen next to ours. Reese Compton and Naya Suarez from the University of Toronto. They were on the program yesterday, meaning they've already won a match. Their information said they were sophomores, so this is their second Monster's Ball. They have that look to them too. I understand how losing would make you more desperate to win the next time.

Reese keeps her weapon balled in her hands so I can't see it, her dark eyes focused and her hair slicked back into a low ponytail. Her brown skin and features make me think she might be Latine, though I can't be sure. Her partner slinks in behind her. Naya's Monster form is a big cat. Slim but with two heads, too monstrous to be anything mundane. Her teeth gnash in matching maws, gleaming pearly whites that look wickedly sharp. Something ripples underneath her hickory fur. Something that

seems alive, but that can't be right. It's probably her muscles moving oddly.

And here we are with no strategy whatsoever. My monster nuzzles against my neck. I ignore it.

I slide a knife into each hand.

Fuck it.

I want to win, and so does Nolan. That has to be enough, because it's all we have.

The horn blows, and Reese tries to rush me. She's fast, but I still manage to move out of the way, glancing down to be sure my ties are still there. I also finally get a look at her weapon. It's a garrote. Fucking medieval. She holds the wooden ends tight, the wire between them so thin that it's basically invisible. The only benefit to me is that it's a close-range weapon. As long as I stay back, I can control the fight.

The ground shakes as Nolan and Naya collide. I realize my mistake in looking at them the instant a wire gleams in the light in front of my face.

I jerk back at the same time that I stab down, exactly where I know my ties are, and Reese swears and dances away. Blood drips from her hands, but she didn't get one of my flags.

Without waiting for her to recover, I throw three knives in quick succession. Reese dodges them, but she's forced toward the arena wall as she does it. I keep them going until she hits the concrete barrier. I let one more knife fly, putting spin on it. The black metal embeds itself in the wall with a blue flag hanging from it. If I threw it straight, it would have just ripped through, but the spin helped it catch the fabric.

Reese's mouth drops open, and the horn sounds.

I grin.

Until something splats onto my arm. I look down as an insect the size of my fist digs its pincers into my forearm.

In the corner of my eye, Reese moves, but I'm preoccupied by the giant bug trying to burrow underneath my skin!

Smoke explodes around us, and something knocks me back. I scramble on the ground and rip the bug thing off of me. Nolan's paw comes out of the smoke and squashes the insect. He has even more patches of fur missing, and some of the bugs are still crawling on him.

Naya. I was right the first time. Something *was* moving under her skin.

"I'm gonna throw up," I gasp. The announcer is saying something about the fog and obscured vision. Nolan snaps his teeth at me, I suspect to get my attention.

One more flag. Just one more.

I do have to hand it to Nolan, the smoke screen is incredibly effective—though it obscures our vision too.

Nolan nudges me again, and I gag thinking one of those bugs is going to crawl on me. He points his paw through the smoke toward the left.

He can see through. Right. It's his smoke, so it makes sense. I'm almost surprised that Naya can't sniff us out, but there is a scent to the smoke too. It probably dulls everything.

I can't see because I'm not at the proper evolution to share Nolan's ability, so all I can do is trust where he's pointed.

I swallow and rush through the smoke, knife out, slashing until I hit something that screams. I smack into Reese, driving her to the ground, and rip off her flag. I scramble to get off her, and she kicks me in the stomach.

The smoke clears, and the horn blows.

I still have the flag gripped in my hand.

The crowd is going wild in the stands. I pant, looking at them. Nolan is too, blinking, swiveling his head as people whoop and cheer.

For us.

I grin. We did it. And *I* did it without my monster. Next step, learn how to use it. To master it.

Reese swears and throws her garrote to the ground before stomping out of the arena.

I crawl to my feet and half stumble to the doors. I collapse onto my knees, still trying to catch my breath. Once I finally get my bearings and turn, Nolan is standing behind me, tugging on his shirt.

My heart is still beating too fast, something sated deep in my belly, something with sharp teeth and amber eyes.

"They were cheering," Nolan says, his voice just above a whisper.

I smirk at him. "What did I tell you?"

He comes over and squats in front of me. He holds out his hand, pinky extended. "You promised me we'd win it all."

I hook my pinky into his. "We will."

"If, for even a second, I doubt you're committed to that, I'm out."

"I wouldn't expect anything less."

We shake, and Nolan releases my finger and stands. "Are you free right now?" he asks.

"Why?"

"I'm going to do you a favor, not out of the goodness of my

heart, but because I have a vested interest in what you find. If there's a connection between who killed your mom and who's framing Wilds now, I want to know."

I beam at him, and he looks away.

A two-for-one win. I could get used to this.

CHAPTER FIFTEEN

Nolan rolls onto the paved driveway of the Murphy compound. His car is a basic Honda Civic, necessary for him since he apparently lives in Kingston but drives over to Sydenham often. The same place where Kendrick Durand's girlfriend, Yati, lives. I step out of the car along with Virgil and Corey and peer at the houses on the strip of land.

It's decidedly suburban. The houses are single-story bungalows that look newly built, with vinyl siding in neutral blues and browns. There's a path to a small park with swings and a jungle gym where a few kids are playing, and a cluster of Canada Post mailboxes. And another path that I assume leads to the forest where me and Virgil were.

The whole area is a lot nicer than I expected. Given the way the Wilds are treated, I figured we would be going to ramshackle sheds or something. Not a neighborhood that looks like it's been planned by a government committee. Not that you need to be living in poverty to be under someone's thumb.

"Okay," Nolan says, turning to us. "You two"—a point at Virgil and Corey—"stay here. August can come with me."

I jolt a bit. Is that the first time he's called me by my name instead of just saying "her?"

Virgil shakes his head. "We didn't drive an hour out here to stand by the car."

"We're going to talk to a woman about her dead boyfriend, not have a cup of tea. It isn't a group activity. And I'll remind you that arranging this to include any of you is already a favor."

Nolan and Virgil stare each other down. I suspected things weren't going to be great when Virgil congratulated us on winning, and Nolan decided that the best response was to tell Virgil that he'd better not lose tomorrow.

"It's fine. We can wait," Corey says, leaning against the Honda.

Virgil scoffs and retreats into the car, slamming the door behind him.

"Very mature," Nolan says, and then turns and starts walking.

I jog to catch up with him. "You're the one who antagonized him."

"By setting a boundary? That's a red flag."

"I mean earlier when he was saying you did a good job in the match, and you responded by acting like you don't trust him to do the same." Nolan rolls his eyes and waves at a couple as we walk past them. Their eyes linger on me and then slide past. If this whole community is made up of Wilds, then they must know that me, Nolan, and Virgil are partnered by now. "Do the other Wilds know the real story of why we're bonded?"

"Like I would spread something that embarrassing around. The cover story is bad enough. The truth is worse." He brushes his hair out of his eyes. "Dad knows."

"What about your mom?"

"She worries enough."

That Master at the banquet said Nolan was a bastard. Meaning that at some point, either Garrett stepped out on his wife or they took a break.

We stop in front of a house with mint green vinyl slats, and their Christmas wreath still hanging on the white front door. Nolan raps his knuckles on the wood and waits.

"Does your mom live on the compound too?"

"Yup."

"Are she and Garrett, like . . . together?"

"Nope."

"Has anyone ever told you that you're an amazing conversation partner?"

He grins. "All the time."

The door opens to reveal a white woman maybe a couple of years older than Bailey with hair the same auburn as Nolan's. I raise an eyebrow at him. He jerks his head toward her. "August, this is my cousin Yati. Yati, this is the girl I told you about."

Yati beams at me, revealing a little gap between her front teeth. "Oh, you're just beautiful! I love your hair! Come in, come in."

"Thanks," I mumble, following her inside.

As we walk through the hallway to the living room, I spy photos of two gap-toothed children with darker auburn hair.

"Kids are down by the park," Yati says over her shoulder as she directs us to sit on the sectional couch. "Just throw those toys off—there you go. Sorry for the mess."

"It's cool," I say as I remove the stuffed rabbit that I sat on.

Yati says, "You really are so pretty."

"Stop being weird," Nolan says.

"Sorry, sorry," she says. "Nolan is so busy that I don't get to see him much. And he hasn't dated anyone in a while, so I get excited. I think maybe a boyfriend a year ago. Two girls before—"

"Can you not give out my entire romantic history?! And we're not dating." He jerks his hands at me. "Bachelor." Then at himself. "Monster. Not happening."

I would feel bad for Nolan if I weren't enjoying this so much. He's not a great conversationalist, but Yati is just fantastic. Gold star for her.

"Okay! Don't bite my head off." She looks at me. "You wanted to ask about Kendrick? Nolan said you help out at the McIntosh Castle library or something?"

I clear my throat. "Yes. We're updating some of the records and looking to identify unknown Monsters. Kendrick had a video of a Monster sighting, and the society said they lost it, so I wanted to check in with you."

Yati bites her lip. "Yeah, I'm sorry, I honestly don't know where it is. I did look for it. Not for those bureaucrats, fuck them, pardon my French. He told them he had work that day, at his real paying job, and they still insisted on him going down to Toronto. Then he got sick anyhow. . . ." She sighs. "Guess we know why that was. Should have gone to the hospital, but he said he was fine, that he'd just lie down."

I furrow my brow. "Wait, so he went to Toronto when he was sick, or . . . ?"

"Nope. Didn't go at all. Not the day they put in the report anyway. He dragged himself down there the next day and got their video. Still sick, mind you." She shakes her head. "We both almost

shit our pants when we got the order from the Doctorate to go take the footage. He'd literally just gotten back from going to Kingston to drop the stuff off, and then he has to go out again?" Yati sucks in a breath, her eyes watering. "I really think that's what killed him, you know? All that back and forth while he was sick. Fuckers. Sorry."

Conceptually, I understood that I was coming to ask a woman about her dead partner, but it's only now that I remember what it's like to rip off that slowly forming scab of grief. This will make it fresh again. I dig my nails into my thighs. "Don't worry about swearing. . . . So then Kendrick brought the video to the Doctorate?"

"Yeah. Dropped it off in his mailbox. That's why I didn't understand why they were acting like we still had it."

"Did Kendrick say anything about the job? Or the Monster?"

"The Monster was gone by the time he got there."

Meaning that if Carrigan was manipulating a Wild to do his dirty work, it wasn't Kendrick, who didn't even get into Toronto until the next day. And if he was that sick, Carrigan maybe didn't even kill him. Which only leaves that reptilian Monster.

That video would confirm if the Monster who had been spotted that day really was there, but it's gone. Whether Cyrus or Carrigan took it, whatever is on there is lost to me.

"Sorry that I couldn't be more help," Yati says.

I shake my head. "No, you were great. I knew it was a bit of a long shot. Thank you."

Yati walks us to the door, giving both me and Nolan hugs before we go. Me and Nolan head back in the direction of the car.

"That's a helpful coincidence," I say. "That she's your cousin."

"There are only three Wild families left in Ontario, and most

of the ones in Kingston live here. Everyone's related to me either by blood or marriage."

That's probably why people keep waving to him and why he seems to know all the proctors. I thought it was something about being the "second son," and it likely is, but it's also that.

"I guess it's useful, too, if you're going to take over one day," I say.

Nolan stops. "Who told you that?"

"Uh . . . I mean, at the banquet, some guy said that after Garrett—"

"Let's get this straight," Nolan says, eyes boring into mine. "I don't give a fuck what grand plans my dad has for me. I'm not going to be his backup."

"August?!" I turn around to see Mia coming out of a house a few feet away from us with Garrett beside her. She hefts a tote bag onto her shoulder, her thick dark hair loose and shiny. "You're back!"

"Shit," I mutter. To Nolan, I say, "I told her that me and Virgil broke into the vault because of a possible tip about my mom, which is true, and that we found you injured, so don't contradict the story."

"Why did you tell her anything?"

"Because she was pestering the crap out of me. How is she in a Wilds micro-town and still doesn't know about them?"

"Through concentrated effort on my dad and brother's parts. They insist she be kept in the dark." He shakes his head. "Useless effort, but I'm not getting into it with them."

"What are you doing out here?" I ask Mia as she gets close, forcing a smile onto my face.

She gestures at Garrett. "Helping Grandad. I decided to stay over for the weekend." She looks at me and then Nolan. "What are you doing here?"

"Research project. Just needed to talk to someone Nolan knew." I jerk my hand in the direction of the car. "Virgil and Corey are back at the car if you want to say hi." The last thing I want is for her to think I came here by myself with Nolan. Mia is way too quick to mentally couple me up with people.

"I don't think we've met," Garrett says, extending a hand to me, when I'm sure he knows exactly who I am. The girl who almost killed his son. He's got the face of a kind older man, but his eyes are steely, the brown flat.

I take his hand and shake it. "August Black."

Mia says, "August's aunt lives in the tiny house community, and she helped me out with the community dinner I mentioned before. We did one for the holidays, too."

"Did she now?" Garrett says. "Sounds like a nice young woman." He turns his gaze to his son. "Thought you'd be busy today."

"I was." Nolan doesn't look at his dad when he speaks.

"Are you coming back tomorrow?" Mia asks Nolan. "We can play Kelp again."

Nolan smiles at his niece with genuine affection. "So I can beat you at Kelp again?" She rolls her eyes. Nolan sticks his hands in his pockets. "Probably not this weekend. I have assignments. Next weekend for sure, though, okay? I can come out to you on the island."

"Fine. Maybe August will want to come too?"

Before I can answer, Nolan says, "It's a two-player game. And we have to go." He turns and starts walking, so I'm forced to follow.

"Nice to meet you, August," Garrett calls from behind us.

"You too!"

"You know he hates you, right?" Nolan says under his breath.

I grimace. "I figured." I can't blame him. A kid pushed me in a

playground once, and Mom would still gripe about him years later. I figure nearly killing and then trapping his son in a bond hasn't earned me any of Garrett's favor.

"After all, if you'd killed me, he might have had to find another replacement."

"Jacques doesn't want the job?"

"He would take it. Dad would love that too. But it wouldn't fly. Jacques abandoned us during the rebellion, and if there's something the community has a fresh memory for, it's the rebellion. Doesn't matter that it was more than a decade ago. He didn't stay and fight." Nolan shakes his head. "Never mind that. What are you going to do about your mom now?"

"I guess what you said. I'm going to have to find out what Monsters she would have known in the society."

Meaning, I went from having a lead to having nothing. One step forward, two steps back.

CHAPTER SIXTEEN

Riley

Joseph S. Stauffer Library is one of those buildings on campus that you can't help but look at. A behemoth of gray brick and dark blue glass, it takes up an entire corner of University Avenue and Union Street. It's not the most aesthetic, but you can't deny that it's eye-catching with its metal spires, blocky decorative arches, and mixture of circular and rectangular shapes.

It makes even more of an impression once inside, where you can see the balconies climbing several stories up. So high that I found myself craning my neck the first time I entered the building.

Now, Stauffer and I are old friends. I stride through the front doors, past the foyer and snack bar, and make my way into the actual library section before heading to the elevators. I booked a study room for eight a.m., though Corey's not meeting me until nine.

The study rooms are mostly lined up along the outside

walls—small spaces with large tables and a whiteboard. Once inside, I tuck myself into a corner, putting in my earbuds and propping my phone up. I make a video call at exactly eight a.m. to no answer. I wait another five minutes, then try again.

On the third call, a Black woman appears on the screen, hair still in her bonnet at what looks like a kitchen table, feeding a baby in a high chair. There are slight shadows under her brown eyes, and her septum piercing is crooked.

I say, "Thank you so much for agreeing to this call, Cece. I know it's early."

"I've been up since five thanks to my hell spawn, so it's fine." The hell spawn in question gurgles and kicks their feet. "I know, huh? You're my little demon boy and I love you but you're a nightmare," she coos. The cutesy tone drops as she turns back to me. "What's this about?"

"I was hoping to pick your brain about the sickle."

Cece, class of 2011, was QBSS president in her senior year, and in that timeframe managed to achieve the full release of the scythe. It was during the Wilds rebellion, and there was a lot of spillover with uncontrolled Monsters running around. QBSS took it upon themselves to help manage the situation, with Cece at the helm.

Now she's feeding a child mushy peas, but in her day, she was a force to be reckoned with, and I'm sure she still would be if I put the sickle in her hands.

Cece leans against her palm. "You having trouble with the release?"

"I'm seeking guidance."

She laughs. "There's that Historic upbringing. I know that life." She spoons more food into the baby's mouth as she tells him, "But

you won't, no you won't. No generational trauma for you."

My lip twitches. I'm hardly traumatized. Cece is powerful, but she's also one of those rebellious types. She was vocal about disliking the Historic designation despite being one herself. Her parents were hard on her because they wanted her to be better.

"Are you able to help, or . . . ?" I ask.

"Why do you want to wield the sickle?"

All I can do is stare at her. What kind of question is that? I collect myself and say, "To protect our society."

Cece sighs. "Girl, listen to me. Do you think I swung that sickle with some grand purpose?"

"I . . . Yes. I thought . . . I mean, you were protecting people from Monsters."

Cece makes a buzzer sound with her mouth like I got a big fat X in *Family Feud.* "I went out there swinging because my friends were in danger. I didn't do it for QBSS or my ancestors. I did it for the people I cared about. The sickle knows you. When you unleash it, you'd better have a damn good reason, and you'd better be willing to die for it." The baby starts to wail, and Cece kisses her teeth. "Sorry, I gotta go."

"Thank—" She hangs up. ". . . you."

There's a knock at the window of the room, and I jump. Corey is there, bundled up in a puffy coat, carrying a tray with two cups from Common Grounds. I gesture for her to come in.

"Sorry," she says. "I'm early."

I rub my face. "It's fine."

"Rough morning?"

"Yeah."

"Maybe this will help," she says, motioning to the coffees. "I got

sugar, milk, and cream packets since I wasn't sure how you take it."

"Black is great, thanks."

It's good, actually, that Corey is here. We can get straight to work instead of me trying to wrap my head around what Cece said. She would never be my first choice for alumni guidance, but she's the most recent president to manage the full release. The one before is closer to my parents' age, and the last thing I need is for them to go yapping about how Riley Townsend called them for advice because she's too incompetent to manage her weapon.

Everyone in QBSS is already looking at me, and so far the only thing I've done in front of them this year is get my ass handed to me by Malachi.

"How's our mutual friend doing in her latest death competition?" I ask.

Corey smiles. "August and Nolan won their first match yesterday. Second match with Virgil is this afternoon."

"Not bad."

"They're good. Brave." Her eyes drop to the table, and she curls her left hand under her right. Almost to hide it. I'm not shy about missing fingers, and I didn't think she was either, but something seems to have changed. "Well, uh, let's get to it. I brought some of Dr. Weiss's journals. Just the ones Henry had me get last year."

"What did he use them for?"

"Oh, uh, he's never said. I think he's just that sort of person. A lot of students study the words of Dr. Weiss. Now I'm doing some apocalypse research for him, which is more practical. I think he wants to help the Doctorate manage the rising spontaneous Monster birth rates."

"Makes sense." All this interacting with August made me forget

how real society members are. They're devoted to their leaders and founder, and believe in things like a Monster apocalypse. The last time I was alone with Corey in the parking lot during the initiation, she was anxious about Virgil eating August and getting put in the Pen. She wanted to talk about anything but the society. I think I got something like thirty new skincare and gothic movie recommendations. But she's grown up as a Learner. I shouldn't be surprised that she's devout.

"Maybe we should establish what we know so far?" I dig in my bag and produce a notebook, opening it up. "It's a tangible object, likely an artifact. Bernie said it killed Gods, so we're operating on the assumption that it's a weapon."

"And someone in the Learners' Society wanted it enough to put together an elaborate plan to get it. Meaning they're someone with some degree of power. Either they want to use the weapon or, like you suggested, prevent others from using it."

"I do also have some historical documents. But of course, none of the notes about artifacts mention this weapon. They don't mention the sickle, either, and that exists. We do keep some things in oral tradition only. Information about this artifact must have either been lost or hidden for its protection."

"Protection from us," Corey murmurs. I don't have to confirm it. She untucks her left hand, leaning her cheek against it. "According to our records, Joseph Lawrence took with him all the information about the artifacts. But something must have remained in the society for someone to know to look for this weapon. You said QBSS has had spies in the society before?"

I shift. It's weird to talk about us spying in the organization she belongs to. "Yes. We keep those records oral between the handler

and the spy. Though there is a code name for the most recent one. It's Healer. Does that ring a bell for August's mom?"

Corey shakes her head. "She worked a consulting job, as far as I know. Maybe a good place to start is to see if there's any overlap in descriptions of something like an artifact. I can look in the journals and you can look in your records, and we'll note down any possible descriptions, and then compare them."

"Okay, let's do it."

For the next couple of hours, we work in relative silence, poring over our documents before comparing our lists. I point at a word that I didn't note myself, but Corey has. "'Osseous.' What's the context for this in your text?"

"One of Dr. Weiss's journals, dated prior to the split with Lawrence. He mentions that 'the Osseous, now formed, may also be undone. As I believe it should be.' I flagged it since it's Latin for bones, and I know that's important to QBSS, and he's used the word before in reference to Lawrence's research, but here he's capitalized it."

I flip through Lawrence's texts and squint at a mention. His handwriting is small and tight, but yes, it's a capital letter. "'The protection of the Osseous is paramount to our survival.' I glossed over it because of course it's important to protect our bones, but you're right, it's capitalized."

"Could the weapon be a bone, then?" Corey asks. "This is the only overlap we've found of an unknown proper noun recorded by both founders."

"It would make sense. All our artifacts contain bones, so one made entirely of bone might have some significance. No idea whose bones."

"Maybe the bones of a Doctorate."

I tilt my head. "You think so?"

"I wouldn't be surprised. The body of the Doctorate has special properties. It's an open secret that something of the Doctorate's body goes into the serum. That's the piece that helps Masters exert control and is likely why Doctorates can break those same bonds. They've never publicized what from their body they actually contribute. Perhaps it's bone."

"Wouldn't you have noticed if Weiss was missing a femur or something? Unless he happened to save his baby teeth."

Corey laughs and sticks her left leg out from under the table. "You might be surprised. Unless my leg is sore or I'm dealing with phantom pains and limping, so long as it's covered, most people don't notice that I'm an amputee."

"Fair point."

"Not to mention that if Dr. Weiss temporarily bonded with a Monster who had a regeneration ability he could sever a limb, or pull a tooth, regrow it, then break the bond. First and foremost, he was a researcher. I wouldn't put it past him. Plus, he and Lawrence worked on those artifacts together. That incorporation of bones into the serum may have led to similar research that eventually became the artifacts."

"And based on that quote, this Osseous was something that Weiss seemed to fear, but Lawrence felt was integral to protect."

"Then it's a strong hypothesis that we're looking for the Osseous." Corey nods to herself. "I'll double-check in the McIntosh Castle collection and Henry's personal volumes. I have access to the latter now, which helps."

"I hope he's paying you," I say.

She laughs. "He is; don't worry. I love history, but I also

understand that compensation is important. I'm actually kind of surprised that you aren't majoring in history. You seem to have an interest."

I give her a tight smile. "It's not practical for me. Academia and research are great, but in all fairness, most people don't become millionaires off tenure."

"Is that your goal?" Corey asks, tilting her head. "To be a millionaire?"

I shift in my seat. "My goal is to be successful. I could contribute effectively to the progress of QBSS, too. Money gives you the power to elevate those without."

I get that. Career choices aren't always as simple as just doing what you like. I'd love to do a master's in library or information studies, but Queen's doesn't offer it, and I don't technically need it. I'll be taking over at McIntosh Castle regardless. Which is the exact reason I can't leave Kingston. Not for that long, anyway. I'll probably do it online in the end. I understand that choices and goals don't exist in isolation."

"Exactly," I breathe. I catch myself and clear my throat. "Just . . . yeah." Corey's phone buzzes, and she checks it, staring at the screen for much longer than normal. "What's up?"

She startles, almost dropping her phone. "Oh, uh, nothing. It's nothing. Let's see if we can find any other references to this Osseous." She puts her phone down but curls her left hand back underneath her right, and for the next twenty minutes she stares at the pages of a journal without flipping them.

"Have you ever had your palm read?" I ask.

Corey jerks her head up. "What?"

"Give me your left hand." Blinking, she reaches out, and I take

her hand in mine. I ignore the way I suddenly have to swallow. Her hand is warm, probably from being tucked away, and shakes a little as I hold it. Even the small nubs of her pinky and middle fingers twitch at the contact.

"Wouldn't you rather my right hand?" she asks, her voice soft.

"Why?"

"I don't know. I think it makes some people uncomfortable."

"I'm not some people." The corner of her mouth twitches up. I trace the lines on her palm with my right index finger. "You'll live a reasonably long life. You know, enough to be comfortable but not so long that you're on TV on your hundredth birthday saying you wish you died a decade ago." A giggle slips through her lips. I trace another line and lick my lips. "This one means you're in a moment of great change and transition."

"Does it go well?"

"Is there any reason it shouldn't?"

She looks at my hand holding hers. "I don't want to be scared anymore. I don't want to feel weak, either."

"Again, I've seen you kick a Monster in the face. When have you ever been weak?"

Corey's eyes widen and get glassy for a moment. "Uh, what about the love line? Isn't that a thing? How's that looking?"

I let go of her hand and fold my own away in my lap. "My grandma didn't teach me that one." Technically, she didn't teach me any palm reading. What she did teach me was how to distract someone who's lost in their thoughts.

"Did something happen?" I ask.

"Just . . . my parents. My brother is out of the Pen." She gives me a grim smile. "He's been staying at their place while he's in the

city for the Monster's Ball. They've been trying to get me to come over. Like, they've been good about it. Not pushy. Just saying they miss me or whatever and wish the family could be back together. Apologizing, too."

"Oh." I don't know a lot about Corey's past struggles. Just what she told me last semester at August and Virgil's initiation: That she competed with her brother when she was really young, and she didn't pass. That's how she lost half a leg and two fingers. "Is that a bad thing?"

She fiddles with the edge of a notebook. "It's not supposed to be. I keep thinking that I should be the bigger person and just go. They're so happy to have him back, and I'm sure he's happy to be back. I can't imagine what that was like for him . . . but I'm still terrified of him, and I'm also still mad at my parents for putting us through that. I was getting better with them, but now it's all coming back, and I feel like I'm looking for him in every shadow and every corner. When I actually saw him, it was like I was back in the Pen again, crawling away with a bleeding stump, crying and thinking I'm going to die."

"What's wrong with being scared?"

"I . . . I just, I don't want to."

"I don't think that's how feelings work."

She laughs. "Yeah, I guess not."

"Take your time. Don't do it at their speed. Do it at yours."

Corey blinks at me, her eyes wide. I clear my throat and pick up my notebook. "We should call it a day," I say, standing. "But I can read your palm again anytime you want."

"Thanks," she says with a smile. I pack away my stuff and then help her with hers. She's got so many books that it takes several

minutes to force the zip on her bag closed. She bites her lip. "I was supposed to pick up more from Henry. I'll have to do a drop-off between classes."

"I thought you guys didn't have a lot on spontaneous Monster birth stuff. What sources are you using?"

"We don't, but I've been looking into Meredith Grant specifically, the fifth Doctorate, and there's tons on her. Her life is really fascinating. She was the third child of the fourth Doctorate, which was already scandalous because it defied Dr. Weiss's single child for Doctorates rule. Then her other siblings died young, so she was kind of a last chance to make sure the line didn't die off. Her father was later conscripted for World War II, and he could have dodged the draft but insisted on fighting and died when Meredith was only seven and—" She flushes. "I'm sorry. I'm boring you."

"You're not. Honestly, I don't know a lot about Learner history unless it intersects with ours or is particularly juicy. I'm intrigued." Besides, the way her face lights up talking about it is leagues away from the tortured expression she had on while discussing her family. If this keeps her excited and smiling for a few more minutes, it's worth it.

"Okay, well, she was only seven, and so they couldn't make her the Doctorate, but they didn't have anyone else because her father had no siblings. That's how the Doctorate's Challenge was created. Do you know about it?"

"Yeah, another death tournament you do in case all the Doctorates die, right? Masters form teams and compete, and if they win, the Master leading them becomes the Doctorate."

"Yes! So it was the very first one, and Gregory Russo won and

was Interim Doctorate until Meredith came of age. He never got the official title of Doctorate since he was just a placeholder for Meredith, which I think made him bitter toward her. She famously despised him. She wasn't popular as a Doctorate, in any case. I think because she was a lesbian."

I raise my brow. "She was?"

"Well, allegedly. She and her husband lived in separate houses, and she pretty much ignored him. If divorce had been an option, I'm sure she would have done it. Meanwhile, she had a close friend, Matilda, who lived with her, and when Meredith died early in a car accident, Matilda wrote and read her eulogy, and Meredith left her house to her in her will. It wasn't honored, but she'd tried. Maybe they were just friends, but I doubt it."

"I thought the Learners were accepting of all, et cetera, et cetera. I wouldn't have thought she'd have to hide it with them."

"Yes, well, it was still the early nineteenth century. The society has always been ahead of the times in acceptance, but ahead of the times doesn't necessarily mean progressive by today's standards."

I would argue that it doesn't necessarily mean progressive today, either. They just moved the targets of their oppression from one group to another. For some people, power never feels like power unless they have someone over which to assert it. "What happened when she died? You said it was early."

"Yes, at thirty-four, when Cyrus was sixteen. They reinstated Gregory for two years instead of doing the challenge again."

"And this relates to the apocalypse how?"

"So! The spontaneous birth rates plateaued during Meredith's time as Doctorate and didn't rise again until a couple years after her death. I thought that gap was too far to be related to her tenure, but

now I'm wondering if I was wrong. I haven't found any other possibilities yet."

"Good luck with that."

Corey grins. When she smiles, it fills up her cheeks like she's bursting with it. Something in my stomach flips. Too much coffee. "Thanks for indulging me."

After double-checking that we haven't forgotten anything, we leave the study room. On our way out of the library, I spy August's brother bent over a series of books and scribbling furiously. He's got about five different empty coffee cups around him. I knew that he had to make up for lost time, but damn, he looks like someone who has to defend their thesis in the next five minutes.

Outside of the library, Corey and I stand across from each other. I shuffle my feet. I don't know why I feel like I should do something. Corey makes the decision for me, folding me into a hug. "Thank you," she says again. "Really."

After a beat, I wrap my arms around her and return it.

Her hair is soft where it brushes against my face and whatever soap she uses is fruity.

She releases me, and I think I say something like bye before she leaves and I'm still standing there. Just a hug. I hug other girls all the time. It's nothing.

"Getting cozy with the enemy?"

I whip around to see Inaya walking out of the library. I forgot that she practically lives here, constantly cramming for chemical engineering courses because she had to pick the supposedly hardest engineering track. I roll my eyes. "Is there something I can help you with or are you just here to make snide comments?"

“There’s a fine line between using the Learners and fraternizing with the Learners.”

“And aren’t you lucky that you aren’t the president so you don’t have to make that distinction?” The expression on her face sours, and I walk home with a spring in my step.

CHAPTER SEVENTEEN

Running to the library as soon as I wake up isn't even old August behavior. It's definitely not new August behavior. And yet here I am, in one of the McIntosh Castle rooms, trailing my fingers over the spines. All the books are shiny and clean from Corey and Virgil's efforts. Not a speck of dust in sight.

I did at least manage to sleep in this time, exhausted from everything that went on yesterday, from the match to visiting the Murphy compound. Me and Virgil decided that during the tournament days, I may as well stay at McIntosh Castle. I suspect so that he can micromanage to make sure I get to the matches on time.

Still, despite looking through the records for the millionth time, I don't find Mom's name. Which means I'm not starting off well in figuring out what Monster in society she could have known.

I pull out my phone and text Dad, *Does Mom have any other*

family besides her mom? My grandma on my mom's side died when me and Jules were little, so we never met her, and Mom never talked about her.

I collapse on a couch and tap my foot as I wait for Dad to text back. Even with the couches, the long drapes, and the fireplace that should make the space cozy, I can never fully relax in these rooms. Like I'm always expecting to be scolded by a librarian.

Dad finally replies. *You're up early.*

I groan. *My question?*

No, just Pattie, who didn't speak with her own family, and Annie's dad took off pretty early.

What was his name?

Jonesy Griffen. Though I think Jonesy was a nickname?

I squint at the phone. *I thought they weren't married?*

They weren't. But I guess she took his name anyway.

I'd assumed that Griffen was Pattie's maiden name because she never married. But it wasn't. *Then what's her maiden name?*

Simmons. I remember because Annie briefly considered changing hers to that, to honor her mom.

Why would Mom want to honor a woman who she never even talked about? *Why didn't she?*

I don't know. I figured she just didn't get around to it.

Getting up from the couch, I find the tome noting society members under *S* and tug it out. While Summerhill houses the society records that are more private or require permission to access, McIntosh Castle has the information that any student can reference at any time, including the student records. Which is how Virgil was able to check on them so easily.

"What are you looking for?" Virgil says from behind me.

I jump and spin around. "Can you make noise or something?"

"I did. I said 'good morning.'" Virgil comes up beside me, looking over my shoulder.

I stab the page. "This is my mom's mom. I thought Griffen was her maiden name, but it was actually my mom's *dad's* name. Simmons is her maiden name, and there she is, Patricia Simmons. They weren't married, but she changed her name. She must have been doing it to, like, hide her identity or something."

"Are we sure it's the same one? That's not an uncommon name."

I bite my lip. The student records don't include a lot of confirming information. It just says that she worked in the Scientist department. "No, but I mean, Mom was friends with Carrigan, and this says that Pattie worked in the Scientist faction. That's at least a connection."

"But Carrigan said your mom wasn't part of the society."

"And we've established that Carrigan is a liar."

Virgil leans in to look at the record, his breath wafting over my ear. I fight a shiver. "She's noted as a member since her birth in 1953 and is on record until her death in 2008. If she had a married name—even if she wasn't actually married—that should have changed in the record if it was on her ID. It definitely should have been recorded that she had a child. The fact that both are omitted would be suspicious if this is your grandma. Or maybe proof that this isn't her." He's so focused on the records that he doesn't seem to realize how close he is to me. "There are a few other Simmonses here. Some are Monsters, which explains how the mutation got into your family. Only one person is still alive. She's had a name update. Georgia Derwood . . . Oh shit."

"What?"

He steps back and gapes at me. "That's . . . that's the woman Dr. Liu is, um . . . It feels weird to call her his girlfriend, but yeah. She's not a Monster and doesn't have a rank or anything, just an ordinary student of the society. They met on his sabbatical, and he's living with her. She was with him when he came to visit us that first time. The Black woman."

She looked at me for a beat too long. Did she recognize me as Pattie's granddaughter? Why didn't she said anything? "Dad said Pattie didn't talk to her family, but it's worth a shot. Can we have a meeting or something?"

"I'll text him."

"Are there any other, like, record places that we should look into?" I ask.

Virgil shakes his head, then stops. "I mean, there's the vault on the Doctorate's island. That's where they store top secret files or historical valuables. Though I doubt anything with your mom would have ended up there. In any case, it's impenetrable. Another reason that the cottage is such an important historical—"

"Is this going anywhere?"

Virgil scowls at me.

My phone vibrates, and it's Mia trying again to set up this game night with her and Nolan. "She's so persistent," I mutter. "I thought Mia would be busy with Isaac and school."

Virgil grimaces. "I think they kind of broke up?"

"What?! When? Why?"

He shrugs. "I don't know. I asked him about her yesterday, and he said they don't hang out anymore. He's been really focused on training. I don't know if he's stressed about defending or what."

"But yesterday Margot crushed their opponents without him even lifting a paw."

"Yeah . . ."

I shake my head. I'm not getting involved in Isaac and Mia's teen romance drama.

"You should get ready," Virgil says.

"Are *you* ready?" He's been weird since yesterday. Happy for me and Nolan, obviously, but he's also been quiet.

"I'll get you the win," he says.

I can't help but notice the difference between what he said and what Nolan said. *I'll get you the win.* Not *let's win.*

"Hey . . . ," I say, chewing on the inside of my cheek. "The monster . . . What does it feel like to you?"

Virgil squints at me. "Like, in the initiation? I guess like rage and anger."

"No, since the initiation. It's not, like . . . in the back of your mind or . . . ?"

"August," he says, staring at me. "What do you mean?"

"What did you think I was talking about at the bus stop after that first training? About mastering the monster?"

"Like . . . getting a hold of your anger. Maintaining control."

I nod. Finally, we're getting somewhere. "Yes. Of the monster."

"Figuratively," he says, stepping closer, "or literally?"

It's a good question. And I'm not sure I can answer it. "Never mind." I turn to leave, and Virgil grasps my hand, keeping me in place.

"If there's anyone who would understand," he says, "it would be me."

I swallow, keeping my eyes on the ground. "Ever since that day

with Nolan . . . it feels physical, like it's living in my head. As soon as I fight or attempt to use any abilities, it tries to come out. To make me lose control again." I look at Virgil, who's staring at me like he's afraid. Not of me. *For me.*

"The bonding," he says. "This might be a side effect of two partners. If this gets worse, like it starts to take over or Adam can't break the—"

"I can handle it. Master it, like I said."

Virgil nods but never once stops looking scared.

Before we can go into the antechamber for our match, we have to check in at the Bachelor league greenroom. They actually call it that, like we're celebrities. The room is buzzing with activity as the Bachelors file in. This is the last day of our league getting the afternoon slots. Tomorrow, we'll swap, and the MiT league will go in the afternoon and us in the morning. They usually run the repechage matches in each league in the same time blocks, so we haven't had a chance to watch any.

I did confirm via text that Jules won his match today. I wanted to pester him about how the fight went and whether he hurt himself or not, but didn't. *He's* the one who shut *me* out of Mom's stuff. I'm not going to act like everything is fine.

Nolan is thankfully on time but with his usual aloofness. Even though he's not competing today, we always have to check in as a trio.

Virgil goes to the food section a few feet down while Nolan comes over beside me at the coffee station, swearing when the thermos runs out with his cup only half full. He flags down a volunteer, who runs off to get a refill.

I grab today's program from beside the creamers and flip through while sipping my own cup of coffee. "What the fuck?" I breathe.

"I'm not going to ask you what you're freaking out about," Nolan says. "I don't care. I'm just waiting for caffeine."

"Violet and Frankie are on the repechage list today. That means they lost their first match."

"Oh, so you're telling me anyway? Great."

I shake my head. "I know they seemed kind of nervous, but I didn't think they'd lose. Even *Hudson* won his first match."

"I'm not engaging with you."

"You know that if we take turns going back and forth, it is technically a conversation?"

Nolan looks down his nose at me. I think he and Virgil may be the same height. Meaning they both have at least half a head on me.

"Black and Hawthorne," a volunteer shouts. "Time to proceed to the arena."

"Don't lose," Nolan says.

"Don't miss our fight waiting for coffee." I drop the program and head toward the door. Virgil joins me, having abandoned the bagel he was eating. As we walk past, a guy mutters about how it must be nice to have an advantage in the competition. It's not the first time I've heard these sorts of titters. I guess because I haven't keeled over, they only see the benefits of our three-way bond.

"Then do it," Nolan says, leaning against the coffee station. The guy in question has a deer in headlights look on his face. "Do it," Nolan repeats. "You want an advantage? Find a second partner and get approval from the Doctorate."

The guy starts spluttering.

Nolan cups his hand to his ear. "What's that? You can't? Then shut the fuck up."

The guy closes his mouth.

My entire body warms, and I can't help the massive smirk on my face.

"Don't get excited about it," Nolan mutters, and I hear it even across the room.

"I'm not," I say as I turn and leave with Virgil.

Virgil doesn't say anything as we wait to be let into our assigned antechamber or as we stand in the dark. Not while I strap on my knives and we stretch.

Finally he asks, "Is it in your head right now?"

I swallow. "Yes." The monster is prepping. Pacing. Wearing a hole in my brain with anticipation. I flex my hands, feeling the ghostly sensation of claws I don't have.

"Just leave it to me," Virgil says, his jaw tight.

"Excuse me?" Does he think this is a solo fight or what?

The light turns amber.

Virgil doesn't respond, only transforms, prowling the space until the green light goes on.

We walk out to applause. The announcer is still saying something, but it's just a buzz in my ears.

Our competitors are already waiting. Arthur Dinh, an East Asian–looking boy who's slim but muscled, holding his own pair of throwing knives. His are the style with holes at the bottom of the handle so you can twirl the blades. His partner, Sutton Hull, is a fluffed-up sheep-type Monster, covered in thick fur with horns curling on her head. Her lips spread in a permanent grin packed with razor-sharp teeth.

I slide my knives into my hands.

The monster, suddenly . . . is quiet.

For some reason, that feels like a bad omen.

The horn blows, and Virgil leaps over my head, charging in front of me. I don't even get a chance at the competitors because he's already out there trying to take them on by himself.

He's trying to Margot me.

I think the fuck not.

I dash forward and almost get a knife to the face, managing to jerk back just in time like I'm out here doing the limbo.

Turns out that Virgil wasn't actually overwhelming both of them, Arthur just wanted him to think he was so he could get a knife out at me. I move away and whip out my own knife, only for it to clash with one of Arthur's in midair and fall to the ground.

I keep my distance. Nobody wins in a close-quarters knife fight. Everyone just gets stabbed, and I'd rather avoid that, even knowing I could heal. Which isn't even a given with how rudimentary my third-evolution skills are.

Virgil attempts to swipe Arthur with his claws while also handling Sutton, which results in him getting bitten. Though Sutton is the one who cries and rears back, pierced by one of the many spikes littering Virgil's body.

That ass. He really thinks he can manage this alone.

I wasn't planning on trying to tap into the monster, which makes fighting feel effortless. Not when I still lack control. But the way it has sunk into my mind, timid and quiet, makes me feel . . . bereft, almost. Like I'm missing something.

It's never been like this before. Even when I was actively trying to suppress it, it fought back. What's different now?

Arthur breaks away under Virgil's feet and throws a knife with spin on it. This dick is stealing my move! I only have two choices. Lose the flag or take a knife to the thigh.

I smother a scream as the blade digs into my leg. "Motherfucker," I hiss. It's clear to me within seconds that I should have just lost the flag. The pain is excruciating, and it's not as if I can pull the knife out. I might bleed to death.

Arthur grins.

Virgil, meanwhile, is still too caught up with Sutton, who's fantastic at keeping him occupied even as she's taking hits from his spikes. All that fluff on her must be providing some sort of protection. She only got hurt before because she went in for a bite.

Arthur rushes toward me. He's going to make it close quarters, knowing I can't run. And once he's got me down, even with the time delay between grabbing flags, it won't be that hard to manage the win. Not with my leg like this.

We'll lose.

No fucking way. Not this early.

Come on, I will inside my head, desperation overriding my fear of losing control. *Do something!* But the monster stays as it is.

Virgil is only across the arena, and yet it's like he's not there at all. I don't know who that is. That isn't the boy who stood up to Caden for me, who roared so fiercely to protect us from that rogue Monster during initiation, who tucked a braid behind my ear while he told me I was a risk worth taking.

It's like we aren't even bonded. Aren't connected in any way.

Arthur grins as he gets in my face, close enough for his fingers to brush against my flag.

I open my mouth and scream. There's no point to it. It's just a

release of rage. But the moment I start, it feels different.

I'm not the only one furious and frustrated. Feeling the walls closing in.

I'm not the only one who doesn't want to lose like this. Fighting this way. As two lost individuals instead of partners working together.

I'm not the only one who can't think of anything else to do but scream to give release to every bit of those emotions churning in my gut.

Even now, with something between us broken, we can still recognize those shattered pieces in each other. After all, it's not as if either of us understands what it means to be whole and untouched. We have only ever been bits of porcelain on the ground being put back together with bloody fingers.

For the first time since the initiation, we *roar*.

Arthur drops to the ground with his hands over his ears, his eyes squeezed shut.

I have seconds.

I dart forward and snatch the first flag away from him. The horn blows. Before he can recover, I drive one knife into each of his thighs. He screams and falls onto his side. I kick him in the face, glancing at the clock. The monster makes a sound that seems suspiciously like a chuckle. When Arthur tries to go for another of his knives, I slam my foot onto his hand. Something crunches underneath. A shiver rolls over my shoulders and shakes me down to my toes, like when you scratch the exact right spot.

I kick him in the stomach. Feel the give under my toe. It's not as satisfying. Sutton bleats, trying to get around Virgil to help, but she can't.

The monster is grinning now. Licking its chops.

More.

More. *More.* MORE!

The timer runs out. Too fast.

I rip the other flag away.

The final horn blows.

I squeeze my eyes shut and tell myself that I didn't like any of it, gasping as the monster slams against the walls of my mind, still roaring.

Because, of course, this is Virgil's monster. It comes from our bond. If I'm disconnected from Virgil, so too is the beast.

Virgil and I walk into the antechamber, and I wait until the door closes to round on him. "What the fuck was that?"

He grinds his teeth. "I thought I had it."

"What am I to you?!"

Virgil stares at me, swallows, the amber of his eyes dimming in the closed chamber. "My partner."

"Good. So you didn't forget. What were you thinking? What could possibly—"

"I was trying to be better!" Virgil shouts. "I was trying to actually have something to offer you. Nolan can already intentionally use a third-evolution skill, and I can, what, make claws come out in human form? Roar sometimes? Passively regenerate?" He turns away from me. "That thing in your head . . . I don't know what it is, but I know enough to understand that it's my fault. Everyone is always protecting me, and I can't let you of all people do the same thing."

"Why me of all people?" My voice is barely above a whisper.

Virgil looks at me like I punched him in the stomach. "You know why."

"Don't ever do that again," I say, walking to the door. I put my hand on the handle. I speak with my back to Virgil. "I didn't choose Nolan. I chose you. Protecting each other was never something that was supposed to go one way. We fight together, or we don't fight at all."

CHAPTER EIGHTEEN

Laira opens the door to Henry's home with a flourish, outfitted in a gray sweatsuit with her locs in a bun on top of her head. "He's been expecting you," she says, voice full of foreboding.

"Is this a bit?" I ask.

She grins and takes my coat. "You don't like it? I'm thinking of spicing up my workdays with catchphrases."

"What exactly do you do? Like, for work?" I ask Laira as I kick off my boots.

"I don't. Not really. I take the odd mission, and I assist Henry. Mostly by dramatically walking guests to his location, or lifting things, driving him around, and providing much-needed comic relief. I find careers to be vastly overrated." She waves me down the hall. I follow after her, expecting to be taken to the parlor, but instead she starts up the stairs.

Laira knocks on the first door on the right, and Henry's voice

welcomes us in. She lets me inside, then closes the door, leaving me and the professor alone. Henry's personal office is similar to the one he has in Humphrey Hall—lots of wall-to-wall bookcases, leather furniture, and polished wood surfaces. I spy a photo of a young Henry and what must be his family, two smiling parents and a little girl stuck to his side.

"Take a seat," Henry says, directing me to the chair in front of him.

I sink into the leather. "To what do I owe the pleasure?" I'd been summoned right after the match, I assumed for a lecture. Except Virgil wasn't asked along. If I was going to be yelled at, then he should be yelled at too.

"Sloppy match today," he says, leaning his elbow on the desk.

I pick at the edge of a nail. "Maybe you should ask your ward about that."

"I will." He narrows his eyes. "You've been holding back."

I scoff. "You call breaking a dude's fingers and stabbing him twice holding back?"

"Not today so much. But the first match, yes."

"We won."

"And still." He taps on the side of his head. "What is going on up there? There was something blazing in you at the start of the semester. A bright fire that's since gone out. You fight like you're afraid to."

I keep my gaze on the surface of the desk. Had Virgil told him about the monster thing? "The last time I decided to let loose, Nolan almost died. I don't want to get into the habit of murdering innocent people."

It's silent for long enough that I finally look up to see Henry staring at me. He points across the room to the portrait of him

and his family. "We went to Gould Lake for a hike the day they died. It had taken all day, and we were exhausted. It's not the most family-friendly trail, but my father loved a challenge. I stopped to relieve myself." Henry laughs a bit. "Picture me, fifteen, a few feet away from my family, peeing in nature without a care in the world. Then I heard the screams. There is no sound like someone being eaten alive."

I swallow, and my nails dig into my palms.

Henry continues, "I stood there, petrified. That was when the Monster pushed through the trees, blood on its lips. And there I am." He pauses for a moment. "The Monster froze then. It took a while for me to realize it wasn't moving. Cyrus came around the corner with Adam at his side. I'd told Adam we'd be going for the hike, and so when reports came in of a spontaneous uncontrolled Monster in the area, Cyrus himself rushed over. I was saved. But do you know what the worst part was?" I do, but I shake my head like I don't. "The hatred that burned in my belly at how weak and useless I'd been. The pity people showered me with because I was so pathetic. From that moment, I decided that I would never be that boy again—caught with my pants down when someone I loved needed me. So yes, you almost killed Nolan, but you also saved Virgil. You cannot fight in a cage, Ms. Black. And quite honestly, I didn't presume you to be the type to put yourself in one."

The monster's hot breath huffs against my neck, bearing down on me. "You told me to control myself."

Henry leans forward. "Yes, to control your power, not suppress it. Release yourself before you become too accustomed to being bound."

"Then teach me," I snap. "Teach me how to."

"I intend to. But first, you need to do something for me. In the next match, loosen the reins a bit. Show me some of that power. Prove to me that you can use even a fraction of it without drowning."

I'm the first of our trio to make it to the check-in the next morning. There's something to be said for rage keeping you up. That, and Henry's words. We won the match, but it was a near goddamn miracle. I opted not only for ignoring Virgil but also for sleeping in my dorm instead of McIntosh Castle.

I get what he said, but I'm still pissed.

Violet and Frankie walk into the room. They must have won their repechage match yesterday. Though Frankie is shuffling around like someone died, and when I raise my hand to wave to Violet, she gives me a tight smile and then turns away. At least she's got her lipstick on. That's something of a good sign, right?

When Bryce and Mitch arrive fifteen minutes later, they come over to say hi. They've been doing well thus far, still in the main tournament like us. Mitch makes a beeline for the refreshment table after his greeting, while Bryce stays.

"Congrats on your wins," he says, adjusting his glasses.

"Thanks. Congrats to you too." I point at his eyewear. "You wearing those aesthetically?"

He laughs. "No. I have astigmatism. It's based on the shape of my eyeball, so the bond can't do anything about it."

"Shit luck. When's your match?"

"Near lunchtime, they said, vague as ever. We do have time to watch some of the earlier matches at least." He looks around. "Where's the other two-thirds of your team?"

"One usually shows up right before he's needed, and the other

annoyed me and so I don't really care as long as he shows up on time."

"Yeah . . . I had a chance to watch and noticed that you and Virgil seemed off."

I shake my head. "Speaking of being off," I say, nodding to Violet and Frankie, who are currently in a corner. Frankie's crouched and hugging her knees, and Violet's looking at her phone without scrolling.

Bryce winces, and Mitch comes back with two stacked bagels, biting through the two at once. Honestly, it's impressive. He chews and swallows. "We talking about team Vikie?"

"Is that their team name?" I ask.

Bryce says, "No, they don't like it," at the same time that Mitch says, "Yeah, they love it." Mitch points to him, and Bryce and says, "We're team Brytch, and I was calling you guys Virgust, but I've adjusted now to Augvirlan!"

I grin. "Thanks, I hate it."

"Don't be like that. Give it some time to grow on you."

"I won't be doing that. Now, can we refocus on the team Vikie stuff?"

Mitch says, "See? You like it." I roll my eyes. "I told Frankie that she's getting too in her head about it, and Violet is just feeding into it."

"What does that mean?"

Bryce sighs. "They haven't reached the second evolution."

"Wait," I say, "like, not at all?"

Mitch nods, finishing off his bagel double-stacker. "No signs of Frankie's ability, either. You can't even attempt third evolution if the Monster isn't expressing something."

"Okay, but they're winning now, so why does it matter? They'll get there before the competition is over."

"You have to understand," Bryce says. "Violet has always done better. She's always top of the class. She always excels. She's always good at everything she tries right away. Struggling is not something she's ever had to do. I think it's getting to her."

Bryce and Mitch are called for registration, and they say their goodbyes to me and leave to get their seats in the audience. Shortly after, Violet and Frankie are called and leave for their match antechamber.

I feel for them. Even when I was the old August, success never came easily to me. But Violet has always had this unflappable confidence. I'm sure Frankie is probably under a lot of pressure to perform too. I also can't help but wonder if Violet's not used to Bryce being the one ahead of her. The whole time I've known them, he's been something of a shadow to her shine. But now he's stepping into the light.

Nolan and Virgil enter the greenroom at the same time. Virgil mumbles something about getting a coffee while Nolan approaches me.

"Trouble in paradise?" Nolan asks.

"It's too early to try being cute."

"I'm not— Never mind. Are you going to be good for our match?"

"Yes. I wasn't the problem in the last one." Though now I have the added struggle of attempting to do what Henry told me. Show him that I can let some of the monster out without losing it completely.

Nolan rocks back on his heels, watching Virgil fuss with his coffee. "Roars don't come out like that. It's a low-level intimidation skill. Annoying at best."

"Not for us."

Nolan regards me for a moment that goes a tad too long. I swallow and look away. What a time to notice that the guy is attractive. Not that I didn't notice before. But now I find myself more aware of the freckles that dot his face in random patterns that also feel perfectly placed, and the way little strands of his hair fall out from its tie.

And I'm confident going into this fight with Nolan. Like he said, it's instinctual. We don't have to work at it.

I wish that were how me and Virgil had fought. It should have been.

We go through registration, and Virgil mumbles something about getting a seat while me and Nolan head to the antechamber. Time rolls by faster than expected and soon enough, the amber light flashes, and then the green, and it's game time.

It almost feels like the applause is louder this time in the arena. Like there are somehow more people, or maybe they're just screaming more.

We're the first ones out and get to wait for our opponents to be announced. The monster rakes a claw down my spine, pushing experimentally. I swallow. No matter how Virgil is acting, something I said must have made it through to him. We're not good, necessarily, but we're not bad, either. He's still with me.

The announcer says, "We have Hudson Barlowe and his partner, Remington Torres, from Queen's University. Barlowe came in fourth in this year's Bachelor candidacy and has been a surprise in this round of the Monster's Ball, beating out the Sharma-Kumar duo, who ranked second in this year's Bachelor candidacy at Queen's. He may be a dark horse!"

Wait, *Hudson* and Remy were the pair who beat Violet and Frankie? *Hudson?!*

At initiation, this boy was practically trembling when he saw me. But that's not the case now. He stands tall with a sledgehammer in his hands. The moment he sees me, his lips spread into a wide grin, teeth bared.

I let out a slow breath, remembering exactly how much it hurts even to be grazed by that weapon. But I also know its weaknesses. It'll be like fighting a less impressive version of Caden.

The horn goes, and fog surrounds us. I glance at Nolan, watching the mist seep out from gaps in his fur where bone and muscle peek through. There are some groans from the audience, whose vision is also compromised. Corey told me last time that the cameras recording us switch to infrared so they can see on the screens. Thankfully, those screens are obscured from our competitors at this height.

I'm waiting for Nolan to point me to where they are when he suddenly surges forward and head butts me to the side. I grunt and am about to swear at him when an insect-like pincer appears and stabs him through the shoulder. Nolan doesn't even cry out, just slashes with his paw and slices the pincer.

As Remy appears out of the fog, the severed pincer on his back grows anew like nothing happened.

Shit. He can regenerate.

I think about the monster and picture it through the bars of a cage. Let a bit out. Just a paw. In that same instant, the beast slams against the metal, and I grit my teeth. Snapping my jaws involuntarily.

I just manage to dodge as Hudson jumps out of the fog, swinging the sledgehammer. I duck under it and roll, ripping a knife out and throwing it, aiming for his hand. But he must have read the move, because he dodges it.

"I'm going to win," he snarls. "For Caden!"

"Oh my God, stop being a minor character in your own life." I would roll my eyes, but I need to keep them on him.

Hudson swings the sledgehammer in a circle, moving his whole body with the motion before he lets it fly. I jump out of the way.

It's a bad move—now he's got no weapon. But when I look, he's gone.

I turn as the sledgehammer comes flying back at me, the metal flashing in the corner of my eye. Something fucking biblical must save me because I manage to do my limbo move and evade.

The horn sounds.

I snap my neck down to see one of my flags gone.

The monster roars, the sound echoing in my head. I gnash on my lip, my breathing getting heavy.

Hudson grins at me from across the arena.

The fog dissipates. It's not helping us right now, so there's no point to it.

Hudson and Remy are at the second evolution. That's the only explanation for how he could move fast enough.

Looks like I was wrong. He's not the minor character anymore. After all, he's got a tragic backstory now. And here he is, fighting the girl who was gleeful over the death of his best friend.

I'm the villain of his story.

I grip my knives harder. I can't lose this flag, but I also need to make sure that I can grab his. The monster paces back and forth, claws clicking, hackles raised. I try again to release a little bit, one paw, but the beast is too greedy. It slams against the bars again. It wants to tear Hudson limb from fucking limb and slurp the marrow from his bones.

Something that I can't allow to happen. Even if it's Hudson.

I only have one weakness to exploit.

If I'm his villain, then I'd better play my part well.

"Beating me won't bring him back. He's still going to be a stain on the ground," I spit. "Or did they clean him up?"

Hudson's face crumples before he screams and runs at me.

I ask, "Did you gather the entrails into a jar like I suggested?" He swings the sledgehammer, moving wildly. It's easier to dodge. "How about Daddy? He was his trainer, right? Had a good cry with him?"

That sparks something in Hudson's eyes.

"Wait," I say. "Is his daddy training *you* now? Are you the replacement son?"

He goes ballistic. His swinging is fiercer, and faster, but also more distracted. I whip a knife at his face, and as he leans to dodge, I snatch one of his flags.

A victory that's short-lived when his sledgehammer smashes into my side.

I tuck and roll. I try to stand up but can't and stay curled on the ground. Jesus fucking Christ, it hurts. Ribs have broken; they must have. Hudson goes for me again and is mercifully intercepted by Nolan kicking him into the wall. Remy reengages Nolan, but at that point the damage is done, and Hudson is dealing with his own pain.

Did one of my lungs collapse? I can breathe, but I can't catch my breath. I keep wheezing. Fuck this dude. Even from the grave, Caden is messing with me. Him and his bigot of a father with his Wilds proposal, and his lackey who's decided to become useful.

I could tear him apart with my teeth and listen to him scream.

Shaking my head, I squeeze my eyes shut and then open them.

Hudson picks himself up off the floor, blood rolling down his temple as he stumbles toward me.

I lift my shirt and look at my deeply purple side. Not a great sign.

Hudson comes and stands over me, grinning. I bare my teeth at him. I don't know where the sledgehammer is, but he doesn't seem to care to use it. He says, "I hear your mom's dead."

"Weak," I gasp, and with the last of my strength, I shoot my leg up, kicking him right in the family jewels.

Hudson crumples to his knees, and I smash my fist into his stomach, one, two, three times. The monster purrs in my ear. Only when I'm satisfied do I rip the flag off.

The horn sounds and I lie next to him. He's crying without making any noise. Tears sliding down his face.

"I didn't make Caden my enemy," I say. "Not you, either. I hope you remember that."

"Eat shit and die," he gasps.

"You keep working on those insults, bud. You'll get there." I force myself to my knees and manage to get up. I clearly wasn't ready because they give out, but then Nolan is there, and I lean against his leg. Grasping a handful of his fur, I limp to the antechamber, where the doors close behind us.

I drop the second we're back in the dark, still trying to catch my breath.

"What are you doing?" Nolan says, standing over me in his human form, clothes back on. How long have I been crouched here?

I wave at the ground. "Checking out the scenery."

"Heal."

"Because it's so easy."

"Yes," he says. "It is. Do you know what your problem is?"

"I'm sure you're going to tell me."

"You still think you're human. You aren't. Humans cannot move like you can, have the strength you can, could not walk away from the same injuries. Yet you insist on acting like you're human in the same breath that you say there's nothing wrong with monstrosity. If you believe there's no fault in being born a Monster, why are you trying so hard to avoid it?"

The monster stares at me from its gilded cage. I reach out, knowing it could snap at me, destroy me. I let it drag a rough tongue over my hand, my panting slowing as I breathe easier. The pain ebbing.

"Nolan," I say. "What's the monster like for you? Like, in your mind."

He frowns. "What are you talking about? I *am* the Monster."

The door to the antechamber flies open, and a small group of people enter. "Let's set up the lighting over there," a white man with a microphone and floppy brown hair says. The team behind him moves fast, putting down chairs and plugging in lights. "August, dear, get off the ground, and we'll have you go in front. Maybe some makeup for her? For the shine? And, Nolan, you'll be beside her."

"Who are you?" I ask, standing, breathing freely.

Nolan smirks at me, and I ignore him.

The man says, "You can call me Dick."

"I'd rather not."

One of the team members ushers me over to the chair setup while another puts powder on my face. I wince. I can breathe now, but I'm not fully healed. Everything still hurts. Nolan falls into the chair next to me and also gets his face powdered.

Dick settles in the chair set at an angle to our right, and the camera light goes red. "I'm here with August Black and one of her

two—that's right, *two*—partners, Nolan Murphy, who you may recognize as the second and youngest son of Garrett Murphy of the Wilds." Nolan's hands flex as he's introduced. "Congratulations on making it to the quarterfinals! You've both amassed a good number of fans, and I admit that it's exciting to see a Wild in the Monster's Ball. August, what's your secret to success?"

I turn to Nolan and quirk an eyebrow. He's the one who wanted the airtime, not me. "What's *our* secret, Nolan?" I ask.

Nolan turns to Dick and says, "If you like seeing a Wild compete, then perhaps you'd also like to protect our rights. This proposal going around would make it so I couldn't continue to attend Queen's University, couldn't have a career, and would let any potential I have be wasted proctoring and doing assigned missions until I die. You voted for a Doctorate who you wanted to bring positive change to the society. We want the same. That proposal is not only an affront to him but to Dr. Weiss's philosophies. And if you won't strike it down, we will, when we win this whole thing."

Dick stares at Nolan, jaw unhinged.

When Nolan stands and walks out of the room, I follow.

CHAPTER NINETEEN

The student volunteers insist that I go to medical to be checked out just in case. I feel like a giant bruise, but they confirm that my fractured, not broken, rib is already mending, and since I can breathe normally again, my lungs seem to be fine.

Virgil sits in the chair beside my bed while Nolan stands at the foot of it.

The nurse who's been helping says, "You're all good. But if any symptoms reappear, come straight back here. No hospitals."

"Will do," I say. The nurse hustles off to help a competitor who doesn't have regeneration abilities. I turn to Virgil. "Did Bryce and Mitch's match start?"

"It's about to."

I swing my legs off the bed and stand. I stumble, and Virgil is over in an instant to steady me.

"You should rest," he says.

"I want to watch. I haven't seen any of their or Violet and Frankie's matches."

"You—"

"Just let her go. She's going to fight you the whole time otherwise," Nolan says.

Virgil and Nolan stare at each other for a moment before Virgil concedes but insists on helping me walk, though I don't need assistance anymore after a few minutes.

"It sucks," Virgil mutters. "Watching from the sidelines."

"Wish I could watch while you and Nolan fight."

He cracks a smile. "I'm sorry for yesterday. I just . . . I wanted to be able to handle it."

"*We* did. Get that? *We*, as in partners, as in a team."

"I know. It won't happen again."

When we get to the arena where Bryce's match is happening, it's so packed that we only get spots because of Henry's Mastery group seating, where Corey is already waiting, her foot bouncing. Part of me doesn't understand why she's putting herself through this, but another part of me does.

"Are you okay?" she asks.

I nod. "Fine. I didn't want to miss this. Are *you* okay?"

"I can do it."

I reach out my hand, and Corey grips it, leaning in close to me. Virgil sits on my other side, and Nolan beside him.

The announcer's voice comes over the speakers. "Welcome to the last main tournament match in the Bachelor's league before quarterfinals. We've got a good one for you! We have Bryce Clark and his partner, Mitch Romano, from Queen's University. Bryce was third in his Bachelor candidacy and has been making

a name for himself with quick, decisive wins."

Bryce and Mitch emerge from their end, Bryce with his sword strapped to his back. I've never seen Mitch's Monster form before. He's gigantic—at least eight feet tall with a gorilla-like form, bulging muscles everywhere you look, and on his chest is what almost looks like a metal breastplate fused into his skin. Mitch bares his teeth and beats his chest.

"And the challenger, Barbara Hu, and her partner, Ellis Yang, from the University of Ottawa. Barbara, better known as Barbie, was first in her Bachelor candidacy cohort and has been an absolute force in this competition. She is the favorite to win in this league, but will Bryce give her a run for her money?"

Corey grips my arm harder.

Barbie and Ellis emerge. I have to admit that she does look deadly in a bubblegum princess sort of way. Her blond hair is tied back in a long ponytail, bangs cut perfectly to drape over her eyebrows, and she's wearing a bright pink bodysuit. Her weapon is a knife on the end of a rope that she keeps balled in her left hand.

"What is that?" I ask.

"Sheng biao," Corey says. "It's a rope dart. And she's very good with it." She's speaking about Barbie but staring at Ellis. At that sleek panther form.

The horn blows.

I can barely see Barbie as she surges forward. I only realize what's happening from the metallic clang of her weapon hitting Bryce's sword as he raises it to defend. Meanwhile, Ellis disappears in a plume of black smoke, and Mitch swings his massive gorilla arms this way and that, looking for him.

"What the fuck?" I mumble.

"You're looking at a high-level fight here," Margot says, walking over with Isaac at her side. Now that Virgil's mentioned it, Isaac does kind of look . . . I don't know, down, I guess. He shuffles his feet and stares at the ground. "They're both comfortable with second-evolution skills."

Ellis appears behind Mitch and sinks his teeth into the other Monster's leg. Corey is holding me hard enough to hurt, though I bear it. Mitch howls and tries to shake Ellis off.

Meanwhile, Bryce and Barbie stop moving. Bryce has sweat dripping down his face, running over the goggles he wears to protect his glasses. He's breathing hard. Barbie, in comparison, only has a bit of dampness on her bangs, and she stands, lazily swinging her sheng biao around in a circle.

That would be the moment I would rush in for a flag, but she's not even bothering.

Bryce grits his teeth and surges forward again, and it begins once more. Mitch seems to have gotten free of Ellis, but Ellis has disappeared from the field again while Mitch limps and swivels, trying to guess where he'll be attacked. Ellis appears and Mitch has a good angle and throws a right hook, only for Ellis to disappear again upon contact.

A scream draws my attention to Bryce, who's jumped back, nursing several cuts on his arms, legs, and face. He's more using his sword to hold himself up than to fight at this point.

"He's slowed down," Margot says, leaning forward.

Still, Barbie refuses to go for his flags. Instead they clash over and over, until Bryce falls to his knees, his sword clattering to the floor.

Mitch roars, trying to turn toward his partner. Ellis appears in

front of him at every turn. And Mitch has his own injuries to deal with.

Finally, Barbie walks over to where Bryce kneels. To his credit, he makes an attempt to grab a flag from that vantage point, which she neatly sidesteps. She kicks him in the chest so he goes down and then plucks the first flag from his person.

A thirty-second timer appears on the screen.

She plants a foot on his stomach, leaning her full weight on him, a smile on her face.

Is that what I looked like when I was running down the clock?

To their credit, Bryce and Mitch don't give up for even a second. When the timer hits zero, Barbie takes the last flag.

The horn blows.

She doesn't have a single cut on her.

The house me, Corey, and Virgil stand in front of isn't particularly standout or impressive in any way. It's certainly a downgrade from McIntosh Castle. But Dr. Liu has chosen to take up residence in this boxy townhouse new build near the ferry dock because of the woman who lives there. Georgia, who may have known Mom and Pattie. Pattie, who I can still only think of as Pattie. My grandma, as far as I'm concerned, was Dad's mom. Pattie was a ghost who I didn't think was relevant to me until now. And Georgia could be a close or distant relative.

"Didn't Dr. Liu say Georgia doesn't know August or her mom?" Corey whispers to Virgil.

Virgil says, "Yeah. But August is insisting on a direct approach."

I tug my jacket closer around me. The grass on Georgia's front lawn is frosted white from the chill. I reach the front door, and as I'm about to knock, the door opens and Georgia steps out. I didn't

get a good look at her before, so I look long and hard now. She's got a tapered afro with gray and white hairs throughout, and her cheekbones are high and defined. She steps back when she sees me.

"Hi," I say. "Georgia, right? I'm August Black. I think you knew my mom, Anemone Black? She went by Annie. Or maybe her mom, Patricia? Pattie? She was a Simmons like you."

"Oh, well, my name is Derwood—"

"But your maiden name is Simmons." I smile wider. "Derwood was your married name, and you're divorced, aren't you?"

"Widowed, actually. I didn't know a Pattie. There's a lot of us." She turns and locks the door, then bustles past me. "I'm sorry, I need to head out."

"You're really going to pretend not to know me?" I snap.

Georgia stops and gives me a look like I'm a naughty child she's not afraid to punish. "Look, I said as much to Harold. I do not know you or your family. I am sorry that you have lost them, and I understand that you are desperate for answers, but I don't have them."

With that, she gets into her car and drives away.

Virgil sighs. "I'm sorry that it's another dead end."

"We can probably check archival records for . . ." Corey goes on, but I already have an alternative in mind.

I walk to the fence and let myself into the backyard.

"Oh, so we're just breaking and entering?" Corey asks behind me.

"August!" Virgil hisses. "Do you not remember this going poorly last time?"

"I doubt she has a Monster in the yard."

I go around the back of the house and try the patio doors. They

slide open. I at least have the grace to take off my shoes once inside. I head up the stairs while Virgil brings over a chair so Corey can sit to remove her boots.

It's not difficult to find the woman's bedroom. I root around in her drawers without managing to find anything more than charging cables and lip balm. I move on to her closet, crouching as I push aside dresses and shirts. I get on my tiptoes and riffle through her boxes, which seem to mostly be empty shoeboxes. Why would you even keep stuff like that?

"You're Pattie's granddaughter, that's for sure."

I snap my neck toward the door, dropping one of the shoeboxes.

Georgia stands in the doorway with her arms crossed. "Pattie could never leave things alone. You have none of her finesse, though."

"Maybe don't leave your patio doors open," I splutter.

"Is that really how you want to lead after breaking into someone's home?"

I clear my throat. "So then you *do* know Pattie?"

Georgia shakes her head. "I was looking for an apology."

"Sorry," I say.

She sighs and walks up to me. "I see it. In the forehead." She steps back. "And the hips. I didn't get them, though; too bad. Well, let's go downstairs and discuss it over some tea. Your friends are already there anyway." Without waiting for me to confirm, she heads out and I follow.

Virgil and Corey are, as Georgia said, at her kitchen table looking miserable. I sit next to them, slouching. Georgia takes her time getting our tea orders and fixing the cups. Then she roots around in her cupboard, extracts a blue metal tin that's supposed to contain those horrible cookies with those giant sugar flakes. I'm dreading

being offered one, but when Georgia opens the lid, inside there's a single photo. She takes it out and hands it to me. "That's the only picture I still have of her."

It's a younger Pattie holding a baby. But . . . I've seen baby pictures of Mom, and this isn't her. I flip the photo over, and the date there is 1981. Mom was born in 1982.

"Your baby?" I ask.

"I never had kids," Georgia says.

"Who is it? Not my mom."

"No, not Anemone. I have no idea who. Pattie would not discuss it. I didn't even know she was seeing anyone, and suddenly she was pregnant and wanted to hide it. Not proper, she said. So I helped her. I don't know where she gave birth, but it sure as hell wasn't a hospital. Showed up with a fresh baby and told me to take a picture. Wouldn't tell me if they were a boy or a girl either, and you know it's hard to tell with babies."

"What happened to the baby?"

Georgia shrugs. "I don't know. Then she met Jonesy, and got pregnant again, totally fine with not being married that time for whatever reason, and she had your mom, and then Jonesy took off."

"Why would you lie about knowing August?" Virgil says, looking between us.

"Because that is what Pattie wanted. She'd gotten herself mixed up in something dangerous, and she had me stage this big fight at a lecture and said I couldn't talk to her in public. Made me get rid of all the photos of us. I kept that one secret because the situation with the baby felt suspicious enough that it might matter one day. You can't imagine how many times I begged her to tell me more or let me help, and she wouldn't have it. So stubborn that she said she would

really cut me off, not even meet me in secret anymore if I didn't stop." Georgia shakes her head. "I didn't want to lose her, so I honored her wishes. She did cut herself off from the rest of the family, I assume for the same reason that she wouldn't let Anemone be registered as a student with the society, and why she took the last name of a man she hadn't even married and who'd left her. We continued to meet in secret while I pretended I hated her publicly. All the way up to the day my sister died."

"Sister?!" I blurt out.

"Yes. She was my older sister by three years."

I stare at Georgia. The woman is my great-aunt, and she's an active member of the society. Potentially she watched me enter the candidacy and said nothing because of a promise to her sister. Now I had forced myself into her life. Not that it was hard to get her to break.

"If I hadn't done this, would you ever have said anything?" I ask.

Georgia stares into her teacup. "I suppose not. Annie knew about me. At any point, she could have reached out but chose not to. I assumed that meant she wanted the same thing as Pattie. But I admit that it's difficult to keep honoring a wish when everyone who cared about it is dead. I resolved not to approach you, but seeing as you're here now, well . . ."

I fist my hands on top of the table. I don't know how to feel about suddenly discovering a new family member. I'm glad for the information source, but otherwise . . . I already feel disconnected from Pattie. There's no automatic closeness with Georgia by virtue of their relationship.

Either way, Pattie had a secret. One that was dangerous enough to require breaking ties with her family, and a baby might or might

not have been involved. Mom might have known about it. Or might have only been honoring a wish like Georgia. "Do you know if my mom was directly involved?" I ask.

Georgia sighs and takes a sip of her tea. "Who knows? Running around with the Doctorate's son while her mom was trying to keep her away from the society, it seems like stepping in the shit would have been inevitable. I tried to bring that up with Pattie in private, but she wouldn't have any of it. 'Carrigan is a nice boy,' she said. 'Not like the rest of his family.' But I've never seen any difference between him and the other Shaws. He didn't even come to Pattie's funeral. And now he's in his hidey-hole just like he was when Anemone took off with you and your brother."

I decide not to get into her feelings about the Shaws. Adam honestly is the only good one in that family, but I can't blame her for seeing them all as the same. "Carrigan disappeared before? When we moved?"

"Yes. He was supposed to be taking over the reins in the Scientist faction, and then all of a sudden, poof. It was a hectic couple of days, let me tell you. First the attack on the Doctorate, then the next day Anemone takes off and Carrigan's gone with her—though not together, mind you."

"Attack on the Doctorate?"

Georgia gives Virgil a meaningful look. He ducks his head and says, "My parents."

The older woman nods. "Lots of confusion and mayhem. A good time to disappear. Honestly, I only met Harold in the first place because I went straight to McIntosh Castle to try to scrub Pattie from the records, only to get caught in conversation with him during my failed attempt. It was a surprise when we ended up on

the same tour group during his sabbatical. He remembered me over a decade later, can you believe it?" Georgia seems to be fighting the smile that threatens to light up her face. "No one came asking about Pattie in the end, so I decided to leave the record alone. Well, until now, anyway."

"So you have no idea what Pattie or August's mom knew?" Corey asks. "Or if it had anything to do with the Queen's Black Student Society?"

Georgia reels back. "Why would they be involved?"

"Just wondering . . ." Corey trails off, turning red.

"I'll tell you one more thing," Georgia says. "I don't believe for a second that Pattie just died. Her illness came on much too suddenly."

"Cancer, right?" I ask.

Georgia furrows her brow. "No. Is that what Anemone told you? She had a heart attack." I freeze. A heart attack, just like Kendrick. "Meanwhile, she had no prior issues with her heart. Someone did something to her. And they must have figured job well done because Anemone didn't run until two years later." She takes a long sip of her tea. "That's all I know."

We finish our tea and stand to leave.

Georgia says, "Well, you know where I am. Just . . . if you wanted to stop by . . . Even if you wanted to bring July . . ." The otherwise put-together woman seems suddenly shy.

I hold out my phone to her. "Put in your number. Me and Jules can come by for tea."

Georgia nods several times, typing in her number with a single finger. I text her so she has mine.

It feels too awkward for a hug, so I just stand there while I thank Georgia for her time. I don't know how much of the Simmons family

is left, but as far as Pattie's branch of the family tree goes, it's only me and Jules. I'll make sure we come back at some point to see her. I know how easily family can disappear. I pause to take a picture of the photo of Pattie and the baby, and then we leave.

I thought this would give me answers, but now I just have more questions. Something was going on with Pattie, Mom, and Carrigan. There's some connection there. And that baby . . .

"When was Carrigan born?" I ask Virgil.

"Not 1981. He's older. Also, gross, considering he had a thing for your mom."

"Just asking!"

I shake my head. Forget the baby. It would be way too complicated to find some random kid. More likely, Mom and Pattie were targeted for something they knew. Carrigan must have known too, which is why he went underground. And we already know what Carrigan was after.

"The weapon," I say. "Pattie and my mom have to have known about it, right?"

Corey nods. "It's the only thing that connects so far. It would explain why your mom thought you and Jules would be safe with QBSS if they were supposed to have the artifact."

This was why Mom was murdered. Why Pattie was murdered. For a weapon.

In my mind, the monster snaps its jaws, imagining itself crunching bone and lapping up blood. I tilt my head back, close my eyes, and soak in the vision.

CHAPTER TWENTY

If there's one thing the society loves to do, it's repurpose Summerhill for their events. The space usually used for lectures has been redecorated to host the closing dinner for the first four rounds of the Monster's Ball. The white tablecloths have been transformed into deep mauve, and the chairs are covered with the same linens draped on the walls. The centerpieces are long-stemmed candelabras, and there's more silverware than I know what to do with. It's very much giving vampire wedding.

Almost makes you forget that a short while ago, there was a funeral for an entire family here.

Me, Virgil, Margot, and Isaac enter as a group, though we haven't been seated together. Thankfully, Nolan is there when we arrive. Attendance is mandatory, and they actually checked off our names at the door.

"Saw your interview before one of the matches," Margot says to me, tilting her head in Nolan's direction.

I tuck my hands into the pockets of the black skater dress I chose for the occasion, thanks to my limited and Virgil-supervised use of Henry's credit card. The dress has a plunging neckline, long draping sleeves, and galaxy sparkles all over, and I paired it with black insulated tights and my Docs. "Well, you know, me and Dick go way back."

She gives me an exasperated look. "I do think it made an impression. It started lots of conversations."

"Positive conversations?" Virgil asks.

"I think so. Younger people seem to admire the sort of devil-may-care attitude that August and Nolan bring to the function." Margot smooths the nonexistent wrinkles in her sleek emerald dress. "Can't imagine why."

I let out a dry laugh that she smiles at.

"Happy to have made it through to quarterfinals?" I ask, looking pointedly at Isaac.

"Yup," he says, and heads toward the bar like he's going to be able to get anything more than pop and juice.

Margot shakes her head. "Teenagers," she mutters as she follows her brother. They'll sit on the other side of the hall with the rest of the MiT league participants.

"Shall we?" Virgil asks, and I nod.

We head to the Bachelor league side of the room and take our assigned seats. It's common for Mastery groups to be seated together, so we're with Bryce, Mitch, Violet, and Frankie. I take a look around the room, where our other cohort peers are nowhere to be found. That's bad luck. Their next ball will be their last.

I try not to wince looking at Bryce. Mitch doesn't have regeneration abilities, so they both have to heal naturally. Which, given the bond, is still much faster than usual.

Nolan joins us, sitting on my other side. He, without a single hint of shame, glances at the cleavage that I have on display and then away, like he didn't do anything at all.

"Enjoy the view?" I ask him.

Virgil chokes on air.

Nolan shrugs. "Sure."

I roll my eyes and return my attention to Bryce and Mitch. "How are you guys doing?"

Mitch grins. "Can't keep me down. This one, on the other hand . . ."

"I'm doing better than I look," Bryce says. "Did you watch?" Me and Virgil nod. "Did it look as much like I was getting my ass handed to me as it felt?"

Virgil says, "No," at the same time that I say, "Kind of."

Bryce takes it in stride, laughing.

"How's your leg?" I ask Mitch.

"Hurts like a motherfucker," he says. "As soon as those doors opened, I was like, okay, this isn't great, but I think we can manage it."

"You handled it as well as you could," Virgil says. "I knew they were favorites to win, but I didn't expect their level to be that high."

If that were us, we would have lost right off the bat. It's a near miracle that we could make it through without using second-evolution abilities. We almost handed the match to Hudson and only won because we could manage the roar. If we can't be consistent with second-evolution skills by quarterfinals, we'll lose.

Hudson is thankfully seated far away from us, though he has been kind enough to make time to glare at me every few minutes. I'm sure it would delight him for us to fall to the repechage so he

could get a second chance to beat us. Another reason why we can't let that happen.

"Yeah," Bryce says. "Henry said we needed to be at the second evolution at the start of the Ball, but not everyone we fought was consistently there. So we could manage better. Fighting Barbie and Ellis was the first time we had to keep it up for a full match, and she barely broke a sweat." At that, he glances at the entrance, where Barbie and Ellis are walking through.

She looks like she's at Toronto Fashion Week, in a form-fitting peach dress that looks like vinyl or rubber or something. Ellis, on the other hand, chose a simple black dress shirt and pants. He stands with his hands in his pockets, slouched, head ducked. Now that I get a chance to look at him properly, it's hard to deny that he's really hot. Like, model hot. He and Barbie look like a celebrity couple.

I glance at Violet, who's staring at the table setting like it's a TV screen. Frankie has physically turned her chair to the side and is observing everyone else, not even looking at us.

I jump when Frankie speaks suddenly. "Our first match was with Hudson and Remy. I fought Remy in human form during that second Bachelor candidacy test last year. Wasn't even a challenge then. I took him down like nothing. But his skill level was completely different. Hudson, too, because they were at second evolution. We lost in minutes. Henry was right. We should have gone in at that level, because you never know who you'll be paired with."

"But you've done well in the repechage," Virgil says.

Frankie scoffs. "It's easier when you're fighting losers. For quarterfinals, we'll be against people who were doing well up till that point like Bryce and Mitch instead of people who lost in the first round."

"Bathroom," Violet says, standing and heading across the room.

At that, Frankie goes back to avoiding eye contact.

Everyone at the table suddenly gets up, and I scramble to my feet too, not sure what's happening until I turn around to see a beaming Adam.

"Just wanted to say congratulations to you three," Adam says, gesturing to our trio. "And unfortunately, no progress thus far on our little issue." He bites his lip. "But I'll keep at it. Until then, you seem to be doing well. I haven't had a chance to see more than the opening parade, but I have a mandatory appearance at quarterfinals and beyond, so I look forward to watching."

"Thanks." I'm not sure what else to say. And then Adam is moving on. It's a quick conversation, but given the way people are flocking to him, I'm sure it was a lot just for him to spare us that moment to share an update.

"There was another attempt on his life last night," Nolan mutters as we take our seats again. "Dad said a bunch of Master-Monster pairs swarmed the Murphy compound, looking for the Monster who attacked him. Found her dead like twenty kilometers away. I assume they were keeping him from the matches for safety, but I guess it didn't matter."

"What do you think is happening?" Mitch asks. "A single Wild attack is one thing, but multiple is a pattern."

"He's not the only one with the power to control Monsters. One is hiding, apparently even from his brother," Nolan says.

Nobody needs to say Carrigan's name. Mitch looks at his lap, and Bryce shifts in his seat. Even if it's obvious, they don't want to blame a Doctorate candidate.

"If someone was manipulating them, they would need to come

out of hiding to do that," Virgil says. "You can't manage it remotely."

"Exactly," Nolan says. "We tried to volunteer Wilds to be part of the security detail so they could search the area, but the request was denied. Despite the fact that any Monster, including the paired ones, could be used just as easily." Nolan crosses his arms over his chest.

Honestly, I get it. There must be some reason that Carrigan is choosing to use Wilds specifically. Maybe because of what Adam said about them being harder for him to control, making the Wilds a weakness of Adam's that Carrigan can exploit. And I mean, two Wilds *did* get the job done when it came to James.

I spot my brother across the room and stand. "I'm gonna say hi to Jules." I haven't had a chance to talk to him in person since he showed up to yell at me, so I head over to him now. I've been keeping an eye on his table specifically to catch him when Natalie was gone.

He sets his jaw. "I don't suppose I can convince you to skip the afterparty?"

"There's an afterparty?" I ask, widening my eyes like I've never heard of such a thing.

He sighs. "Please don't stay out too late. You have classes tomorrow."

"You could benefit from taking a night off. You look like shit."

Jules presses his lips into a line. But he must know I'm right. He's got a nice set of dark circles developing, and it looks like he's breaking out. "I'm working on getting my grades back into good shape and making time to train. It's the least I can do."

"The least you can do for who?"

"Please, not today."

"If this is penance for Mom, pay it by finding her murderer, not

denying yourself a life. Besides, what could you have even done in the moment?"

"Anything!" Jules snaps. "Literally anything."

I shove my hands into my pockets. "I didn't come here to argue with you."

"Could have fooled me," Jules mumbles.

I assess my brother from head to toe. He looks like he's in good shape other than looking tired. Not injured in any way that I can see. "I met our great aunt."

"Who?"

"Georgia Simmons. She's Pattie's younger sister. Pattie is—"

"I know who Pattie is. How did you find her?"

"I have my ways."

"Legal ways?"

"We're supposed to have tea with her at some point. Let me know a day and time that works for you."

"Are we going to address that you didn't answer my question?"

I pin him with a look. "Are we going to address the fact that you seem to think Mom's death is some special burden for only you to bear?"

My brother scowls and is stopped from saying more when Adam taps the mic on stage and asks us to return to our seats. I go back to my table, but it doesn't feel like the conversation is over.

Despite what Jules says, I do go to the afterparty because I haven't been out in ages, and I want an excuse to dance. Which is how I end up walking into Ale House. Unexpected is who comes with me. The afterparty is open to all society students, and Corey insists on going because she wants to have a night out with me and doesn't want to

be held back by the idea of seeing her brother. Which means Virgil insists on going as moral support. Margot comes because she "does like to have fun sometimes," though Isaac is forced to stay home. And lastly, Nolan joins because he was promised an open bar, and he's legal.

They check IDs and give out wristbands at the door for people who are of drinking age. I scowl. Wristband systems suck. It's better when they put the big "X" on your hand because at least you can wipe that off. Though usually people rip the bands off and toss them on their way out, and if you tape it just right, bartenders don't notice.

"Don't even try stealing someone's wristband," Margot says to me. "All the bartenders are Learners tonight and everyone knows you're underage."

"Do you get joy from my suffering?" I ask her.

She rolls her eyes. "I'm going to hang out with my friends. Don't—"

"I thought *we* were your friends." I press a hand my chest.

"*Don't* get into trouble," she finishes before leaving us.

"Wow, she fully ditched us."

Nolan says, "Good idea," and walks to the bar.

Corey keeps scanning the crowd every few seconds as we perch at a stand-up table.

Ale House feels like less of a club than Stages. I think it's more known as a venue for bands, so there are no fancy strobe lights outside of the stage area, and they just play the music over the speakers instead of using a DJ. The "dance floor" is basically wherever you can stand.

After five minutes of silence, I understand why Margot and

Nolan ditched us. Virgil and Corey are entirely consumed with waiting for Barbie and Ellis to show up.

"How's the research for Henry going?" I ask Corey. Maybe if I attempt to make conversation, I can shake her out of it, and she can actually have fun.

Corey purses her lips. "It was going well. I learned a lot about Meredith Grant but nothing that would explain the plateau of births. I went to get the most recent records of the birth rates only to learn that Carrigan moved them to the Scientist offices in Toronto. I've been trying to recall them to Summerhill without any success, primarily because Carrigan isn't here to give permission for them to be released, so that's great."

Well, that went well. I hold out my hands to her. "Let's go dance."

She shuffles her feet. "I'm not that coordinated. . . . I practiced getting used to fighting with my leg, not dancing."

Shit, I hadn't thought about that. A room full of people probably isn't the greatest environment for it either. "If you really don't want to, you don't have to. But if you *do* want to dance, let's do it, and screw what other people think." Taking on that sort of attitude is the only way I could get myself to dance in public after gaining weight. I know what it feels like when you're the center of attention for the wrong reason.

"In a bit," she says, eyes still scanning the room, giving me the feeling that lack of coordination isn't the only thing occupying her mind.

"I'll go out, and I'll come back and see if you've changed your mind later." She nods absently, and I sigh and move to the floor space where some people are dancing. Maybe once I'm here, she'll join me. I would give anything to be drunk right now. It's hard not

to be aware of people staring, but I close my eyes and dance anyway. I love this; it's still something that's just for me.

When I look across the room, I make eye contact with Virgil, and he doesn't turn away. I don't stop moving either. I twirl to face the opposite direction and break the eye contact, wiping sweat off my forehead.

"You're walking a fine line," a male voice whispers in my ear. I jerk around to see Nolan with a plastic cup in his hand.

"Don't know what you're talking about."

"Right." He doesn't step back to give me personal space, but I don't step forward either. He's let his hair down and has that singer-songwriter look, which does, in fact, work for him. "I didn't peg you as a girl who holds back."

It's an echo of what Henry said with a different timbre. "I don't."

"Don't you?" He laughs. "I saw you in the Bachelor candidacy, you know. You were different then. Now the society's gotten to you. You're a good little rule follower, just like him."

"Fuck off," I snap.

I want to rank well in the competition. I need to get stronger. And I don't want to risk Virgil being punished for something that I did. Breaking and entering is one thing, but spitting in the face of a rule I was explicitly told would result in bond-breaking is another thing. So yeah, I don't mess around as much as I used to. But to compare me to Virgil is criminal.

"Here comes trouble," he says, looking away from me across the room.

That's when I spot Barbie with a wicked grin on her face as she talks to Corey, while Virgil is nowhere in sight.

"Shit," I mutter, striding over to them.

". . . too much of a coward—" Barbie's saying when I make it over.

"What's going on here?" I cut in, sliding beside Corey. The girl's shoulders are hunched, and she says nothing.

Barbie gives me a flat look. "Just having a conversation with an old friend."

"Amazing. Catch me up to speed."

"It's not really any of your business."

"I think it is."

She scoffs. "I'm just trying to understand why Corey has no problem cozying up to a boy whose parents are literal mass murderers but can't have a conversation with her own brother." She looks directly at Corey. "You should be happy that he's not rotting in a cell. Some of us didn't give up on him. Some of us kept our promise."

"You should have told me," Corey says finally. "Instead, you ambushed me—"

"Ambushed you?!" Barbie laughs. "Are you forgetting that you blocked me on every platform? Besides that, my mom told your parents what was happening. If you just talked to them, they would have told you. And why do you even need a warning?"

"Maybe because it's traumatizing?" I say.

"Traumatizing to see her brother?! Are you listening to yourself?"

"Stop it, Barbie," a voice says. I was so concentrated on her that I missed Ellis coming over. He stares down his partner while Corey stiffens.

Barbie says, "She has no concept of what you went thr—"

"Just *stop.*"

"No!" Barbie shrieks, tears pricking at her eyes. She points a pink stiletto nail at Corey. "I used to think you were a good person.

I loved you even after we broke up. You were always there for me. So was Ellis. Then in an instant, all that was gone. You wanted nothing to do with him *or* me. That's not how friends work." Ellis attempts to pull Barbie away, and she shakes him off. "I'm going! I'm fucking going."

Ellis mutters something in Korean. I assume he's talking to Corey, but he doesn't look at her.

Corey immediately glances around us, flushing.

Ellis and Barbie leave. "You okay?" I ask.

"Fine," she mumbles.

"What did he say?"

She shakes her head. "Just that he was sorry. We're not supposed to . . . not supposed to talk in languages other people can't understand at society functions. It's like he's trying to stir things up."

Right. The Learners prefer a melting pot approach and dislike any highlighting of individual culture. I guess counting in Korean during taekwondo isn't applicable. "Maybe he wasn't antagonizing you?" I say. "Maybe he was just trying to, like, I don't know, speak directly to you."

"He knows my Korean is bad," she says, turning even redder. "I don't want to talk about it."

I understood that the society had stolen things from Corey—her relationship with her brother and parents, her leg and fingers—but I hadn't truly realized the sacrifice of culture she'd made. The Learners promised so much, but they took even more.

CHAPTER TWENTY-ONE

You would think a crowded coffee shop on a Monday afternoon would be the worst possible place to have discussions about the society, but as it is, everyone at CRAVE Coffee House & Bakery is so wrapped up in their own conversations and laptops and phones that I doubt anyone is going to pay attention to us. Which is probably why Margot asked to meet here for our first mentor session. I thought she'd be hungover after the party last night, but I guess not. She probably drank responsibly because she's so good.

I make a beeline for the baked goods display at the front of the shop. Because Virgil is the only one trusted with regular use of a credit card, he orders for both me and Nolan. Nolan is wearing sunglasses inside, I assume because he didn't drink responsibly. I wouldn't know, since we left right after the Barbie-Ellis confrontation.

We grab our orders and head to the table Margot chose near the back. She puts away her laptop when we reach her. Midterms are

happening soon, and I'm not surprised she's getting a head start. I peep the leather gloves on her hands. She had gloves on with her outfit last night, but I assumed that was a fashion choice. Wearing them inside feels more like she's hiding something.

I gesture to her hands. "New fashion statement?"

"Eczema breakout," she says.

"Bullshit." Margot has never struck me as the sort of girl who would hide her hands because of a rash.

"I wasn't aware that you knew my medical history enough to dispute it." I give her a long stare, and she sighs. "I'll be fine for quarterfinals."

Quarterfinals start the first week of March, giving us roughly three weeks to prepare. It's not a lot of time to master the second evolution, but we don't have a choice.

Margot says, "Today we're just doing a debrief. You tell me how you think things are going so far performance-wise. So, how was it?" Nolan drinks his coffee while staring at a wall, and Virgil picks at the brownie he got. "August," Margot says.

I poke my finger into my lemon square, making a circular dent in the icing sugar and curd. "I mean, we made it through."

"By the skin of your teeth, I hear."

I throw my hands up. "If you already know, why are you asking us?"

"Because I want to hear your perspective." She turns to Nolan. "What did you think?"

"Like she said, we won our matches."

Margot sighs. "Virgil?"

"If we can't be consistent with second-evolution skills before the quarterfinals, we're going to lose."

"Finally! Someone with some realistic remarks and goals. Do

you have a plan for how you're going to accomplish this?"

I cut into my dessert and eat it. What's the point of saying anything when apparently nothing I say is what she wants to hear?

"Stop sulking," Margot says to me, and I scowl. "You'll feel worse if you lose. You've shown some ability to use second- and third-evolutions skills. The goal is consistency. You should be concentrating on that instead of unnecessary side quests."

"What does that mean?"

"You tell me. Why were you breaking into Dr. Liu's girlfriend's house?"

"Jesus Christ, he's like sixty years old, don't call her his girlfriend."

"Why?"

"Because it just sounds weird. Partner, maybe?"

"August!"

I shrug. "I had my own personal reasons, and Georgia was fine with it in the end."

"Your own personal reasons for breaking the law, which, if she had chosen to charge you, could have disqualified you from the competition." She glances at Virgil. "I'll note that you were there too, enabling her. Care to share with the class?"

Virgil hunches in his seat.

"What is it? What could be so important that you're once again risking disqualification for it? Enlighten me, please."

Georgia wouldn't have called the cops on us. Decent Black people don't tend to like doing that to other Black people. We wouldn't have gotten charged. But I doubt Margot would care if I said so.

Margot looks into my eyes. "I'm serious. Tell me. If I can help or Henry can help, we will. But we can't do that if you keep us in the

dark. I did everything I could to help with Jules, didn't I? Give me a bit of credit here."

She did help a lot with Jules, even when it meant defying direct orders from Henry. I know Jules wanted to keep this hush-hush, but he isn't exactly being helpful right now, and the first thing he did was tell Natalie. If Virgil and Corey know, why not Margot?

I lick my lips. "Jules told me that a Monster attacked him and my mom. In exchange for his safety, Mom . . . she sacrificed herself. Someone in the society targeted her and she's dead because of them."

Margot leans back in her chair and takes a deep breath. "And you want to find them." A statement, not a question. "This is why you broke into the Wilds' files—because you know they've been used for assassinations." Nolan grits his teeth, but Margot ignores him. "And Georgia?"

"Is my great aunt who pretended not to know me because of her sister—my grandma on my mom's side, Pattie. Pattie *was* in the society and insisted my mom be kept out of it. That's why my mom wasn't in any records. Apparently she and Mom were mixed up in something dangerous. We think it has something to do with the weapon Bernie was sent after."

Margot exhales, setting her chin on her steepled fingers. "Why are you doing the Monster's Ball this year?"

I falter. "That's . . . well, Virgil—"

"No. Adam gave you a chance to postpone a year. It would have been easier on both you and Virgil to wait and use that time to train and see if Adam can release you from this extra bond. Sure, it's better to win sooner for opportunities, as Henry said, but it's not necessary. And then you would have even more time for your investigation. So I ask again, why are you participating in the Monster's Ball *this* year?"

I swallow.

She continues, "Maybe during the Bachelor candidacy, you wanted to help Virgil and save your brother, but that's not what's fueling you now. Why you have this urgency."

"I don't know what you want me to say!"

Margot levels a long stare at me. "You need grief therapy."

"Fuck off."

"I'm serious."

"Maybe don't try diagnosing people when you don't even have your BA in psychology yet. I don't understand why I'm getting the tenth degree. We won. And we didn't get to second or third evolution through all this training or whatever. We did it in the fights when it was necessary." I gesture to Nolan. "He was right. It's instinctual. Finding my mom's killer has had no effect on our progress." I'm handling it. I don't care what Margot thinks. I stand. "I'm done."

Nolan stands with me. "Amazing. So we can go?"

"August," Virgil says. "Can you at least listen to what she's saying? I . . . It's not a bad suggestion."

My jaw drops. "Excuse me?"

"When my parents died—"

"I'm not you. All I want to do is kill the asshole who killed my mom."

Margot says, "So we've escalated from finding the person to homicide?"

"I don't need this," I say, and walk out of the coffee shop. I stomp south on Princess Street without any clear idea of where I plan to go. I just want to get away. When I hear footsteps behind me, I whip around, ready to cuss Virgil out.

Nolan holds up his hands. "I just happen to be going this way. I'm not here to force you into therapy."

My shoulders relax. "Then at least walk beside me. It feels creepy with you back there."

We make our way down the street together in silence. I guess that I could catch a bus back to campus. But we reach the bus stop and Nolan keeps walking, so I keep going too.

"What are you studying at Queen's? I never asked."

Nolan says, "Economics."

"Thrilling."

"There's a reason people say the only guarantees are death and taxes. It's a stable degree. I figured it would be less networking-heavy than doing commerce, too." He stops in front of a store called Minotaur. "This is me."

It's a brick building with a bunch of seemingly random things in the window, from plants, to socks, to board games, and more. "What's in there?"

He shrugs. "Come if you want."

I follow him into the store, which is brightly lit and packed with the same random assortment of items inside. There are displays of succulents, and marbles, and clothing, and books. Nolan walks to the back of the store, where they have a bunch of board games displayed. But not the ones I'm used to like Monopoly or Clue.

Nolan makes a selection and brings it to the register, where the cashier and him have a conversation about the game and some new stock they're going to get in at some point.

We leave the store, and I'm kind of mourning not taking more time to look around.

"What's the game?" I ask.

Nolan stops and considers me for a moment. To be honest, I'm shocked that he hasn't shaken me off yet. "Want to play it?"

"Sure."

What do I have to lose?

I sit on Nolan's couch while he unpacks the game he bought and sets up the pieces on the coffee table. The more pieces he punches out, the more I start to reconsider what I've agreed to. It's the most complex thing I've ever played. Though he insists that it's simple once you understand it.

Mia's probably going to be pissed that we're playing something without her.

His apartment is a small bachelor unit, though he's made good use of the space. He has a bookcase and curtain blocking off his bed so it feels more separate from the couch and TV.

"Why don't you live at the compound?" I ask. Sydenham is about an hour away. Which, sure, is a rough commute, but being from Toronto, I'm used to people doing that sort of traveling every day.

Nolan says, "Because it's the least my dad could do given the shit I have to put up with because of him."

"The second son stuff?"

He grinds his teeth. "It is exhausting to be reminded every day that you were your parent's second choice for a role that you don't even want. And your description is the child who was created when your dad hit up your mom because he and his wife were on a 'break,' and he wanted to fuck around. He spent the first six years of my life treating me like a dirty secret and then wanted to hold me up to the light all of a sudden. I don't even understand why the community insists on having a leader in the first place. It's never worked out for us."

And I thought I had daddy issues. Nolan's are next level. Meanwhile, Jacques and Garrett have had this sudden reconciliation. Sure, maybe the Wilds can't have him as their new leader, but that doesn't mean Garrett doesn't have a personal preference. "People like to have someone to look up to," I say.

"Look up to yourself and you're less likely to be let down."

I don't know that I agree. I used to. I even used to think that when I did let myself down it was fine, because it was just me, but there were ripples outward to people I cared about.

"Okay," Nolan says, apparently satisfied with his setup. He goes on to explain the rules, which actually aren't that complicated, like he said. You're building a city using the little hexagon tiles, hence the name Suburbia. Apparently this is a newer version that he hadn't gotten around to buying yet. Now that I know he's an econ major, I get why a game that's basically about creating economic infrastructure would appeal to him.

Clearly board games are very much Nolan's thing. His entire bookcase is filled with them.

"Who do you usually play with?" I ask.

He shrugs. "Cousins. Or Mia."

"So, like, are you and Jacques cool, then? He's not mad that he can't lead, but you can and don't even want to?"

Nolan snorts. "He's too much of a saint to have grudges against anyone. He's like Virgil. Golden boys you can bring home to mom."

"Golden boy who ditched his community?"

"Yeah, well. I guess that was his only rebellious streak—him and his mom leaving. I don't have a problem with him."

"How come Mia doesn't know about the Wilds?"

"Because that's how Jacques wants it." He sets his piece down.

"Your turn." He watches as I make my selection, not putting nearly as much thought into it as he did. "It's a lot of information to take on. Both Dad and Jacques did assassinations."

"I knew Garrett must have but I didn't realize that Jacques did too."

"Eighteen is old enough to be assigned targets. He had five years under his belt before he left. It's a lot to dump on someone, that their parent was a hired killer."

Nolan plays his piece, and I try to take some time to decide before I play mine. "How was it for you? The rebellion?" Now that Nolan is actually answering things I ask instead of just ignoring me or being cryptic, questions keep coming out.

"I was six. I didn't know what was going on. I was more preoccupied by the fact that my family members kept dying." He shakes his head. "That's why I can see that the current situation is different. Say what you want about my dad and Natalie, but they were organized when they targeted the society in the rebellion. This comes off as messy. Someone else is responsible."

"Yeah, I mean, I would also assume that people trained in assassinations would be more efficient."

Nolan shrugs. "Not that you had to be for the sorts of missions the society would dispatch. I mean, yes, Wilds were trained in targeting Master-Monster pairs. But the assassinations almost always had regular people as targets."

"Wait, what?" I gape at him.

"Yeah," Nolan says. "Not even powerful folks with money or anything like that. Regular people. There were rumors that maybe these were Monsters who hadn't turned yet. That we were running out of room in the Pen, so they were being preemptively killed.

Which is ridiculous, because you can't predict the existence of spontaneously born Monsters ahead of time. It's like a bite. The mutation develops and expresses all at once."

"Do people in the society not know this stuff?"

"Not about the assassinations, no. But Adam must realize we're a bad fit. I assume that's why he defended us right away. Not that it matters. The Wilds are the society's favorite scapegoat. There's a reason the rebellion happened in the first place. You can't oppress people and not expect backlash. But of course when it happens, they act like it came out of nowhere, and you get played off like the villains. How dare you fight for your rights, you know? Well, I'm sure *you* know."

I do. Can't help but know being Black. "Sucks," I say, for lack of any better response.

He shrugs.

"So games are kind of your thing, eh?"

"Games like this. Clear sets of rules and outcomes. Unlike whatever game Henry is playing."

My brow furrows. "You noticed that?"

"Hard not to."

"It's kind of fucked, but it's the way he is. He's always been a huge help anyway."

"And why is that?"

"What do you mean? Virgil is his ward or whatever."

Nolan looks up from the game board. "You don't do everything he does out of the goodness of your heart. He wants something. And as long as you don't know what that is, you're going to be his plaything."

I stiffen. "He wants Virgil to be safe and for Adam to do well."

"You're assigning a lot of altruism to him." Nolan moves his piece. "I bet they know. Virgil and Margot. Maybe Corey, too."

"Know what?"

"The endgame. There's always an endgame." He nods to me. "Your move."

I take some extra time to decide where to put my piece. Nolan isn't just saying shit to be contrary. A few days ago, I would have believed that, but not now. Despite his resistance to it, we're partners. It feels that way. I'm even comfortable in his space, which he didn't have to bring me to.

He's right.

I don't believe Henry is that altruistic. But I had never considered that Virgil could be keeping me in the dark too.

CHAPTER TWENTY-TWO

Riley

I can't help but wonder what I'm doing as I drive toward McIntosh Castle with a massive gift bag in the passenger seat. I shouldn't be going to a birthday party. And I should have picked a generic present like a gift card. I definitely should *not* have been fighting on eBay with some woman and paying extra for rush shipping.

I park in front of the house and get out, retrieving the bag on the way. There's a guy already there on the front stoop, just staring at the door with a gift box in his hands.

"Are they not answering?" I ask as I approach him. "I can text August."

He whips around and splutters, "Ah, n-no, that's okay." There's something about his face that's familiar. He looks East Asian, but I don't think I've seen him on campus. I'm good with faces. Plus, he's, like, very attractive. I don't think I would forget a face like that even without my parents training me to catalog everyone I meet. It's a great skill for a future lawyer or real estate agent to remember

someone at a glance along with two to three facts about them.

He shoves the box in his hands at me. It's beautiful, an off-white with a golden satin ribbon tied in a bow. "Could you give this to Corey for me? I just wanted to drop it off."

"Okay. . . . What's your na—"

"She'll know."

Before I can ask anything else, he speed walks down the steps and around the corner. I furrow my brow as I use the intricate knocker on the door. *Where do I know him from?*

The door opens, and August says, "Thank fuck you came. I was prepared to go to your house and drag you here."

"No need," I say, rolling my eyes.

"Wait, you brought *two* presents? Way to flaunt your wealth."

"No," I snap. "I brought one present. A guy at the door just gave me this box. He said he had to run and asked if I could give it to Corey."

"That's suspicious."

"Just take it."

August collects the package from me, and I follow her through to one of the many sitting rooms in the house. The space has been loudly decorated with balloons in gold, black, and white, along with streamers and banners. It looks like someone did a line of coke and then went to Party City.

"Virgil decorated," August says. She points at a table, which already has a couple of gifts on it. "You can put your bag there."

Virgil himself is moving around the room, adjusting the decorations in a way that's clearly busywork. "You came!" He beams when he spots me.

"I was threatened," I reply.

He nods, pleased.

I always forget how unhinged these people are until I'm spending time with them. I quirk a bit of a smile. Sammie would have loved them.

Margot is also here with her brother, who she introduces to me. I give him a wave and stifle a laugh at the way his eyes widen when he learns I'm the QBSS president.

"She's coming!" Virgil says suddenly, looking at his phone. "Hide!" He shoves party crackers into everyone's hands before shutting off the lights and practically diving behind a sofa. I share an eye roll with August. I tuck myself behind a velvet curtain while August crouches behind a chair. Margot and Isaac choose to squat under the present table, Margot grumbling as they do.

Corey's voice filters in from the hallway. The lights flick on.

We jump out and shout variations of "Surprise" and "Happy birthday." The party crackers explode confetti, all except August's. She gives up quickly, throwing it to the side.

Corey presses her hands over her mouth, actual tears in her eyes. Virgil and August envelop her in a hug. August jerks her head at me.

Uh, absolutely not.

Isaac, however, does join in while Margot and I stand off to the side.

After Corey breaks from the others, she gives us individual hugs. I stiffen, anticipating mine, and then my body traitorously melts when she throws her arms around me.

Virgil sits Corey down, gets everyone drinks, and announces that she should open her gifts.

Though August is here and supposedly also a host, she barely speaks to either Virgil or Margot. Mostly talking to me, Corey, and

Isaac. Even Corey herself seems . . . off, her smile a little too wide. Strained. And whenever the attention turns away from her, it drops.

"This is from Riley," Virgil says, handing the gift bag to Corey.

I say, "It's not—"

"Don't disclaimer the gift," August says from beside me, and I glare at her.

Corey pulls out the large spider Squishmallow. She reads the tag, "Her name is Bella and she's . . . a talented palm reader." She laughs, and my body heats, because that . . . that feels real.

It was worth fighting with the eBay lady for that laugh.

Margot and Isaac get Corey a gift certificate for the indie bookstore downtown, Novel Idea. Virgil gets her a rare book about Parisian Victorian architecture and decor, and August gifts her a leatherbound notebook with her initials stamped on the outside. Virgil lifts the final gift.

"Uh, a guy gave that to me outside the door," I say. "He said you would know who it was from."

"Probably Dr. Liu," she says.

I frown. No, I met Dr. Liu when I came to see August after the fight with Nolan. He was definitely not that guy. But I say nothing, letting her open the gift.

Inside, there's a clothbound book sitting on a bed of pink tissue paper. It doesn't have any sort of title or author name. Corey studies it, turning it around before opening it and staring at the first page. She sits there just looking at it for a moment before turning the pages. They're thick and shiny in a way that doesn't seem to match the vibe of the binding. I glimpse what look like sticky notes tacked inside.

"What is it?" August asks.

"It's a travel guide. For Korea." She swallows, still turning the pages. "Lonely Planet, I think, but rebound by hand. I always used to look at these sorts of guides in the bookstore. But I worried it wouldn't be proper to ask my parents to get me one. That it would imply . . . I don't know. Something."

Not proper in the society's eyes, she means. But they love diversity *so much*, supposedly. That's how cults work. They need their members to be singularly devoted to their cause. If the Learners let people participate too much in their individual cultures, they might realize that they have community outside of the society. God forbid Corey want to travel and learn more about her background.

I want to say to Corey that she should have never questioned if she could have a book. But it's not like a couple of words from me is going to undo years of brainwashing. Besides that, the society is her past, present, and future. The people within it, her family and friends. It's not that easy to walk away, even if it just starts with reading a book that others might side-eye. After all, didn't I ignore Sammie when she first left QBSS because it wouldn't be proper to keep clinging to her after she abandoned us? It's not the same. Could never be the same as the Learners. But it's similar enough for me to, at least a little, understand where she's coming from.

Corey closes the book and sets it back inside the box, forcing a smile. "Is there cake?"

There is, in fact, cake.

Virgil brings it out with candles, a wish is made, and the slices are handed out.

Corey says, "Nolan didn't want to come? You could have invited him."

Margot scowls, and Virgil stiffens. Aha, so that's the point of

tension. The new addition to the group. Or to August and Virgil's partnership, in any case. Nolan's become a sticky cog in the engine.

"I invited him but didn't expect him to show," August says. She shrugs, but I can tell she's disappointed in a way the others aren't. It seems like Margot and Virgil are happy they didn't have to see him.

"Maybe he wants to lie low," Isaac suggests as he grabs a handful of chips. "Wilds stuff is getting worse."

"Worse?" August asks.

Isaac starts speaking with his mouth open until Margot throws him a look. He finishes eating before saying, "People are talking about a civil war."

"You mean another slaughter," I say, because that's what it is. There's only so much Learners bullshit that I can stand before I have to call something out.

He cringes. "Pretty much."

Margot says, "Hopefully Adam won't let it get that bad."

There's silence as everyone ponders that. Eventually, Margot and Isaac leave, and it's just the four of us left.

"How has the weapon progress been?" August asks. "I assume Corey updated you on the stuff we found out about Pattie?"

I nod. I got a text from Corey that August suspects her mom and maternal grandmother were murdered by Carrigan for their knowledge of the Osseous. But if Carrigan and August's mom were so buddy-buddy back in the day, why wait until years later to attack? I don't believe he just lost track of her. I say, "Can we please refer to it correctly as the Osseous instead of 'the weapon'?"

"Fine," August says. "How has progress with the *Osseous* been?"

"I have new stuff," Corey says.

Virgil crosses his arms over his chest. "Is this really the time?"

"I don't mind." Corey goes upstairs to retrieve her notebook and comes back down. "Okay, so after August said she found her grandma's registration, I did some more research on her, and she was a nurse. Riley said the last QBSS spy was code-named Healer. Maybe it's not her, but it's a pretty good link. Plus, she worked at the student clinic, which would have given her easy access to any QBSS students to pass on information. She was probably the one who put August's bones in the artifact, not her mom. Though it doesn't necessarily mean she knew about the Osseous. Maybe it's like when Bernie targeted Riley—her murderer might have just *thought* she knew."

I would have to email whoever was president around the time Pattie would have been a spy now that we had a time period nailed down. I'm pretty sure Grandma was active around that time too. Hopefully I could get something out of them.

I ask August, "How old were you when Pattie died?"

"Like, two?"

"Not old enough for teeth to be falling out naturally unless you hit your mouth or something. They must have surgically removed it, which your mom at least would have had to sign off on. And you agreed to it, I assume because you were two and didn't understand what was happening. Either way, Pattie was desperate to get your bones in an artifact, meaning she already knew she was in danger. Probably knew your mom was in danger too."

"Then they should have used their bones and protected themselves with the artifacts," August says.

"But they didn't. Instead they set you up for a legacy within QBSS that could have potentially given you access to it. It would put you in danger too, but maybe it would be worth it for whatever reason they had. Or maybe they trusted that we would help you. In

that case, it makes sense that it would be you, not Jules. After all, we can't stop someone from turning. Maybe your mom sent Jules to QBSS not so he would get in, but so you would follow him there."

"Then she should have told him to tell *me* to go," she snaps.

"Would you have listened?"

August swallows, dropping her gaze to her hands. I know August used to be rule-abiding, but that's not the person I met. With this much planning going into it, maybe her mom accounted for that. Still, none of this answers the question of why they did this or how they even came into knowledge of the Osseous in the first place.

Corey rifles through the pages of her notebook. "I know we still have a lot of outstanding questions, but our goal is to find the Osseous. To that end, Riley and I made a list of locations mentioned in each of the texts, and I found matching notes of a fortress by the bay and a cache there. What better place to hide information about a dangerous artifact?"

"Where's this fortress by the bay?" August asks.

"Fort Henry," Virgil and I say at the same time. I add, "It's on Deadman Bay."

"That's colorful."

"What matters is that we have a location." We can finally *do* something. I can stop feeling like I'm not going to make the council's deadline. "We'll need to put together a plan to go. Ideally, in a group. If there's something there worth protecting, it won't be easy to get to."

Virgil frowns. "Is this . . . urgent?"

"Yes," Corey says before I can. "This is what the person who was manipulating Bernie was after. Likely the same person making moves with the Wilds. If we don't go now, we might miss our chance."

Virgil deflates but doesn't speak against her.

A couple of hours later, it's time for me to head home, and Corey insists on walking me out. In the entryway, she leans against the doorframe. "Thank you for coming, and for the gift."

I rub the back of my neck. "It's fine." This is the point when I should leave. Just say goodbye and go. "Are you okay? You seem kind of . . . off today."

"The book . . . it was from my brother." My eyes widen. That's why he looked familiar. Because I was seeing Corey's features in his face. "He should have already been back in Ottawa, but I guess he took the train to bring the present. Our parents had a wedding portrait of themselves in traditional Korean clothes from back before they joined the society. Tucked away, of course. But he and I found it when we were little. We used to talk about traveling to Korea someday and doing all the stuff we weren't allowed to do here. He must have bound the book himself and put in all these sticky notes about places in the guide he thought I would like, or things we mentioned when we were younger. Ellis and I . . . we weren't close. It was more that we shared the same close friend. But when we talked like that . . . it felt like we were."

I lick my lips. "Are you still scared of him?"

"Yes . . . And Barbie said something—"

"Barbie?"

Corey swallows. "That shared close friend I mentioned? We used to date, actually. . . . It was a long time ago, and we were only fourteen. Anyway, she's Ellis's partner now. That's how he's out. And she said . . . she said I abandon people."

"Since when? You're one of the most loyal people I know. You have to be to deal with August."

She laughs, but it trails off. "She's right, though. After I lost, I left her, and Ellis, and my parents. I was terrified, and they all just reminded me of it."

"There's a difference between pulling back because you need space to heal and abandoning someone."

"Yeah," she says, but I don't think she believes me. She steps forward, reaching out, and my heartbeat speeds. She touches the sickle at my neck. "How's this going?"

I shrug, trying to feign nonchalance. "Got some useless advice from an alumna." Corey raises an eyebrow. "She said the sickle knows me, and when I unleash it, I should have a good reason, and I should be willing to die for it. But I *do* have a good reason. I'm trying to protect QBSS."

Corey tilts her head. "It sounds a lot like the Master-Monster partnership." I bristle, and she says, "Just hear me out. To bond, you and your partner need to be aligned. Isn't that what the alum was saying? That you and the weapon need to share a purpose?" She licks her lips. "Even if I had managed the flesh exchange, my brother's and my bond wouldn't have worked because I wasn't there to save him. I told myself I was, but really I was there because I wanted the approval of my parents and the society. Even then, I was scared. Scared of disappointing everyone, which is exactly what happened. I think . . . I think we always hope to be motivated by altruism, but there's nothing wrong with being motivated by something else. Even something selfish. As long as you realize it."

I flex my fingers. Last semester, I wasn't just trying to protect QBSS. I was trying to avenge Sammie. If I'm honest, I cared about the revenge more than anything else.

But now . . . what am I doing now?

CHAPTER TWENTY-THREE

What's left of our Mastery group cohort meets in the courtyard of McIntosh Castle the day after Corey's birthday. It's an odd meeting place, but Henry explains that he needed our activity to happen outside, and the Grad Club can't accommodate, whereas the castle's yard is surrounded by high stone walls and therefore more secluded. I'm huddled in my jacket with my hands stuffed into my pockets. Though of course, Nolan and Virgil are perfectly comfortable in the cold weather, since Monsters regulate their body temperature better than typical humans.

Henry stands at the front of the group, which consists of our trio, Violet and Frankie, and Bryce and Mitch. We fan out in a semicircle around him. There's a Black guy and girl next to him who he's yet to introduce. From the similarities in their noses and face shapes, I'd guess they're related. Laira is lounging on the patio furniture in the corner with Corey.

Henry says, "Congratulations to those of you who are still in the running." He gestures to the pair next to him. "I have Jacinta and Derrick Benson here with me. They successfully defended last year and have agreed to join us today to help with a task." The two of them wave at us. "But first, I would like to address the ongoing threat to our Doctorate. You may have heard titters of civil war between the society and the Wilds, and I encourage you to use your critical thinking skills."

Beside me, Nolan squares his shoulders.

Henry continues, "Many of you will be too young to remember, but the rebellion days were dark times. The population of Wilds was also about five times larger than it is now, guided by central leadership, which became fractured after the fact. What we are seeing now are the clumsy efforts of individuals, and we are doing everything within our power to thwart their plans. I will remind you that the life of the Doctorate is integral to our success in the apocalypse. Should you be put in a position to protect him, you must. There are no ifs, ands, or buts. Do you understand?"

There is a chorus of "Yes, sirs" from the group. Henry looks directly at me. "Yes, sir," I say.

"Good. Now, progress reports. When I call on the Bachelor, they will state the highest evolution they have reached, a moment of pride, and a moment of weakness." He looks around the circle as if he's got a choice of more than three people. "Bryce."

Bryce adjusts his glasses, looking fully recovered from his last match. "In training we've reached level three, though we haven't been able to replicate the results in matches yet. I'm proud of the teamwork that Mitch and I have been able to maintain, and our second-evolution skill mastery. And I can see that a point of weakness is our stamina."

"I would agree with that," Henry says, nodding. "You benefitted from ending matches quickly for the most part, but that's caught up with you. If you two can manage third-evolution skills in training, you can do it in the matches. You need to push yourselves."

Henry talks like he's been watching the fights, but I didn't see him during Bryce and Mitch's last one. Knowing him, he must have a secret special spot where he sits. "August," he says. "Your turn."

I say, "We've reached the third evolution. Or, I guess we have with Virgil's ability. The roar and regeneration. I'm proud of winning. And I mean, I hadn't fought with Nolan before, and that worked out, so that's good. For weakness, I'd say consistency."

"Correct. Even now, you and Violet are uncomfortable in the cold when you shouldn't be." I glance over at Violet, who's also bundled up for the weather, as opposed to Bryce, who's only in a light jacket. "This is why our session today is outdoors. Jackets off. Accessories, too."

He's acting like he came out of the womb having mastered the second evolution. I shrug off my jacket and hand it to Corey, who gives me a sympathetic look. The Monsters and Bryce don't look as comfortable now, but they aren't actively shivering like me and Violet.

"Now, Violet, your progress report," Henry says.

Violet keeps her hands at her sides, refusing to hug her body like me. "We . . . we remain at the first evolution. However, I would say that I'm proud of the progress we've made in the repechage regardless. But I understand that we need to progress further."

"Don't be proud."

Violet blinks. "Sir?"

"It is by sheer luck that you two have persisted in this

competition despite your failure to show even a hint of second-evolution mastery."

Violet's eyes water, and she bites her lip.

I cross my arms over my chest. "They still fought and won. They don't get to be proud of that?"

Henry turns his cold stare to me. "Pride is something to be felt by an accomplishment. Not something you feel when you happen to dodge a bullet. You've noticed that two pairs are no longer with us. Both of them have second-evolution mastery. They just happened to get poor matchups."

"I understand, sir," Violet says. And actually throws *me* an annoyed look. Frankie keeps her head down.

Henry says, "Now, for today's practical. One by one, the Bachelors will lie on the ground, and your task is to stand up by any means necessary. Let's start with Bryce."

"You got this!" Mitch says as Bryce steps up by Henry and lies on the cold patio slabs with his arms and legs splayed out.

Henry observes him and, apparently satisfied, he waves to Derrick. "You may begin."

Nothing different seems to happen physically, but Bryce grinds his teeth and struggles to push himself up from the ground. I glance at Derrick, who just stands and stares at Bryce.

"Third-evolution skill," Virgil mutters beside me.

"You can use them even if your partner hasn't transformed?"

"Yes. Remember last year? Margot used hers against Jules even though Isaac hadn't transformed. You don't even need to be near your partner, technically, though it helps."

Bryce manages to get his arms and legs underneath him but is still struggling to get up.

"Come on, Bryce," Mitch says, clapping his hands like he's a coach on the side of the ring.

I figure Henry is going to call it, but then something changes, Bryce's arms and legs bulge as if muscle mass has built over seconds. He grunts as he shoves with his newer muscles, pushing until he manages to stand, every vein in his neck straining.

Henry raises his hand. Abruptly, Bryce sags and almost falls over. "Very good!" With a shaky smile, Bryce heads back to Mitch, and the boys fist bump. "Next up, Violet."

She looks like she might puke, her brown skin washed out. She lies down on the ground, trembling either from the cold or the pressure.

We watch her struggle for what feels like a lifetime. She does manage to tuck her arms, getting her palms close to her chest to press up, but the actual pressing up part is not happening.

Henry raises his hand.

"I can still— " Violet says.

"No, you cannot." Tears appear in her eyes, and all I want to do is look away but that would make it worse. Henry gestures to Frankie. "What were you thinking about while you watched her?"

Frankie gapes at our professor. "I . . . I don't know."

Henry points to Mitch. "Consider the difference between the two of you while you're watching your partners." He looks at Violet. "You think about it too as you observe your peers. Even when you are doing something by yourself, this doesn't stop being a partnership."

"Yes, sir," Violet mumbles as she heads back to her spot.

"August," Henry says. "Let's go."

I swallow and step forward, lowering myself to the ground. It's cold under my hands, almost stinging. And I'm already freezing.

"You can do it," Virgil says, taking to heart what Henry mentioned. Mitch was encouraging Bryce while he did this. Apparently that matters. Nolan just gazes at me as I lie on my front.

Henry gives the signal, and a pressure shoves me into the stones. It's punishing and feels like it's everywhere. It's a strain just to lift my head. The monster thrashes in my mind as if the place where I've caged it has shrunk. It's not helping the situation at all. I imagine this is what it might feel like to be crushed underneath a building. I grit my teeth and shove with my arms. I'm not doing any better than Violet, honestly. Virgil is still cheering me on while Nolan continues staring. Bored.

"Let it out," Henry says, his voice booming. "Show me what you couldn't in your match."

Shit. I should have known he would bring that up. It's not that easy. I try to give the monster an inch, and it tears off a foot. If just telling me to do something is how Henry's "teaching" me to control it, I'm no better off than I was without his help.

I shove harder, snarling at the beast the same way it snaps at me, and something gives as I manage to get up on my hands and knees. My limbs shake, and it hurts to breathe. I swear this motherfucker is pressing me down harder now.

"Stop holding back!" Henry shouts.

I grit my teeth, blocking out both his voice and the monster's howling. *Get up. Get up. Get up!*

Nolan glances away. And that's what fucking does it.

A bar of the cage snaps, and the monster reaches out with carbon steel claws. I open my mouth and scream, expecting a roar. But what comes out is a plume of smoke that envelops the group. I look at Nolan, who's watching me with a smirk on his face.

The control snaps. The pressing sensation gone. I leap to my feet.

I inhale, and all the smoke rushes back into my mouth. It's suffocating. I'm drowning in it. The cage is compressing. It's going to get free! I'm going to—

"Just breathe," Nolan says.

I exhale, but the smoke keeps coming until I've pulled it all in. I'm practically panting in the end. But the monster is where it's supposed to be.

I look to Virgil, but he's staring at the ground instead of me.

Henry is beaming. "Well done," he says.

"Agreed." We all turn toward the back door of McIntosh Castle, where Adam is leaning, Corey beside him. I didn't even notice her going to get the door.

Henry's expression sours. "You're unaccompanied?"

"I wouldn't dream of it. Corris and Amelia are inside. She wanted to borrow one of the fable books."

Henry's shoulders drop at that. "At least you have some sense."

Some sense? Amelia, I learned at the Bachelor crowning, is the name of Corris's partner. The girl Monster who I fought in the last candidacy test, not realizing she was just a kid until later in the fight. Why would Adam use a child like her as protection when the Wilds after him have already slaughtered children? What the actual fuck is he thinking? I know Amelia is good at defense, but she's eleven years old. Isn't it enough that she had to help with the Bachelor candidacy? She should be at home playing video games or something. Not protecting a grown ass man.

Adam grins. "When Corey mentioned you were conducting a lesson, I figured I could peek in. Blame it on nostalgia."

As a Doctorate candidate, Adam wouldn't have even needed to compete in the Monster's Ball, so why would a Mastery group be nostalgic?

Henry says, "I wasn't aware that the Doctorate had so much free time."

"I like to take any opportunity I can to encourage the next generation of Masters and Monsters." He nods to me. "Third evolution with a partner you've only been bonded to for a month is quite a feat."

"Thanks," I manage to croak. My throat feels . . . not sore, but odd. Like it's still unsettled by the sensation.

Adam raises his hands and steps back. "Don't mind me, Henry. Go ahead."

"I'm just about done," Henry says. "That was the end of the exercise. You can replicate it by having your Monster partner sit on your back while you work on pressing up. You can also push your second-evolution mastery by not wearing your coat around campus. Challenge yourself to use these skills innately in your everyday life until it becomes second nature. Dismissed."

Bryce, Mitch, Violet, and Frankie say their goodbyes to the Doctorate and thanks to Henry and the sibling duo. The siblings then draw Henry into conversation about a lab they're doing for psychology.

Corey hands me my coat, and I blink at it. I hadn't realized that I didn't feel that cold anymore. "I'm fine," I say, waving it off, attempting to do Henry's homework.

I head over to Adam, who is still standing in the doorway. "Is it necessary to use Amelia in your security detail?" I ask him.

Adam sighs. "It wasn't my choice."

"You're the Doctorate."

"I'm aware, and yet I still rely on others for counsel and guidance. And Amelia has strong defensive skills. Many Masters insisted upon her use. Besides that, being guard for the Doctorate is a well-paid job. More so than doing random missions away, and at least it lets them stay in Kingston."

It's technically a fair enough reason, but I don't like it. Adam nods to Nolan and Virgil, who are by the patio furniture speaking with Laira and Corey. "I admit that I was expecting a roar, not smoke."

"You're not the only one," I say.

"It's a good sign, nevertheless. I'm not making much progress on figuring out how to break your bond, so I'm glad to see you're getting along well with Nolan."

I shrug. I don't know why I'm downplaying it. Nolan isn't exactly a people person, but we have an understanding. Though I have to remind myself that no matter how well we work together, this bond isn't what he wants. It's not a real partnership. It's an exchange of services on a time limit.

Adam says, "I find myself relating to Virgil in this moment." I raise an eyebrow at him. "You, and Henry, and Nolan as well, you have this sort of righteous fury. It fuels you. Makes you stronger. But Virgil and I, I suppose we're afraid to let ourselves feel that. And when you don't have that fuel, what makes you fight?"

Virgil is still afraid. After initiation, I wanted to use the monster. And he . . . I suppose he wanted to let me use it. Virgil doesn't need righteous fury. I have enough for both of us.

"August!" Amelia shouts from behind Adam, appearing with a book in her hands, her cheeks still red from the cold despite her

brown skin, and a knit hat over her two braids. Her hair is long enough to reach the middle of her back, black and silky smooth. Corris smiles at me from behind her. "Were you training?" she asks.

In some ways, it's odd that I primarily know this girl from her more monstrous woolly mammoth form. It's almost disarming to see her in a human shape. "Yup. Can I see your book?"

She hands it over, and I flip through the pages. It's a Learner publication with illustrations throughout. I stop on one with a girl at her window, a bird on the sill, remembering the fable that Virgil told me about a hated bird with a poor temperament. The bird who was saved by a girl who asked for sweet songs after helping it when no one else would. That vicious little thing, tamed because it wanted to be loved.

Nolan's words come back to me. *"I saw you in the Bachelor candidacy, you know. You were different then. Now the society's gotten to you. You're a good little rule follower, just like him."*

The monster raises its head, and I swear it smiles at me.

"I have this exact volume from when I was a child," Adam says with a smile. "From my mother before she passed. I read it so many times that the pages had to be glued back in."

"Lucky," Corris says. "I heard only five copies were ever printed."

"Yes. The privileges of being the Doctorate's son." Adam tries to maintain his smile, but there's something emptied out from it.

I give Amelia her book back. Before the three of them go, I ask Adam, "No news about Carrigan?"

He shakes his head. "No. To be honest, I hope it stays that way. If hiding keeps him safe, then that's what he should do. I already lost one brother. I would rather not lose two."

I bite my lip. Adam's not even entertaining the idea that one

brother is likely responsible for the death of the other. I wave to him, Corris, and Amelia as they leave.

Nolan stalks off without saying goodbye, and Corey invites the rest of us inside for tea. Laira takes her up on it, while Henry says, "I have to be off. August, walk me out."

Sensing that this is a demand rather than an ask, I follow Henry outside to the gate attached to the courtyard. The same one I came through drunk last year, meeting Virgil for the first time, though I did forget the encounter and needed to hear the story from him.

"Had a good chat with our Doctorate?" Henry asks.

"Sure."

He holds my gaze for a moment like he's trying to figure something out.

"What?"

"I'm trying to decipher why he has any sort of interest in you."

"He's not being creepy."

"I didn't think—" Henry pauses and pinches the bridge of his nose. "I didn't think he was 'being creepy.'"

"Don't you have an interest in me too? I heard you have a whole dossier on my family."

"It's important for me to vet the people who come into Virgil's life."

"You knew my mom, though, didn't you? She and Carrigan were friends."

"I met her once or twice. She was very much like you. No sense of hierarchy and who should be spoken to in what way. That's the extent of it. To my understanding, that's all the contact Adam had with her too. She wasn't part of the society and therefore wasn't relevant." He tilts his head. "You seem to feel that there is a

conspiracy here, but I can assure you that your lineage is not so remarkable."

"You really know how to make a girl feel special."

He's holding something back. He must be. Because I'm certain now that he set me up. He wanted Virgil to meet me, to pick me, but at the same time acted like he wanted the opposite. Henry is questioning Adam's interest in me, but he seems to have his own reasons beyond protecting Virgil.

Henry smiles. "You did well today. You released the reins a bit, and what happened? You succeeded. Most importantly, you maintained control. Now stop being afraid of your power."

I jerk back. "I'm not—"

"You are. You wish to be powerful, but you fear the cost of it. If you're just as scared as Virgil, then what use are you to him? I expect to see further progress in your next match."

"I won't let you down, Daddy," I say sweetly.

He grimaces and leaves, I'm sure regretting having paid me a compliment at all. And I pretend that his words haven't rattled me.

CHAPTER TWENTY-FOUR

I descend the stairs of the ferry to the parking lot with the other passengers and get more than a few odd looks for carrying my jacket in my arms instead of wearing it. For the last couple of days, I've been going without it, and annoyingly, it's been working. I'm freezing at first, but once I stop thinking about it, I settle into not being warm, per se, but fine.

Still, I assume that Dad and Bailey will have something to say if I show up for the long weekend without a coat, so I pull it on once I'm outside and adjust my backpack. I'm glad that the Family Day weekend also falls on Valentine's Day so I don't have to be confronted by a bunch of happy couples.

I already didn't have any plans other than studying, and unfortunately still have to do that. We're going to have a quiz right after reading week, and I need to be prepared. So after this long weekend, it's back to campus to study more during the week off.

Someone nudges me in the back, and I spin around to see Nolan.

He's got on a backpack and a jean jacket too thin for the weather.

"What are you doing here?" I ask.

"Visiting." He points at Bailey's yellow Honda. "There's my ride."

"*Your* ride?!"

Bailey pops her head out of the driver's window. "Hi, Nolan!"

"Hey," he says, going straight for the back seat.

"How do you know him?" I ask Bailey.

"He's Jacques's younger brother. Jacques asked if I could pick him up since I was coming here anyway. How do *you* know him?"

"We're . . . friends."

Bailey is kind enough to not question the pause. This is the worst. We drive out to the tiny house community with my aunt asking Nolan questions about his major and stuff. It's a little too similar to drives with her and Virgil. When we arrive at the lot, Jules is waiting outside, having come ahead. Dad will be on a later ferry, but he'll make it in time for dinner. It's a tight squeeze in Bailey's place, but we all managed to fit last Christmas.

Jules gives Nolan a hard stare. "Nice to see you again," he says.

"Yeah, you look thrilled," Nolan replies.

Bailey gives me a look and mouths, "What's going on?" I just shake my head.

Nolan says goodbye to the two of us and walks to the Levesques' house while the three of us head to Bailey's house. She must have been doing Valentine's Day content for her social media, because there's a giant arch over the doorway decorated with a bunch of fake pink-and-white flowers.

Me and Jules collapse on the couch while Bailey goes to the bathroom on the other side of the tiny house.

Jules asks, "How's it going with him?"

"Nolan? Better than I expected."

"Good." Jules nudges my foot with his socked one, which he knows I hate. I kick his foot, and he doesn't even grunt. "You mentioned this great aunt and neglected to mention breaking into her house."

I scowl. "She was fine with it in the end."

"So you're ignoring what I told you about staying out of it and investigating anyway?"

"No. I was having a nice conversation with a relative."

He shakes his head. "I wish you would listen to me."

"You have a lot of company there."

Bailey comes out of the bathroom and starts assigning us kitchen duties. She's decided to do a crab curry because she got a deal on crab legs. My job becomes cutting the dumpling dough she made into squares while Jules chops apples for a galette for dessert. Whatever that is.

"Is there any more of Mom's stuff here? Like, besides what Dad dropped off?" I ask Bailey. Me and Jules have already torn through everything Dad stored in her shed. But it can't hurt to ask if she has more.

Bailey hums as she massages the crab legs with the curry mixture. "Nope, that's it. Everything was in that box I brought you."

"What about from Pattie?"

"Annie's mom? No, but Mike would know better—"

There's a knock on the door, and Jules goes to open it. Dad comes in, shivering dramatically. "Freezing out there," he says. He's still as bald as ever, but he's been keeping up with his shaving, and he looks good. I admit that after learning how Pattie died, with her and

Kendrick both having heart attacks, I was a little paranoid about Dad having had one too. But he's alive, so it's probably just a coincidence. I hope so, anyway.

Bailey says, "August was asking about Pattie."

Dad brushes his beard. "What's with this sudden interest in your mom's family tree the two of you have?"

Me and Jules shrug at the same time.

"Did you know her well?" I ask Dad.

He shakes his head and comes up behind Bailey to see what's in the bowl. "I like the look of that! Smells just like when Mom made it too. How can I help?"

"By not touching anything," Bailey says, waving him away. "Your cooking is cursed. And August and Jules are already helping."

"Dad!" I say.

"What? Oh, yes, no, I didn't know her well," Dad says. "She liked Annie's little friend more. *Carrigan*." If Carrigan has no haters, then me and Dad are dead.

"Male egos are so fragile," Bailey mutters.

Dad makes a face. "Pattie was kind of closed off, but Annie said she'd lost a child when she was younger, and then Annie's dad left her, and she had this falling out with her family. Rough life."

"She . . . lost a kid?" Did the baby in the picture die?

He nods. "The child didn't live to see their first birthday. Annie didn't know anything else."

I guess it's a good thing I didn't spend time trying to figure out who the baby was. They're already gone and buried. Damn, Pattie did have a rough life.

Dad starts telling stories of the professor drama at St. Lawrence while we finish up cooking. When the curry is ready, we eat until

we're suitably stuffed and squish on the couch to watch a movie. As usual, Dad and Bailey fall asleep within the first twenty minutes.

"I don't know why Bailey always suggests a movie when she knows she's gonna fall asleep," I say, shaking my head.

Jules says, "I feel like they both use it as an excuse to nap after eating."

I snort, and Jules laughs. It's like how we used to be. Before all this. Not the way we are now, having to hide things from each other and fighting over what to do about Mom's killer.

There's a knock at the door that makes me jump, though Jules is unmoved. Possibly because he heard the person coming up to the door long before they knocked. I should have too.

I answer it, and Mia and Nolan are standing on the stoop. Nolan looks like he would rather not be there. Which is his default, honestly.

"What's going on?" I ask.

She lifts up her cell phone, showing the multiple messages she's sent asking to hang out that I kept canceling because I needed to train. "Real nice way to treat your friends."

"I've been busy!"

Mia says, "Fine. But I need your help now. Dad and Grandad are both being suspicious, and I'm going to follow them. *Or* you can tell me if you know what's going on." She jerks her thumb at Nolan. "I gave him the offer too, and he won't say anything."

"Why would I know what's happening?"

Mia narrows her eyes. Then she spins on her heel. I throw a desperate look at Nolan, and he shrugs.

"Mia, wait!" I throw on my coat and boots only to realize that Jules is doing the same. "Where do you think you're going?"

"Where you're going," he says. "You need supervision."

"Nolan's gonna be there."

"Even more reason to come."

Which is how the four of us end up following Mia across the property to the Levesques' garage, where she fires up some giant motorcycle thing with four massive tires. "How are we all supposed to fit on that?" I ask.

Mia says, "Jules can ride with me, and you can ride with Nolan on the other one. Since I assume neither of you knows how to operate a four-wheeler. Quick, while there are still tracks to follow."

We take the offered helmets, and Jules hops behind Mia without issue, awkwardly reaching for handholds on the back that don't require grabbing onto her.

Nolan gets on the second machine, and with a sigh, I climb behind him. Unfortunately, there isn't any way to avoid having to hold on to the person in front of you on this model. Nolan glances at me. "What are you waiting for?"

I flush and wind my arms around his middle. The machine jolts as he takes off, and I cling harder, pressing my body into his back. I swear he laughs, but I can't be sure.

We fly across the flat landscape of Wolfe Island until we come to a forested area. Nolan stops short of the entrance. Mia pulls up beside him and flips the opening of her helmet up. "Why did you stop?"

"If we get closer, they're going to hear us. Let's go the rest of the way on foot."

Mia scowls but obeys, and we trudge forward on a rough dirt path.

I text Nolan, *What are you going to do? What if she finds out about the Wilds?*

I hear the phone vibrate in his pocket, and he takes it out. I watch the screen go black as he turns it off without reading the message.

I'm starting to remember why I didn't like Nolan before.

Finally, we reach a section of trees with the flickering light of a fire glowing between the branches. We crouch just out of sight. There's a group of four people gathered around a campfire. Two of them are Jacques and Garrett. The other two are a Black man with short russet curls in maybe his forties, and a woman in her fifties who looks like she may be biracial, but I can't place the races.

Thankfully they're engrossed in their conversation, and we've been quiet enough that we don't get noticed.

Garrett says, "We need solutions. Pointing fingers isn't helping anything. We're not playing Hardy Boys out here trying to find the real culprit. We need to figure out how to mitigate what's happening right now. How to protect ourselves from being used in the same way."

"Easy for you to say," the woman snaps. "They're avoiding using Murphys. They see you as the rebellion trigger and don't want the heat. But the rest of us? Fucking fodder. It would be great if we could just take off, but we have to proctor, and that's how they're getting us."

"That's what I mean! Nolan made some real traction with his interview, but that proposal is still gaining ground. We have the opportunity to join together and facilitate a new agreement with the Doctorate. One in our favor."

"He won't do it," Jacques says. "Because they won't cancel the Monster's Ball, and they need us as proctors. If we're gone, they'd have to use Master-Monster pairs, and now they've branded that job as something for us—the lower class. They won't want to take it,

and they'll push back. Shaw is not a pusher. He'll fold."

The Black man says, "We need to ferret out Carrigan. It's obvious this is him. Who else? We do that, and we're the heroes. It would then be easy to say we shouldn't be bound by anything at all. The rebellion was over a decade ago, and we've atoned enough."

"Maybe we should let Carrigan or whoever this is finish the job," the woman mutters. "Getting rid of the Doctorates was always something we wanted."

Garrett sneers, "Let them do what they want while Wilds are being killed in the process? You want us to get wiped out?"

"Funny coming from you."

"Stop," Jacques says, his voice iron. "The last thing we want now is dissent in our ranks."

I glance at Nolan, whose expression is impassive. For all this talk about how Jacques can't be Garrett's successor, it looks like that's exactly what he's doing. It's not like Nolan was invited to this. He says he doesn't want the title, but I wonder how he feels about watching his dad's first choice stepping into the role.

Garrett licks his lips. "Natalie Soer has presented an option." There are immediate groans and swears from the two strangers. Jules stiffens beside me. "I know! But we need allies in this."

"The second they see us and any known Pro-Libs together, there's going to be a riot. They hate us now—can you imagine how they'd react if they caught us working with her again?" the woman says.

"Listen! She has new members who aren't known. They can help us form cells. Basically, a pair assigned to each Wild with the idea that they will monitor and try to contain any Wild being manipulated so that an attack cannot happen."

There are more mutterings and grumbles around the group.

"Fine," Garrett says. "We can put it to a vote. Working with Natalie, going after Carrigan, or letting things be as they are."

The vote happens, and the decision is made that they will work together to ferret out Carrigan. Which nicely lines up with what I would like to see happen. But no one seems happy about it. Only Garrett voted to do the Natalie team-up. They file out and leave, with only Garrett and Jacques left, and I hope the four-wheelers are hidden well enough.

I think we've gotten away with it until Jacques says, "Out. *Now.*"

"Shit," Mia mutters.

We slink out of the trees. Jacques shakes his head. "I cannot believe you."

"I can't believe *you*!" Mia shouts. "You're hiding all this stuff from me!"

Jacques sighs, scrubbing his face. "Anything that I hide from you is for the purpose of keeping you safe."

"You used to say that you showed me things so I could be *empowered*. Now you've changed your mind?"

Garrett says, "Maybe it's time. . . ."

"No!" Jacques snaps. "She's *my* daughter." To Mia he says, "I'm keeping you out of this because—"

"My grandma tried to keep my mom out of it," I say. "Now they're both dead." Jacques stares at me. "I just . . . I don't think she's going to give up. She's not the type."

"Just tell her," Nolan says. "Now isn't a great time for this to be a secret. She could be a target without even knowing."

Jacques laughs at that, but I don't see how it's funny. He spots something behind us and freezes.

We turn, and there's Izzy. "You're not very sneaky," she says to her daughter, and Mia hikes her shoulders up to her ears. Izzy looks at her husband. "It's time, Jacques. You were afraid she'd see you differently, but it's already happening because of everything you've hidden."

He deflates and stares at his daughter. "Once you know, you can't go back."

"I'd rather know than not," Mia says.

Jacques takes a deep breath, and his form shifts, his clothes ripping, his body changing. He becomes a giant bird with brown-and-black feathers, huge talons, six massive wings spread out, and three sharp beaks.

Mia's eyes are wide as she stares at this version of her dad. Looks him in the eyes.

One of those beaks opens and starts to sing the way birds do. Trilling sounds. I'm so used to Monsters growling or snarling. It's disarming to hear music.

Mia drops to her knees and then scrambles backward.

When she stands and runs, her parents let her go.

I twist in the direction she disappeared, then back to Izzy. "Should we . . . ?"

"Let her be," Izzy says. "Give her a few minutes to herself."

Jacques's song dies, and the only sounds are the footfalls of his daughter fleeing from him.

CHAPTER TWENTY-FIVE

I find Mia outside the next day, on the porch swing of her house covered in a blanket. I don't know where she went yesterday when she bolted, but she made her way home at some point. I imagine Izzy and Jacques wouldn't have let their fifteen-year-old daughter stay out all night.

I step onto the wood planks with my hands in my pockets. Bailey, Jules, and Dad are still sleeping. The latter two shared the bed in the loft that used to be mine while I shared with Bailey. Thank God, because I could hear Dad's snores from the other side of the house. I wish I'd slept longer, but I woke up without meaning to.

I lean against the porch railing, facing Mia as she swings. "How are you doing?"

She picks at the blanket. "At least I'm not out of the loop anymore, I guess. I got what I wanted."

"It's still a lot to take in."

She eyes me. "Mom said you only got involved last year." I nod.

"She said Isaac and Virgil are Monsters too. You think that's why Isaac stopped hanging around me? Too hard to keep the secret?"

"I don't know. He didn't seem to be concerned about that before. . . . I think something's going on with him. You know about the Monster's Ball?"

"Vaguely. Some competition thing that Wilds have to proctor, whatever that means."

"I think he's feeling the pressure and struggling to deal with it."

She pulls the blanket closer to herself. "They're still hiding something."

"What do you mean?"

Mia licks her lips. "I've heard that song before, the one Dad sang in his Monster form last night. Exactly that melody."

"Wait, when?"

She stares out at the expanse of land. "We used to live in Ottawa. Mom and I. Before she met Dad."

"Before . . . ?"

Mia tilts her head at me and then laughs. "Dad, uh, well, he's not my biological dad. I guess I thought Bailey told you."

I shake my head. I'd just assumed. I guess that explains why she's not a Wild. Not every child born to a Wild becomes one, just like regular Monsters, so I figured Mia was one of those. Turns out she's not even in the same gene pool.

She says, "He's the only dad I've ever known. But I was two, and we were in this apartment building with a forest out back. Mom set me down to play on the swings, and this other lady called her over. I don't know. She left me for a bit. And I heard that song. I went toward it. I mean, I was just a kid. Then I saw him, that bird, those three beaks and hard oak eyes." Mia shivers and hugs her arms

around herself. "Something about the music drew me in. Made me move toward him even though all I wanted to do was run."

The music must be a third-evolution ability. That would explain Mia's experience.

Mia continues, "Mom came back before I could get too close. She was panicked and crying. Scared. She begged the bird to leave us alone. To stop. Put her body between us as she grabbed me and ran away." She grips her hands in the blankets. "There are stories among the kanyen'kehá:ka of creatures in the night who try to lure you away. For years, I was afraid of that bird coming back to get me. And you know what made me feel better?"

I shake my head.

"The fact that Dad was there to protect us." She scoffs, shaking her head. "That same night was the first time I met him. He showed up at our apartment, as a man, of course. Whisked us away to the island, where he said we would be safe, and we've been here ever since. Turns out, the thing he was keeping us safe from was himself."

I swallow, a dark thought growing in my mind. "When were you born again? 2007?"

"2008."

If she was two years old, it would have been 2010 when Jacques appeared. A year before the rebellion. Wilds would have still been doing assassination missions. Nolan said the targets were normal people. . . . Had Jacques been there by chance, or for a very specific reason? And if so, why hadn't he followed through? "Did you tell your mom about it? The memory of the bird and everything?"

Mia cracks a smile. "She said it must have been a dream, and I believed her. I mean, I was two when it happened."

"And now?"

She plays with the end of her braid. "I couldn't make myself ask. This is my dad, you know? I still love him. It's already so much to realize that he's the same creature from my childhood nightmares. Do I really want to know what he was doing trying to lure me into the forest? Or should I just focus on the fact that he helped us? Mom knew at some point that it was him, and we stayed. I've felt safe with him. I . . . I don't want to lose that."

"Do you regret asking to be let into this?"

She shakes her head. "No. I wanted to know. I just . . . Dad was scared I would see him differently, and he was right. I ran from him. Everything is the same, but it feels different."

The door to the house creaks open, and Nolan steps out. He says to Mia, "Go inside. You're gonna freeze out here."

She stiffens at first before relaxing. She'll probably be like that for a bit. It's a lot to realize that the people around her have always had the ability to become massive Monsters. She gets up and gives me a tight smile. "See you later."

"See you."

Mia heads inside, and Nolan stays where he is.

"She thinks her parents are still hiding something from her," I say. "Are they?"

Nolan says, "Probably. But I don't know either."

"Jacques wasn't sent to assassinate Mia or her mom, then?"

He shakes his head. "There's no record to confirm that. If there's a secret, no one is letting me in on it." He crosses his arms over his chest. "Did you catch up golden boy on the goings-on?"

I assume he means Virgil. I did text him, but he hasn't texted me back. He was odd after our last Mastery group. Withdrawn, almost. Even Henry had complimented me, so I have no idea what's crawled

up his ass and died. "Are the Wilds really going to go after Carrigan?"

He scoffs. "Apparently. Not that it's easy to know where to start. The Scientists are tight-lipped."

That's a problem. Pattie was in that faction too, and she was devoted to Carrigan even before he was leading it. I can't imagine the sort of loyalty he's garnered among them now. "It would be great to have a Scientist contact."

"You do."

"No . . . I don't."

Nolan narrows his eyes at me. "At the club night, you were talking to that guy. Killer Barbie's partner."

"Ellis?! Wait, he's in that faction? How do you know that?"

"I pay attention. At the opening gala, he was speaking to some other Scientist faction people. Apparently he's interning in their Ottawa offices. I've been watching the faction, given that Carrigan mysteriously disappeared right when this all started." He crosses his arms over his chest. "You're not good at investigating."

"Okay, Sherlock." I pull out my phone. "Let me text Virgil and see what he can set up." After a moment, I add that we should maybe leave Corey out of it. It could be triggering for her. Why risk it when Ellis may not even have anything useful to say to us?

"I'm coming," Nolan says. I balk at him. "I gave you the information, so I'm coming."

He does have a point. Honestly, it could be helpful if working with Nolan in some capacity also gets me access to Carrigan when the Wilds find him. *If* they do. "Hopefully he actually texts me back," I mutter.

"Doesn't it get annoying?" Nolan asks. "The back and forth. The insecurity."

"He's not insecure." Nolan laughs, and I hike my shoulders up. "Virgil is hard on himself. That's all."

"He plays the victim, and you enable him. All of you."

"You don't know him."

Nolan just smiles and returns to the Levesques' house.

I stand there on the porch repeating what I said in my head.

You don't know him.

The bus ride to the Cataraqui Centre is only twenty minutes, but it feels like it takes a century, given that Virgil has barely spoken during that time, and Nolan definitely hasn't. Glad that having an entire long weekend to stew hasn't changed whatever's up with Virgil. We're lucky Ottawa U has the same reading week period as us so that Ellis could come for this meeting. Otherwise, I doubt a Monday afternoon would have been convenient.

Me, Virgil, and Nolan get off the bus at the mall terminal and walk to the main entrance. The giant gray building has probably seen better days, the CATARAQUI CENTRE logo on the stone faded and scummy. But most importantly, it's far from campus, and Corey is busy doing an all-day training session with Dr. Liu on McIntosh Castle library stuff today.

I try not to think of Corey as we spot Ellis in the food court. I was half afraid that he'd bring Barbie, but he seems to have sense. He smiles awkwardly as he waves to us.

We sit down. "Nice to see you under better circumstances," he says.

"Yeah," I say.

"I suppose we all know each other in one way or another, but I'm Ellis." He nods to each of us in turn. "Virgil, August, and Nolan."

I say, "That's us."

Ellis wrings his hands. "Cool, cool. Uh, you had some questions for me?"

"Just what I mentioned in my message. Wanting more information about Pattie Simmons."

"I looked her up. She worked as a nurse on campus, and she also helped out as a nurse in the faction. As we do experiments, we tend to require things like having blood drawn and professional care for patients volunteering for studies. But otherwise, that's it." He kind of shrugs. "The Toronto and Ottawa sites are more hubs for the faction than Kingston. Kingston is more of a political hub, if that makes sense. So she wasn't even really in the right place."

"But Carrigan was in Kingston."

"Attending Queen's . . . All the Doctorates go to Queen's."

"Right."

"I'm sorry I don't have more for you. . . ."

Nolan takes this as a signal that it's his turn. "How has your faction been dealing with the fact that Carrigan's disappeared?"

"He hasn't disappeared; he's on sabbatical."

"Jesus Christ," Nolan mutters, and I can't help but agree with him. What a spin to put on it.

Ellis shifts in his chair. "He's always had a system in place so that, should he need to take an emergency leave, he would be able to. He's very thorough in that way. So it's been business as usual. In all honesty, the length of his presence in Kingston was unorthodox to begin with but necessary due to the election."

"Weren't you . . . ," I start and then trail off. He would have been underground last semester.

He clears his throat. "Barbie caught me up."

"What was it like?" Virgil asks, voice so quiet that I almost miss him asking. I don't think he meant to say it aloud either, because he splutters, attempting to take it back.

Ellis licks his lips. "People act as though it's like waking up from a dream, but it isn't. You're conscious the whole time. Fueled by instinct, unable to stop it. It's worse when you're there long-term because they drug you to keep you more docile, and it makes your brain slow, and you can start to think more. But the thoughts are just being confused about where you are, and why you're there, and why you can't leave, and why you can barely move. Sometimes they need you for whatever reason. The Doctorate comes, and you have this sudden clarity. That's when the agony starts. Because you realize you've been there so long, and you're going to be there longer, and once the Doctorate is gone, you'll lose everything again. It's better when you lose that clarity. Animals don't feel their mortality. Don't have regrets. Suffering is just simple suffering. People act like the Pen is mercy, but I'm telling you right now that if there's no guarantee that someone is coming for you, it's better to die."

Without realizing it, I've gripped my hands into fists.

Virgil is pale, his skin washed out.

"Sorry," Ellis says, cracking a weak smile, but he doesn't take it back.

If Corey knew all that . . . would it make things better or worse for her?

"I admit that I had an ulterior motive for agreeing to this meeting," Ellis says, glancing between me and Virgil. "Corey . . . I . . . I mean, I'd like to reconcile, somehow. And I just . . . I don't know where to start, and I figured that since you're both so close with her . . . I don't

know. Maybe you can bring it up? That I want to? Our parents have tried setting up dinners, but as you can imagine, that hasn't gone over well. I did put a card with my number on it in her birthday gift, but she hasn't reached out. . . ."

"After all that shit Barbie said to her, are you surprised?" I ask.

Ellis winces. "Barbie is her own person. I can't control her. In the same way that I'm my own person. I want to have a relationship with my sister. I want my family back. I know our parents have messed up, and Corey is still on her own journey with them. Maybe she's not as willing to forgive and forget as I am. That's okay. I'm just looking for a chance to have a relationship that isn't based on obligation or external pressure. *Please.* If you could just even suggest it, I would appreciate it so much."

Me and Virgil look at each other. He says, "We'll test the waters and see."

Ellis beams. "Thank you so much. Sorry again that I didn't know more about Pattie. I guess she passed too early for you to know her. Must have been hard for your mom."

"Yeah," I say with a shrug. "It is what it is."

We say our goodbyes, and as we're leaving, I pause. Pattie and Mom don't have the same last name. Her last name isn't the same as mine, either. All I said was that she was my grandma. I never said on which side.

"Did you mention my mom to Ellis?" I ask Virgil.

"Uh . . . I don't think so? But maybe?"

He probably did. How would Ellis know otherwise?

I look back over my shoulder at Ellis still standing where we left him, watching us walk away.

"Never met a Scientist who I trusted," Nolan mutters.

Virgil glances at him. "Is there a faction you *do* trust?" Nolan scowls. "That's what I thought."

Nolan says, "Some of them are supporting the proposal."

"Scientists? Why?" I ask.

"Because part of our agreement said that Wilds cannot be experimented on. My dad knew the Scientists would use us falling on hard times to lure us into paid studies. So he made it impossible for them to do that. This new proposal allows for voluntary participation in the same breath that it restricts the work Wilds can do. It would be easy to get back into the habit of using us as test subjects. As if volunteering wouldn't only happen because of desperation." He looks at me. "Another reason we have to win."

"We will."

Virgil looks at me out of the corner of his eye, I'm sure questioning why I would make that promise. We've had a hard enough time just staying in the running. But I have to at least pretend at confidence. Our potential to win is the only thing keeping Nolan in this game, and we need him.

Virgil turns away, and I wonder if he knows it too.

CHAPTER TWENTY-SIX

I can't help but have complicated feelings about gyms. I step into the ARC, which, as usual, is busy. Filled with students lining up for Tim Hortons, sitting at the tables, or heading up the stairs. This portion of the building I'm very familiar with, having spent a good chunk of the summer shilling coffee at Tim's. Since then, I do also like coming in between classes to grab snacks from the grocery store or a coffee from Common Grounds, because I can use my meal plan card for both.

But I haven't gone to the gym section of the building since the Bachelor candidacy. Gyms are where I went to punish myself. I thought of them and pictured myself running on the treadmill, sneakers slamming on the belt, dripping sweat and hating every moment. But I wouldn't stop until the screen lit up, showing that I had burned five hundred calories. Only then did I deserve to eat. Just got here and I already can't wait to leave.

I scan my student card to gain entry to the athletics center and

take the elevator to the third floor. I'm double-checking my phone to make sure I get the directions right when Corey flies out of a door down the hall.

"What's up?" I ask. Corey's dark hair is thrown into a hasty bun on top of her head, and her cheeks are splotchy.

She sighs, and the sound drags through her body, her shoulders slumping. "The Scientists sent the spontaneous birth rate records but said they can't find the ones from last year that Carrigan was looking after. Henry thinks Carrigan falsified them to try to push whoever became the Doctorate—either Adam or James—into funding his faction more and hid the evidence."

"That's kind of fucked."

"Yes, well, that's politics for you. The Scientists have shown the current spontaneous birth rates, which seem steady. So if they did spike last year, either it's over now or Carrigan lied. Meaning a rising birth rate is no longer a threat, so Henry no longer cares. He suggested that I focus on my studies and take a break."

"I mean . . . isn't that good?"

Corey shakes her head. "It's good that they're not spiking but"—she lowers her voice—"I was using the Meredith studies as an excuse for borrowing Henry's copies of Dr. Weiss's journals, which I need to look into the Osseous. But since I don't need to research anymore, he took them back."

"Shit."

"Yes, shit. I have a lot of notes, but it's not the same as having the sources. We have to hope we find something good at Fort Henry."

"Can't you just say you want to do a project on Meredith?"

"No. Apparently Dr. Liu personally approached Henry to say he wanted me to have a lighter workload for the latter half of the

semester. Our training yesterday . . . well, I admit that I've kind of been neglecting the collection."

"I shouldn't have agreed to let you do the research stuff with Riley. It's too mu—"

"It's not!" Corey says, her voice echoing in the hall. She winces. "It's not. I want to keep busy."

I was right to not get Corey involved with the Ellis thing. I assume that's why she's so desperate to keep her mind occupied.

"See you later," she says. I wave as she heads to the elevators, and I go into the room she just left. The sign on the door says COMBAT ROOM.

The space is massive. A huge room with blue mats lining the floor and walls, QUEEN'S written in big bold letters across both. Inside, Henry stands with his hands in his pockets while Laira sits cross-legged against the wall, scrolling on her phone.

"Should I get out my knives?" I ask, assuming we're going to do sparring or something. This is my first training without Virgil and Nolan, so I'm not sure what to expect.

"Weapons aren't needed for today," Henry says. "Within every physical battle is one that takes place on the mental plane." He taps the side of his head. "What happens up here creates results in the outside world. I've chosen to do this specialized one-on-one training with you to strengthen your mind. Perhaps this can help you get over your fear and tap into the power that I know you have."

"What are we going to do?"

He gestures to Laira. "You're aware that Laira has a rather special third-evolution skill. You saw some of it in play with Ms. Mathers."

"Torturing people in their minds."

I don't miss the slight flinch from Laira. Henry says, "Some

reptiles have a secretion on their bodies which can create hallucinations. Laira cannot control what you see, per se, but you can be primed. Once it's in action, she and I are both privy to what you see. Your task is simply to break out of the illusion."

Laira jerks two fingers toward herself, and I go to her. She holds out her arm, and as she does, liquid beads on the surface. It looks like sweat, thin and clear over her ochre skin and fine dark hair. "Place your palm down."

I raise my hand, ignoring the tremble, and put it on her arm. It's hard not to remember the way Ms. Mathers screamed, though Margot insisted that the woman wasn't in any real pain. That everyone in her Mastery group cohort experienced this.

Henry says, "Tell me, do you still believe that you could have saved your mother?"

A tingling sensation travels from my hand up my arm. I gnaw on my lip. I don't know why he's talking about that right now. "Is it working?" I ask, and turn, then blink.

Wait, who was I talking to again?

I shudder as the cold hits my arms. Around me the trees swaying in the breeze seem sinister with the cover of night. I've been to the Scarborough Bluffs enough times that it should feel familiar, but we've always come during the day when it was populated by people walking, running, and cycling along the various trails.

"Come on," Mom says, pulling me forward. She doesn't usually manhandle me like this, but we also usually aren't out at nearly two in the morning. "We're almost there."

"Almost where?"

Mom's hazel eyes are focused, like she can see in the dark. She pushes her curls off her forehead and keeps dragging me onward.

I guess I don't get an explanation. I rarely do. It's not on me to ask. I'm just supposed to do as she says. We break out of the trees into the open air. We're on top of one of the cliffs, Lake Ontario spread out below us as far as the eye can see.

"What—"

Mom holds a finger to her lips, eyes narrowed.

I follow her gaze to the trees, where a pair of glowing yellow eyes peer back at us. A shiver travels down my body.

The thing bursts from the trees, heading straight for Mom. I barrel into her, pushing us both out of harm's way. I reach for my thighs, pulling out a blade and whipping it at the shadow. But the thing only bats aside the metal like it's nothing.

"Run!" Mom shouts. "Run!"

But I won't. I can't.

Inside me, something growls and flexes its claws. It wants to be let out. Wants to rip, and tear, and—no. I can't let it.

I raise the knives in my hands and plant my feet, keeping myself in front of Mom even as the thing charges toward us. But she gets the jump on me, sweeping my legs out from underneath me. When I fall, she lures the shadow away, waving her arms and shouting.

I scramble to my feet, but it's too late.

The beast slams into her, and she flies through the air, arms and legs pinwheeling, off the cliff and into darkness.

I'm on my knees, breathing hard, tears on my cheeks.

The thing that attacked her, the Monster, regards me with its glowing eyes and flees into the night.

"That didn't go as you planned, did it?" a man says, coming out from the trees, his locs pulled into a ponytail. "I hoped your fear for

your mother would be greater than your fear of yourself. I suppose that I was wrong."

I know this man. . . . Henry.

This is Henry. And I'm in a hallucination.

"Why did you choose me?" I spit at him. "Don't fucking lie. I know you did. You put me in Virgil's path. You wanted me here. Why?"

Henry stares out at the view. "It was strategic, really. I learned that Carrigan was having a girl followed. Of course, at that time, I knew Cyrus was dead and there would be an election. I was keeping eyes on both Carrigan and James. When I did a bit of research on you, I discovered that you were the child of the girl Carrigan had been obsessed with in university. Unremarkable to me, but not to him. At first, I assumed it was leftover infatuation. But I wanted to see how involved he might get. So yes, I sent one of my Mastery group pupils to push your buttons. Not to say sexist drivel, mind you. But to antagonize you a bit."

I laugh. *He* was the one who sent that guy after me. "They pushed me, all right."

"You were drunk. A toddler could have pushed you. Nevertheless, I set my pieces. Sent an alert for Virgil so he'd see you on the cameras and had him turn off the exterior light hoping it might guide you. Neat bit of psychology there. I'm sure you thought you picked a house at random, but no, you picked one that appeared unoccupied. The rest is due to your own stellar social skills."

"Thanks for the compliment," I drawl. It's so neat when he lays it out like this.

"I brought your file to Adam, James, and Carrigan so I could see Carrigan's reaction. Like a professional, he kept his cool. I admit that

once I met you, I regretted my meddling. Vulgar, uncooperative, and disrespectful."

"I aim to please," I say with a grin.

"Yes, well, from there on, Virgil insisted upon you. I couldn't move him from it, and so I was forced to see you through. I never did find out what Carrigan wanted from you, but you've proven useful on your own, and it is something of a victory over him to have you."

Had Adam not done it, would Carrigan have nominated me for the candidacy? Did he want me in the society like this, or had he just wanted to make contact? And why? Mom specifically wanted him to help Jules, and he didn't do shit for him. "You don't have a guess as to what he wanted with me?"

Henry shrugs. "Sentimentality, I assume."

I don't believe it. What I do believe is that Carrigan may have wanted to know if Mom had shared anything with me. If I knew about the Osseous. Probably the same reason he spared Jules. Maybe the plan had been to play nice with me while he had Bernie manipulate Jules. But once I was under Henry and Adam's influence, it wouldn't have been so easy to pull the wool over my eyes. Henry meant to use me but had inadvertently protected me.

I stare at him as he comes to stand in front of me. "I would not test you this way if I didn't expect you to succeed," he says. "So, do you want to succeed? Do you want to be powerful enough to say with conviction that you could have saved her?"

"Yes," I breathe.

"Then stop being afraid!"

"It's not that simple!" I snap. "What if I let it out again and kill someone?"

Henry frowns. "It?"

I shift in place. "In my head . . . since we bonded to Nolan, the feeling of the power that comes from Virgil, the monster, it's become . . . well, it looks like Virgil's Monster form but it's like a manifestation of the monster? Virgil thinks it's a side effect of having two partners. When I let it out, I get powerful, but I also, like, *become* it. I want to hurt things. So I've been keeping it in a cage. I try to let out a bit, but it's not easy."

Henry stares at me for a long moment. "Is it like this for Virgil, too? Since the attachment of Nolan to your bond, that is."

"No."

"Interesting," Henry says. "Who have you told about this? In this amount of detail?"

"Just Virgil."

"Let's keep it that way. If it is indeed a side effect, then it's volatile. We don't want the society to get the impression that you may become a liability or threat. We should keep it a secret at least until you have firm control over it." Henry nods to himself. "This is helpful context. Now, we'll go again, and you'll let it out."

My heart rate spikes. "I can't—"

"Ms. Black," Henry drawls. "If someone of your skill level can kill me just because you use your full strength, then I prefer the grave." I scowl at him, but something in my shoulders unwinds. "Let's go again."

For the first time since nearly killing Nolan, I'm not afraid to let the monster go. To sink into the feeling of its flexing claws and jaw crowded with sharp teeth. If training like this with Henry is what will help me master the beast inside, I'll do it.

CHAPTER TWENTY-SEVEN

Despite my love for dance, I've never been in a traditional studio. I was more the type to watch videos online and practice alone in my room. I wanted to learn more formally but never got the chance. I didn't expect that my first time at a studio would be with two boys who happen to be able to transform into Monsters. But honestly, it's about time I started to enjoy some condition-free perks of being in the society. Virgil fidgets beside me, even more obvious because we're in a room full of mirrors with nothing else to stare at but our reflections.

Our instructors are also alumni of Henry's Mastery group. Silas, whose broad, sculpted chest is covered by several sheer strips of fabric that are almost a shirt, paired with tight black pants, and their partner Zokia, who's in tights, a unitard, and a sheer wrap skirt—every item soaked in glitter and rhinestones. Both are white with very good tans considering that we're still suffering through winter. There's also Kris, a Black man, lean in

that dancer way, lounging against the wall and observing.

Zokia tilts her head, regarding us. "Three at once was the right move."

"I know," Silas says. "It's going to be perfect."

Christ, this is going to be a nightmare. Unfortunately for us, it's tradition that before the start of the quarterfinals, there's a formal ball where each pair does a dance. Typically a sort of ballroom number, but any style is permitted. I suggested that we skip it, but it's another one of those parts of the Monster's Ball that *cannot* be skipped.

If it were just me, I'd be excited to learn choreography and do a performance, but when it means coordinating with both Virgil *and* Nolan? Yeah . . . not so much.

"Wouldn't it work better if we danced separately with August?" Nolan asks.

Both Silas and Zokia look aghast at this idea. Zokia actually holds a hand to her heart. "*No.* What would you do while August and Virgil were dancing? Just stand there?"

From Nolan's expression, I'm sure that's exactly what he assumed would happen.

"This is the tale," Silas says, spreading their arms out. Nolan groans. "August is the wolf, and Nolan and Virgil are lambs." Nolan groans louder.

Virgil, meanwhile, looks vaguely ill.

"It's a subversion," Zokia adds.

Honestly, I'm into it. Silas continues, "Virgil and Nolan have been living a life ignorant of violence or wickedness. And then August comes into your pen, prepared for slaughter. The blood and carnage are frightening but also enchanting and erotic."

"What the fuck?" Nolan mutters.

Virgil actually sits on the floor, like he feels too queasy to stay standing.

Zokia steps in. "You wrestle, fighting for your lives, but also against your forbidden desires. And in the end, August emerges victorious, but who has truly won?"

"Cool," I breathe.

Silas and Zokia beam at me.

Nolan, on the other hand, looks at me like he can't believe I would cosign this. For the first time, he and Virgil are on the same page. Virgil buries his face in his hands.

Drama queens.

"So," Silas says. "We'll start with Virgil and Nolan together, and August will be stage left doing a solo. Then we'll have her come in, and it'll become the three of you dancing together, and then Virgil and Nolan will die, finishing poses on the ground, and we'll have August do her final pose standing. Understood?"

We nod, though I feel like I'm the only one who does it with any sort of energy. I get a solo! It'll be a mess once the three of us have to come together, but at least I'll get my own moment so the audience knows that one of us has talent.

"I want to die," Nolan mumbles.

Zokia grins. "And so you will! But not until the end." She shoos us backward. "We're going to perform it once through for you. I will be August, Silas will be Nolan, and Kris will be Virgil.

The three of them get into position, Silas and Kris with their backs against each other, and Zokia off to the side. The music is slow at first. Silas and Kris wrap around each other and then away, dancing playfully with big leaps while Zokia does her solo, creeping ever closer. As she engages the two lambs, the music shifts to

something darker. She leaps onto Silas and the two of them fall to the floor, tumbling in a way that's definitely on the edge of intimate while Kris wrestles to pull her from Silas. As the music goes on, the fight becomes something that's more difficult to differentiate from a romantic encounter. Finally, just as they seem to be settling into harmony, the wolf that is Zokia strikes, and Silas and Kris fall to the ground while she finishes in a pose with her hands up to her head, a mime of wolf ears.

They finish, and I clap enthusiastically. Virgil stares with his jaw unhinged. Nolan just shakes his head.

While I go through the starting solo with Zokia, Virgil and Nolan are being instructed by Silas on the moves. They grasp onto each other in a way that looks like it's a touch too hard and avoid eye contact. I don't think it's because they're both guys. Both of them grew up in the society, where orientation beyond heterosexuality is commonplace, and Nolan is at least bi or pan. I suspect that it's more because they don't particularly like each other.

I ignore them and enjoy the process of learning the moves with Zokia, who is delighted by how quickly I'm picking everything up. I am too, honestly. I can't help smiling as we run through the whole solo.

When I finish, there's clapping, and I turn to see Silas giving me applause while Virgil and Nolan stare. I avoid Virgil's eyes. He's looking at me the same way he did at the afterparty. Like he might be willing to take a risk. "You're made for this," Silas croons. I didn't think I could smile harder, but I do. "Perhaps if you two perform better, she might have someone on this end of the room to admire besides Kris and me," Silas adds.

Maybe I'm imagining it, but it feels like the boys start doing better after that.

. . .

Having never been to Fort Henry, something I underestimated is how absolutely massive the place is. It's a huge, sprawling piece of land fenced in by multiple stone barricades, a literal moat (though without any water in it), and restored canons. As Riley drove us out, Corey gave a quick lesson on the history of the place. It was a nineteenth-century British military fort built during the War of 1812. But the one we see today is a restoration done between 1832 and 1837, and it was additionally fortified during that time. It was abandoned by the British in 1870 and then by Canadian troops in 1891, at which point the society came in and made the fort part of the many underground routes throughout the city. Eventually, it was opened as a museum in 1938.

"I saw a wrestling show here once," Nolan says.

I jerk around to stare at him in the third row of the SUV. "Why were you at a wrestling show?!"

He makes a face at me. "To watch wrestling."

I shake my head and turn back to the front. I'm tempted to mention how pleased Riley seems to be having Corey ride shotgun but decide against it. I've already gotten too involved in that matchmaking for my own good. Virgil reminded me almost every day for a week to make sure Riley came to Corey's birthday party.

As we get out of the vehicle, Virgil glances at Nolan for what seems like the fiftieth time since we picked him up. I don't want to get into how many texts I had to send to beg Nolan to participate. We need his smoke ability, since only a few blocks away from the fort on the other side of the parking lot are homes that apparently belong to the armed forces who actively police the property. If we don't want to get caught, using his fog is our best bet. Especially since I can't trust

that I'm practiced enough to use the ability in his stead.

Honestly, I expected him to just ignore me, but here he is.

"Is no one going to think it's weird that we're parked here?" I ask, glancing around.

Riley says, "It's a public space. Lots of people park and walk around here. I mean, look at the view." She waves to the city that sprawls out in front of us. The fort is up on a high enough elevation that you can see the downtown waterfront and Deadman Bay sprawling out. "As an additional precaution, I changed my plates before we left."

"You changed your plates? You just have extras around?"

"Why are you acting like you have no idea how a secret society might operate?"

This girl is so mouthy. "Have you ever been told that you have the demeanor of low grit sandpaper?"

"No, but I'm sure you have." My jaw drops, and she plows on. "Here's the plan. Nolan will cast a fog around the area to obscure us from the cameras. Then, with his and Virgil's assistance, we jump over the moat and onto the wall. There should be stairs on the other side. From that point, still using the fog, we break into the interior rooms where they host the exhibits. I spoke with some members who have worked at the site, and only the cameras on the outside are functional and monitored during the offseason. So once we're inside, we'll be good. Corey and I think we're looking for a secret entrance in one of the displays, so just follow us there, and then we can spread out and search."

"What would you have done if I hadn't come?" Nolan asks.

Riley looks him in the eye when she says, "Changed the plan."

I seriously have to side-eye Corey because the girl looks like she

just became more into Riley with that sentence. I do not get the appeal.

Nolan is apparently more than capable of casting fog without transforming. Which, I mean, Monsters are supposed to be able to do, but I think Virgil's only managed to transform parts of his body and use healing in a more passive way thus far. He studies Nolan as he casts the fog like he's learning something.

I nudge Virgil with my shoulder. He glances at me. "What?"

"You're looking really hard."

"Just wondering if there's a trick to it," he mutters.

"You know that you can ask him for advice, right?" I say. "We *are* a team."

Virgil mutters something unintelligible under his breath.

Once the fog is thick enough, it's time to move. The challenge isn't just the height of the wall. It's also the width of the moat area that itself spans a few feet. Nolan lets Corey get on his back so he can jump her over. We might need to run, but she decided to wear her taekwondo leg instead of the running blade, citing that it's stealthier and she can still run in it, just not as fast. Nolan stares at the wall, bending down and swinging his arms back before leaping. Corey lets out an involuntary squeak, and they land at the top of the stone barricade, disappearing over the other side.

"I'm sorry," Virgil says to me. "For being weird for the last little bit."

"You're acknowledging it?"

He bites his lip. "He's better than me. The skill gap between us is so obvious."

"Is this really the time for this?" Riley hisses under her breath.

Virgil shakes his head and crouches so she can get on his back.

Riley climbs on, muttering about "fucking freshmen" as Virgil jumps. He gets on the top of the wall as Nolan is coming back. They nod at each other before Virgil goes over with Riley.

I wait for Nolan to drop down, but instead he takes out his phone and types something, and mine vibrates. He's texted one word.

Jump.

I lick my lips.

Virgil reappears on the top of the wall, and he and Nolan exchange words.

We ran the hallucination five times on Tuesday before Henry called it a day. Laira thought I was getting better, but Mom still died every single time. Even with the monster inside unleashed, I still wasn't good enough. I have to get stronger. I can't do that if I don't push myself. Their skills are my skills. If Virgil and Nolan can do it, I should be able to.

The monster stretches, languid. It almost feels . . . sated, in a way. Maybe because of letting it loose with Henry. Closing my eyes, I feel for the strength and flexibility in the muscles of its legs.

I squat down and tense my thighs. Easy as pie, just do what they did. I push up, jump, and . . . I'm doing it! It's actually happening! My arms windmill as I get close to the wall, and then my legs flail as I realize that I am, in fact, *not* doing it, because I'm just short of the stone barrier.

I start to fall toward the moat only to have my arms jerked up, the right by Nolan and the left by Virgil. My feet land on the stone, and I breathe heavily.

"Close," Nolan says, dropping my hand.

I glare at him, and Virgil shakes his head. We're on the uppermost section of raised seating. In the middle of the space is a giant

empty area. I guess that would be where they hosted the wrestling. It has the feel of an empty concert venue or coliseum.

Nolan hops the railing, a drop of at least twenty feet, and lands beside Corey and Riley on the lower level of the fort. Virgil, of course, heads toward the stairs off to the right that Riley mentioned before.

Instead of following him, I take a deep breath and jump over the railing, following Nolan's lead. I land with one knee down, whipping my head up after so my braids fly behind me.

Corey squeals. "You did the superhero landing!"

"Don't encourage her," Riley says.

"Too late," I say with a beaming smile.

Riley rolls her eyes as Virgil joins us. "Glad at least one of you isn't too good for the stairs. Now can we refocus on the task at hand?"

"After you, fearless leader." I make sure to bend at the waist and twirl my hands a few times.

Riley stomps toward the closest door. I couldn't see from above, but now it's clear that lining the oval-shaped perimeter of the space are rooms. She heads to the closest door, using a key that I guess she got from whoever at QBSS works at the fort. Corey and Nolan follow her inside, but I hang back with Virgil for a moment.

"He's better than me too," I say to Virgil. "I could feel insecure about it, or I could let him help me get better. I choose the latter. You should too."

Virgil stares at me for a moment before nodding. "Maybe he's better at the combat, but you're definitely the superior dancer."

I'm smiling too much probably, looking at Virgil for too long. But he's doing the same thing.

Nolan was wrong about Virgil. He doesn't play the victim. He just isn't shy with his emotions. He wants to keep them controlled,

but they seep out anyway. I haven't missed the fact that he feels indebted to me. To all of us, really. And he wants to make up for that. Desperately. Nolan may be more advanced in his skills, but he doesn't care the way Virgil does. Or, at least, I thought he didn't. But his presence here is making me question that.

We step inside and are met with the grim expressions of our friends. "What?" I ask.

Riley says, "Someone else is here."

CHAPTER TWENTY-EIGHT

Riley

I chew on the inside of my cheek as we move through Fort Henry. It has the feel of a haunted building at night without anyone around. The exhibits don't help—rooms featuring empty tables with full place settings, a four-poster bed with army regalia laid on a trunk, and a gift shop. Because what would history be without opportunities for capitalism? Though I do admire that their bakery uses the same ovens that would have been operated during the fort's time. *"It's the details,"* Mom and Dad always say. The right details in a staging can be the difference between selling at asking and selling *over* asking.

I wouldn't mind a haunted vibe if the place felt abandoned too. Though it's been made clear that we aren't alone. It was only a brief flashlight beam, but it was enough. I shake my head and plow forward. I need to keep this expedition focused. Especially because August and her partners are acting like this is a playground, wasting time with side conversations and practicing jumping like

we aren't infiltrating a military-guarded historical site.

I double-check against the map I printed at home. "Okay," I say, my voice low. "There should be a hidden entrance between this exhibit and the gift shop. We'll split up to search. Corey with me, and you three can stay a trio." August smiles at me in a way that I don't particularly like. A sort of shit-eating grin. "Do you have any objections?"

"Nope," she says, turning and walking off with Virgil and Nolan.

Corey moves ahead, and I join her, checking for any hidden panels or switches or latches. This is the worst part of this whole endeavor. If we can't find anything, we'll have to come back another day, and that'll increase our chances of being caught. Not to mention that the woman who was QBSS president at the time Pattie would have been an active spy isn't responding to any of my emails, and her phone number on file is out of service. Grandma knew her but insisted the woman wasn't going to talk, so that was a bust. I need this to work out.

After forty-five minutes of searching, we've circled back to the exhibit depicting barrels of imagined alcohol, and I'm about ready to tear my hair out. Anything but keep trying to find this fucking—

"Here!" Corey says, too loud and giddy.

I rush over to her. She's found a switch tucked behind a barrel that I swear I checked a dozen times, which has opened an entrance in the wall that was partially hidden by a hanging tapestry. Pushing the cloth aside more fully reveals a set of stairs leading down.

"Yes!" I say, also too loud. "You're amazing! I could kiss you!" She flushes, and I gape. "I . . . um, so we should go down there, right?

I'll text August." Thankfully, texting her gives me the opportunity to stare at my phone.

I can't believe I said that. Not that there's anything wrong with kissing a girl. Like, I don't have any issues with Corey being a lesbian. That's great for her. But I can't just be saying shit like that. I mean, I've thought about it, but every girl has thought about it. We're naturally open in that way. Also, it's a figure of speech.

I have a lot of admiration for Corey, is all. Sometimes you admire a girl a lot, and she happens to be pretty, and so those kinds of thoughts come up. If I were gay, I wouldn't have enjoyed sex with Jackson. He was a bit mushy with it sometimes—I didn't need to be told he loved me a million times during—but it was good. I looked forward to it. Initiated, even.

Though there is, of course, the option of liking *both* girls and boys.

"That's not creepy at all," August says, and I spin around. She reels back. "Why are you giving me the stink eye?"

"Nothing," I mutter. "Let's go."

August shares a look with Virgil and then Corey before they follow me down the stairs. We leave Nolan at the top to let us know if anyone shows up. Namely the other person who's skulking around.

The stairs lead us into an underground tunnel. It's made of stone and without even candle or torch holders on the wall. Obviously it wasn't meant for people to be using it casually. With my phone, I light the way.

Both girls and boys . . . I mean, I like Corey, but not like that. Sammie was . . . I shake my head. That's a bad comparison. I knew Sammie for years, and we were best friends. It was easy to get mixed up about things. Does a passing thought about kissing a girl

automatically make me bi? I don't think so. I wouldn't have done it. I nod to myself. *Right. I wouldn't have done it.*

"Why are you moving your head so much?" August asks.

"I can't move my head now?" I snap at her.

She holds up her hands like she thinks I'm going to attack her. "Chill! Christ."

I force myself to focus, and when we come up against a door, I'm glad to have something to do other than think about things irrelevant to our current circumstances. I stare at it, reaching out and tracing the symbol there.

"Is that . . . a scythe?" August asks.

"Sickle," Corey and I say at the same time. I look at her. Corey says, "I guess there was always a chance that it could be a QBSS cache as much as one for the society."

I take off my necklace and press it to the symbol.

August leans forward. "What are you doing?"

"The bones in the artifacts can be affected by other things that hold bone. They create reactions like chemicals. It's also believed that artifacts hold the memories of the wielder—it's another reason why we always add bones, never taking any away. Meaning if anyone else opened this door with the sickle, their bones remain in it, and it should open for me too."

I activate the artifact, the sickle pendant glowing gold.

And . . . nothing happens. The door doesn't move. A muscle in my cheek twitches.

"Should we smash it?" August asks.

Virgil gets to it before me. "Smash it and risk the whole tunnel caving in?"

"Just a little smash," she mutters.

I grind my teeth. "It should have worked."

"Does it respond to the sickle at this stage?" Corey asks. "Maybe August was right. It's not the sickle. It's the scythe."

"I love you, Corey," August says. "You're the only one who ever admits that I'm right." I think she was about to say more but suddenly she jerks her head toward the mouth of the tunnel. I would brush it off except Virgil does it too at the exact same moment.

There's a crash from above us.

"Nolan," Virgil says.

August turns and runs back the way we came, and the rest of us rush after her. Corey swears, lagging behind me. She's not using a running leg. Shit.

I turn back, "Are you—"

"Fine," she grunts. "Keep going. Leave me behind if you need to."

I spin around and keep pace with the others while Corey falls behind. There's nothing dangerous in the tunnels, so she'll be fine. Even if there were, she can handle herself.

We get up the stairs and into the gift shop, where the room has descended into chaos. There are broken desks and overturned post-card and key chain displays, shattered FORT HENRY mugs and other merchandise scattered on the floor.

Nolan is baring his teeth, his nails extended into claws, his lower lip bleeding. Across from him, unfathomably, is Jackson, a glowing shield in front of him.

"What are you doing here?!" I shout at him.

Jackson glares. "I could ask the same of you." He shakes his head. "I knew you would fuck around. Your presidency is in danger, and this is what you're doing?"

"I'm looking for the weapon that I told the council I would find!"

He gestures toward the group. "With *them*?!" His eyes dart to Corey before coming back to me. "This is a little more than just using your connections."

Jackson has always, *always* been so weird about my female friends. Sammie most of all. Bernie's voice invades my mind then, talking about how I seemed to prefer Sammie over my boyfriend. I mean, yes, isn't that just friend code? You love your friends more than your partner because they'll always be there.

"You guys go back down," I say. "I'll deal with him."

"Dramaaaaaa," August drawls as she turns around.

Nolan retracts his claws and wipes his split lip, taking the time to flip Jackson off before he follows the others.

Corey lingers for a moment, but at a nod from me, follows the rest of them.

"You two have been spending a lot of time together," Jackson says, gazing after her. "You don't even realize the way you act. How you get obsessed. First it was Sammie, and now it's her?"

He makes me sound like a stalker or something. "Spending time with someone to do *research* doesn't make me obsessed. Also, Sammie was *murdered*. God forbid I try to get justice for my dead best friend. And again, what are you doing here?!"

Jackson lets the shield return to its chain form, putting it around his neck. "The elder council are monitoring you. I've been following you too, and trying to distract them, but you make it hard when you do things like this."

Wait, what? "Monitoring me? Like . . . using members?"

"Members. Alumni. Whoever. You need to be more careful."

Shit, shit, shit.

Jackson continues, "I was able to get the guy who was here tonight to leave. Told him I had already patrolled the area and hadn't found anyone. I doubt he believed me, though. I was going to leave you to it until I came up against the redhead, who was way too ready to fight."

"Why wouldn't you just tell me?"

He laughs. "Would you have answered a call from me?"

"If you just supported me when it matt—"

"I can't. Because supporting you and protecting you are two different things."

"Well . . . thanks. But now that I know, I can handle myself."

Jackson gives me a long look. "You're different this year. I know I wasn't a fan of Sammie, but . . . you were always more yourself when you were with her." He averts his eyes. "I was jealous of that, honestly. I always felt like I was getting this curated version of you. You were the same way even after she was gone, when you were fighting to find her killer. The Riley who thew me and Malachi up against the wall. The girl who was too good for me. The girl you were with Sammie. That's who you are, Riley. But this . . . this isn't it."

It's not like I don't know what he's talking about. I felt it too. When I was with Sammie, I wasn't thinking about everything I did or said or how she saw me. But I could never be that version of myself with Jackson. When I was with him, I wasn't just Riley. I was a Historic. I was a prospective wife and mother to his children. I was part of a couple with a certain level of visibility.

"I did love you, you know," I say to him. "You were the one always looking around to see if there was anyone I loved more."

"Was it so wrong to want to be loved the most?" he asks, his eyes glassy. "And for you, were you ever really going to be happy being with second best?"

I press my lips into a line, saying nothing.

Jackson cracks a smile. "Just be careful. I hope one day I can see that girl again. The real Riley. I know I wasn't her favorite person, but she was mine." He turns and walks down the hall to the exit.

I swallow and squeeze my eyes shut, practically slapping my face to get rid of the tears. I spin on my heel and head down the stairs, jerking to a stop when I find Corey there waiting.

"Sorry," she says. "I just . . . I thought I'd wait for you." She keeps her head down, hunching her shoulders. She opens her mouth and then closes it.

"What?" I ask. "Just say it."

"I don't think what he said was much different from what your alum said. The sickle . . . Maybe if you think of the person you were with Sammie, your real self, you'll have better luck connecting with it." I don't respond, and Corey waves down the tunnel. "We should go."

I follow her in silence until we reach the others.

August starts to say something but shuts her mouth at a look from Corey.

I practically yank the necklace from my neck to press it to the symbol again. If I entertain what Corey said. If I think of who I was with *her* . . . I close my eyes. I have a goal. I want to find the Osseous. If Sammie were here, she'd say that we're getting that door open no matter what. Not for any grand reason. Just because it's what we came here to do. She wouldn't take no for an answer.

I snap my eyes open when the stone grinds against the floor, the door slowly sliding open.

I look at Corey, who stares back at me with a smile that doesn't reach her eyes.

And of course, after all that, the chamber holds nothing more than dusty books.

CHAPTER TWENTY-NINE

I wipe sweat from my face as the music ends and Zokia snaps at me to finish properly, prompting me to push myself back into the ending pose until she signals I can stop. Our progress in the dance studio hasn't been as terrible as expected over these two weekends of practice. Nolan still spends most of the time rolling his eyes, but he and Virgil are trying. Silas and Zokia have made it clear that we're not going to become technical dancers overnight, so the goal is making it look nice and expressing the right emotion.

Honestly, this is the thing I look forward to the most every week. Between training and classes, it feels like everything else in my life is something that the society is taking from me. Never thought I would be so desperate to have a hobby.

Silas narrows their eyes at us. "There's a tension between you three, but also a refusal to release it. You have to be free with your bodies."

"For fuck's sake," Nolan mumbles.

Silas zeros in on him. "Whether you like it or not, you're a representative of your entire clan in this competition. Don't you want to dazzle them? Change the minds of those who doubt you? Or were you just spouting empty words at a camera?"

Nolan presses his lips into a flat line, his face reddening.

"And you two," they say, pointing to me and Virgil. "The outsider and the outcast. Don't you hope to change the tides of your fortune? They're moving, but not as much as before."

"I don't know that a dance is going to do that," Virgil says, stuffing his hands into the pockets of his slacks. His insistence on formal wear for these sessions means he always sweats the most, and his collared shirt is soaked through at the neck as usual.

"You've never watched a dance that entranced you?" Zokia asks, staring him down. "That captured you? Tempted you? Inspired you?"

Virgil swallows.

I don't know if he has, but I remember watching a music video and seeing the way the dancers moved. How I immediately wanted to do that too. Was willing to spend hours in my room copying them. Up until that point, I'd never had anything that felt like my own. I had Mom's lessons and her and Dad's pressure to do well in school. I thought that was all I ever would have. Until that moment.

Silas says, "No one is going to read anything into this. Yes, we know Monster-Master romance is forbidden, blah, blah, which is precisely why people enjoy these dances. It's just on the line enough to be exciting. You don't have to be shy or guarded. It's a performance." They smile. "If it feels real, it just means you've done your jobs well."

"Let's go through it one more time," Zokia says, clapping her

hands. "Make this last one count. This is your final session with us, after all."

We get into our starting positions and go again. It's not like anything drastic changes, but it also feels different. The touches and more intimate moments of the dance are still kind of awkward, but during the times when we're supposed to make eye contact, it happens. Usually, Virgil is too embarrassed to do it, and Nolan can't be bothered.

And of course, that's when I find myself wanting to turn away.

At the end, we thank the instructors—even Nolan—and head out of the studio. It's warmer today, more fall jacket weather than winter puffer. Though I've been keeping up with not wearing either.

"We have the Margot thing, right?" Nolan asks.

We had her move our meeting from its usual time to today so we could get in a practical session before the quarterfinals. We'll have private training with Henry tomorrow too. Though there's also an alternative reason for the change in timing.

We head back to campus, entering the ARC and heading to the gym section on the third floor, where we're meeting Margot and Isaac. Since our previous session with her was mostly about advice, Isaac wasn't needed, but now that it's more practical, he's supposed to be helping.

The brother-sister duo are waiting for us in the middle of the room. At Margot's instruction, I lock the door behind us.

Isaac's head turns suddenly, and his eyes narrow.

"What?" Margot asks.

He blinks and shakes his head. "No, sorry . . . It's nothing."

Margot plows forward as Margot tends to do. "Let's do some sprints. Isaac will participate so you can understand the benchmark

of speed that you should be able to reach. Line up." We arrange ourselves at the far wall of the space, and this girl pulls a whole ass whistle and stopwatch from her pocket. When she blows it, we run.

Predictably, the boys leave me in the dust. But by the fifth sprint, something shifts. I remember the feel of tapping into the monster's strength, thinking of its movements, its amber eyes locked on me. I know that I'm moving faster, confirmed by Margot's nod at me. By sprint number eight, it feels like we're actually competing.

Margot says, "That's ten. Virgil took six of those, by the way. Three for Isaac and one for Nolan." She nods to me. "August was second in three."

Virgil grins, looking at Nolan, who rolls his eyes. Virgil holds out his fist to me, which I bump. I never won, sure, but three times I was faster than two Monsters, and that's something.

"Jumps now," Margot says. "Just vertical." The ceiling of the room must be at least twenty feet tall, meaning we have a lot of space to work with.

"Starting to feel less like I'm helping and more like I'm being tested," Isaac mutters.

"On my signal," Margot continues. "Ready? Go!" We do ten rounds of jumping, and by the time we finish, I'm sweatier than I already was from dancing. The guys manage to touch the ceiling multiples times. I think I get close once. "Isaac took five of those—"

Isaac lets out a triumphant "Ha!"

"Four to Nolan, one to Virgil. August second for five times this go."

Now Nolan is the one throwing Virgil a shit-eating grin. They're competing against each other like we aren't on the same team.

Margot looks around the space. "Now for strength . . . not a lot

of options, and I don't want to go to the weightlifting room since it's not private. . . . Maybe I'll just have August lift Virgil."

Virgil balks. "She could lift Isaac?"

"He's too light. You've got enough muscle to be a challenge." Margot waves at me. "Let's go."

I walk over to Virgil, not sure how I'm supposed to be lifting him, and settle for squatting and locking my arms around his knees. With a grunt, I shove up with my thighs and manage to get him in the air. He lets out a sound that's suspiciously squeal-like. Nolan is fully laughing at him.

"Let's see how you react when she picks you up," Virgil snaps.

"Actually, not a bad idea," Margot says. "You can transform, Nolan. August will pick you up like that."

Virgil looks like Christmas came early, his smile is so wide.

"Please be serious," I say to Margot. "You don't actually expect me to pick him up in Monster form." Lifting Virgil is one thing, lifting a giant Monster is another.

"I'm always serious." Margot levels a stare at Nolan. "Do it."

With a sigh, he strips down as we look away, and transforms. Once he's ready, I walk over to him, trying to figure out how I'm supposed to lift a six-foot-tall fox.

"Just get in there." Margot gestures to his stomach.

"*Just get in there,*" I mutter, high-pitched and mocking.

I line myself up underneath Nolan, pressing my hands to his stomach. I do have to squat, which helps because it gives me room. But for fuck's sake, I'm really supposed to lift him?

Margot says, "If you believe that Virgil or Nolan could do this, then you can do it too."

I take a deep breath and shove upward, my thighs screaming and

Nolan moving not at all. *Come on, come on.* I can do this. I have the strength. Monsters smash into and toss each other around all the time. I shove, and this time, my thighs move, almost too fast, and Nolan lifts abruptly, making a similar squeal to Virgil, followed by something like a resigned sigh.

Virgil is beside himself. He's laughing enough that I wonder if this is the most fun he's had all year. But I care more about the fact that I'm lifting a Monster. "Holy shit!" I gasp. I take a couple of shaky steps forward and then a few more.

Margot says, "Don't get carried aw—"

I give Nolan a little toss. Meaning his whole flailing weight comes crashing back down toward me. But I get my hands up and he lands, sending me down to one knee. I release him fully and collapse, panting hard.

Virgil falls onto the ground, he's laughing so hard—wheezing, actually. I shake my head at him as I roll out from underneath Nolan, who glares at me.

Margot gives me a flat look. "I was saying, don't get carried away."

"Right," I reply with a sheepish grin. "Sorry." I really did it, though! Before, it felt like I could maybe manage this stuff in a pinch, but I'm more confident now. I think I could replicate what we did today in the ring. Between this and actually doing well on my PSYC100 quiz, things finally feel like they're working out.

Nolan transforms back and changes, his face definitely the reddest I've ever seen on him. Virgil recovers enough to compliment me on the lift.

Margot says, "Now that you have running, jumping, and strength up to second evolution, you'll be able to do more combination

moves together. Like, you could jump on Virgil's back and fight on top of him."

Virgil says, "I don't know if that's necessary. . . ."

I tilt my head. "What? You don't want me to ride you? I feel like I'd be really good at it."

Virgil splutters a lot of things, and not a single one of the words is coherent.

"You can ride me," Nolan says. "I don't mind."

"Okay, children," Margot snaps. "I was making a legitimate suggestion. So I'll just leave it to you three to decide what you do or don't want to do." She mutters, "This is why I can't stand freshmen."

"We love you too, Margot," I chime.

She shakes her head and leads the way out of the combat room and back down to the ARC's main floor. As we exit, Isaac freezes.

Mia leans against one of the pillars, her hair down around her shoulders, wearing a light green coat and pair of wide-leg jeans.

Margot's gaze immediately snaps to me and Virgil; we both feign ignorance.

"Oh my God, Mia!" I say, and make a show of slapping my forehead. "I totally forgot we were going to meet here today." I was worried earlier when Isaac seemed like he might have smelled her, but it worked out okay. Also, I can't believe this boy is ignoring a girl whose scent he picked out from three floors away.

Margot shakes her head. "I'm not getting involved in this." To Isaac she says, "I'm going to get a drink. Grab me when you're done." She stalks off upstairs, I assume to the CoGro coffee shop. I expect Nolan to take off, but he stays where he is, apparently curious enough to hang around.

"Hey . . . ," Isaac says to Mia.

She rocks back on her heels. "You've been doing a lot of training lately."

"Yeah, um . . . well, my track—"

"I know about Monsters, and you never once mentioned track last year."

"Public place," Virgil says under his breath.

But neither Isaac nor Mia are paying attention to him. Isaac's jaw unhinges. "You *know*?! Your dad told you?"

She's holding her ground, but I don't miss the slight shake to her hands. I did ask several times if she was up for this confrontation, and she insisted. "What I'm interested in is what he told you," she says. My eyes jerk to Isaac. That . . . I was not expecting. "He mentioned having a conversation with you in the new year, but he said that he never forbade you to see me or anything. Just to be careful because I don't know about"—she pauses at a panicked look from Virgil—"about you know what. Well, now I do, and I'd like to hear a real reason for why you ghosted me."

"I didn't want to scare—"

"Bullshit," she hisses. "And yes, I'm scared. I'm fucking terrified, but at least I'm being honest with myself. Are you?"

Isaac swallows and looks at the ground. "My whole life . . . my sister has protected me. It's, like, her thing. Even when we fight, she still does it. Last year, I finally did something on my own, and I . . . It was horrible. The screaming . . ." He scrubs at his face. "Your family has done a good job of keeping you out of the dangerous parts of being around all this. I just . . . I don't know that I'm strong enough to do the same."

Well, fuck.

"Don't I get to decide what I am or am not a part of?" Mia says.

Isaac hunches his shoulders.

Mia shakes her head. "I am so done with everyone thinking I'm some precious princess who needs protecting. Don't act like you're doing something noble for my sake. Maybe if you want your sister to see you as an adult and stop protecting you like you're a little kid, you should stop acting like one."

Isaac's eyes get big, and Mia whips around and stomps away.

Me and Virgil look at each other.

Well, that was not how that was supposed to go. I was expecting more of a tearful reconciliation, but I'm on Mia's side. Isaac fumbled this.

Isaac turns to Virgil. "I don't get it. She's mad at me now?"

"Your first mistake was being helped with your relationship by these two," Nolan drawls, shaking his head. "Yikes." He decides to exit on that note, heading toward the doors without saying anything else.

I slide my hands down my face. "Ignoring her to protect her?" I say. "You didn't want to run that genius idea by literally any woman you know?"

Isaac hunches his shoulders. "I just . . . I can't do this right now," he mumbles, heading up the stairs after his sister.

"Encouraging," Virgil says to me, his voice flat.

"He's the one who fucked up! I didn't know he was doing all that!"

Virgil takes a seat at one of the nearby tables, laying his head on the surface. "Nolan is right. I don't think either one of us is equipped for matchmaking."

"What happened to your rizz?" I ask, dropping into the chair across from him.

He quirks a smile, and my chest warms. "I get it, though," he says.

"You get the misogyny?"

"No, he definitely should have been up front with her as much as he could. But I get why he's scared. The whole Bernie thing was hard for him. It was for me too. And Jules . . . Imagine if he had bitten you. It's a risk to be in proximity to us. It's one thing when someone volunteers to be in our lives and another when they don't understand what they're getting into. And honestly, I don't think Mia gets it yet. It's too fresh."

I lick my lips. I don't want to think about what would have happened if my brother beheaded me. But Jules probably thinks about it all the time. He even mentioned it to me. To be a Monster is to be in constant fear of hurting the people you love.

I lay my head on the table so me and Virgil are facing each other. "You all keep acting like you're a minute away from losing control again. You aren't."

Virgil meets my eyes. "Just because we have control doesn't mean we feel in control."

I think of the monster inside and swallow. Yeah, I guess I do have some idea of what that feels like.

CHAPTER THIRTY

Me, Virgil, Nolan, and Corey stop short as Riley's house comes into view. It's not the house itself, which remains unchanged from the last time I was here. Still cookie-cutter and immaculately kept, I'm sure by someone Riley's parents hired. No. It's the fact that Margot is standing on the front stoop.

"What's up?" I ask her as we approach.

Margot grins. "I'm here for the meeting."

"What meeting?"

Her smile drops. "Cut the crap. It's bad enough that Henry has me out of the loop, but now you guys too? Fuck that. I know you're doing something, and you aren't very sneaky, so Henry knows too. You children require supervision."

"You're only a year older than us."

"In number, but I feel many years more mature somehow."

Virgil asks, "What's Henry leaving you out of?"

Margot grinds her teeth. "How he plans to handle the potential assassination of the only man fighting to give my brother more rights. It is, apparently, not my concern." She looks at me. "I can only assume this is something to do with your mother, and you've made no secret of suspecting Carrigan. And I admit that I also find his sudden absence suspicious." She turns and raps her knuckles on the door.

I sigh. Margot isn't the sort of person who you can shrug off. If she wants to be involved, fine.

Riley greets us in the entryway and blinks at Margot. "Oh. It's you."

"Glad to meet again under better circumstances."

Riley gives me the stink eye, like I'm the cause of this. "Fine, whatever." She leads us into the living room, where she prepares drinks with Corey's help while I catch Margot up on everything we've done thus far.

"For someone who didn't want to be involved, you seem very involved now," Virgil says, eyeing Nolan, who has spread out on an armchair, both of his legs casually thrown over the arm of it.

Nolan shrugs. "I'm curious."

When we left the fort, it wasn't empty-handed. Corey and Riley collected the stack of books and journals that were hidden inside. Because Riley is currently the only one with access to the sickle, no one else should be able to check on the cache either. In the week since, the two of them have been poring over the books, and now we're getting to hear their findings.

"What happened to Malachi and Jackson?" I ask. "I didn't notice any boy shoes."

Last year, Riley's house also doubled as a sort of QBSS

headquarters. Though Malachi is obviously no longer the president, I figured he might still keep living here, if only to mess with her.

Riley says, "Our new clubhouse was finished at the end of last year. It's large enough to accommodate all the artifact-wielding members, and so this house is back to being a private residence."

"Where's the new headquarters?" I ask.

"It's on the lakeshore," Margot says. "By the water treatment plant, right?"

I gape. "Wait, is it that big ass mansion we passed on the way here? Oh my God, it *is,* isn't it?"

Riley eyes Margot. "You keeping tabs on it?"

She shrugs. "It's a mansion; it's not a secret."

Riley and Corey bring over the steaming mugs and set them out on coasters for everyone. "Can we get to the matter at hand now?" Riley asks. I make a grand gesture for her to continue. "I'll let Corey lead."

Corey digs her notebook out from her bag, flipping to the page marked with a ribbon. "What we found were some journals of Joseph Lawrence, but also a notebook of new research. Like, very recent." Corey holds up a leatherbound journal that does look newer, now that I think about it. She grins. "And it's stolen."

"Or found," Riley adds.

Corey pouts, preferring the drama of what she said. "The writing in the notebook has annotations in the margins, commenting on what was written. And those annotations match the writing in some of the other notes we found. Making it seem like they stole, or *found,* the newer notebook. And most importantly . . ." She opens the book and shows a handwritten note on the front page of the journal. It says, *Happy Birthday, Love, Dad.*

"Okay . . . ," I say. "So it was a birthday present?"

Margot actually throws her head back and groans. "Please use your critical thinking skills and ask more relevant questions—like, who is 'Dad'?"

Why are all my friends so goddamn antagonistic?

"Glad you asked!" Corey says. "It's Cyrus Shaw's dedication! It took me a while to do cross-referencing and the like, but it is definitely his writing. And it's the only writing in the whole book that's his. Meaning the late Doctorate Shaw likely gifted the blank notebook to one of his sons, and that son is the one who was originally researching the Osseous and potentially is the puppet master who set everything with Bernie in motion. It makes sense. Someone in power, just like we thought. And that's not all." She says to me, "Remember that I asked for samples of your mom's and grandma's writing?" I nod. "I feel confident that the annotations and notes in the margins are from Pattie."

I sit up straight. "She could have taken it from Carrigan. Or maybe he even gave it to her?"

"He could have tasked her with finding the Osseous," Margot adds. "He would have needed someone who could access QBSS, after all. Get her to do the dirty work, and then . . ."

"Kill her once it was done," I say, clenching my fists in my lap. "Can you confirm that it's Carrigan's writing?" I ask. "That Cyrus gifted the notebook to him?"

Corey shakes her head. "I couldn't tell. . . . The writing is super messy, and there are some similarities with each of the Shaw brothers' handwriting. They don't have as much personal flair as the late Doctorate Shaw or Pattie. It could be any of them. Honestly, I got lucky being able to match any of this writing. It's not an exact science either."

"It's gotta be Carrigan. Why would Adam even be researching this? And James is dead."

Nolan says, "Doesn't mean James couldn't have been doing research before he died. And you could question why Carrigan would be looking into this as much as any brother."

"But why leave all this at the cache?" Virgil asks. "Did Pattie fail, or did she realize it was dangerous and hide it? Besides that, she would have needed a QBSS president to open the cache for her. Unless she put her bones in the sickle?"

Riley shakes her head. "No. The sickle is the most protected artifact. It is possible, however, that her handler was a past president. Which makes it even more confusing why they wouldn't have shared the information she found. Unless she didn't even let them know. Either way, Pattie must have realized that she couldn't get the Osseous for whatever reason and left the research so someone else could. Probably August, whose bones she planted in the chain."

"The inscription doesn't sit right with me," Margot murmurs. "Cyrus never favored Carrigan. I can't imagine him giving him something with 'Love, Dad' on it."

I shrug. "Maybe he stole the notebook from one of his brothers when it was empty. Could explain why he kept the inscription. To stick it to them or something. Daddy-issues people have a lot going on." Margot doesn't say anything further, but her expression remains pensive. "What about their notes on the Osseous? Anything useful?"

Riley sips from her cup and crosses her legs. "Only that the original writer was aware that QBSS likely had it. And they felt sure that it's a weapon. According to their notes on Weiss, it was something that he and Lawrence created accidentally. Weiss wanted

to destroy it, and Lawrence wanted to keep studying it."

"Which is in line with our theory that Bernie's puppet master didn't want to use it but to get rid of it," Corey adds. "And that's where Lawrence's journals come in!"

"They're less journals than random notes," Riley says. "The sort of thing you'd write on a spare piece of paper and keep just in case. Except he shoved them into one journal. Like, some of this is literally grocery lists." She raises a finger. "But whoever was putting together all this information—Pattie, I guess—made some sort of connection. Because she ripped out passages from Lawrence's notes and collected them on a blank page in the Shaw journal. The last pasted Lawrence passage says, 'And with this, the Osseous will create a meeting between God and patella.'"

"Patella? What's that?" I ask.

Riley says, "It's the name of the bone of the kneecap. They mean it will bring a God to their knees."

"That's it, then," I say. "A weapon that kills Gods."

"It seems to be."

Corey says, "The first passage is, 'Where the canons bellow and the dead bow to the bay and the blade, I remembered why I am a pacifist.'"

"Fort Henry," Virgil says.

"Not just Fort Henry. 'The canons bellow,' as in, below. The cache was underground. And 'bow' to 'the blade'—the sickle is a bowed blade, as in curved. Scythes, too. We used the sickle in a cache below the cannons and found notes from the dead. We found their memories."

I rub my temples. "It's a fucking scavenger hunt."

"It's a scavenger hunt!" Corey squeals. "With riddles as clues!"

"And the Osseous at the end," Riley adds with significantly less enthusiasm.

"For fuck's sake," I say with a groan.

"It's not that bad," Virgil says. "Pattie already picked out the passages for us. We just need to solve the clues."

Corey says, "The only thing we haven't figured out are these symbols Pattie wrote in the margins beside the clues. One is definitely a sickle, but no idea about the others. A code, maybe? But we're sure we can at least proceed with what we have now."

With one mystery after another, it's refreshing to have a map to the end.

The power to kill a God, and finally, it feels like I'm close enough to taste it.

It's convenient that Henry's house is between Riley's home and campus, so me, Virgil, and Nolan are able to make our way here right after our Osseous chat.

Laira meets us at the door in a maroon jogging set, her locs piled in a bun on her head. We take off our shoes, and she leads us to the end of the hall, where we head down a set of stairs, the passageway made of stone. Medieval-looking.

"Sex dungeon," Nolan mouths.

I snort.

At the bottom is a door that brings us into a large underground chamber. The ceiling isn't very high but pretty good for a basement. Eight feet at least. On the right wall is a cache of hanging weapons.

Henry is already in the room waiting for us, leaning against the wall. He pushes off and comes to stand in front of me while Laira deposits herself on a couch in the corner, slouching into the

cushions. He nods to the weapons. "Each one was used by a member of my family as their chosen weapon when they became Masters." He walks to the wall and taps a thick broadsword. "My father's." He gestures to another, thinner sword—a fencing one, it seems like. "My mother's."

I ask, "Which one is yours?"

"I prefer to parry with my mind."

I roll my eyes. I'm convinced that he spends his spare time thinking up mysterious lines to use.

Henry is unfazed by my attitude, likely used to it by now. "I've heard good reviews about your progress from Margot. She feels that August's second-evolution mastery has come along nicely. Meaning we can focus on the third-evolution skills. August has done well enough with healing, but regeneration is one of those things that tends to kick in instinctively." I read as much in Corey's notes from the first Mastery group meeting. "She's also managed to use Nolan's fog and Virgil's roar by fluke. But I do think there's more to be discovered."

"Like what?" I ask.

"Virgil hasn't even begun to explore the limits of his body, I would gather." Henry gestures to Nolan. "How did you come to discover your third-evolution skills?"

Nolan shrugs. "My dad taught me to imagine what I could do. He says all skills have limits, but they can also have levels. Expansions to unlock even if most Monsters won't have more than one to three third-evolution skills."

"Exactly," Henry says. "Remember, August cannot use a skill that you yourself haven't mastered. You need to push yourselves. Consider what you may be able to achieve." He gestures to Laira,

who comes over, stretching out her already secreting arm.

"What is this?" Nolan asks Henry.

"An exercise. Using hallucinations to help you feel the pressure of a real fight. August and I have already done this in our private training sessions."

Nolan looks at me, and I nod. "It helps," I say. After all, it helped me realize that I'm still not strong enough to avenge Mom.

Henry says, "Better you meet a challenger who pushes you here in your minds before the actual arena."

I place my hand on Laira's arm, and Virgil licks his lips, reaching out, but Laira pulls away. "You boys touch the other arm."

Virgil obeys, holding onto her left while I grasp her right. Nolan is the only holdout. I say, "Do you want to win or not?" Finally, he puts his hand down.

It takes a few moments for the environment to change, the room shifting and transforming.

A Monster roars across the room, a shadow that feels familiar. Hulking and massive, ten feet tall on two legs with dark bulging muscles, five-inch-long claws, and pearly white fangs covered in saliva. Somewhere in the back of my mind, I know the room is too small for it, but it still looms over me.

The monster inside me opens its eyes. This is usually the point where I would release it. But that's when it's just me, Henry, and Laira. I can't be sure that I won't hurt Virgil or Nolan.

The shadow races across the room toward me, and I throw myself out of the way. Virgil in Monster form smashes into its side, leaning with the spikes on his body, though it kicks him in the stomach, unbothered by the sting of the blades. Nolan steps forward, fog pooling around him, covering everything. I don't see him but rather

hear the pounding of his paws as he runs at the Monster.

I wait, watching the white smoke, and then see him fly back. I have the sense to jump out of the way, tucking and rolling.

The monster hurls itself against the barrier of my mind, gnashing its teeth.

"What are you waiting for?" Henry says from behind me. "Are you just going to watch?"

I grasp my blades in my hand and sprint forward, jumping several feet in the air and coming down at the beast, who bats me aside like a fly. I hit the wall and gasp, spitting out blood. I force myself up in time to watch the Monster rip a chuck out of Virgil and slash Nolan across the chest.

Blood splashes onto my face. Stinging and hot.

Both boys lie on the ground.

The monster is thrashing in my mind, but I'm frozen, staring at their bodies. Virgil's chest is moving too fast, and Nolan's too slow. The shadow raises both its massive claws and slams them down, right into each boy.

The monster inside roars where no one can hear.

No one but me.

Mom dead.

Virgil dead.

Nolan dead.

And me, here again. Alone. The sole survivor.

What's the point in holding back so I can't hurt anyone when there's no one left?

I fly at the shadow with a roar that shakes the walls, ripping and hacking. It stumbles but doesn't fall away, advancing on me. It reaches out to slice me, but I'm too fast, and it only clips my shoulder. I don't

even feel it. All I care about is ripping this thing apart.

Blades come to my hands without even thinking about them. No, not blades. The shape isn't quite right—too jagged at the ends and too rounded along the body. It doesn't matter. I throw them. I slide between its legs, lifting the blades and tearing through flesh as I go, black blood splashing on my face. I spin, whipping out more blades. Something in me tears with every single one. Still, it doesn't hurt.

And it's not enough.

I need to make the shadow suffer.

I sink my teeth into its thigh and close my eyes as it screams. I don't know when I start laughing. Who knows? But every slice brings another giggle out of my mouth. There's enough blood that I'm soaked in it. It makes my skin tacky and my clothes cling. But none of that matters while I'm making this thing scream.

"That's enough," Henry says, materializing in the corner.

I hack away at the Monster again, taking a chunk of its back. It cries like something weak and frail.

"I said, *that's enough.*"

The blade I throw nicks Henry on the cheek. It's metallic and shiny.

The shadow Monster bleeds away until the room reveals the truth of reality. Nolan and Virgil across the room, fine but confused, furrowed brows and wide eyes, staring between me and Henry.

"What happened?" Nolan asks.

"I . . . You were there," I say. "You . . . you saw."

Virgil shakes his head. "No . . . nothing happened to us, and then you were moving around the room on your own. Faster than I've ever seen you move."

I stare at Henry, the crimson slice on his cheek.

Something laughs in the back of my mind. The monster there, licking black ichor off its paws.

Henry says, "The boys were there to prime you. Only you touched the secretion. I suspected you would show greater progress if they were nearby. Not a necessity for use of skills, but given your personality, could be a benefit. Which we saw." He waves around at the room. At the gouges in the walls and floor where I must have thrown the blades. But . . . I didn't even bring my knives with me.

"August," Virgil says, laying a hand on my shoulder. I glance at his fingers; they shake the slightest bit. "Those knives . . . they came from your body. I . . . I mean, I grow my claws through my fingernails, but I've never, like, separated anything. But you did."

Henry says, "As you said yourself, Virgil, it's an ability that you have mastered; she just used it in a different way. The base skill is the same." I expect a reprimand from Henry for hurting him. I mean, it wasn't an incidental injury, I did it because he'd annoyed me. Instead, the professor grins. "See what you can do with that power of yours? And look, you unleashed it and we're all still standing. A little cut on me, sure, but otherwise no harm done."

The monster purrs, pressing itself against my back—a caress, almost.

He's right. I didn't hurt Virgil or Nolan like I was worried I would.

And I was stronger than before. Having something to fight for, people to fight for, that helped.

I can do this. Virgil's monster—the rage and bloodlust—I can give it purpose and direction. As long as I'm brave enough to let it go when I need it.

CHAPTER THIRTY-ONE

Tonight, the underground chamber where we had the welcome banquet has been decked out in even more finery for the event before the quarterfinals. They've erected a stage at the far end of the room, raised four feet or so off the ground. It's difficult to dress up plain concrete walls and floors, but they've done their best with thick crimson drapes from floor to ceiling, matching the napkins on the tables. Otherwise, the linens are cream-colored, covering the chairs and tables, with dramatic tall centerpieces of winter bouquets with masks on sticks tucked into the arrangements.

I take a deep breath. *You just* had *to wear a corset, August. You just had to fucking wear it.*

But how many other times am I going to attend a masquerade ball where I do a dance performance? I mean, at least once more when defending next year. But not for the first time again! I had to take the excuse to dress up.

Honestly, the corset isn't squeezing me much more than my strapless bra would have, but it's not comfortable. Given the fact that we're dancing, I couldn't do a huge skirt; instead, the black, silver-studded corset leads to a skirt with rouching in the front and small black bows on either side of my hips to keep my legs free, and it drapes in the back. I've chosen fishnets to cover my legs, because of course. And the sleeves of the bolero I wear are a delicate black lace dotted with Swarovski crystals.

With the help of a video tutorial, I managed to get a curl out of my box braids and pinned them into an updo. I potentially have a hundred bobby pins in my hair right now. Corey helped with my makeup, which required more of a dramatic flair than I'm used to. It takes her longer maneuvering with her missing fingers, so I appreciate her spending the time on it. She did amazing, too, creating an ombre effect with my eyeshadow and even sticking tiny crystals at the corners of my lids, plus a stellar blood-red lip with a creamy brown liner.

Finally, the look was finished with a mask. I was initially annoyed about it covering the makeup, but you can still see the look through the larger-than-normal eye holes. The design is some unholy mixture of wolf and fox that's both grotesque and gorgeous. Every Bachelor and Master wears a mask to match their partner's Monster form, and in my case having two means I get a mash-up.

Nolan stands on my left and Virgil on my right as we take our seats in the middle of the room. The tables in front are reserved for senior Masters and the Doctorate. There's an hour of dancing followed by dinner, and then mingling—aka networking. Not my favorite pastime, but it's a must in these competitions, apparently.

As the lights dim, the first pair comes onto the stage.

"Nervous?" Virgil whispers, close enough to my ear that I shiver. He's wearing cream from head to toe—his suit, shoes, and even his mask. The mask is a maw curving into an impressive display of teeth. It's obvious it's a wolf, even though it's not his coloring.

"I'm fine." If anything, I'm impatient.

Nolan seems to feel the same way, if his tapping feet are any indication. Like Virgil, he's in a cream ensemble, but his mask, of course, is of a fox. The costuming was Silas and Zokia's idea, to mirror their roles of lambs going to the slaughter.

With each partnership called to the stage that isn't us, my dress feels tighter. Constricted. Margot and Isaac do a dance that's actually sweet—a girl and her dog type theme. According to Virgil, Isaac is in a "don't want to talk about it" mood regarding Mia, so that blew up in our faces. On her end, she said that he knew her number if he wanted to talk to her.

Ellis and Barbie take the stage. She's not dressed in pink as I expected, but black. At one point the lights go out, and their outfits glow with bone embroidery. They become dancing skeletons and finish falling into their graves together.

A volunteer comes to our table to lead us backstage, since we'll be next after the performers heading up. I catch Barbie's eye as she leaves, and they're as cool as glass in winter.

We take off our shoes, leaving them with a volunteer, and then crowd in the wings. My hands shake, and I clench them. It's not like this counts for anything competition-wise, but still, I want to do well.

I glance at Virgil, whose lips are moving like he's counting the steps, and then Nolan, who's staring impassively at the pair onstage doing a tap routine. Virgil tried to broach the topic of what had

happened in the last training session, but I struggled to explain beyond the fact that I'd used the monster. I wasn't sure how he felt about seeing me like that. Honestly, I didn't want to know how he might see me when I took advantage of a side of himself that he despised.

"Even though this doesn't really matter," I say, "I'll be doing my best up there."

Virgil says, "It matters to *you.*" I swallow, watching the dark amber staring at me from within the confines of the white mask. "If it's important to you, it's important to me. We're a team, right?" He holds out his hand to me, elbow bent, smiling.

Even after seeing me use the monster, Virgil is still content to stay by my side. Sure, he doesn't have as much choice in the situation as he should, but he's still here. Maybe he hates the monster inside him, but he doesn't hate it within me.

I reach out and grasp his hand, pulling close. "I just want it to be perfect."

Virgil laughs. "When have you ever been perfect? The best thing about you is that even when you smash something to pieces, you only make it better than it was before." I fight not to gasp, because it feels like I've been breathing through a straw all semester and I've only now managed the full range of my lungs. "I've been perfect my whole life. The reason I'm here now is because you helped me break the rules. That's why I went onto the Murphy compound with you, why I broke into Georgia's house with you, why I keep doing not entirely recommended things with you. Because some, *not all,* but some things need to be broken. And you know that better than anyone."

The monster stares back at me through Virgil's eyes.

Now I have something to lose. I have Dad, and Jules, and Bailey.

Virgil, and Corey, and Riley, and Margot. Last year, I had nothing to be afraid of because I had destroyed everything I had left.

A volunteer says, "Okay, you can get in your starting positions."

Me and Virgil drop our hands, and Nolan's eyes follow us. He said nothing during our conversation. Just stood on the periphery.

I walk onto the stage, doing my best to estimate where to stand while Nolan and Virgil walk to the other side. The stage is dark. I wait for the music, trying to control the thumping in my chest to no avail.

It's one thing to do the routine in front of Silas and Zokia, and another to do it in front of a room full of people. I've never danced like this before, for others instead of myself.

No. I *am* dancing for myself. Why should I dance for them? I spent months performing for these people. Following their rules and customs, and kneeling at the altar of their Gods.

Henry was right. Nolan, too. I've lost something of myself to this society. I'm less than I was. It's one thing to follow the rules and another to tame myself to their wills.

And if Virgil, the pinnacle of rule-following, has told me to break some of them, who am I to say no?

The monster purrs, sliding its paws onto my shoulders, resting its soft cheek against mine. There is no cage. There never needed to be. This isn't something to be restrained, because it's a part of me. I made it so when me and Virgil brought our bond to life with a roar.

The music begins, and I move. I stretch my arms and kick my legs. When I drop to all fours it feels natural, as if this is how I should be as I prowl toward Virgil and Nolan.

I leap onto Virgil, pressing his shoulders into the ground while he grasps my waist and lifts me—a touch that used to be tentative,

but now he holds me like he's not sure he plans to let go, fingers digging into the sides of my corset. I tug the red cloth hidden inside his jacket while he holds the other end.

Nolan leaps at me, and we roll. In practice, the movement was often half-hearted, but now he tackles me. When we roll over each other, every point in our bodies presses against one another. When I land on top, something comes alive in those still-water eyes.

He slips out of my grasp as Virgil pulls him away, tugging him close to his chest, and they press their cheeks together. What was in practice a light touch is now an insistent melding of skin.

We twirl and leap around each other, maneuvering the red cloth between us. There's no chasteness. No moves are being marked. Every single one of us is going full out. Fingers and nails dig in, and something rips, and I don't care.

The touches and glances that were missing are here now, even in the way Nolan caresses Virgil's face, and Virgil leans into it, grabbing the other boy by his lapels, until I rush between them and we tumble to the floor. There are holds that are too hard and others that are so gentle they almost seem to not happen at all. Every single part of my body is heated and at attention.

When they've both been torn apart, I bare my teeth and swear that there are too many inside my mouth.

The two boys lie dead at my feet, covered in scarlet.

The lights go out.

I hold the pose until the music has stopped.

Applause thunders through the room, and I stumble off the stage. Our volunteer ushers us into the backstage area.

The next pair moves toward the stage, and one of them whispers to the other, "Would you look at that? Even Wilds can be trained."

Nolan mutters something about the bathroom and leaves, his shoes unlaced.

I reach out, but it's Virgil who grasps his hand.

Nolan whips back, eyes hard. "What?" he says.

"Don't let them get to you."

Nolan laughs. "That's not what's getting to me." He jerks his head at the stage. "Look at me, performing like a trained pony. My goal has always been to escape the society, not entrench myself in it further." Nolan tugs himself free of Virgil and throws me a look that's too difficult to decipher—it's wounded, almost, but I can't say how I've hurt him. "When this is over and I've gotten what I want, *we* will be over. I'll be free of the both of you."

That was always the plan. This trio isn't meant to be permanent. And yet, the thought of Nolan leaving us behind doesn't feel like a restoration of what used to be. How it's *supposed* to be. It feels like a loss.

Whipping the backstage curtain aside, Nolan disappears in a swish of fabric.

Me and Virgil return to our seats and watch the remainder of the performances, including Jules and Natalie, who do a bit with a lot of swishing dark fabric. My brother is concentrating so hard that his face is almost stonelike. He really does struggle to loosen up.

Nolan doesn't return.

As I expected he would, Adam comes over to congratulate us on our performance. Like Henry, I'm starting to wonder what I did to earn the favor of this man. Usually, attention from powerful men is conditional. Yet Adam doles it out to me like an overeager parent on Halloween. It's something that I haven't taken nearly enough advantage of.

I intend to correct that.

CHAPTER THIRTY-TWO

Riley

I sit with a coffee near the wall on the upper level across from CoGro. I told Corey that I would meet her here since she wants to grab a smoothie before we head to the library. The space is packed now that most midterms have finished up and students are emerging from their study caves. I cracked down hard over reading week, chugging energy drinks and coffee like it was my job so I could study for twelve hours a day. Usually, I strike more of a balance, but between Osseous stuff and QBSS council duties, my spare time has been zapped dry.

Corey comes up the stairs and beams at me, waving before motioning to the CoGro line. I give her a thumbs-up. It should honestly be illegal to be as cute as she is in that puffy pink jacket. Really, she and Sammie are like night and day, but they both have that sort of infectious energy.

When Corey walks back with her smoothie, grinning at me, my face gets hot.

I don't know what I'm supposed to do with these thoughts. Ignore them, I guess. I always have. It's easy because I still like guys. How often do you need to notice how attractive a girl is before it becomes *a thing*?

I stand and sling my bag over my shoulder. "Ready to go?"

She nods. "Yup. I've got some good guesses about the next riddle. I think we can probably crack it today."

When the pressure is stacked against me, all I can do is hope to learn and grow stronger. And yet, I cannot help but feel that I am many years too late.

I have my own theories too. Chances are we have the same thoughts. It seems like whenever we meet, we're both automatically on the same page.

Corey freezes in place so swiftly that I almost smack into her. In front of us is an East Asian–looking girl with platinum-blond hair, skin so pale it seems to be glowing, and literally the same jacket that Corey is wearing. The girl looks Corey up and down with her dark eyes. "We did always have a bad habit of accidentally matching."

I find myself stepping forward so I'm beside Corey, who's yet to say anything despite the fact that she seems to know this girl. "Riley," I say by way of greeting. "And you are . . . ?"

The girl slides her eyes to me. "You should know."

I can't help the bark of a laugh that comes out. "Well, I don't. Sorry that you seem to have overestimated your importance." There's no need to be snippy with her, but I don't like the effect that she's had on Corey, making the girl who was seconds ago beaming and bright turn sullen and silent.

"My God, you love an assertive girl, don't you?" she says to Corey. "Ready to jump to your aid at any moment."

"We're *friends,*" I say. *Just friends.*

Corey hunches. "Is there something you need?"

"Not from you. Apparently you don't need anything from me, either, going behind my back and summoning Ellis all the way over here."

My jaw tenses. This girl is talking about Corey's brother in a familiar way. Meaning this is likely Barbie. Corey's ex.

Corey's forehead scrunches. "I haven't talked to Ellis."

"No, you had Virgil text him."

"No," Corey says, voice firm. "I didn't."

It takes a moment before Barbie's eyes go wide, and she laughs. "Holy shit. *They* went behind *your* back and reached out to him. Wow. I guess now you know what it feels like to be betrayed."

"We're going," I say, grabbing Corey's hand and maneuvering her toward the stairs. She follows without a hint of resistance, confirming my theory that she wanted to escape.

The two of us are silent as we walk out of the ARC and down the block to Stauffer. What were Virgil and August thinking? Probably Nolan, too. They're a three-headed nightmare. I know Corey has a messed-up relationship with her brother, but the girl isn't that fragile. They should have just told her. Which isn't even getting into why they needed Ellis at all.

I turn toward Corey as she slips her hand out of mine. "Don't want people to get the wrong idea," she says.

"I don't—I didn't say that like . . . I just—"

Corey shakes her head. "It's fine. I don't think I've done well at hiding how I feel, so . . ." She sighs. "I don't want it to be weird. I want us to keep being friends."

The way she feels . . . ? Wait, about me? I think of how much

August pestered me to come to Corey's birthday, and about that label of "hot friend" that August insisted she hadn't given me. It had never once occurred to me that Corey might have any interest in me.

Just friends.

Corey walks into the library and my hand twitches at my side. I grip it into a fist and follow her. We make our way upstairs to the room I booked. As soon as we sit down, I say, "You're not made of glass. They didn't need to hide it like that."

She ducks her head. "They probably thought they were protecting me. It's not their fault. I could barely say two words to Barbie, and none to Ellis."

Before she can curl her left hand under her right, I reach out and hold it, stopping her. It's a habit I don't even know that she's conscious of—hiding her hand with the missing fingers. "I'm afraid too. I'm scared of what will happen if I can't find this weapon. If they take the presidency away. Of what my parents and my grandparents will think. What the rest of QBSS will think. I'm afraid of . . ." I trail off, staring at our linked hands. I'm afraid that she'll let go again. I could ignore the little observations I made about her, the feelings that bloomed when we interacted, when it was just me. When I didn't know that she might . . . I look into Corey's eyes, the exact shade of the bark of the tree outside my house in summer. "Do you think I'm weak because of that?"

"I would never think that," she breathes.

"Then don't think it about yourself." I pull my hand back and cross my arms. "And your ex is a bitch."

Corey snorts. "You shouldn't say that."

"I call it like it is."

"She's just upset. She and Ellis were always close. I think she thought the three of us were close. But really, Ellis and I were close with *her*, but not with each other. Sometimes I think . . ." She bites her lip. "Sometimes I think I only wanted to date her because then I could have something he couldn't." She cracks a smile. "Shitty, eh?"

"As shitty as staying with a boy because he makes you look good?" I ask.

"You ended it."

"So did you."

She shakes her head. "By ghosting her."

"Better than pinning her to a wall with bone magic."

Corey laughs then, the mirth spreading to her whole face, and I sag a little. She says, "You must have liked him at some point, though, didn't you?"

"I did. He's a bit of a follower, but he's kind. A little goofy. I loved him, really." The problem was that whenever I was with Jackson, I was thinking about Sammie. When I wanted to go to a new restaurant or store, I thought to go with her first. If I saw something funny online, I sent her the meme. It was never that I didn't love Jackson; it was that I loved Sammie more.

"And for you, were you ever really going to be happy being with second best?"

I clear my throat. "What are your theories about this riddle?" I need something to focus on so my thoughts can stop whirling.

"Oh! I was thinking maybe a library? Like, getting lost in the stacks and learning? But when Lawrence was attending Queen's, the first library wasn't even built yet. So he could only have meant Summerhill, right?"

I shake my head. "Summerhill is a society building. How could he have gotten in there to hide anything?"

"But the oldest library is Douglas, and that wasn't built until 1924. How old would he have been then?"

I do the mental math. "Like eighty-six."

It takes a moment before both of our mouths drop open. "He said he was many years too late!" Corey says.

"Because it was so far after the time he was a student!" I add.

"Dr. Weiss had passed by then too. I wonder if he meant that, as well. Like, he was hiding the Osseous, but the only other man who knew about it and had wanted it destroyed was dead."

"Now, the challenge will be finding where in Douglas he hid it."

"I found something else, too." She reaches into her backpack and withdraws one of the journals. We'd split them up to look through. As she does, I also notice a familiar book whose spine is blank. The travel book that her brother got her.

"You've been reading it?" I ask. "The book that Ellis got you."

"Sometimes . . ." She shrugs like it's not a big deal. "It's interesting."

"Sorry, I interrupted you."

"Oh, right, uh, so this passage says, 'The three of us are brothers in death: mine, and his, and the one who started it all. One of us an origin, and he and I, thieves both. We thought only to make instruments of death with a life. He with his Monsters, and me with mine.' I think he's talking about Patient Zero. But I don't get how that was connected to QBSS. You guys didn't have anything to do with Francis."

"Thieves . . . Wait, so, Patient Zero is the origin of the Monster mutation, yes?"

"In a sense, yes. He's not the only Patient Zero–type person, so technically they're all the origin. But Francis was the first of his kind that Dr. Weiss discovered."

"And something they stole from him . . . Well, Weiss changed the mutation with the serum. I suppose someone could view that as stealing? Like he created something new from Francis." It was shaky, though. "But our artifacts are only made from our . . ." A chill snakes down my back.

From our bones.

How the artifacts have power is something that has never been explained to us. It was said to be a gift from our founder. Something he created that, when embedded with our bones, gave us gifts. The power came from him.

Except it didn't.

He with his Monsters, and me with mine.

Patient Zero's bones are in our artifacts. That's why they work against Monsters. That's why there's a finite number of them. Why we can't make more. When Joseph Lawrence left the society, he took Patient Zero's bones with him. That's why he and Weiss had that huge falling out. And that's why the Osseous is named as it is. It must be made purely of bone instead of mixed with metal and gold. An artifact with maybe the highest concentration of Francis's bones. And I doubt they waited for him to die naturally to take advantage of his body.

An instrument of death that cost a man his life.

"Riley?" Corey asks.

"I . . . I need to go. I'm sorry, I just . . . I need to check on something."

I'm up and out of the chair before she can say another word. I

practically run home, throwing my bag on the floor in the entryway and pulling out my phone. While it rings, I pace, willing her to pick up.

The line clicks. "To what do I owe the pleasure?" Grandma says on the other end, voice chipper.

"Did you know whose bones were in the artifacts? Bones not given but taken." The silence on the other end is too loud. They always said *"bones given"* like it was an iron-clad rule, and I never questioned it. "Did you know?!"

"Don't raise your voice with me, Riley Jane."

I snap my mouth shut.

She sighs on the other end of the line. "You should have just practiced more with the sickle and challenged that boy again. Not made these promises to go after this artifact and—"

"*You knew.*"

"I did not know. I had some inkling. My grandad was prone to loose lips by his fourth brandy on Christmas evening. I used to sit at his knee and listen to all he had to say about Joseph Lawrence. Of course, he was just a child then. Six when Lawrence died. But I guess Lawrence had an eager tongue when he'd had a brandy too. He asked my grandad if he didn't think our enterprise and the society were two halves of the same dirty coin. That he'd done his best to shine our side, but the grime of theirs was inescapable because we were made from the same bit of copper. So yes, they bind their people to Monsters, and we bind ourselves to objects. Same as my grandad, I figure that means there is something fundamental shared between us."

"Then why do we act as if we're better than them?"

"Because we are," Grandma hisses. "Did you hear me, girl? We

are the shiny head of that coin. Money is a dirty business. Lawrence evened the odds for us. He wouldn't have had to do that if it weren't for Weiss. As it has always been, a white man raised a weapon, and we were forced to raise our own to survive. Do you dispute that?"

"No," I mutter.

"You want it to be pure and simple, yes? Well, it's not. Sometimes you have to get down in the ditch to wrestle your way out. You can't just stand on the edge and hope not to fall in."

"I am trying to be perfect for an imperfect institution," I spit out, choking back a sob. I have given everything that I am, everything that I have to QBSS. I turned my back on Sammie for QBSS. I give, and give, and at every turn I'm told that I'm not good enough. Not good enough for a society built off the bones of a man who'd only wanted help.

"Riley Jane," Grandma says. "Being perfect for the imperfect is how Black women keep our heads above the water."

The sob comes out then, despite my effort to keep it in. Tears come with it. I'm on my knees, bawling. "I'm tired," I wheeze. "I'm so tired of this."

Grandma sighs. "Your parents would give me hell for this, but Riley, baby, if you're tired, then stop. You are always going to be a winner because you are *you*. You don't need the title, or QBSS, or anything."

But I do. What would I be if I weren't a Historic? What did I sacrifice Sammie for, then? Why did I lose her?

I need QBSS so I won't spend my life regretting it.

"No more lies or concealment," I say, voice hoarse. "The woman who was president when Pattie Simmons was a spy for QBSS . . . I know you said you can't help, but please—"

"She's not going to tell you anything."

"I have to try to—"

"Listen to me," Grandma says. "She has a brain injury. Had a head-on car collision. I know you think I don't do anything for you, but I did meet with her, and I can say with confidence that she doesn't remember a damn thing. She could barely remember who I was. Retrograde amnesia, they said. She's great with people she sees every day, but good luck with anything from the past. Assuming she was this woman's handler, she didn't say a thing to anyone, as is our custom. Any information she had is gone."

It's so classic Grandma to act like she couldn't help me, then go behind my back and help anyway, then say nothing. Still, she tried. "Thanks," I say.

"Riley Jane?"

"Yes."

"Please think about what I said."

"I will."

I wouldn't. But I felt like I owed her the lie.

CHAPTER THIRTY-THREE

I sit on a supple leather couch between Virgil and Nolan while the Doctorate serves us tea and I contemplate whether interrogating Adam is my most ingenious idea or my worst one.

Adam's private residence isn't what I expected. I pictured dark, brooding colors and antique furniture like Henry's home. Instead, his house is on a street literally called Country Club Drive by the golf course and he has a bag of clubs by his door like that's something he just does on the daily. Sure, the leather furniture is nice, but it reminds me of the home of a rich uncle with bad taste, not the leader of an influential secret society. This man even has a Canadian flag out front—like, who casually puts up a flagpole?

Settling on the couch opposite us, Adam says, "I'm happy that I was finally able to take you up on that chat. I know last year was too busy, but my schedule is less constricted now that my movements are limited, given everything going on. You two didn't get

to talk to me on Doctorate Day, either, so I'm glad you asked to come by at the ball last night."

"Thanks for having us," I say. Pleasant as a peach. I can be when I want to.

Even Nolan is on his best behavior. While he never returned to last night's event, I let him know my intention to see what Adam might know about his brother's whereabouts, information relevant to both me and the Wilds. Without Henry pointing it out, I would have gone on assuming that Adam was just this nice. But there's something more there. Enough for him to trust me inside his home during a time when he's an active assassination target.

First, I'll confirm Carrigan's alibi. I can ask Adam about Carrigan's time at school with my mom too and see what he knows. Something has to bring up a clue we can go off of.

Adam says, "Sorry that I could only do this so early in the morning. And on a match day, too."

"We'll be fine," I insist. "We're in the afternoon rotation."

"Ah, good, good. Well, what sort of questions did you have? Henry is already a capable tutor, but I'll try to advise on whatever I can."

"Any updates on our entanglement?" Nolan asks.

My eye twitches, but I don't say anything.

Adam winces. "Not particularly. This would be easier if Dad were still around. My research has shown that exchanging more blood can sometimes heighten a blood bond, make it stronger. In the past, some who wanted to break a blood bond without Doctorate intervention tried draining as much blood as possible from one Monster and replacing it with donor blood, the idea being less shared blood between them. But it was unsuccessful." Adam wrings his hands. "There's more . . ."

"More?" There's a bark to Nolan's voice.

"Yes, well, I've been observing your bond. I admit that I didn't want to alarm you, so I tried to be discreet, approaching you at events and at your training to check in."

"Don't you need to, like, close your eyes and concentrate and stuff?" I ask.

"No . . . As I've become accustomed to seeing the links, I can do it with only a few minutes of observation with my eyes open."

That's why he keeps coming over to us at events. He was just trying to check our bond without freaking us out. It's nothing to do with me specifically. Shit. He might not tell us anything, then.

"May I ask what you discovered?" Virgil says.

Adam sighs. "The bond has changed shape. These ties are a lot more complicated than it seems on the surface. As time goes on, it has only tangled more. I fear that it's beyond me."

I chew the inside of my cheek. Is the bond reacting like that because of how much me and Virgil have been relying on Nolan? Or has he maybe, just a little, gotten attached to our trio?

"So it's unlikely to ever be undone," Nolan says, his voice flat.

"Yes. At this point, the only way to break the bond would be death."

Nolan keeps his expression neutral. Stiff and closed. Even if we win, he's not going to get away from us. This is permanent. Though on the bright side, we also can't be punished with a bond breaking. We can't have that fucked-up partial break thing done to us either. Or maybe it's worse in that we *can* be punished, but the only option is fatal.

"Well," I say. "As a consolation prize, maybe we can get an invite to that fancy Doctorate ball in November."

Virgil winces beside me. Too forward for him. I don't care. We

need to get something useful from this conversation, and if Adam doesn't actually favor me, then maybe guilt will help him get talkative.

Adam blinks. "Doctorate . . . oh! The one Dad used to throw. We didn't have it last year, but the year before we hadn't publicized that Dad passed that month and had to run it like usual. Such a mess. But I suppose there will be an expectation of one this year."

If Cyrus was dead by the time the Doctorate Ball happened the year before last, then he couldn't have been the one who sent the order for Kendrick to collect that video. Carrigan must have given the order, forging his dad's signature.

Adam continues, "Honestly, I find it to be kind of a nightmare. At the last one, I spent the whole time being accosted about succession plans. It was the worst." He laughs, and I fight to keep the smile on my face.

Professor Chen said that Adam hadn't been feeling well. That she hadn't seen him the whole night, and Henry even had gone to check on him. No, she said she'd *heard* that he might have been sick. But why would Adam lie to us about his attendance? I take a chance that I hope I won't regret. "Yeah, we talked with Professor Chen, who said she was lucky to get to chat with you, and that you seemed kind of stressed."

Virgil tenses at my side.

Adam says, "Yes, I was. We had a great conversation. She's done wonderfully in her position. I'm sure I'll put on a ball at the end of the year, and while we don't usually invite Masters-in-training, which I have no doubt you'll be by then, I'll see what I can do."

Why is he lying? Does he honestly not remember and wants to save face? Or is he hiding something?

I beam at him. "Thank you. Actually . . . can I use your bathroom?"

"Sure," Adam says. "There's one right by the entrance—"

"Do you mind if I use the upstairs one?" I ask, making a desperate face. "I have really bad bladder shyness, and if I feel like anyone can hear—"

"No, that's fine, go ahead. Second door on the right."

"Thank you!"

I rush toward the stairs with Virgil's and Nolan's eyes on me.

The first thing I do is go to the correct door and open and close it loudly. I stand in the hall, working to calm my breathing.

I ease open the doors to the other rooms. One is the primary bedroom, which I leave alone in favor of the office. I slip into the room and quietly close the door behind me.

It's not a large space, maybe the size of my dorm room, with a wooden desk in the middle, a window behind it, and wall-to-wall bookshelves on the right and left sides. The top of the bookshelves hold books, but the bottom halves are cupboards. I start opening them to see if there's anything of note inside.

I don't even know what I'm looking for, but I just need evidence of *something*. I mean, that journal could belong to any of Cyrus's sons. I didn't suspect Adam of anything until he lied to my face. But for me to believe he's involved with all this somehow, I would need to find something that tied him to Mom. Not just Pattie and the Osseous.

It hits me then. The video Kendrick turned over that was mysteriously lost. It was on a USB-C key. Whoever has that is the person who wanted to cover up the footage on there. Footage that could include Monster activity from the day Mom was killed.

Metal. It would smell like metal.

I close my eyes and inhale. This ability is as much mine as it is

Nolan's or Virgil's. I open my eyes and concentrate, smelling the bits of metal. I follow them to the desk, opening the drawers just in case. But they're things I expect. Staples and paper clips, and the computer itself.

Crouching on the ground, I sniff around and find an Allen wrench and a fallen screw under the desk.

Amazing, human metal detector. You're helping clean his office.

I pace around the room, pausing when a hint of a metal smell comes from the bookcase. I follow my nose, pressing the tip of it to the spines, ignoring how fucking weird this is, until I find where the scent is coming from.

It's a book of fables. The same one Amelia borrowed from the library that Adam said he had received a copy of from his mom, who had died when he was young. The moment I tug it out, something falls from between its pages.

I stoop and pick up a USB-C key. Neon green.

The rush of blood in my ears is so loud, it drowns out my thoughts.

I shove the book back into its spot while I put the USB-C key in my pocket with shaking hands and close the office door behind me.

I would have sworn that the architect of Mom's death was Carrigan, but . . . he has an alibi. Adam doesn't. He was supposedly sick, but Chen didn't actually see him. She only saw Henry going to check on him. But what if Henry hadn't found him? Adam had even given a convenient excuse for why he kept coming around me, just checking our bond. But what if that wasn't why? I mean, he had been attentive to me even before this whole blood bond thing.

Henry said he'd tried to put me and Virgil together because he'd heard that Carrigan was interested in me. Who had he heard it from?

It would be easy for Adam to steer Henry my way. Henry's always thought he was manipulating his friend, but what if it was the other way around?

I go into the bathroom, flushing the toilet and washing my hands. I grip the porcelain and stare into the mirror.

I was wrong. I was so fucking wrong.

There are thundering steps up the stairs, and the door to the washroom is ripped open. I'm faced with a panting Virgil.

"What if I was actually using the bathroom?!" I say.

"We need to go. *Now.*"

I stiffen. *Fuck.* Did Adam realize what I was doing? "What?"

"Wilds have Amelia. She was in human form, and they got the jump on her. I have no idea where Corris is. Adam and Nolan went after them. I think the Wilds are headed to the Meadowlands, where they can actually transform."

"Wait, the Wilds are in human form too?"

"No, partial. Just, we need to go!"

I rush down the stairs with Virgil, and we hop the fence to the golf course, sprinting across the green. The monster opens its eyes and cracks its back. I know Nolan's scent instinctively—drugstore all-in-one shampoo and conditioner in some sort of mint. It's a crime for that boy to have beautiful, luxurious hair while using that shit.

When we enter the scene, there's a Wild with Amelia pinned to her chest, the small girl crying as a claw is held to her throat. My eyes dart to Adam, who's trying to talk the Wild down. Nolan is too.

Adam's the one doing this, right? He must be. He's the puppet master. He killed Mom! The monster in my mind slashes and screams at the air. My vision blurs at the edges. I struggle to breathe. It's him. It's *him.* He pretended to be sick and went to Scarborough

and sent a Monster after my mom, then covered it up. He sent the Wilds to kill James and his family and then pretended he couldn't control them to stop them. But he was right there.

He's been *right there* all along.

"I'll come with you," Adam says. "Just put her down and leave her alone." The Wild is crying too, caught between Monster and human forms.

Adam is the one who benefited from everything Bernie did that made the Traditionalists look like traitors and got him voted in. He's the only one who gains something by killing off the other Doctorate candidates. Then he went after Mom because she knew about the Osseous, the thing that could bring him down.

He manipulated me. Made me trust him. He allowed Bernie to talk to me last year, which is how I learned about the weapon in the first place. He's using me to find it, and it's working. This is why he kept me and Jules alive. To use us.

I'm moving before I can comprehend it, fast, straight toward Adam, the monster roaring in my ears.

But something else is faster.

A Wild, fully transformed, comes from behind and spears Adam through the gut with a massive scorpion-like pincer.

I'm breathing too fast, and it also feels like I'm not breathing at all. Blood spurts out of Adam's mouth as the Monster raises him up, impaled. Blood drips from Adam's stomach as he gasps, his mouth wide open.

This . . . this isn't supposed to be happening.

I don't understand what's happening. I . . . I . . .

The other Wild, still in a horrible mash-up of human and Monster, lunges for Amelia.

No.

I see James's children. Little kids reduced to blood and guts on the ground.

I open my mouth and roar with everything I have, tears spilling down my face from the force of it, the monster screaming with me.

The Wild stops in her tracks, falling to her knees, holding her head. The other Wild rips its pincer out of Adam, dropping him to bleed on the ground. They both look . . . confused and disoriented.

"Nolan?" The woman gasps, fully transforming back to a human. "What's happening? What's going on?"

Nolan stares at her, open-mouthed. "Polly, that's you, right? Who's doing this to you? Who's controlling you?"

"I don't know. . . . I don't know what's happening. I—"

"No!" Virgil shouts, running in front of the woman, but all he does is delay the inevitable. The other Wild skirts around him and whips that wicked tail, severing Polly's head before disappearing into the trees.

Nolan collapses, his hands out like he still thinks he can save her.

Amelia is screaming and screaming and screaming. Virgil goes over to her, trying to comfort her. I'm staring at the woman's severed head, her eyes wide open, expression shocked.

Adam gasps, and when I turn to him, he's still covered in blood, but the wound in his stomach is knitting itself back together.

"How . . . ?" I gasp. "How are you . . . ?"

Adam cracks a smile. "Thank you, Virgil, for being here."

Virgil . . . ? His regeneration ability. Adam is using Virgil's healing.

This, all of this, was part of his plan. Agree to meet with us knowing that Virgil would come. Set up a Wild attack during a time

when he must have been sure that Corris was gone. Because now we're witnesses. The Wilds tried to assassinate him. They almost succeeded. Thank God Virgil was here. It's a fucking miracle.

Now, even if Adam is the one who killed Mom, there's no way for me to kill him. Not only can he control Virgil and Nolan, hurt them before I get to him, but he can also use Virgil's healing to protect himself. He's invincible.

A God.

Me and the monster gnash our teeth.

Any God can be killed.

CHAPTER THIRTY-FOUR

Everyone in the room is silent after I share my theory about Adam. Virgil has his head in his hands while Nolan leans against the doorjamb with his arms crossed. Corey keeps opening her mouth to say something and then closing it. Margot is massaging her forehead and staring at her lap. Riley is the only one in the group who will meet my gaze, I assume because she's not being told that her leader is a manipulative and corrupt murderer.

It's only been an hour since everything that happened at Adam's house. Corris appeared and broke down over Amelia. A bunch of senior Masters, including Henry, swarmed the place. Henry sent us to McIntosh Castle, and the first thing I did was text Margot and Riley.

"Let's see the video," Margot says. "It could be anything."

I scoff.

Corey brings over her laptop and plugs in the USB-C key. We

crowd around the screen. All except for Nolan, who stays in the doorway. The footage is hours long, and Corey is forced to scrub through it. But from the first frame of the video, I know I'm right. It's of the Scarborough Bluffs. There's a flash of something huge and green. Even frame by frame, it's too hard to make out what it is, but it's reptilian for sure. And then, most damning of all, Adam walks into frame about half an hour after.

I turn to Margot to say some version of "I told you so" and pause at the wide-eyed look on her face. "What?"

She swallows. "The Monster. It's Laira."

"What?!" I say again, louder now.

"Who's Laira?" Riley asks Corey.

"Henry's partner," Corey says, biting her lip. To Margot, she asks, "Are you sure?"

"Yes," Margot says, and steps back from the computer, her hands on top of her head. "Fuck. I— Fuck!"

Virgil says, "It could be like the Wilds. She might not know. Even then, just because she was there doesn't mean she's the one who—"

"Then who else?!" I ask, incredulous. First Adam, now Laira. These people who I not only trusted but *liked*. Though at least in Laira's case, she might not have been aware of what she did. But still. How am I supposed to interact with her knowing that she . . .

"I'm leaving," Nolan says, pushing off the wall.

I jerk toward him. "Just like that?"

"The deal was that we win so I could use the reward to block the new proposal. Now I learn that the man who's supposed to grant said reward is the same one who's using Wilds? The game is rigged. There's no winning."

"So you're just giving up?" Virgil asks.

Nolan laughs. "What's your plan, Mr. Perfect? You going to kill the Doctorate?"

Virgil is opening his mouth to respond as I say, "Yes, that's the plan." Everyone in the room stares at me. "I'm sorry, are we supposed to let him get away with this?"

Nolan shakes his head. "That man was speared through the stomach and still managed to control a Wild actively fighting against him. Besides that, I'm sure Virgil could tell you that the one and only assassination attempt of the Doctorate by a non-Doctorate did not go well. It's over."

He walks out of the room, and I sink onto the couch. Today's match is with Virgil, but the semifinals are in two weeks. We need Nolan.

Riley says, "He was very dramatic about it, but Nolan had a point. I agree with August that Adam needs to be stopped, but it's not going to be easy."

"Are we just cool with murder now?" Virgil says, swiveling his gaze between me and Riley.

"I'm cool with doing what needs to be done," Riley says.

I nod. "The plan hasn't changed. We're still seeking a weapon that kills Gods. Just now the purpose is a little more immediate."

Corey wraps her arms around her body. "A candidate is one thing. But we're talking about *the* Doctorate. No matter what he's done, going after him is treason. Punishable by death."

"I agree, homicide is not the way. But there is a solution," Margot says, and we turn to her. "If he confesses to everything, including the manipulation of the Wilds, it'll show the society that he's corrupt. Remember, he's not the only option for the Doctorate. As long as Carrigan lives, there's an alternative."

"Henry will never allow it," Virgil says. "Even if Doctorate Shaw did kill August's mom, he won't care."

I say, "He'll care if he suspects that his friend killed his family." Now I'm the one everyone's watching. "Adam was there when that Monster killed Henry's parents and sister. Henry was favored by their dad. And I've always gotten the impression that the brothers resented him for it. Henry said Adam knew his family was out there camping, which is how he knew to get Cyrus to save him."

Virgil crosses his arms over his chest. "There are a lot of leaps there."

"Sure. But chances are Adam also manipulated Henry to get me involved with you guys in the first place. Henry admitted that he set it up for me and Virgil to meet." This is apparently news to Virgil, whose eyes go wide. "He felt Carrigan was interested in me because of some tip—"

"A tip from Adam," Margot says. "Adam told Henry about Carrigan's interest in you. Henry thought it was because Carrigan had a thing for your mom, but Adam insisted it was something more."

I lick my lips. "So you knew he set me up."

She crosses her arms. "I *suspected* and confronted him. He confirmed. I didn't see the point in saying anything to you. In the end, you and Virgil chose each other." She perches on the edge of an armchair. "What matters is that if Henry even suspects that Adam might have had something to do with what happened to his family, it could be enough to sway him. That's not even touching the fact that Laira was probably used without her knowledge or permission."

"Okay, fine," I say. "We gather evidence, and then we kill him."

"For someone who was so shook up over almost killing Nolan, you sure are trigger-happy now," Margot snaps.

“Nolan was innocent! Adam has murdered multiple people, including my fucking Mom!”

“Allegedly!”

I throw my hands up and pace around the room. I cannot believe we have this much to go on, and I’m still getting all this reluctance. From Virgil, okay, fine. Considering the trauma of everything that happened to his parents, I understand why planning the murder of a Doctorate wouldn’t sit well with him. But with all the planning and scheming that Adam has done so far, how is anything short of death going to stop him?

“Okay,” Riley says. “I think that’s fair. Start with an interrogation, get support, and we can deal with what comes next.”

I throw an annoyed look at Riley. She barely needed any convincing. Fucking turncoat.

“How do you plan to manage that?” Virgil asks.

Riley grins. “With a little intimidation from a weapon that scared even his ancestor.”

“We would have to get him alone,” Corey says. “And we would also need to guarantee that he won’t just attack us or have other senior Masters intervene before we extract the information. Not to mention we’d have to escape retaliation long enough to get proof to Henry.”

This, I’ll give Corey credit, is a legitimate problem for both interrogation and assassination. Now that Adam has made it look like he was almost killed, the senior Masters won’t let him be alone again under any circumstances.

“The vault,” Margot says.

Corey nods. “Yes! That would work.”

“The place on the Doctorate island where you keep artifacts and stuff?” I ask.

Virgil says, "That's not its only function. The vault is made of a special material known only to the Doctorates. When you're inside, it blocks your ability to access bonds. Within it, Doctorate Shaw would just be a normal man. It's so fortified that not even Monsters can break in. But there's wired access to the outside world. It was made for the apocalypse. So the Doctorate could hide there if needed and still be able to send out commands."

"The savior of the apocalypse made a panic room? That really inspires confidence."

"It's supposed to be a temporary measure."

Riley says, "We use the Osseous to threaten him into the vault—"

"We won't need to," Corey says. "The prize for the winner of the Bachelor league includes a tour of the Doctorate cottage. The vault, too. That's part of the appeal, since you normally wouldn't get to see inside."

"Even better. Once they're inside, August makes him confess. She has knife skills; he doesn't. Then she sends out a video from the vault, which we use as evidence. She can also have him share something more concrete. In that case, the fact that he's under duress won't matter." She holds her gaze on me for a moment, and I don't think I'm mistaken when I read the intention in her eyes. Not so turncoat after all. Riley, unlike me, read the room. No one is getting on board with murder. But if I'm the one in the vault, the one who gets the confession, I can also finish the job.

After all, under the assumption that Adam is the puppet master, which I believe he is, he's also the reason Sammie is dead.

Me and Riley have a personal stake in his death. This is why she's outlined this plan. I just need to keep my mouth shut about my

continued intention to murder Adam. I need everyone on board with this plan so we can execute it.

"The Doctorate will be able to open the vault from the inside," Margot says. "You also need to prevent that. Plus, I'm sure they'll send a senior Master along on the tour. You'll have to deal with them, too."

"I can do it," I say. "So, we have a plan?" I look around the room to be met with nods. I meet Virgil's eyes. "We'd have to win. Not just place within the cutoff."

"Like it's hard?" Riley asks.

Despite myself, my lips quirk up. I look at Corey, who's been quiet for a bit. "Corey?"

She swallows. "As far as the interrogation plan goes, I think it's feasible. I just . . . Sure, Adam could fool us. But it's hard to believe that he fooled Henry, too."

"They're not as close as you'd imagine," Margot says. "When Adam was explaining what happened with the Wilds today to Henry, I was there, remember? He said he used Virgil's ability to heal, and Henry was . . . stricken is putting it lightly. He was under the impression that Doctorates could only operate at a first-evolution level when it comes to controlling Monsters. He grew up in close proximity to the Shaws, but it seems like they concealed a lot from him."

"Family secrets, I guess," I say.

Margot nods. "That's my impression. But Henry and Cyrus were close. I think it really affected him not only that Cyrus hid that, but that the Doctorate did too. According to Henry, Doctorate Shaw wasn't always able to do this much. Something changed after he graduated to the title."

"Which begs the question," Virgil says. "If he's more powerful

as a Doctorate than he was as a Doctorate candidate, why is he picking off his brothers at all? I just . . . What if we're missing something? We need more guidance and insight."

"You want to tell Henry," I say, voice flat.

"Is that so wrong?" Virgil asks.

"Yes! It is when he's Adam's best friend. He's biased! We need the confession first."

Virgil stares at me. "Confession, and we bring it to Henry, and we don't do anything else until multiple people have denounced him and we have concrete evidence to use against him. We are only using the Osseous for intimidation."

"Yes," I say.

"When you take a life, there are ripples outward. And they start with you. You can't still that water once it gets going. You think that's what you want, but it won't make you feel better. Promise me that you'll stick to this plan. Interrogation only." The room is silent while me and Virgil stare at each other.

"Yes! I wouldn't do that to you. I wouldn't do what your parents did."

His shoulders drop, and he nods. He believes me even as I lie through my teeth.

"Well," Riley says, clearing her throat. "We have a plan, so like, yay team or whatever." To Corey she says, "I'll text you later."

Margot also decides to leave, and I go with her, making my way back to my dorm room.

I wouldn't do that to you.

The monster stares at me with dark amber eyes, lips peeling into a sharp-toothed grin.

. . .

I'm so focused on the upcoming match that I almost miss Jules walking by. Only him grabbing my arm stops me. Competitors and spectators alike surge past us. In the morning, while I was discovering who Mom's real killer was, they had the repechage matches carried over from the last rounds. Meanwhile, those of us who have advanced will be starting the first of two days of quarterfinals, which is what most students are here to see. This will be our only match for this section of the competition. Then we have a two-week break before semis. Even if you lose, you go straight through to the semifinals repechage.

Natalie waves at me from over Jules's shoulder, and I treat her to a scowl before turning to my brother. "What?" I ask.

Jules steps back. "That's what you have to say to me after not answering my texts all day?"

"You said to concentrate on studying."

"And that's what you've been doing, have you?"

"Of course."

I wish I could trust Jules with this Adam plan, but I know he would try to stop me. This is more dangerous than investigating, and he didn't even want me doing that much.

Jules says, "So you weren't hanging around the Doctorate when he was almost killed by Wilds?"

"He's fine."

"He's fine because Virgil happened to be there."

"That's not supposed to be public knowledge." Jules turns and gestures to Natalie like it explains everything, which it does. Annoyingly. How the hell does this woman always get the inside scoop but somehow has fewer leads on Mom than me? "I'm fine. Both Virgil and Nolan were there, and I wasn't the target. And even

if I had been speared through the gut, now I know I would have survived."

Jules takes a long, deep breath. Composing himself.

Virgil nudges my shoulder. "We need to go."

"Good luck," I say to Jules, and walk away with Virgil.

I need to concentrate on our match.

We reach the antechamber, and I stretch. All we need to do is win. It's that simple. Win, and win, and win. Get Adam alone. Wring the truth from him. And then kill him where he stands. I could cry self-defense. No one else will be there to challenge my story. And now that Carrigan is apparently innocent, maybe having been in love with my mom will get me some brownie points. He can pardon me, and everything will be fine. Virgil is the one who said that even when I break things, they turn out better. This is the right move. We can't give Adam a chance to retaliate or get away.

It's kill or be killed.

"Thank you," Virgil says.

I raise an eyebrow. "For what?"

"I know you want to get justice for what happened to your mom. I'm sure agreeing to the interrogation plan wasn't easy on you. But I just . . . You told me it was my job to stop you, remember? If you go too far. So I'm glad you're listening." He grins at me then, and my stomach clenches.

I just need to open my mouth and reassure him. Keep on with the lie. But when I look at Virgil with that earnest smile on his face, I falter.

And he sees it.

His smile dips. "August . . ."

The light turns amber. "That's your cue."

"August," Virgil says again, his voice lower now. Rougher. "You're going to stick to the plan, right?"

"The light."

"August!"

"You need to turn. It's going to go green!"

Shit. Why couldn't I just lie?!

I turn away from him, and slowly, the shadow behind me grows. The light turns green just as Virgil finishes transforming, and I stride toward it. Outside the doors, the crowd roars. I walk out, and Virgil follows behind me. But for the first time, having him at my back doesn't make me feel any better.

CHAPTER THIRTY-FIVE

I swear the ground shakes with the force of the shouting and cheering, mixed in with jeers and boos. The concrete of the floor is unyielding under my feet. I slide my knives into my hands, clenching and unclenching my fingers around the cool metal to ground myself.

The crowd has turned against us, I see. I imagine that the latest attack on Adam has something to do with it. Even if Nolan isn't fighting today, we're still known as the team with a Wild.

I just need to strike a balance between using the monster's power and staying myself.

But when I reach for the beast, it turns its back on me.

I whip around to look at Virgil across the arena. His shoulders are hunched and his expression pinched. *No.* Not again. Fuck! I could have kept up the lie if he just hadn't looked at me like that. Like he was so proud. Is he really that bothered by the idea of me killing a *murderer*? This isn't good. If Virgil is disconnecting from

me, not only will I not be able to use the monster, I won't be able to use second- or third-evolution skills either.

"Virgil," I hiss, knowing he'll hear me. "I'll do the plan! Just get your head in the game."

He doesn't even look at me. He definitely doesn't buy my lie like he did the first time.

The doors across from us open, and our opponents walk out. The announcer says, "We have Melani Tobin and her partner, Shay Monterri, from McMaster University! Tobin has been slaying the competition in her first Monster's Ball, frequently winning in under five minutes. She's been a sleeper hit, ranking last in her Bachelor candidacy but quickly outpacing everyone in her cohort who originally placed higher. She came to win!"

Melani is a Black girl with a wicked grin and a narrow face. Her head is shaved on the sides, and the remaining hair is sectioned into tiny braids that she wears twisted into a high bun. Her weapon, a knife whose blade is the length of her forearm, is strapped to her thigh. From the wraps on her hands, I'd say she has some boxing experience too. She winks at me. I press my lips together.

Her partner, Shay, makes me think of what a raccoon might look like if it were giant and both on steroids and infected with rabies. She lopes forward, transitioning from a four-legged walk to a two-legged one with ease. So bulky that it feels like her muscles have muscles, with foam casually bubbling at her lips.

The announcer helpfully reminds everyone that as these are the quarterfinals, there will be no flag pulling. The match ends when one of the Bachelors either yields by raising a closed fist, is rendered unconscious, or dies.

Dying is obviously not the ideal outcome, but I won't yield. The only option is to win. Virgil has to know that too.

The horn blows, and I only have seconds to raise my knife to defend as Melani flies at me. Instinct is the only thing that saves me. She's relentless, throwing hooks and jabs at me. I'm thankful for my forearm guards, but I need to make some space between us.

I bend my knees and jump back several feet into the air. I gasp. I have my second-evolution skills. Virgil isn't completely disconnected. I fling out knives, which Melani avoids. As I fall, she's there to meet me, striking me in the gut. Since I'm in the air, there's no purchase, no way to get my footing until I smack into the ground. I hear the echo of Margot's voice from last year when we were training for the final test, screaming at me not to fall. I jump to my feet in time to block Melani and hear Virgil cry out.

I jerk my head toward him to see the foam from Shay's mouth eating into his flesh like acid.

"Pay attention," Melani sings as she shoves her knife toward my gut.

I push into a full back handspring to avoid it, something I've only done a few times before, but with second-evolution skills, it's easy. I limit my airtime. I don't want to get caught again. Sweat slides down my brow as I fling out more knives that don't meet a target.

I'm not fast enough.

Not for her.

The monster in my mind still won't turn to look at me. Motherfucker! I can't win with this thing! It shivers, and the sensation runs down my spine like ice cold water. It's . . . afraid? Of what?

Out of the corner of my eye, I spot Virgil, pink flesh exposed. He's not in a great position because he needs to operate on all fours, but Shay can go bipedal and tower over him.

But most importantly, he's not regenerating. *Why isn't he healing?!*

"You should have more confidence in your partner," Melani says, standing and twirling in her blade in circles. "Trust him to handle his own shit. You trusted the other one." She tilts her head. "Or is this one weaker? Do you need to mind him more? It's a little pathetic, don't you think? With two partners, you should be the baddest bitch in here. But look at you—you can barely catch your breath."

"Stop commentating and fight."

She grins. "Oh, sweetie, I was giving you a moment. These five-minute fights are starting to bore me. I want it to last."

"Fuck you," I snarl.

All she does is laugh and rush forward. She's only got one blade, but she's swift with it. I wince as cuts open up on my arms and legs whenever we parry. It's a useless exercise. My knives are small and not meant for close quarters.

The monster is quiet in my mind. Curled into a ball.

I feint with a knife and then backhand her as hard as I can. Her neck snaps to the side. She laughs again. "That's more like it!"

Fuck this noise.

I open my mouth, and a scream is all that comes out.

Just me.

Nothing more.

Melani, however, stopped to brace herself, and I use the moment to fling a knife her way. She's caught off guard enough that she can't block with her knife and raises her arm, taking the blade deep into her forearm. She rips it out, and blood gushes from the wound.

I grin.

The smile drops off my face as I watch the wound knit itself back together.

Now I'm the one caught off guard, and the punch to my nose comes too fast to defend. I hear the crunch and cry out, flailing, tossing every knife I can while I literally sprint around the ring, trying to get away from her. The pain is excruciating. It radiates from my nose to my temples and even into my mouth.

I'm still sprinting as Melani follows me, giggling as she does. Like it's just a game to her.

The crowd is chanting something. It takes me a moment to finally decipher what they're saying.

Yield. Yield. Yield.

Another sucker punch to the gut sends me flying into the concrete wall. It smacks my back with a force that knocks the wind out of me. I fall to my knees, panting.

No. I'm not yielding. We have to win!

I glance at Virgil, and he's worse. He's trembling, and half his torso is melted away.

No. We just need to fight harder. Do more.

Virgil's in so much pain. Enough that I know through the bond. Terrible, excruciating pain. I could make him fight. I can make him keep going. We have to win! We have to—

Virgil howls as Shay spits more acidic foam at him. It cuts through me as surely as Melani's blade.

He still won't heal.

He's going to die.

I can keep going, but he can't.

The monster looks at me with Virgil's eyes.

Melani towers over me.

I raise my hand in a fist and hold it there.

The horn blows.

The chanting stops.

Virgil has to be dragged out of the arena on a stretcher to the sounds of cheers and boos. He's reverted to his human form. Naked and shivering, even with the reflective blanket they threw over him. I limp behind the medics, going as fast as I can.

"Virgil!" I shout. "You need to heal! You're going to die!"

His eyes are rolling in his head, and he's not paying attention to me. To anything. The blanket slips enough to see that his ribs are visible through the mess of skin and blood on his side.

"Virgil!" I cry, and I hate the way my voice sounds. Trembling and broken.

I should have yielded sooner. I should have paid more attention to him. The second I noticed he wasn't healing, I should have stopped it. But I didn't.

Because I wanted to win.

I wanted a chance to kill a man more than I wanted to protect Virgil.

I think of Mom flying over the cliff to her death. Of Virgil and Nolan bleeding out.

They set Virgil down on a bed in the medical room. He isn't responding anymore. His face is pale and washed out, his chest moving so slowly that it barely seems to be moving at all. Meanwhile, the staff are talking over each other.

"Are you going to do something?!" I scream at the medic closest to me.

He narrows his eyes. "We're trying! You need to get out of the way."

I stumble back, giving them space.

They keep asking each other why he's not healing, but they don't seem to have any answers. The door to the room opens, and I spin around to see Nolan striding over to us.

"Nola—" I start, but he moves around me.

One of the medics says something, and he shoves them aside, growing his hands into claws.

I don't even think. In an instant, the tip of a spike is kissing the side of his neck, indented into the skin. Its origin is the base of my wrist, where the metal has torn through the flesh, the obsidian color shining in the lights. Only the second time I've managed this feat. We hover there, him with his claws, and me with mine.

Nolan doesn't do anything more than look at me.

I lower my hand, and the metal slides back beneath my skin.

Nolan turns to Virgil and uses his claws to slice open his other arm, dripping a stream of blood into Virgil's mouth and tilting his head to make him swallow. I stare, transfixed, as Nolan runs his tongue against Virgil's limp arm, taking in more of his blood.

Slowly, the wounds start to close.

I touch my nose, feeling the bones shifting, and wipe the blood away with my shirtsleeve.

Adam said that exchanging more blood could strengthen the bond between them. Maybe enough that Nolan could force Virgil to heal if he can't do it himself.

It also means that if there was *any* chance our bond could be undone, now Nolan has guaranteed that it would be impossible.

Till death do us part.

I sag, falling to the floor.

Nolan hoists me up by my elbows, pulling me out of the room.

He half carries, half drags me to another enclosed space. It's small and empty, more a storage room than anything. He sets me on the couch, forcing himself into a position of kneeling on the cushions to lay me down.

I look at him. We're both breathing hard.

I reach up, tangling my fingers in his hair, which is just as soft as it looks despite his poor taste in shampoo. I drag him to me, and our lips meet. I don't have the headspace to be embarrassed by the moan that comes out of me when we kiss. It's rough and desperate. Our teeth knock against each other more than once.

He tugs my legs up onto the couch so we're horizontal and presses me into the cushions, sinking his whole body on top of mine. I bend my knees, making space for him to lie between them as he sucks my lower lip into his mouth.

I don't know who's shaking, one or both of us. The heat pooling between our bodies is too much. It hurts. The burn of it.

I'm only peripherally aware of pulling the hem of my shirt up because Nolan leans back to let me get it off.

And that moment breaks the entire spell.

The two of us are panting, on a couch, and I'm lying here in my bra.

He trails his fingers up my stomach and between my breasts and then behind my neck. He leans down pressing his forehead to mine. "You're so hot," he whispers.

My already heated body flushes even more. It's not that I forgot, but I'm now more concious of the fact that this is my new body, and no one but me has seen it. I didn't even think about that as I tore my shirt off.

Nolan presses a kiss to the shell of my ear and says, "Do you want this because you want me? Or because you're grateful I saved him?"

I swallow, saying nothing.

I want to tell him to stop making it into something else because I'm burning, and I feel like the only way I'm going to cool off is if we do everything that I need us to do right now. If we both let ourselves be set on fire, then maybe the flames will eventually die out.

Nolan leans back and pulls my shirt over my head. Helps me put my arms into it and tug it into place.

I sit up. "You came to watch? Even though you said there was nothing for you?"

"You're lucky I showed up."

"You wanted to be here."

I wait for him to deny it, but he doesn't.

We arrange ourselves as much as we can with swollen lips, and Nolan's face as red as it is. I shove the door to the room open, and almost collide with Barbie, of all people.

She glances between me and Nolan, but I don't have time for her bullshit.

I need to get back to Virgil.

CHAPTER THIRTY-SIX

Nolan pulls onto the driveway in front of a nondescript house on the Murphy compound. We were mostly silent for the full hour drive into Sydenham, letting Nolan's playlist of crooning indie tracks fill the space.

I check my phone, but Corey hasn't texted me any updates on Virgil. She stayed behind at the Pen to wait until he wakes up.

But Nolan insisted that we had other places to be, and so here I am.

I follow him up the steps, assessing the house with its beige vinyl siding. It's unadorned. Like a show home.

The door is unlocked, and I follow Nolan inside. The walls and trim are white, the closet doors mirrored, and the floor that millennial gray wood tone. No pictures on the walls or artwork. Not even a rug.

"Dude," I say. "What's up with this house?"

Nolan says, "Legally, it's occupied, though the Wild who owns

it doesn't actually live here. So unofficially, we meet here sometimes. It would put the society on alert if we were meeting, say, at my dad's home. They don't like us to gather. So we do things like this."

We walk through a long hallway to a dining area where a group of people already wait. Mia waves at us from beside her mom. The two others are the same people who were in the forest before, the Black man and the possibly biracial woman. While Mia and Izzy are happy to welcome me, the others don't look as jovial about it.

"Well," Garrett says, "since our guests of honor are here, we may as well get started."

Nolan told me on the ride over that he'd updated his dad on the whole Adam situation. And Garrett had told a small but trusted group. Obviously, some Wilds were compromised, and it wouldn't be wise to have Adam learning that we were onto him.

"You know Mia, Jacques, Izzy, and Nolan." Garrett gestures to the two strangers. "This is Clay and Xenia. They represent the two other Wild families in Ontario. Clay is based in Peterborough and Xenia in North Bay. However, due to the present circumstances, their families are staying with us here."

"Isn't that worse?" I ask. "Like, bringing them closer makes it easier for them to be used."

"It's happening anyway," Xenia says, curling her lip. "They get called here for missions by themselves, and that's when this shit goes down. At least this way we're around."

Garrett looks at me with barely concealed contempt. I guess I'm still on his shit list. "I've updated them on what you said, but we have questions about the interaction. Nolan said you broke the Doctorate's concentration."

I furrow my brow. When did I— "Oh, the roar," I say.

Nolan nods. "Maybe it was a one-time thing because you surprised him. But it broke Polly out for that moment. It's a good strategy to keep in mind."

"Has that happened before?" Clay asks.

I shrug. "I've never done it around a Doctorate before. But it doesn't affect regular Master-Monster pairs beyond hurting their ears."

"Must have just distracted him," Garrett says. "We have to avoid transforming. That's the only thing that'll keep us safe. No more missions, no more proctoring."

Jacques furrows his brow. "They won't like it."

"Tough."

I see now why Garrett was the one to lead the rebellion. He's willing to make the difficult calls to protect his people.

Clay glances at Nolan. "What about your second son? He's competing. Is *he* going to stop transforming?"

Nolan doesn't hide the hostility in his gaze when he looks at Clay. "Call me that again. I dare you."

"Stop," Garrett bites out.

Clay scoffs. "I'm saying the quiet part out loud. You've got both sons here, but there's no confirmation of succession during a time when we're being killed off." He points at Garrett. "Who's it going to be? The turncoat or the second choice?"

Garrett stands to full height, stepping toward Clay. "You are on my property, under the protection of my people—"

"It's a fair question," Jacques says, tucking his hands in his pockets. "The phrasing lacks a certain *je ne sais quois,* but he's right."

"Leave me out of it," Nolan says. "I came here to help. Not to be your backup. So just tell us what you need from us and get on with it."

No one says anything for a moment, leaving Garrett to stare at his sons.

I say, "I mean, I would like to know why I'm here."

Garrett says, "For the same reason Mia and Izzy are here. We need people who aren't Wilds to help us investigate and find Carrigan since it's become too risky for us to be connected to him as these attacks continue. But we need him because he's the only person who can confront his brother. So, will you help?"

"Of course," I say. We need Carrigan as the replacement Doctorate and I want to be sure that taking him off my suspect list was the right move.

The meeting ends, and Mia walks us to the door. "How are you doing?" I ask her.

"Good," she says, voice firm. "Being involved is helping a lot. I'm feeling more a part of the family and the Wilds. So don't worry about me."

I roll my eyes. "I wasn't."

"Yeah, sure."

We leave and Nolan drives me to Victoria Hall. He pulls into the driveway in front of the stairs and parks.

"You know the 'second son' thing is more a dig at Garrett than you, right?" I tell him.

Nolan grips the steering wheel. "It's a dig at both of us."

"It doesn't have to be."

He makes a noncommittal noise, which I take as my signal to leave. As I reach for the door, Nolan mumbles, "Thank you. For helping the Wilds, I mean."

"I have my own motives."

"Good." He holds my gaze, and then, "I don't regret it."

I lick my lips. I don't have to ask what he's referring to. "Then why did you stop?"

"It's complicated."

"I'm sure." I get out of the car and close the door behind me. Yes, it's complicated. But in the moment, I wanted to pretend it was simple.

I head into the dorm and up to my floor. Just as I'm about to go into my room, some random white girl waves to me. I raise an eyebrow. "Your friend was looking for you," she says.

"Who?"

The girl scrunches her face. "Uh . . . she was, like, Asian? I don't know. I don't want to guess."

Corey. "Thanks," I say, and retreat into my room, texting her a check-in on Virgil.

She writes back, *Sorry! I meant to text. We just got to McIntosh Castle, and then he was hungry, so I was warming up food. He woke up like half an hour ago, and they immediately got him transferred home. I didn't get a chance to text until now. He's eating. Seems like he's doing okay.*

I reply, *Okay, glad he's doing good. I'll see you both tomorrow.*

Corey wouldn't have had time to swing by Vic Hall, so what was that girl talking about? I shake my head and flop onto my bed. I'm not in the mood.

Virgil is okay. That's what matters.

Still. We lost. We're lucky we'll have the break to recover before the repechage, but now our chances are down to one. Any more losses and we'll be dropped from the competition.

I fist my hands in my sheets.

CHAPTER THIRTY-SEVEN

I glance sidelong at Virgil as we walk through the tunnels toward the arena where Margot and Isaac's match will be held. He's walking steadily, as if he weren't on the brink of death yesterday. Still, at least we don't have to fight again for another couple of weeks so he can recover. The crowds almost feel thicker today as they press in on us.

"You should have rested at home," I say to Virgil.

He clenches his jaw. "I'm fine. I want to watch."

"You almost—"

"He said he's fine," Nolan cuts in, hands in his pockets. He insists that he's only here because he thinks there's a lot to learn from watching Margot. But the fact that he's trying to learn anything at all already exposes him.

Virgil glances at Nolan and then away.

I shift. It's ridiculous to think he's going to somehow know that me and Nolan made out yesterday. Almost more . . . Which I'm

allowed to do. Not within the constraints of the society, but as far as me and Virgil are concerned. We aren't a couple. And honestly, what is Adam even going to do? He told us point blank that he can't break our bond. He's not going to kill us either. Not while he needs me. I wouldn't flaunt anything, but the big, scary consequences for this particular entanglement no longer exist. Which Nolan may or may not have worked out for himself.

Fuck Nolan. I thought kissing him would release something. Instead, I'm more wanting than I was before.

I let the others walk into the arena, holding Virgil back by his elbow. Nolan glances at us but keeps walking. Virgil looks at my hand on his arm, and I let go.

"Are you really okay?" I ask him.

He glances down the hallway, which is emptying out as we get close to match time. "I messed everything up again. You were right. It was the wrong time to talk about the Doctorate. But you also lied, and I'm not going to forget that. We agreed to a plan that I can't trust you to stick with. How are we supposed to move forward now?"

"I'm being realistic! We'll still get evidence, but do you honestly think that's going to be enough to stop him?"

"If it isn't, that bridge will be crossed by Henry or another senior Master, not you. You act like it's going to fix everything, but it won't."

"I know that it's not going to fix anything!" I snap. "My mom is dead. She isn't coming back. This is for *me*. I'm sorry that I'm not some perfect angel like you."

"August," he says, and my name on his lips when he speaks that softly makes me shudder. "You were in my head in the initiation. Hell, I even told you the sort of thoughts that I've had. I'm not judging the kind of revenge you want. I care about how this will affect you. I care about *you*."

All the walls I've tried to build between us crumble in that moment. Pressure builds behind my eyes, and I swallow. "I'll follow the plan, okay? I'll get the evidence, broadcast it, whatever. I'll make sure what I do can't come down on you. But that's all I can promise."

Virgil shakes his head, shifting his gaze away from me. "We should go. I need a program too."

"I already checked," Virgil says. "Jules is in the repechage."

"Shit," I mutter. Guess my brother didn't fare any better than me yesterday. I didn't think Natalie would ever lose.

"How long do you plan to shut him out?" Virgil asks. "Last semester, you were ready to put your life on the line to save him."

"Yeah, and he pissed me off right before he went missing then too. He has a talent for that, and a lack of talent for apologies."

I walk past Virgil into the arena, trying to brush off the weight of his words about caring about me. We're not a couple, but it feels like I've betrayed him by kissing Nolan. At the same time, if Virgil wanted me enough, he could have me. And he has to be the one to make the move. Only I know he won't. So why should I be waiting around for something that won't ever come?

When we enter the arena, the lack of Wild proctors is obvious. Instead, there are two pairs of disgruntled-looking people who must be senior Masters and Monsters. Look at that—they *can* find other people when they need to.

Based on the sneers thrown Nolan's way, others in the society have noticed the strike and aren't happy.

We settle in our seats, where Corey is already waiting, and unexpectedly, so is Jules.

I guess Virgil will be happy that I'm now forced to interact with my brother.

"I heard you lost," I say to him.

Virgil doesn't hide his groan. A muscle in Jules's cheek tenses. He says, "I heard you did too."

Fine. I guess I deserved that. "This is bold, researching your competitors from their mentor's section."

He grins. "Virgil invited me."

I swivel around to my partner, who only straightens in response. I cannot believe this boy was half dead and still made time for this. "Of course he did," I say, plopping next to my brother. Virgil sits on my other side, with Nolan next to him. "What lecture am I getting today?" I ask Jules.

"No lecture. I'm just here to watch the fight."

I lean past him to Corey, who sits on the other side of my brother. She said that Virgil seemed agitated once he'd woken up. I want to tell her about the Nolan thing, but I also don't want to put her in a weird position of hiding something from Virgil. Then again, me and Virgil are hiding something from her. "I assume you told Virgil to rest too?" I ask her.

"Yup. He said—"

"I'm fine," Virgil finishes. And Corey makes a gesture like "That's what he said."

Jules studies Virgil. "Nat says that third-evolution skills more than anything else are a test of the Monster. If you have doubts or get in your head, you're going to struggle. Whatever is bothering you, leave it at the door. Deal with it after."

Virgil hunches his shoulders. He's been living with the knowledge of being a Monster much longer than Jules, but Jules also has a senior Master as his partner.

"He knows," I say at the same time as Nolan, of all people.

Our eyes meet for a second before we both look away.

Virgil says nothing.

Since when does Virgil let *Nolan* speak for him? Corey widens her eyes meaningfully at me and gestures to her phone.

I look at the text she just sent, tilting my phone so Virgil can't see.

It says, *Nolan came by McIntosh Castle last night to see Virgil. They talked for a long time. . . .*

Fuck.

I glance sidelong at Nolan and Virgil, who are now both concentrating on the arena. Nolan wouldn't . . . he wouldn't *tell* Virgil, right? Maybe they weren't even talking about me. Helping Virgil would have strengthened their blood bond, so it was probably about that.

"You good?" Jules asks me.

"Fine. Everyone is fine."

The lights dim and then flicker and flash to alert that the match is beginning, followed by some truly cheesy music. This is new. I guess I didn't notice at our match because we were in the antechamber while this was going on.

The announcer comes on and says, "Welcome to the Shaw Arena match. This is our first round of the MiT league quarterfinals! And it's going to be a fun one!"

"Jesus Christ," I mutter. This announcer guy has no tact.

"We have the dynamic sibling duo, Margot Bouchard and her partner, Isaac Bouchard, from Queen's University. Margot is a favorite in this league, and you'll want to keep your eye on her." The doors open, and Margot is turned, her back to the audience, snapping something at Isaac, who is only partially transformed and is snapping something back.

"That's . . . weird," Corey mutters.

Margot whirls around, eyes wide as she realizes the doors are open, and strides forward. Isaac finishes transforming as they enter the arena.

"Not good," Virgil says, wringing his hands.

This is exactly what Jules was talking about. Leave it at the door. But Margot and Isaac couldn't even stop as the doors were opening.

The announcer stumbles a bit as he continues, "Uh . . . and um, the challenger is Samuel Yoke and his partner, Donovan Li, from Western University. They've had a surprising . . . uh, should we . . . ?"

Isaac is stomping his feet behind Margot, who's had to turn around and snipe at him to stop, and now it seems like they're arguing again, Isaac nonverbally.

"They're fucked," Nolan says, leaning back and crossing his arms.

The competitors' doors have opened, and they walk out to mutters and buzz from the audience with Margot and Isaac still arguing. Samuel is wielding a large, curved sword, while Donovan is behind him in reptilian form with multiple tongues and tails, walking on two feet. Meaning Margot and Isaac will likely have the same issues that me and Virgil had with Shay.

A new voice comes over the loudspeakers. "Competitors will be silent and face the front or risk disqualification."

Margot whips to the front, grinding her teeth.

The previous announcer returns to finish off introducing the challengers, though I don't know if anyone is paying attention now.

The horn blows, and there's a moment when neither competitor moves. Then Isaac jumps into the fray, bounding toward Donovan, leaving himself completely open. Samuel brings up his sword to slice the kid on the way, and Margot sprints forward to

keep him back, barely making it. She's running at a normal speed. Not accelerated.

Fuck. It must be bad if she can't even use second-evolution skills.

"It's done," Jules says.

Even I have to admit that it doesn't look good. Margot is pushed into the defensive. Samuel is moving at a ridiculous speed, and she's still managing to defend, but not well.

Virgil hunches, head in his hands.

"What?" I ask.

"I told Isaac to talk to her. I didn't think he'd do it right before the match!"

"For someone who was half dead, you sure had a lot of time to do stuff."

Virgil says, "I had a lot of texts! Some from people *you* should have been texting back. And some were from this morning, not last night."

I look at Jules, who purposely stares forward. "What did you talk to Isaac about?" I ask Virgil.

"I think what Mia said really got to him. Like, about growing up. Their strategy is they let Margot go out hard and Isaac stays back. Isaac thinks the only reason they do that is because Margot is trying to protect him, treating him like he's a little kid. I told him to talk about it with her."

"Seems like that's going well," Nolan drawls.

Isaac's fighting is so messy. He's jumping all over the arena without any sense of strategy. And nothing is working against Donovan, whose skin seems to be rock-hard and impervious to most attacks. Meanwhile, Margot is fighting for her life. Bringing brass knuckles to a sword fight when the sword guy is moving at that pace and you're not is less than ideal.

Margot runs underneath her brother's belly and then literally climbs onto Isaac's back. She's shouting something, but it's hard to hear this far away. Isaac is also having to fend off Samuel, who is attempting to cut his feet, though Donovan stays back.

Samuel gets a slice in, and Isaac whines. Margot's face crumples. But she stays where she is on her brother's back. Isaac keeps going on his own, getting cut, and crying out with every one. Margot stays the course, sitting in place.

"Why isn't she doing anything?" I ask.

"I think she's letting him do his thing," Virgil says. "But . . . it's not like it's helping."

Margot's fists are gripped in Isaac's fur, and even from up here, I can see how much this pains her. I'm thrown back to yesterday, when I watched Virgil suffering, dying. I had to call it, but Margot isn't doing that. It's not even that dire yet, but it will be soon enough.

Isaac reels back to evade another jab, leaving his stomach on display. Samuel grins, raising his knife, and Margot squeezes her eyes shut. But then, just as Samuel runs in, Isaac shakes the spit off his lips. Samuel screams as the saliva burns him, and Isaac's ears go flat against his head, but he comes back down on four legs and stands his ground.

Margot opens her eyes, her jaw slack.

Isaac *does* have a strategy. He's doing something. That wasn't a fluke, and I think Margot now knows it too.

She says something and leaps off Isaac's back, landing in a crouch. She rolls her shoulders back and blows out a breath.

Samuel diverts, running toward her. Margot slams her knuckles together, and red sparks fly off the metal.

I grin.

When Samuel brings his blade down, she traps it between her

fists, the metal glowing red. Samuel attempts to pull back, but as he does, the blade bends. He manages to get away, but he's left with a half-melted sword. There's a crash on the other side of the stadium, where Isaac has headbutted Donovan into the wall.

Samuel's face drops just in time for Margot to sucker punch him. Blood spurts out of his mouth and onto her face, but Margot doesn't react to it. Instead, she bombards Samuel, her fists moving too fast to follow, more and more blood splattering onto her face. By the time she relents, Samuel keels over on the ground, shaking.

His eyes roll into the back of his head, and he collapses.

For a few seconds, no one moves.

Then the horn blows.

Me and Corey immediately get to our feet, screaming and clapping. Virgil sags, like he might fall out of his seat, while Nolan is applauding at a more resigned pace, but it's clear he's impressed.

Jules stands.

"What did you learn?" I ask him.

"That the Bouchards are not to be fucked with." His brow furrows. "I sincerely hope we won't be matched up. But it's also inevitable."

"I mean, you don't have to win to have defended."

Jules stares me down. "You think Nat would be satisfied with anything other than a win?"

I don't even have to answer. I know already that she would accept nothing less than first place. My brother is going to have his work cut out for him.

Still, this has been a lesson for me too. Me and Virgil should have done a better job of dealing with our shit. He's not like Nolan.

We need to have conversations. I can't just rely on him being driven by wanting to win.

Me and Virgil share a glance.

Our next match will be very different.

CHAPTER THIRTY-EIGHT

We gather at the Grad Club the Wednesday after quarterfinals for that week's Mastery group. Regardless of what he said about there being nothing in it for him, Nolan is here as he's meant to be. Maybe because I agreed to help with the Wilds, and he has a conscience. Or maybe because of what we did in that room in the Pen. Meanwhile, Virgil sits near the edge of the squishy leather couch the three of us are on, eager to learn.

I glance out of the corner of my eye at Laira sitting by the piano. Somehow, I have to ask what she was doing in Toronto. I like Laira. The idea that she might be the shadowy Monster who pushed Mom to the brink . . .

Henry says, "Glad to see that everyone made it through." Bryce, Mitch, Violet, and Frankie have evidently been killing it in the repechage. It was always inevitable that I'd have to go up against my friends, but I didn't realize it would be so soon. There are only four

teams in the semifinals repechage, and we'll have to beat them all—including the people in this room.

Henry continues, "By now, I'm sure everyone is aware of the most recent attack on our Doctorate." I stiffen in my seat. "I would like to assure you that his guard has been increased, and as the Wilds have declared a strike, they are not transforming—aside from our Mr. Murphy here. This is not something the Doctorate himself ordered, but it does have a potentially positive outcome."

"Potentially?" Nolan says, glaring at Henry.

"You wouldn't want to suggest that this is the work of a Doctorate candidate, would you? Because that's the only reason that not transforming would definitely, instead of potentially, halt this issue." Nolan doesn't reply, and Henry moves on. "All right, progress reports."

We do our usual run-through. It seems like the others are making positive strides, and Violet and Frankie have finally achieved second-evolution status. I'm forced to discuss the discord between me and Virgil causing issues in our last match, which Henry surprisingly doesn't comment on much.

The practical component for the day is a repeat of the first exercise we did, which we can all now do easily. The Monsters are then made to do small third-evolution demonstrations, followed by attempts from the Bachelors to call on the skill, which only Bryce succeeds at doing. For homework, we're meant to work on third-evolution skills.

Henry dismisses us, and I stand to leave. "August, Virgil, and Nolan, stay back."

I sigh. Bryce and Mitch give us sympathetic looks as they leave. I think Violet and Frankie are still feeling too downtrodden to manage sympathy for anyone else.

I'm trying to think of a time when we had a private meeting with Henry that didn't feel like being lectured and am coming up short.

Henry crosses his arms. "I greatly underestimated the level of difficulty that I'm sure Margot has had in dealing with you. Even more so now that you've become a trio." Virgil hunches, and Nolan looks as bored as he's looked all day. "Watching the three of you at the quarterfinals opening ball, I felt that we were finally seeing cohesion. Which is one of the reasons that dance is mandatory. It forces you to collaborate in a different way to help you understand how to work together in matches. And yet, you are regressing. Why?"

He looks directly at Virgil when he asks.

I say, "We had a disagreement right before. But we've dealt with it now." For some reason, Nolan rolls his eyes. "Something to add?"

"Nothing," Nolan says.

"Doesn't seem like nothing."

He slides his eyes toward me. "You can't even let him answer the question himself. You don't have to jump to his rescue at every moment. He's a big boy."

I scowl. "Says the person who was speaking for him the other day."

Virgil rubs his head. "He's right. It was my fault. Things you say to me before we go into a match shouldn't have any bearing on my performance. I should be able to compartmentalize."

"Wrong," Henry says, and Virgil's eyes widen. "You cannot compartmentalize the bond. You watched Margot and Isaac—is that what you thought they did?"

"No . . ."

"Then why would you?" Virgil snaps his mouth closed, and I narrow my eyes at Henry. Does he always have to be such an asshole?

"The three of you act like separate individuals with separate goals. The only reason Mr. Murphy and Ms. Black have managed to perform well thus far is that they can align quickly on winning. But in between matches, you fall out of it again. You cannot turn your connection on and off. You are always bonded. And as far as things seem to be progressing, this will likely be a permanent situation."

I gnaw on the inside of my cheek.

Henry gestures to us. "Align on something. I don't care what you choose. But it must be something that can apply to all of you either in or out of matches." He jerks his head at Laira, and she reaches into her bag, pulling out a box that she presents to us. Henry says, "Play three rounds. That's your homework. Semifinals are in a week, and now you'll be in the repechage. Lose again, and you're out. You might be lucky enough to still make the cutoff even with another loss, but there's no guarantee unless you reach the finals."

I stare at the colorful box, which declares TWISTER. I gawk at Henry. "You can't be serious."

"When am I not?" he says. "I expect to see a better performance in your next match." Henry walks out of the room without another word, leaving Laira to gather her things by herself.

"Actually, could I talk to you for a minute?" I ask her.

"Okay . . ." She eases back into her chair.

I wave off Virgil and Nolan, who go ahead of me. "Can I show you something?" I ask.

Laira shrugs, her brow furrowed. "Sure."

I grab my backpack and pull out my laptop, sitting next to her. I set it on the table and play the video file. Corey isolated the clip for me. It's just the flash of the reptilian Monster darting across the

screen. I examine Laira's face as she watches the video.

At first, her expression is bored, and then it sharpens, and she tugs the laptop close to her. "What . . . what is this?"

"Is that you?" I ask.

She slams the laptop closed. "What the fuck is this?" For the first time since I met her, Laira sounds dangerous. She sounds like the sort of partner Henry would have.

"It's from November twenty-fifth the year before last. I've been looking into what happened to my mom. She was attacked on that day, and there was a reported Monster sighting. So I thought . . . anyway, yeah. That's the place where she was murdered. The Scarborough Bluffs."

Laira shakes her head. "No . . . no, I mean, I went to visit my sister for her birthday around then. But I didn't . . . I wasn't running around in Monster form." The older woman looks sick, her skin washing out.

"Who knew you were going to see your sister?" I ask.

"Uh, anyone, I guess? You have to block off unavailable time so you don't get booked for missions. They don't usually schedule them during that time because of the Doctorate's Ball, and I don't do many anyway, but I did it just in case. The twenty-first to the twenty-sixth. Who did you show this to?"

"Not Henry," I say.

She nods to herself several times. "Okay . . . Can you not—"

"I won't."

She keeps nodding, like a bobblehead on a bumpy road. "I just . . . I don't remember. But I wouldn't have done anything to your mom. I don't even know her."

"I know. Sorry, I just, I thought maybe you'd know something or

had seen someone. That's it." I pack away my laptop and leave Laira at the table, still nodding her head.

I believe that she didn't know Mom and wouldn't have intentionally hurt her. But I also believe that Adam knew where she was going to be and took advantage.

Corey really should consider a career in event planning. She insisted that the best way to carry out Henry's assignment to bond better would be with a sleepover. She's off to do more research with Riley, so we're on our own, but she still took the time to set down a blanket and pillows on the floor in the spare room, along with one of her signature charcuterie boards. No wine, though.

"Are we seriously going to play this?" I ask. "Can't we just . . . not and say we did?"

"We have to do it," Virgil says. "Besides, what if Henry asks us specific questions about how it went?"

"We can align on lies. That's basically what he told us to do."

Virgil stares at me flatly. "We're playing." He lays out the play mat and flicks the spinner. He gets right hand red, and smacks his hand on the red dot in the corner. "Easy."

With a sigh, I spin the thing and get left foot yellow. I put my foot on the edge near Virgil, and Nolan's eye twitches. "What?"

"All games have strategy," he says. "Even kids' games. You two"—he looks between me and Virgil—"are probably going to regret those choices."

"Just spin the thing!"

Nolan flicks the spinner, getting right foot blue. This loser actually takes time to assess the mat. He sets his foot in the middle.

"How is that a smarter move?"

"I'm not sharing my strategy."

Virgil makes a noise that sounds suspiciously like a laugh, but when I look at him, he's settled his face into something neutral. He gets left hand green. Immediately, I understand what Nolan meant. Virgil is now forced to stretch over my foot to put his hand on the green dot in the corner.

Nolan makes a sound in the back of his throat.

"What?" Virgil says, craning his neck up.

"Nothing," Nolan hums.

I flick the spinner, getting right hand blue. Shit. Virgil is stretched across all the nearby blue dots, so now I have to lean over him. I put my hand on the blue dot next to Nolan's foot, just to fuck with him. Though of course he's unaffected and looks pleased to stare at me and Virgil struggling to reach over each other.

By the third go-around, me and Virgil realize how badly we've messed up, and he falls attempting to position his foot. I fall the next move, and Nolan wins. The second round goes similarly, despite me and Virgil trying to move more to the center. Which, once again, makes us end up stretching over each other, meaning we both fall first, *again*, and lose.

Nolan, of course, is extremely pleased with himself. It occurs to me then why he might enjoy games like this so much. Not just the straightforward rules like he said before, but the winning. He wins a lot. And if he's ever second best, it's because of how he played the game, not because he was the only spare option. I'm starting to understand how much being his dad's backup has affected Nolan.

By the third round of Twister, me and Virgil have aligned in wanting to beat Nolan.

"Let's change the turn order," Virgil says.

Nolan shrugs. "If you want."

This time, we make Nolan go first. He always picks spots far away from us, so we crowd in on him. Which seemed smart until we're all tangled around each other.

A bead of sweat rolls down Nolan's forehead. "I hope you two are happy with yourselves. If you played to win instead of to spite me, we wouldn't be in this position."

The position he's describing is Virgil struggling to do a backward bridge on the bottom, Nolan squeezed overtop, and me tangled around them both, attempting not to fall.

"But then we wouldn't have gotten the satisfaction," I say with a grin.

"Now we'll just lose together."

"Good!" me and Virgil say at the same time.

Nolan rolls his eyes, and in the next move, Virgil tickles my leg trying to move his hand, which unbalances me, so I fall on Nolan, who falls on him. In the seconds after being triumphant that at least Nolan didn't win this time, I realize that the three of us are kind of compromisingly tangled in each other. We manage to get out of it and sit on the mat, sweaty and flushed.

"Well," I say. "Are we aligned?"

By the flat looks on Virgil's and Nolan's faces, I would say we aren't.

I shake my head. "How are we supposed to handle Adam if we can't even manage the Monster's Ball? Winning isn't just what we need to do for the plan, it's also a measure of how we stack up, and we're lacking."

"Which is exactly why *we* shouldn't be handling the Adam thing," Virgil says.

Nolan laughs. "Always want to have your cake and eat it too."

"What does that mean?" Virgil snaps.

"You know what it means."

"We can't do this again!" I shout, standing. "Aren't you sick and tired of being so fucking weak? I am. Melani was right. There are three of us. We should be coasting through this competition." I shake my head and collapse onto the bed. It's dramatic, but I don't care.

If we lose again, it's over. We might not even make the cutoff for Master-in-training. Never mind getting Adam alone. I think again of Mom flying over the edge of the cliff.

"You can bunk with me," Virgil says to Nolan. "Let August have this bed."

Nolan says, "I can sleep on the floor."

"Sure. In my room."

A few beats pass, and then finally they leave, Virgil flipping off the light.

I gather the leftover cheese and crackers on the bed and eat by the light of my phone, scrolling through videos just to do something. Once I've finished, I dump the board on the floor and curl up under the sheets, only bothering to put on my bonnet and nothing else.

Hours later, I'm awake again. There's murmuring coming from outside the room. I ease off the bed and walk to the door. Even without getting close, my senses sharpen, and I can hear as if I were in the hall with them.

"Do something about it, then," Nolan says.

Nothing from Virgil.

I push open the door in time to see Nolan step back from the wall, where he was leaning close to Virgil. Much closer than you

need to be to talk to someone. Virgil rubs the back of his neck, turning away from me.

"Everything okay?" I ask.

Nolan nods. "Fine." He turns and heads back into the bedroom.

I walk over to Virgil. "Is it?" I ask.

"Yeah," Virgil says. He stares at me for a moment, which is when I remember that I'm wearing my bonnet. He tugs it down on my forehead so it covers better.

"What's up with you and Nolan?" I ask.

"Nothing."

"Right," I scoff.

"What's up with *you* and Nolan?" Virgil says, throwing it back at me. I swallow. He knows. He has to know.

I lick my lips. "I asked first."

Virgil doesn't say anything for a few seconds, staring at the space beside my head. "Imagine there were only two people left on Earth, you and someone you can't stand. You could try ignoring each other. That would work for a while, sure. But eventually, you understand that you need each other because that's what the circumstances require. You have no choice but to be each other's best friend and companion and partner. And then, suppose you discover that someone else exists. Everything between you doesn't disappear, but now you have a choice. This person becomes the North Star, in a way. To both of you. And so, despite the animosity, despite not wanting anything to do with them, you're linked together by your connection with that one shining star. And between you is an understanding that can only be felt by your shared circumstances, and this same understanding is also probably why you don't like each other."

"Who am I in this equation?"

"Don't do that," Virgil says.

Henry told us to find a North Star, and I don't know that I want it to be me, the way Virgil is implying. But I also don't know that either he or Nolan is giving me a chance to change that.

"Are you still mad?" I ask. "About my plans for Adam."

"Yes. But I'd rather hear the truth from you than a lie." He reaches out, rubbing the satin tie of my bonnet between his fingers. "And my truth is that I'm going to do everything I can to stop you from killing him. That's my role, remember? To stop you."

"That's not what I meant when I said that."

"Wasn't it?" He blows out a breath, dropping his hand. "Good night." He turns and heads into his room.

"Good night," I mutter, still standing in the hall.

CHAPTER THIRTY-NINE

Riley

Douglas Library has a more gothic quality to it at night. The gray stonework looks blacker and the height of the four floors grander. Though of course, you don't enter the building through those fancy double doors anymore. They've added a modern opening on the left—tacking on glass doors with stainless steel handles. There's something about it that feels sacrilegious.

But we won't be going through either of those entrances on University Avenue—not with its bright streetlights and students strolling by even now, at one in the morning on a Sunday.

August yawns loudly, and I resist the urge to snap at her to be quiet. Corey murmurs to her that this shouldn't take too long. That girl has the patience of a saint, I swear.

Corey still hasn't talked with the others about their secret meeting with her brother. If it were me, I would have confronted them already, but she's kept quiet. I would guess it's because she thinks

that was the right move. She said as much the day we encountered her ex.

We've been meeting like usual, but ever since seeing Barbie, it's been different. Those shy smiles that used to almost feel like they were saved for me are gone. It's not like she's not herself. It's that she's started to treat me the way she might treat August.

Because we're just friends.

I take out the keys to the back maintenance door of the building and slide them in. The inside of the library, in contrast to its exterior, is heavily modernized—shiny white linoleum floors with scrapes and scratches from foot traffic, and walls painted white in some areas and yellow in others. We leave the fluorescents off, so the only thing lighting the way is my phone.

I look back at Corey, who's already consulting her notes. Based on what else we could find, we're pretty sure we've narrowed down a location.

"Another QBSS member got you the keys?" August asks.

"An alum, actually." I gesture to Corey. "I'll let you lead from here."

Corey strides forward with Virgil at her side. There is a distinct lack of Nolan, but neither August nor Virgil have mentioned it. August drops back to my side.

"So . . . how are things?" she asks.

"Please be precise with what you want."

"Corey seems . . ." I stiffen, but August doesn't finish the sentence.

"Seems what?"

"Do you like girls?"

I stop in the hallway, though Corey and Virgil don't notice, too

focused on the map. August and I stare at each other for a long moment. Then I turn and walk at a faster clip to catch up. "What would even be the point?" I say finally. "I like guys. I would be perfectly happy doing that. Obviously it won't be Jackson, but I have lots of time to find the right guy."

"Yeah, for sure, if that's what you want." She squints. "How far away is this pl—"

"What does that even mean? If that's what I want?" No way I'm letting her bring this up and then just switch subjects.

August tilts her head. "It means . . . if that's what you want."

"Are *you* doing what you want with your little love triangle deal?"

"It's forbidden or whatever."

"Fuck off," I mutter. "You've really never done anything with either of them?"

August's eyes dart ahead to Corey and Virgil. She takes out her phone, types something, and then shows it to me.

I made out with Nolan the other day. Me and Virgil kissed before, but he was all like "We can't do that again."

Oh my God, this girl really *is* in a love triangle. "Do you have a preference?" I ask.

"There's no point in having a preference when things have to go both ways," she says. "Even if it's not ideal, it's also hard to ignore. And to be honest, I don't want to ignore it." She meets my eyes. "Don't you ever want to give in to what *you* want?"

I look away from her and stare straight ahead. There's a way that things are supposed to be: become president of QBSS, graduate with honors, become partner at a prestigious firm, marry an equally successful man, and be a shining example of the Black nuclear family and Black excellence. There's a blueprint that I'm

meant to follow. The goal of not only achieving what my parents and grandparents did before me but surpassing them.

I think about the time I'm not supposed to think about. When Sammie and I were buzzed, stuffed full of poutine, and curled up in my bed watching *Pretty Little Liars.* There was this scene where one of the main girls and another girl kiss, and we were quiet. Sammie asked me if I'd ever thought about kissing a girl. I lied and said I hadn't. She looked away and laughed like, *"Yeah, me neither."*

She fell asleep, and I thought, what if I weren't with Jackson? What if, hypothetically, I were single? What if I hadn't lied? I played the whole scene out. I would say that, yeah, I had thought about it, and Sammie would look at me, and I'd lean down, and she'd lean up, and we'd kiss.

I fell asleep dreaming of that reality, and when I woke up, I told myself that the thoughts were normal for straight girls. And they were just thoughts. I would never follow through.

Couldn't follow through, because it didn't fit the blueprint. It isn't that I think my parents would have a problem with me being bi, but more that they would be disappointed. And I've already disappointed them so much. Them, and Grandma, and the elder council, and the student council, and the QBSS members. It all just keeps piling up. I don't know how much more I can take. But I also don't know if I can keep pretending to be something I'm not.

"Here!" Corey says. And though she whispers, her voice still jolts me to attention.

I swallow and approach her. The door isn't particularly novel. It looks like it leads to a service area, and when Corey opens it, there's a smattering of custodial supplies inside.

Virgil knocks on the wood in the back. "There's a scent behind

here. Like . . . earth? Something?" We squish ourselves into the already tiny room, looking for any sort of trick door or latch.

Corey stumbles back, tripping over something on the floor, and I rush forward to catch her. She mumbles an apology and holds onto me as she regains her footing. "You okay?" I ask. She nods, the flush on her face obvious even in the dark.

"Sorry," she says. "Balance isn't my strongest suit."

"It's fine." Feeling my neck prickle, I turn to find August giving me a significant look. I ignore her.

"Got it," Virgil says, squatting on the floor and revealing a latch. "There's a symbol. . . ."

I stare at the thing, squinting and trying to make sense of the random assortment of circles. August squats next to me. I glance at her—specifically, at the chain on her neck and then at the symbol. Maybe . . . "Hold the chain to the symbol and activate it."

She seems skeptical but unlatches the necklace anyway. We only had one training session. We should have had more, but I've been swamped. Still, she manages to make the links glow, pressing the chain to the latch until it pops open.

We stare into the open cubby.

At nothing.

August laughs, rising her to her feet. "Yet another dead end. Dead end after dead end after dead end." She shakes her head. "Can barely manage in the Monster's Ball and can't find the actual weapon we need to make Adam confess. This entire plan is doomed."

I dig my hand around in the hole, hoping that something else comes out. I say, "Something should be here."

"But it's not."

There's no way. It can't end here. I need the Osseous. I need to

have something to show the elder council. I can't have spent all this time and energy to come away empty-handed.

"There has to be some other trick to it." I'm digging around in the space while the others stand. I look back at Corey, who's gripping her printouts.

She says, "This . . . I don't know. It had the symbol. It worked. If nothing's there, then . . . whoever was researching before took it. Pattie or Adam, or someone."

"So we skip ahead to the next clue."

"The next clue was an offshoot of this one. We were supposed to use whatever came from it. If we don't have what was supposed to be in there, then we don't have anything."

"It's over, Riley," August says.

"Is it? Or do you just want to give up on the plan? I shouldn't be surprised that you're flaking on me."

"I'm not flaking on you."

"Yes, you are. What? You lost one fight in your little competition, and now you can't hack it anymore? Or did lover boy convince you that his magnanimous leader is magically innocent?"

August grinds her teeth, staring me down.

"This is the man who had your mom killed. And you're just done?"

August spits, "You know what? Fuck you, and fuck this." She throws the chain at my feet, spinning on her heel and taking off. Virgil sighs and follows her, so I'm alone with Corey.

I cannot give up on this. There's no way I just let this shit go.

Corey says, "We should leave too. Either way, we'll need to regroup."

"No, it's fine. You don't have to stick it out with me or whatever."

"I don't mind."

"Why?" I bark. "Because your ex said you give up on friends, and so you need to prove her wrong?"

Corey's eyes narrow. "If this is going to turn into you saying some hateful crap to push me away, we can skip it. I already dealt with that with August, and I don't want a repeat. I wasn't a good friend to Barbie, but that doesn't mean I'm not a good friend. *I am.* I know that. That also means I don't have to accept being shit on. So you deal with whatever emotions are churning around in you, and when you're ready to be a good friend *to me,* text me. And I'll be there. But I'm not a ready-to-go emotional punching bag just because I'm nice."

I stand in the same spot as I watch her leave.

Eventually, I make my way outside, and everyone else is already gone.

CHAPTER FORTY

At university, St. Patrick's Day is a big deal. It's ten in the morning on Monday, but it's rowdy outside my dorm room, as if it were midnight on a Saturday. I open my door and peek out to see floormates running down the halls decked out in green clothes and matching face paint. They're all grasping reusable water bottles that I assume are filled with green beer.

This is when I regret not being more friendly with the people on my floor, because there's no way I'm going to get a hold of alcohol like this. And I could really use a day off.

I've been reading my psych textbook so much that I'm dreaming about the content, and my so-called easy courses have started to get annoying. Mostly because I kept not studying and relying on common knowledge to get me through, which isn't cutting it anymore if the 55 percent I got on my last astronomy quiz was proof of things to come. Now I have to actually try with all my courses, not just psychology, and I'm exhausted.

I lean my head against the door before returning to my bed, flopping onto it to check my texts. I have one that I missed at 9:45 a.m. from Nolan: *Do you have something green?*

A grin spreads across my face. I jump up and root through my closet. The only green thing I own is a black-and-green-checkered skater dress. It'll have to do. I text Nolan back to ask where I'm supposed to meet him.

I'm outside, he says. *Bring a water bottle. One you can't see through.*

I pull on my Docs, grab a sling bag and a tumbler, and head out. Nolan drags his eyes over my form and shakes his head. He pulls off his green hoodie and gives it to me. I eye the fabric. Nolan isn't a big guy, but the hoodie is a baggy fit. I check the tag and confirm it's a size I can fit into before pulling it over my head. Oversized on him, but it's perfect on me. I don't need it, since I'm used to managing in colder weather like a Monster would, but I appreciate the gesture. Plus, it's comfier than wearing the dress alone.

Nolan has on a green long sleeve underneath.

"How do you have so many green clothes?" I ask him.

He raises an eyebrow. "I'm Irish. Murphy, remember?"

Right. He also literally has red hair. I probably should have put those things together earlier.

He gives me a serious look. "There's one thing you need to promise if we're gonna do this."

"Okay . . ."

"You call it St. Patrick's Day or St. Paddy's, with a *d* sound. If I hear a *t*, we're done."

"Noted." I tilt my head. "Is this whole thing like low-key offensive to you?"

He shrugs. "It's all I've known, since I was born here. But our

family was originally in Newfoundland, which has a pretty large Irish population, especially back then. We honestly claim that more than the Irish ancestry, since our family was there for so long. Our ancestor came to Kingston to work and then, well, you know everything that happened from there. So we've been here for a while. But even disconnected, there are just lines you don't cross. And saying the right name of the holiday is one." He turns and starts walking. "Come on."

Nolan must be talking about Francis, aka Patient Zero, whose son was the first Wild who the Murphys are apparently direct descendants of.

I fall into step with him. "Where are we going? Aberdeen?" From what I've heard, that's the party street.

Nolan makes a face. "So we can stand around like sardines in a can with a bunch of cops breathing down our necks? No. Have a little faith in me."

I roll my eyes but follow him to the west side of campus. I'm technically skipping classes, but there's no way Margot and Henry can blame me for ditching on St. Patrick's Day. Henry even pushed our scheduled training session because he claimed that he finds students don't concentrate well on this day.

Nolan walks up the steps of a house blasting hip-hop through the speakers. There are students in green sitting on the roof and milling on the front lawn. No one says anything to us as we walk inside and head to the keg. He fills up my tumbler with a liquid that I assume is beer from the foam, but it's neon green, like Mountain Dew.

"Hey! You made it!" a white guy whose whole face is painted green says as he ambles over and glances at me.

Nolan says, "This is August. August, Randall."

Randall grins. "Freshman?" I'm not sure who he's asking, but I nod anyway. "Robbing the cradle," he says to Nolan with a laugh.

"Fuck off," Nolan replies, but lightly, like he's not that bothered. I mean, he's only a year older, so hardly.

My cheeks heat, and I sip from my tumbler.

Someone calls out to Randall, and he waves goodbye to us before leaving. Nolan says, "Let me know if you feel sick or need to gscoff back."

I scoff. "I'm not an amateur."

Nolan laughs and leads the way out of the house. There's an ease in his shoulders. I'm used to seeing him leaning against walls or in corners looking perpetually petulant. I wish I could have the same level of good cheer. Between school, the dead end with the Osseous, and our lack of progress as a team, I'm not in the best mood.

He nudges me in the shoulder, and I jerk away. He raises his hands. "You okay?"

"Yeah, sorry, just surprised me." Or rather, I felt the nudge and looked over, half expecting Virgil to be there.

We walk into another house that's somehow rowdier than the last one. Two white guys are helping an East Asian–looking guy do a handstand while they organize a funnel. People actually do this shit in real life?

Nolan motions for my bottle, and I chug the rest before handing it to him. "So what?" he asks. "Are you a sad drunk?"

I reel back. "Um, no. I'm a fucking fun drunk."

"Doesn't seem like it. Care to explain why?"

A group of people surges past, and I'm forced to step in close to Nolan while they squeeze by. If this is bad, I guess Aberdeen would have been unbearable. Nolan rests his hand on my lower back,

slipping it under the hoodie, and I lean in more, though I don't have to.

"Just thinking," I say, biting my lip. "Last night we were looking for the Osseous again and came up empty."

Nolan eyes me, his fingers trailing up and down my spine in a way that makes it feel like there's no fabric between his hand and my skin. Anyone could see us here like this. Society people are always around. He doesn't care, obviously, but I should. "You're giving up, then?"

"No. I just don't know what to do. It feels impossible. You said as much. It's like he can't be beaten."

Nolan pulls his hand away to cap my tumbler an give it to me, then starts filling his. I lick my lips, wondering if he's going to put his hand back. I sip the beer, my head getting lighter as I do. I look up at him. This close, the height difference is more prominent.

"Yeah," Nolan mumbles as he caps his tumbler, tips his head back, and chugs from the spout for what feels like a solid five seconds. We head to the next house, and the next, and the next.

We walk out of another house—I've lost track of how many we've been to. Nolan stumbles into my back, and I laugh. He rights himself and strides forward with those impossibly long legs of his. I follow and realize that we're walking through the Victoria Hall parking lot. We come around to the side door, and Nolan gestures at it. "End of the line," he says.

"Seriously? It's, like"—I check my phone—"only one." It hadn't felt like we'd been house hopping for three hours, but apparently we had.

"Sleep it off for a bit. Eat something, whatever. Text me if you want to go out after. You have to pace yourself. I'll walk you to your room."

I roll my eyes but open the door and lead him up to the dorm. We enter the hallway, and with the number of people running around, it takes me a moment to realize that Virgil is leaning against my door.

He turns, taking in me and Nolan. "You missed class," he says.

"We don't have the same classes. How do you know I missed class?"

He gives me a look that says he's not even entertaining my question.

Nolan says, "She's going to have a nap." He nods to me. "Text me later if you want."

"Bye," I mumble as I enter my room. I drop face-first onto my bed, and the door closes. I glance over my shoulder to see that Virgil has followed me in. I groan. "I don't want a lecture. Can I just have fun for once?"

Virgil sits at my desk chair, picking up my bottle. He opens the lid, I assume to inspect it, but instead, he tilts it back and chugs the remainder of the beer.

I lift myself off the bed and walk over to him. For once, he's forced to look up at me instead of down. He didn't come to lecture me. If he had, he would be doing it now. Closer like this . . . and away from the chaos of the hall, it's easier to notice. It's not just my breath that smells like beer. Virgil's does too. It's even on his clothes. "Holy shit, have you been drinking?" I ask. "Like, before you came here?"

He adjusts his glasses. "Some guys from my English class invited me."

"And you went?!"

He shrugs. "They're not society kids. It's nice sometimes. To forget about being a Learner." He reaches up and tugs on the hoodie that I neglected to return to Nolan. It's slight. But enough that I

lower myself, sitting on his lap. The desk chair creaks but doesn't give. Virgil winds his arms around my back and pulls me closer. I rest my forehead against his.

"You're the one who said you didn't want this," I breathe.

He laughs. "I never said I didn't want it. I said we couldn't have it." He stares into my eyes. "I'll always want you."

It's too warm. The flush works its way up my body from the heat at my back where his hands are, through my chest, to where our foreheads touch.

Virgil leans forward.

"Don't do it if you're going to say we can't again," I whisper.

"Don't act like that's going to stop you," he breathes.

And he's right. Because when he presses his lips to mine, I immediately respond, sinking into him. I've wanted this too badly to say no. He lowers his hands, running them up and down my thighs, pulling me closer as if we could physically meld to each other.

We break for air and then come right back, tongues sliding in a way that's more languid than our first time. Virgil grips my thighs, and I make a noise that just makes him kiss me harder.

It's not going to be enough. He has to know that.

I gasp as Virgil stands, lifting me at the same time. He walks me to the bed and tosses me onto the sheets. I'm breathing hard, staring at him. And he's looking down at me. He puts a knee on the bed.

"Be ready to finish it or don't start," I say, still panting. "I'm so fucking serious, Virgil. Either we are or we aren't, but you can't keep walking the line, constantly hopping between we're doing this and we're not. Adam can't break the bond, and he won't kill us. He needs me. The only thing stopping this is you. Make a choice and stick to it."

He stares at me, his dark amber eyes molten. Frozen in this moment.

For a second, I think he's going to do it. To choose me over everything. To pick me.

Instead, he pushes back and stands, running his fingers through his hair.

I sit up, hunching. I can't keep doing this. What I said to him applies to me, too. Either we're in or out, and he just made his choice. I won't be this girl sitting here and wanting him while he says no. "We'll be partners. We can be good at that. We were once, and we will be again. We just won't be more."

Virgil stares at me for a beat and then casts his eyes down and opens the door. Nolan is on the other side, in the hallway. He holds up a water bottle in explanation. A clear one actually filled with water instead of beer. With a single glance at me and Virgil, it's like he can read everything that's passed between us. For a second, I'm sure I see something crumple in his expression.

Nolan has always been cool and collected. Even among the jeers of second son and second best. Impenetrable, in a way. I can make him angry and annoyed. Definitely. I didn't think I could hurt him.

Virgil leaves without saying a word to our partner.

"I'm not going to apologize," I say, avoiding Nolan's eyes. "I didn't promise either of you anything."

"Do you hear me asking for an apology?" he says, stepping into my room and kicking the door shut behind him. He sets the bottle of water on my nightstand and sits on the bed next to me, his face close to mine. His breath still smells like beer. He tucks a loose braid behind my ear, and I try not to think of last year when Virgil did the same thing. We're only an inch or so apart. I can count the freckles

on his cheeks and the bridge of his nose. See the blond of his lashes as he watches me.

Nolan leans closer, so the space between us feels more fantasy than reality. "Tell me you want me, and I'll give you what he won't."

I know I've made Nolan the backup, just like his dad. Second son, second partner, second choice, second best. Second, over and over again. But right here, right now, he can win.

We're both drunk, and we're both hurt. This isn't a good time for making important decisions.

The past version of me, that other August, the good girl, would know the right answer here.

But I'm not her anymore, am I?

"I want you," I say.

Nolan kisses me and tugs off his sweatshirt and jeans before pulling his hoodie off me and pushing up the hem of my dress. He asks me again and again if I want him, if I want this. As he trails kisses down my neck, and slides down my underwear, and fishes a condom out of his discarded jeans pocket. And every time, I say yes.

Because I do want him.

Do I want him the most?

Well, we both know the answer to that.

CHAPTER FORTY-ONE

Corey opens the door to McIntosh Castle and beckons me inside. I can't believe it's the same day. There are still students walking down the streets in green face paint with their tumblers, even louder now that it's actually nighttime.

"I was just about to go out and find Virgil," she says. "He hasn't been answering my texts."

"Yeah . . . that's kind of what I wanted to talk about. . . ." I take a deep breath and remind myself that even though Corey is Virgil's best friend, she's still my friend too. "I hooked up with Nolan."

Corey's brow raises. "As in . . . ?"

I give her a long look, and she steps back. "Maybe we should talk for a bit." She leads the way to one of the sitting rooms, collapsing onto the couch. She must have been doing some work here, because she has several books laid out, including the one her brother gave her.

"You've been reading Ellis's book?" I ask.

She shrugs, fiddling with the three fingers on her left hand. "I mean, it's a good travel guide. And the notes are . . . I guess this feels safe. You know?" I nod. The version of her brother within those pages can't hurt her. "I didn't realize how much he wanted to know me. Or how much I didn't know about him." She waves her hand. "Let's focus on you. Tell me everything."

I go through the full day's events from hanging out with Nolan, to making out with Virgil, to ultimately sleeping with Nolan, followed by a long nap with him, and ending with waking up very, *very* sober.

She asks, "Wait, so what happened after?"

"Nolan got a text from his dad about a Wild meeting or something, so he had to go. He texted me later basically saying that he didn't regret it."

"Do *you* regret it?"

I scrub my hands over my face. It's not like I did something I didn't want to do. And . . . I liked it. Liked that he touched the places on my new body that I'd yet to show anyone, that I still felt a type of way about, and found it all beautiful and kissable. Even when I was thin, I was never comfortable during sex. I spent half the experience anxious about how I looked.

Though I never voiced the thought aloud, it was hard to feel confident that I would be wanted by someone in this body. I could do it a lot of the time. But the thoughts still surfaced. Every glance in the mirror or at a photo was a confrontation. And I didn't always win.

Nolan hadn't lied. He'd given me everything that Virgil wouldn't.

But the fact remained that if Virgil had said yes, I would have been with him instead. "Do you think I should tell Virgil?"

"It's not ideal to keep secrets between friends."

I wince and lick my lips. "Speaking of . . . me and Virgil . . . we met up with Ellis and—"

"I know." Corey wrings her hands. "Barbie told me. Riley and I had a run-in with her. I assume you contacted him to find out about the Scientist connection with Pattie?"

"Yeah. He didn't really know anything, but . . . I also got the sense that he wasn't being fully truthful?" I pause before saying, "He wanted us to help you reconcile with him."

Corey nods slowly. "Makes sense."

"I'm sorry."

"I'm not condoning it, but I get it. You thought I was going to break down or whatever because that's what I've been doing all year."

"I mean, you have a legitimate reason for reacting that way."

"I'm tired of it," she mutters. "We were talking about you. Okay, so I get what you're saying about the repercussions of a relationship being different now given the Adam stuff. But even so, there are other punishments. Being kicked out of the Monster's Ball, for one. It's not without its risks, so I understand Virgil's feelings about being cautious. But I also agree that it's unfair to say you're going to be platonic and then keep pushing those boundaries. Given that you established that, I don't think a line was crossed with Nolan. But I do think you all should talk about it. I mean, do you want to be with Nolan?"

"I don't know that I want to, like, *be* with him. I dunno. There's something there." I stand. "Let's just go find Virgil."

Corey looks like she wants to discuss more but lets it drop. "I'm pretty sure I know where he is."

We leave McIntosh Castle, and she leads me down King Street

and then farther south to a set of small townhouses. Whereas the other houses have welcome mats, or parked cars, or porch decorations, this one has nothing. Corey uses a key on her ring to open the door, and we step inside.

It's a tiny entryway with a place to rest your keys on a small table, and above it, a photo of a family: a handsome Black man, tall and built a lot like Virgil, plus-sized and muscled with his hair in twists, a thick beard, and glasses on his nose, and hugged to his side is a Black woman, though with a much lighter skin tone, big and beautiful, wearing a killer form-fitting dress, makeup done to the nines, with curls that reach her shoulders. In her arms is a baby boy. It's obvious, even this young, that it's Virgil.

"This is Virgil's childhood home," Corey says. "He inherited it, but he refuses to live here. Henry manages the upkeep."

We walk into a large open-concept kitchen and dining room. There's furniture—a couch and tables and chairs—but all the other things that make a house feel homey are gone. No throw pillows, or discarded books or magazines, and no appliances on the counters. Besides that photo in the entry, it looks like it's been staged for sale with the absolute minimum.

"Where's their stuff?" I ask.

"Storage," Corey says. "When Virgil turned eighteen and took possession, he started packing things away. He wanted to get rid of it. But he just did this area and then stopped." She nods to the staircase at the back of the room. "I'll give you two some space."

"You sure you don't want to come with?"

She shakes her head. "I feel like this is an overdue conversation. A private one."

I sigh and trudge up the stairs. I find Virgil in the first room on

the right, sitting cross-legged on the floor with a bunch of photographs laid out in front of him. The entire room is filled with boxes. There's a child's bed in the corner where I guess he used to sleep, and lettering on the wall spelling out his name in pastel green.

"Hey," I say.

"Hey."

I sit across from him. Fuck, this is terrible. I open my mouth, ready to just spew it out. "Me and Nolan—"

"I know."

I blink. "He told you?"

Virgil wrings his hands. "Our bond . . . it's stronger now. From the blood exchange he did to help me heal."

"How does that relate to you knowing? Like you have a telepathic link or something? What does that even mean?"

"It means I know how it feels to touch you in places where my hands have never been," he says, his voice rough enough to make my heart jolt and my throat dry up. "It's not like we read each other's minds, but I just know things that he does and vice versa, and some . . . sensations come through."

"Oh."

I imagine what he's describing as a lot like the initiation, when I knew all these things that Virgil was thinking as more of a feeling than words coming through my mind. Minus the . . . sensations thing.

Virgil hunches. "I'm sorry. I meant to tell you when I came by, and then . . . he should have told you. It's kind of odd, consent-wise, so . . . you should know. And I'm sorry I can't be like him."

I get what he means; it's kind of murky. I appreciate him telling me. Not that I imagine knowing beforehand would have stopped me.

"You'll really have to elaborate on that particular Nolan statement."

"I cannot break every rule in the book. I know that, sure, the bond can't be broken, and yeah, Adam is unlikely to kill us for that particular infraction, given what we suspect about him. But even still, I owe my life to Henry. I owe him my focus and my effort, and I owe him my full attention. I have obligations that Nolan doesn't. I just . . . I thought that I could do both. Because I owe *you* my life too. And more than that, I wanted . . ." He swallows. "It doesn't matter what I want. Henry has always been transparent with me about his goals, and I've always been on board. My focus has to be doing well in the Monster's Ball. That's all."

"Fine." It's not much different from what I said in my dorm. I won't be chasing Virgil anymore. We'll be partners, and we'll get through this competition. And I'll try very hard not to think about the fact that every time I'm with Nolan, Virgil is there too. In the back of both our minds. "What's in the box?"

Virgil shrugs. "My parents' old pictures. Just feeling nostalgic, I guess. You can look too, if you want."

Me and Virgil lapse into silence as we flip through his family albums. His parents seemed sweet together. I can see he didn't get his eyes from either of them, but he has his mom's nose and his dad's smile. Virgil inhales sharply, and I look up. "What?"

He hands me a picture, his hands shaking ever so slightly.

It's his parents, and next to them are Pattie and my mom.

Virgil says, "I . . . I think I saw this once before. Must have been a long time ago. That's why your mom seemed familiar in that picture at Bailey's place."

Virgil's parents knew my mom. Knew my mom and Pattie. Probably Carrigan, too.

"Let's go get Corey," I say.

Virgil follows me downstairs, and after showing her the picture, we return upstairs to dig through the boxes and papers to see if there are any more details about his parents and their connection to mine.

"You had a home birth?" Corey asks, holding up a set of files.

Virgil shakes his head. "No, I was born at Kingston General."

"Not according to these. There's, like, notes from a doula and stuff. Home birth, and there was a nurse, too—uh, hold on . . ." Corey consults the paper, and I know who she's going to say before she says it. "Patricia Griffen."

"Is a home birth bad?" I ask.

Virgil says, "No, but . . . my birth certificate says I was born at the hospital. So, like, they forged it? Why?"

"When were your parents born?"

"My dad was 1979, and my mom was 1981—no, no, no." He shakes his head, already seeing where my train of thought is going. Pattie had a secret baby in 1981. And there she is in that picture with Virgil's parents, and she helped his mom give birth to him. "My grandpa was an asshole who made my grandma get a paternity test. My mom is theirs. Neither of them talk to me now, of course. But she's not the secret baby."

My shoulders sag. Thank fuck for that.

"Now that we've cleared up any possibility of incest," Corey says, "look at these medical notes."

"Medical notes?" Virgil says, coming over and taking the papers. He scans them. "I never packed these. I've never seen these before."

"What's on them?" I ask.

Corey says, "Just, like, lots of blood tests and stuff."

"My parents were sickle cell carriers," Virgil says. "They used to

take me in for tests a lot because they worried I might have it."

"Virgil . . . look at the records. Neither of them are carriers."

Virgil jerks his head up to stare open-mouthed at Corey before flipping through the papers faster. "This . . . Then what were they testing for?"

I swallow. "I mean . . . the thing with you bending the bars last year—bars specifically made to keep Monsters in. And even your blood bond with Nolan and how that got wrapped up with me is odd. You're, I mean, you're not like other Monsters. Even the roar. It's not supposed to be this strong ability, and yet with you, it is. Plus, Pattie was in the Scientist faction. . . . And chances are Carrigan may have been involved too."

"What are you saying? That they experimented on me, and my parents cosigned it?"

"I don't know! Maybe you were just born that way, and they were trying to figure it out?"

"But how would they know there was anything to figure out in the first place?"

Something clatters in the hall, and we turn to the door. Virgil strides toward it and flings it open, and then sprints through the house at high speed before coming back into the room.

"What is it?" Corey asks.

He shakes his head. "I didn't see anyone. A picture frame fell. Nail was loose, I guess."

Corey keeps staring at the hallway, her eyes narrowed.

I follow her line of sight. "What?"

She shakes her head. "I just . . . I thought I saw, like, smoke? Must be the dust."

But there's no dust in this house. It's clean.

"No odd scents?" I ask Virgil.

"Not that I can pick up." He crosses his arms. "But scents can be hidden. And these records weren't here before. Someone put these here."

My mind goes straight to Carrigan, but now that I know about Adam, I have to consider him, too. It was likely his journal that Pattie stole, after all.

"They were friends with Adam, too," Virgil mumbles. "They were in the same Mastery group."

"Wait, why would Adam have been in a Mastery group?" I ask.

"He's the Doctorate's son. He can do as he likes. He wanted to be with Henry, and so he was in the group."

Corey says, "Wasn't it, like, a big controversy, too? Because the senior Master of the group was a Progressive, and Cyrus didn't want his sons to show any faction allegiance."

"Carrigan did," I say.

"That's different. The Scientists are the only legitimized faction. They're seen as apolitical."

Virgil adds, "But Henry said James joined a group too, so Cyrus couldn't say no. That's how Henry and Adam became friends with my parents in the first place. It was weird, because you would think they would be friends with the other Bachelors too, not only their Monster partners."

I say, "And Carrigan disappeared and my mom moved the day after everything went down with your parents. That's what Georgia said." I meet Virgil's eyes. "You always said you never understood why your parents went after the Doctorate. Someone controlling Monsters to make them murder the Doctorate . . . Sound familiar?"

Virgil freezes.

I continue, "Pattie is dead. Your parents are dead. My mom is dead. Carrigan is in hiding. This is starting to look less like a picture of friends and more like a hit list. If Pattie and my mom knew about the Osseous, and Carrigan, too . . ."

"My parents may also have known," Virgil says, voice quiet. He turns and starts to go through the boxes faster, trying to find something, and me and Corey rush to help.

I don't know how much time passes. Hours. Corey forces us to stop, and we order takeout from the roti place in town at my request. Careful not to touch anything with curry-stained fingers, we keep searching. I've looked at so many papers that my eyes are starting to cross.

"There are a lot of books and notes about bonding," Corey mumbles. "Like they were studying it."

"I mean, it's an interesting subject," Virgil says, his eyes on the papers he's sorting through. "I've been reading up on it too."

Me and Corey share a look over Virgil's head. We already suspected that the reason his, mine, and Nolan's bond is so unique is because of Virgil. I don't know if he's unwilling to entertain the possibility that his parents greenlit experimentation on him or what, but the details are starting to add up. Still, what were they even trying to do?

"This is it!" Virgil says, waving around a book. Me and Corey go over to him. "It's an agenda. An hour before the attack, they have 'meet with A' in here."

"Well, fuck," I say.

Even Corey, who's usually the voice of reason, seems pressed to find any way to say that their meeting with Adam just before they went on a suicide mission was a coincidence.

"This is it!" Virgil repeats, shaking the book. "'Meet with A'? Come on! Adam was in Summerhill that day too. He would have known exactly where his father was. He was definitely old enough to take the title by then."

"But is it enough evidence to convince Henry?" I ask. Virgil crushes the book in his hand and slumps. "You get it now, don't you?" Now he understands what this has been like for me. Knowing the person responsible for my mom's death and desperate to make them pay. "Still think grief therapy is the way to fix this? Or leaving it to Henry?"

"It wouldn't hurt," he says, and I scowl. "But I know what you mean. I'm sorry I didn't try harder to understand." His hands twitch at his sides, smooth metallic claws growing and then shrinking, over and over.

Corey says, "We can still do the plan. We can get the Osseous—"

"What if we can't?" I ask. Just hours ago, I felt like there was no way to make this happen. But now, I'm not the only one motivated. "There has to be some other weakness we can exploit to get a confession." Without Adam admitting what he did, I have zero chance of getting away with killing him.

"How exactly are we supposed to find this weakness?" Virgil asks.

I grind my teeth. "There *has* to be something. We still have time as long as the Monster's Ball is going on."

Corey rises, picking up our discarded takeout containers. "I'm going to make some tea." She leaves me and Virgil alone.

He's still crushing the book. "I feel like Frankenstein's monster," he says.

So he wasn't ignoring what his parents might have done after all. "Don't you mean Frankenstein?"

"No. It's the monster—"

I grin, and he sighs, rolling his eyes. It's so easy to mess with him.

Despite my attempt to lighten the mood, his voice gets serious again. "They did something to me, made me something else, and now I've been abandoned by them. Not by choice, but still. I thought I was already at the pinnacle of any rage or hate, but it keeps going up. . . . I'm worried about the day it boils over. It's like the apocalypse. This catastrophe that I just keep waiting for."

"Who says you have to be afraid of it?" I ask, as if I haven't spent my own time scared of the monster in my mind. "It's a part of you." I hesitate, not sure if I even want to say this. "When I use the monster, it's the best feeling. Euphoric, even. Like I'm powerful and nothing can hurt me."

Virgil shakes his head, smiling. "I know. That's how I feel. And that's what scares me."

"Why would you be afraid of being powerful?"

"Powerful people have a tendency to hurt."

I swallow. Because yes, we've done exactly that with the monster. And yet, I can't give up on it.

CHAPTER FORTY-TWO

I swallow, caressing the knives on my thighs in the dim light of the antechamber. Being in the repechage wasn't part of the plan. Now, we'll have to make it through three matches to claw our way into the finals, while those already in the winner's round only have to do one. The repechage isn't only demoralizing, it's harder.

Nolan rolls his neck beside me, calm, as usual.

I haven't seen him in person since we hooked up, leaving his message unanswered. If he feels any way about it, he doesn't show it.

Virgil was on the fence about Adam before, but now that's changed. Even here with Nolan, I feel the difference. There's something solid between the three of us. Adam is the reason my mom is dead. The reason Nolan's people are being framed and pushed to further oppression. And likely the reason Virgil's parents are not only dead but were painted as villains, something that colored Virgil's entire life.

And we won't even have a shot at Adam if we can't win.

I need the monster now more than ever. Need that edge.

The monster stretches, extending metal claws and digging them into the soft meat of my mind.

There's something new in Nolan today too. A resolve that I thought was gone. "What happened at the meeting with your dad?"

"Adam showed up to say that the proposal is gaining a lot of ground, and he wants to sign an interim agreement that 'benefits both parties.'"

"Benefits him, he means, but also lets him look like the good guy."

"Yes. It'll create more pressure on us between the strike and the Doctorate himself offering a comprise. He's forcing our hand." Nolan licks his lips. "This isn't the time for mercy. Win by any means necessary."

"Obviously."

The light turns amber, and he strips down and transforms. I look away as if I haven't seen all there is to see of him. When the light turns green, the doors open, and I take two steps forward before freezing as our competitors come into view.

"No." The word slips from my lips.

Across the arena, Bryce grimaces as he spots me.

I know this was inevitable, but I'm not happy about it.

Bryce squares his shoulders, and his facial expression flattens.

A loss for either of us means we're out of the competition. We've made it to the semifinals, so we're within the cutoff, but the higher you rank, the better. Bryce isn't the sort of guy who would be content with just skating by.

Mitch snorts, his gorilla-like nostrils large and flaring. He's as committed to the win as his partner. And he's got a bipedal advantage.

But we *have* to win. There's no other option.

And no room for mercy. Even among friends.

The horn blows, and Nolan casts a fog around the arena. The audience groans. Now they'll be forced to watch heat signatures on the screen. I couldn't give a fuck.

I close my eyes and take a breath. The fog obscures our scents, but Nolan can still navigate through it. And he is, judging by the sudden roar that comes from Mitch off to my left. *Concentrate.* My nose twitches. The fog . . . it smells like Nolan. That three-in-one soap, bland laundry detergent, and cardboard and wood, like the pieces in his games. The fog doesn't obscure our scents; it just makes it smell like Nolan everywhere.

And knowing his scent, I can tell right away which bit is wrong. The tang of metal.

I surge forward and toss a knife, listening to the clang of steel as Bryce blocks with his sword. I throw three more, staying within the cover of the fog, and each one he blocks. He may not be able to see me, but he has the reflexes to defend.

I'm not throwing fast enough.

I can't be that girl again. The one scrambling through the Pen, terrified and weak. Or the one standing by in frozen horror as she watched children slaughtered, and once again while a woman was beheaded.

I can't be the girl who was at a party while her mom was murdered.

Inside me is the strength of two Monsters. It's about time I started using it to its full extent.

This is called the Monster's Ball for a reason.

That boy with his sword? He's only human.

I'm much more.

The monster grins at me, black lips splaying wide, showing off gleaming teeth.

I let go.

I dash through the fog, no longer concerned about being seen. Let him see. He won't be able to keep up this time. He screams as I fling three knives at his thigh, one after the other, each hitting the same point. Three blades driven deep.

The sword comes down. It's impressive, really. That he can still swing through the pain. It's accurate, too. The blade descends, and I catch it with one hand, the metal clanging against the sharp claws that have shredded through my skin. Not as careful as how Virgil does it, extending his nails. The tips of my fingers are wrecked, split and bloody.

The boy's eyes are wide as he stares. "What the—?"

No time for what and how when there's a match to be won. I toss a fourth knife with my left hand, and it lodges once again in his thigh. He yelps and moves to jump back, but I won't let go of the sword. A fifth knife goes in. One too many, because it knocks two of the other knives out. Blood spurts from the wound.

The boy abandons the sword and retreats. I pick up the two blades from the ground and run my tongue over the cold steel edge, warmed now with his blood. It's like wine, rich and heady.

He's bouncing around the arena, keeping moving so it's harder for me to find him. But, of course, I know where he is at every point. He's dripping blood. I don't even have to try. The scent is almost overwhelming.

I let the knives fall from my claws. The new appendages are beautiful, truly. It's hard not to be mesmerized by the shine of the dark metal.

I wrinkle my nose, staring through the fog at Nolan; those pond green eyes stare back at me. He wants me to finish it. Doesn't he know that's exactly what I'm doing? He should concentrate on his own match.

I'm going to win.

It's funny. I was legitimately concerned about winning a few minutes ago, and now it feels guaranteed.

I'm the Monster. How could I lose?

The boy is behind me—hoping to strike, I suppose. He's found some way through the fog, not that it matters. When he jumps, I spear my claws through his leg, in the same spot where the blades are. He's pulled the small knives out and discarded them somewhere, hastily bandaging the wound. But the claws go through like butter, and he screams and screams.

His hand goes up in the air, and the horn sounds.

I rip my claws back with a squelch.

And he's just there, writhing on the ground.

But it's over, and I won, and that's all that matters.

I head to the antechamber, shaking the blood off my claws. I don't care to taste it anymore. Not now that he's been defeated so easily. I roll my neck as the doors close and we're bathed in darkness. Nolan catches my arm as I go to leave.

"You have blood on you," he says.

I let him collect a towel and wipe off my fingers where the blood is still warm and sticky. I sway a little as the moment between now and the fight stretches, feeling like it was hours ago instead of minutes. The monster curls into a ball, lapping leisurely at blood-soaked paws.

I squeeze my eyes shut. When I open them, Nolan has my chin in his grasp. He lets go and steps back. "You did what needed to be done."

Did I? Or did I lose myself for a win?

We leave the antechamber and find Violet and Frankie waiting for us outside. "What the fuck is wrong with you?!" Violet screams.

My arm is cold now.

In the moment, everything was perfect.

It was.

We won.

We're one step closer to Adam.

But now, something else has settled in my gut, weighty and putrid. The blood that tasted so good is cloying on my tongue, and all I want to do is spit or throw up. Anything to get rid of it.

Powerful people have a tendency to hurt.

"It's the Monster's Ball," Nolan snaps at Violet. "We fought, and we won. That's it. You want to be defeated nicely? Don't compete."

Violet doesn't even look at him. She's incandescent. Spitting as she talks while Frankie hovers behind her, glowering at me. "You targeted a single leg! He might not be able to walk on it again. You didn't need to do that."

"I needed to win," I say, but my voice is too low. Too quiet.

"We all want to win, but what you did was destruction. Like you wanted to hurt him when he's only ever been kind to you. I thought we were friends!"

I laugh. "Friends? Is that what you call it? When you've spent the entire semester barely containing your jealousy because I happen to be doing better than you? Because perfect Violet could never be anything but number one. You want to talk about how I treated him? How about how *you've* been treating him? Now that he's not playing second fiddle to you anymore, you're not as magnanimous."

Violet's mouth drops open, and she steps back.

"I hope you've enjoyed your time being queen of the losers. But I'm here now. And I plan to win."

And that's not the monster talking. That's all me.

I shove past her and Frankie, stomping away. At the exit of the Pen, Virgil and Corey wait. I stare at them. "You have something to say?"

Virgil says, "We won. That's what matters."

"Good."

Corey looks between the two of us and bites her lip. In the end, she doesn't say anything either.

In the back of my mind, the monster laughs, head thrown back, fangs catching the light. I promised to use it. Instead, it's the one using me.

I lean back in Nolan's car, resting my feet on the dashboard. We're headed to Sydenham to talk to the family of Polly—the Wild who was beheaded—and see if there's anything we can learn from them. Mia's apparently friendly with them and is supposed to meet us there.

Nolan parks, and I move to leave, but he's just sitting there. "What?" I ask.

He turns in the seat to face me. "Are we not going to talk about it?"

"What's there to talk about?"

"Do you want to do it again?"

I choke. I don't know what I thought he was going to say, but I wasn't expecting that. "You don't think it's kind of weird that Virgil is inadvertently involved? Thanks for mentioning that, by the way."

He laughs. "Don't act like that doesn't make it better for you."

I flush. "Does it make it better for *you*?"

"No, but there's nothing I can do about it. The bond is the

bond. Actually, how much do you think *he* wants us to do it again? He can still pretend to be a good boy while we do the dirty work."

"Fuck off," I say, throwing open the door.

I try to speed walk to the house, but Nolan is faster and stands in front of me, blocking my way to the door. "Who are you?" he says. "Today you were like a fucking fire. You lit your own way. And yet you barely made it five minutes before you let them trap you again. Stop being ashamed of being powerful."

"I'm not ashamed of being powerful! I'm ashamed because I hurt my friend!"

"You won. *We* won."

I scoff. "Because that's all that matters, right? Winning. Is that why you want to have sex again so badly? Because of me? Or because it lets you win something that Virgil can't? So you can stop remembering that you're still the second son?"

It hasn't escaped my notice, the fact that Nolan sees both Virgil and Jacques as these golden boys, prodigal sons who are so beloved, it's like they can do no wrong. They follow the rules, walk within the lines, and are rewarded for it. Meanwhile, Nolan gets a slap-in-the-face nickname for the crime of being born a bastard who Garrett needed. He gets into university on his own merits and now faces a proposal that would take it all away. He's forced into a bond he never wanted. At every turn, he's reminded that his mere existence is as a second-class person.

He stands close enough to press his chest against mine. "There's no second place when I'm the only participant. He wants you, but he won't ever let it happen. Not for real. Not like I did. And when you finally understand that, then we can talk about who's winning and who's losing. You can rage inside that gilded cage of yours, but all

you're doing is hurting yourself while they watch. You say you want power, but when you get close to it, you back off."

I step away from him. "And you say you play for yourself in your own game, but you only ever move for other people."

I sprint around him to the front door, crossing the distance in seconds so he can't cut me off again. I knock, and Mia is the one who answers, looking from me to Nolan and back. "Everything okay?"

"Fine," I say.

We head into the living room, where a white girl around Mia's age sits next to an older white woman who must be her mom. The woman smiles, and me and Nolan take the open spots on the couch across from her. Mia settles next to the woman, who holds her hand. "I'm Jen. Polly . . . Polly was my little sister." She gestures at the other girl. "This is my oldest, Merry."

"Thanks for talking with us," Nolan says.

Jen nods. "Well . . . Mia said you were there, so . . ." I'm not even surprised that Mia has already had such an impact on this community that she only joined recently. She's always cared about where she belongs. Has always made strides to immerse herself in the people she belongs to. She carves out a place for herself and fits well enough that you start thinking her spot was always there. Even among these Monsters who she was initially afraid of.

"I tried to help her," Nolan says, wringing his hands.

"I know you did. You're a good boy."

His cheeks go red, and despite the fact that he's pissed me off, it's endearing. I don't know why he pretends he doesn't care about these people as much as his dad does. I get that he doesn't want to be trapped here, but that's not what it feels like. It feels like this is his home.

"Was she on a mission, then?" I ask.

Jen shakes her head. "No."

Nolan furrows his brow. "She wasn't?"

"No. That's why I've been confused, because she didn't have any reason to transform. She was supposed to be at work, but she didn't show up. I was shocked when I found out about this whole attack. I mean, last I heard, we're thinking it's Carrigan, yeah? But he could only get her if she transformed, and I don't know why she would."

"Do you think he can force us to transform?" Merry asks, eyes darting. Mia reaches out with her other hand, and it's almost instant, the way Merry relaxes. As if the touch alone has magic.

"That's impossible," Nolan says, but it lacks conviction.

Adam has already been demonstrating Doctorate abilities that we weren't aware existed. We thought stopping transformations would help, but maybe that's not enough. I grind my teeth. I didn't want to need her, but the situation is desperate now.

I have to visit Natalie.

CHAPTER FORTY-THREE

I fidget on the stoop of the house, standing in front of the ornate glass door without knocking. The street is a block of repeating vibrant redbrick townhouses, unlike the homes closer to campus, which have the feel of being ancient enough to be Victorian.

"You know, you could just come in," a voice chimes.

I jump. There's an electronic doorbell system. I spy the cameras neatly recessed in the brick. I guess I shouldn't expect anything less from Natalie.

I reach for the door and open it, stepping into the foyer, where a husky bounds down the corridor toward me, bumping his nose against my palms. Atticus, I know because of Jules's instant enthusiasm about the dog.

The door locks behind me.

"That's not ominous at all," I mutter.

"Oh no? It's meant to be." Natalie sweeps around the corner in a literal floor-length black robe. This woman loves drama too much.

"Come along." She snaps her fingers, and Atticus trots beside her as she leads me into the combination living and kitchen area, where Jules is hunched over a desk set up in the corner.

"August?!" he says as he spots me.

"I found her lingering outside the front door," Natalie says. "I'll leave you to it."

"Actually," I say, stopping her mid-turn, "I was hoping to speak to you."

Natalie's lips slide into a grin. She drops onto the plush green velvet couch, and I sit in the one across from her. Atticus jumps up beside her, and Jules sits on that couch—I assume to be close to Atticus, who he's petting.

"Caught your match earlier today," Natalie says, leaning forward. "Riveting. Right, Jules?"

My brother's forehead wrinkles. "I thought you two were friends."

"It's a competition," I snap. "And that's not why I came here. I have a theory about what's happening with the Wilds . . . and who killed Mom."

"Do tell," Natalie says while Jules's forehead wrinkles increase significantly.

I spill everything that I've discovered about Adam. I didn't want to come to her, but it's not like I can go to Henry with this. And Natalie has connections, and she knows things. Maybe even a Doctorate's weakness.

Jules looks at Natalie. "What do you think?"

"I admit that I never took him for the type. He was rather unremarkable when we were younger."

"You knew him then?" I ask.

Natalie nods. "We were in the same Mastery group. Though I was a freshman when he and Henry were juniors. It was considered the best group at the time for Progressives. I didn't dare approach a Pro-Lib circle—there would have been no faster way to stall my progress. But Adam struck me as a follower. He lacked the ambition of his brothers to my eye. But I've been wrong before." I open my mouth, and she silences me with a finger. "Still, something's missing."

"What—"

She raises her finger higher. "I'm not saying that your evidence isn't good. But there are holes. Primarily, if your mother knew something worth killing her for, why let you and Jules live? Yes, you think that maybe Adam felt like he could more easily get the information from the two of you than her, but still. If he killed you both, the information would have stayed buried the way he seems to want it to. If you knew what he really wanted, you would have leverage. But what are you planning to do with that leverage?"

I stiffen. I told her about the theory, not our plan. And especially not *my* plans for Adam.

"I'd like to know that too," Jules says.

"The plan is to get a confession from Adam."

"And how shall you pry this sudden honesty from the mouth of a proposed master manipulator? Even with this leverage that you've yet to discover."

"With a strong enough threat," Jules says, his voice flat. "That's why you're running around with the QBSS treasurer, isn't it? You want the weapon Bernie talked about. And what you haven't considered is how you get yourself out of threatening the Doctorate."

"I'll have the power. He'll do whatever I want."

Natalie laughs. "You sound so young when you say things like

that." I sneer at her. "And if you can't get the weapon?"

"Do you know of any other weaknesses a Doctorate might have? Adam hinted to me last year that there might be one." In the Jeep after that first test, when I asked why Virgil's parents would have even attempted to assassinate the Doctorate, he said that Doctorates weren't as untouchable as they seemed.

"Why would he tell you that?"

I shrug. "I don't know! I guess because he wanted me to find the weapon."

"The weapon you insist he fears and doesn't want discovered while you simultaneously believe he's manipulating you into getting it? Was manipulating Bernie? Either he wants it found or he wants it buried—it can't be both."

I glower at her.

Natalie tilts her head while me and Jules watch her. "As for weaknesses, Doctorates are much like Monsters. They share a mutation. People don't think of that often. The weakness of a Monster can also be the weakness of a Doctorate."

"What does that mean?"

Natalie leans back into the cushions. "You aren't learning any critical thinking in those classes you take?"

I grit my teeth. I think back to when me and Virgil got our asses handed to us. We were fighting, and Virgil was struggling and emotionally disconnected from me, so the bond suffered. "Mental discord or distress," I say.

Natalie claps. "There she is!"

"He doesn't seem have emotional attachments to people, given that he's either killed or attempted to kill his own brothers and father. There's Henry, but I get the impression that Adam low-key

hates him. And he doesn't have a partner or kids. Maybe he'd panic if he thought his plan was failing, but I don't know how to make him think that."

She sighs, and I get the impression that I've disappointed her somehow. "Then I suppose you ought to get your hands on that weapon."

I stand. She doesn't know any special weakness. She doesn't even know more than I do. The only thing she did was annoy me trying to poke holes in my shit.

Natalie gazes at me. "But will you have the strength to leave it at words?"

"That's the entire goal."

"Of course," she says, with a smile that makes my stomach roil.

I mutter a goodbye and leave the room, only to find Jules hot on my heels. I ignore him, putting on my shoes in the entryway.

"You don't talk to me anymore," he says.

I get both shoes on and turn to him. It used to feel like me and Jules against the world. He was my defender. No matter what, he came to my rescue however he could. Even when I messed up. But that's changed now. "You don't trust me anymore."

It's as simple as that. It started last year in his room, before he disappeared, when he said nothing to me. When he hid what happened with Mom. He's the one who did this, not me.

He sticks his hands in his pockets. "Then give me a reason to trust you."

"I never had to prove myself to you before!" I shout. "When did that change?"

"When I told you to stay away from Monsters, and instead you tied yourself to one forever."

I shake my head, scoffing. "You're just like Mom and Dad. Because I didn't do what *you* wanted, I'm dead to you?"

Jules gives me a pained look. "You're still doing it. You're still torpedoing your life. You think this isn't the same because you're not drunk off your ass? You think this isn't still living for someone else? Think about something you want that has nothing to do with anyone but you. What is it?"

"I could ask you the same thing," I say, before leaving.

Me and Virgil stand silently in the antechamber as we wait for the lights to come on. This time, there's no need to guess who will be behind the doors. Violet and Frankie won their match yesterday. That guarantees we'll be facing each other today. I can't help but wonder what it would have been like had Bryce and Mitch been forced to go up against their friends. Difficult, I imagine. Maybe Violet will be happy that it's me instead. She can fight without restraint or reserve. I doubt she considers us friends anymore.

I have no idea how Bryce is doing. I don't know who to ask who would tell us anything. Maybe it's better not to know.

My stomach clenches like I have cramps coming on, even though my period isn't due anytime soon.

This is no different from any other match. We just need to win.

I glance at Virgil, who stares stone-faced at the indicator light. I can't read him anymore. Not since what we found at his childhood home. And standing with his glasses off, he looks even more like a stranger. Brutality wasn't unknown to Nolan. Nor rage. Bitterness. None of that changed who he was. But it doesn't fit on Virgil. It's as if he's pulled a mask over himself.

I don't like it.

But I need it.

The monster stretches and rolls its shoulders. Hungry for blood.

I won't let what happened with Bryce happen again. I won't lose who I am inside its power. *I* use *it*, not the other way around. I know Henry just wants me to let go, but it's not that simple. No matter how often I do it, I always drown in the monster.

"I'm sorry." Virgil's voice is so quiet that I almost miss it.

I blink at him. "For what?"

He presses a hand to his chest. "For the monster. If I were stronger or better, it wouldn't be this hard for you to manage it." His fingers dig into the material of his shirt. "I want to do better by you, but I don't know how."

I gape at him. How could he think this is his fault? "This is my problem. I told you I would master it, and I will. I just . . . I just need some time. That's all. Don't get in your head. We need to win this."

"I know. Whatever you need to do to win . . . I support you. Okay?"

"Okay."

Whatever I need to do to win. I ball my hands into fists and release them.

The light turns amber. Virgil grows behind me. When it flashes to green, we walk out.

The crowd is pumped up tonight, if the screams and cheers are any indication. The semifinals have gathered a larger crowd, and even this arena is bigger than the ones we've been in before. There's only one repechage match left after this one. The winner of that will go against the winner of the main competition, the promised second chance.

The doors across the arena open, and Violet steps out. She's ditched the bow and arrow she had in the Bachelor candidacy for a pair of twin curved blades. Her face is set and stern, the expression she saves for opponents. Behind her, Frankie looms. I've yet to see the girl's form, and as she appears, part of me wishes I hadn't. She's a four-legged ball of quills and spikes without even eyes.

Virgil has his own spikes, but not nearly so many. It feels almost impossible that this pair lost so early on in the competition. Or that they struggled so hard to get to this point.

We're both going to be Masters-in-training. We're firmly within the cutoff. But that's not what this match is about.

We each want to win.

The horn blows, and before I even realize, Violet has sliced through my cheek, and I'm diving to the side to evade her. But she won't relent. She cuts my Achilles tendon with the other blade, and I cry out, struggling to dart away as I toss a knife. The metal pings off the concrete wall without hitting its mark. And she clangs her blades together like a battle cry. I realize too late that I'm stumbling backward into a giant spike ball.

I'm saved by Virgil barreling into Frankie from the side. He takes a bunch of quills that sink into his fur, but he doesn't flinch or cry out.

Any one of those quills could have speared me right through.

I grit my teeth against the pain as my ankle heals, reconnecting the tendons and tissue while I force out breaths. Virgil blocks both Violet and Frankie, buying me the few seconds I need for it to heal fully.

Turning, I try to make eye contact with Virgil, but he's focused on our opponents, not me. There's a stiffness to his body, not just

from the quills, and an absence in his eyes. He's not detaching from me, but he is from this fight.

I reach for the monster but the shadow of it is immediately overwhelming, and I shove it back.

As Violet swipes with her blades, I throw myself out of the way into a back handspring, then run headfirst toward the arena wall while Violet chases me. I run up the side vertically and flip over, landing behind her, then whip out two blades. One misses, but another catches her in the shoulder, giving me some room. I huff out, breathing fog. It's not as powerful as what Nolan could do, so it doesn't cover the whole arena, but it gives me some time.

I squeeze my eyes shut. My ankle was healed enough for me to move, but it still hurts. *Stop being a little bitch, August.*

The monster looming, raking its claws against the barrier of my mind, just makes me want to shrink.

I can't win without it. But I also can't let go like I did with Nolan. Not anymore. And I can't just accept losing either.

Across the arena, Virgil's attacking as he should, but he doesn't seem like himself.

It's almost like he's bracing himself for something . . . or . . . someone. I bite my lip. In the last match, I used the monster and beat the absolute shit out of Bryce. Virgil didn't speak against it because he wants to win. He said he'd support me. But there's no way he could ever be okay with hurting our friends.

He wants to be like Nolan. Wants to have that drive to win no matter what it takes. Wants to give me permission to use the monster like I told him I would.

Violet slices through fog, perhaps thinking that she found her way in, not that I made an opening for her. I wait for her to leap into

the air before I open my mouth to scream. She falters, bracing for the roar, and I use the moment to slip into the fog I've set up beside me so I can get closer to Virgil.

I run up his tail, avoiding the spikes that belong to his body and the quills that Frankie has put there. I squat just behind his ears.

"Stop trying to be Nolan," I hiss. "I need you to be Virgil. We need someone to have a conscience in this trio. We need someone to hold us back. We need you." I lick my lips. "*I* need you." Because this is the truth of it. This is Virgil's monster in my head. I let him think it was the problem. Hell, I *did* think it was the problem. Nolan was right. I kept telling him it was fine to be a Monster while also saying that the part of Virgil in my head needed to be tamed and controlled.

But it's only Virgil. It's always been Virgil.

I'm the one who wanted to use him to hurt. To maim and murder.

Frankie isn't attacking for whatever reason, and Violet is still lost in the fog. But she won't be forever. She should know our scents better. She'll eventually figure out how to cut through the way Bryce did at the end.

I say, "I was wrong. I can't master the monster for you because you're the one who makes the monster what it is. We can do good things. We can win without losing ourselves. I need that from you. Because I can't be that good. But you can."

Virgil rotates his head toward me, staring at me with huge dark amber eyes. Trapped within them is the monster. The rage, and anger, and pain. But there's also Virgil. There's a boy who has never wanted to hurt anyone. Not really. And he's terrified.

It scares me, too, the power. But in Virgil's hands, it feels safe. Safer than it does in mine. It's part of the reason why we make a

good team. "You're the Monster, Virgil," I say. "You always have been. So just be you, and everything will be okay."

Frankie rolls through the fog toward us at a high speed, with Violet right behind her, clanging her blades together. I grip Virgil's fur, open my mouth, and hope for the best.

In my mind, the monster stares at me, its lips tilting up. And for the first time, the sight of its smile doesn't scare me.

I roar.

Violet goes to her knees, but Frankie keeps rolling.

No eyes . . . She can't see . . . so how has she been . . . ? Violet. That constant clanging of her blades together—that wasn't for intimidation; it was to help Frankie know where to go. That's why she wasn't attacking when Violet was in the fog.

I watch as Violet's blades fall and slap on the ground, making a sound similar to when she smacks them together. Frankie shifts position, but instead of heading toward us, she's coming straight at Violet. Violet, who's still on the ground with her hands on her head.

Frankie will crush her.

And we'll win.

I sweep Violet off the concrete and roll her out of the way. I move fast. Virgil fast. Monster fast. Still, it's not enough to avoid Frankie's quill tearing through my leg. "Motherfucker," I hiss, yanking the quill out. Blood oozes from the wound, and only seconds later, it's knitting itself up at double the speed that my ankle healed. The monster is there; it's free. I can feel the power running through my veins. But when I see its eyes, Virgil is in there too.

Violet stares at me through sweaty bangs, her black lipstick smudged, a streak against her cheek.

"You could have won," she says.

"You could have died." She laughs. I give her a second before I whip a knife up under her neck. "Yield."

"I don't think I will."

I only have a split second to jump back before a dozen quills explode from Violet's body. One of them has nicked me. She stands, tottering with the new weight of the quills. This is the elusive third-evolution skill that she and Frankie couldn't manage before now. And it looks like it took everything in her to bring it out. Her eyelids flutter like she can barely keep them open, and her entire body is trembling.

She pulls on two quills, screaming as they rip from her body, wielding them as she did her swords, the blood from the wounds joining the rest of the crimson liquid soaking her clothes. She slaps the quills together, and Frankie rolls toward Virgil.

"I did know you were a tough bitch," I say, spitting out a wad of blood. She grins.

I pull two knives into my hands.

She totters forward, then sways. Her eyes roll into the back of her head, the quills retract, and she falls forward.

The horn blows.

I drop to my knees, my blades clanging on the concrete.

Fuck, that girl is scary.

CHAPTER FORTY-FOUR

Riley

I told myself that the next time I was in this basement facing the dais of elders, I would have something to show for my efforts. Instead, I'm in the dimly lit chamber with my metaphorical pants down. I have nothing, and from the smug looks on some of the faces, they know it.

Dr. Michaels wastes no time with preamble. "Do you have any updates for us?"

"I was told I had until the end of the semester."

"And so you shall. Like I said, we're only looking for an update."

I force myself to remain at attention. No fidgeting and no bowing of my head. "I've uncovered documents that I believe will lead to the acquisition of the weapon. I am closing in on it." Never mind that I am, in fact, *not* closing in on it. I haven't texted Corey either, even though she told me I could. I shouldn't need her. I should have done this on my own from the start.

"Let's have a report from the social chair," Ms. Howard says, leaning forward.

I'm too late in masking my expression, from the responding glee on her face. But I don't turn as Jackson parts from the crowd and steps next to me. I bite the inside of my cheek.

"She's been working diligently on finding the weapon," Jackson says, "often spending her free time in the library and using our resources." He pauses and swallows. "However, she has been neglecting presidential duties. The welcome for the elder council today, for example, was carried out and presided over by several members in her stead."

There are murmurs among the council. I clench my teeth. I can't expect him to lie for me.

"What do you have to say to that?" Dr. Michaels asks.

"Delegation is a tool of leaders."

The corner of his lip quirks, but he manages to smother the smile.

"You're the president," Ms. Howard snaps. "Delegation does not mean parceling your role out. If you cannot handle the demands of your post, then perhaps you should consider stepping down."

"I will delegate less, as I understand now that that's the preference."

Ms. Howard's lip curls.

But it's Dr. Michaels's call, and in the end he lets it go, with a note that we will reconvene in just over a month at the exam period for my final judgment.

Jackson catches up to me on my way out of the clubhouse. "Riley, wait!"

I keep walking.

"I'd rather not follow you home."

I stop and sigh, tilting my head back. I spin on my heel to face him.

"I had no choice but to report."

"I know. Can I go now?"

"Are you okay? Lately you've seemed especially stressed."

"Why should I tell you? So you can report it?"

He gives me a look that says I'm being unreasonable. When we were dating, it was the sort of expression he'd share when I said we could study for another couple of hours, or that of course I could balance two more extracurriculars with an internship. He was the metric I used to keep myself from doing too much and burning myself out. He kept me grounded. Not anymore.

"You're isolating yourself," he says. "Not just from me. But even from the student council, who you're supposed to be in community with."

I laugh. "You mean Malachi and Inaya? The two people who not only want to see me fail, but also want to replace me?" I don't even mention Darius, who's barely clocked into his own role.

"You're supposed to be our leader."

"I have to go," I say.

This time, he doesn't follow.

I blink awake at the buzzing of my phone. I rub my eyes and rise off my bed with the noise of crumpling papers in my ears. I was supposed to be doing research but felt too tired to go to Stauffer, so I'd opted to work at home. Then made the rookie mistake of lying on the bed and resting my eyes for just a moment.

Now the room is bathed in darkness with only the fluorescent glow of my phone screen. I jerk to attention when I see Corey's name on-screen. I squint at the pictures she's sent over.

We thought the clues were leading us in order, but that's not it. They're

just different caches, and Pattie was checking them all. That means there won't necessarily be items in every area. And she knew that! The little weird symbol things, they're a code.

I pull out the journal. Corey had been using photocopies of pages while I kept the original. The first symbol in the journal beside the Fort Henry clue is a stick with two overlapping triangles. If I look closely at it, yeah, it does kind of look like a scythe. It looks more like a flag, but I guess Pattie didn't want her code to be too obvious. As opposed to the symbol that was on the wall itself at the fort—a stick with a curved triangle—that was clearly a sickle or scythe. The two triangles Pattie used in her code must represent phase two of the sickle. The Douglas clue has a circle. The chain, I assume.

I look over the journal riddles and find one that has the sickle symbol with only one triangle, the circle for the chain, and then three additional symbols. It's the only clue with that many symbols. That has to be where the weapon is hidden. Though if I needed the artifact matching the symbol to open the other caches . . . Screw it. Maybe I can force my way in with just the sickle and chain. I check over the clue again.

I keep finding myself entombed in the past even as I start anew. I cannot help but think that perhaps my learning is shuttered. If I could collect the right pieces, I could build something better.

"Entombed," so something buried. "Learning" likely references an on-campus building. "Collect the right pieces"—that's harder.

I text Corey, *Do we know which buildings on campus have basements?*

Most of them.

Basements that are maybe covered or buried or something like that?

Give me a minute.

I look at the passage again. There has to be some other hint. "I keep finding myself"—could that mean it's a repeat location? I grab the blueprints of Douglas. It's the only place we've been to already that's on campus, though there may be other on-campus locations within the riddles. But at least this is a start.

I sag with a little laugh when I find a tunnel that seems like it may or may not be paved over. Sounds like a tomb to me.

Grabbing my purse, I shove in the blueprints, the key to the library's back entrance, and the chain.

Douglas is abandoned when I arrive. I take several looks around, half expecting to see Jackson hiding behind a tree. I slip inside, follow the blueprints to the other end of the building, and open the basement door. It creaks, and I wince. I tread lightly down the stairs into a space where there are boxes of books labeled by year. A storage area for learning. Shut away. Shuttered.

I grin.

I consult the blueprint again and turn in the direction mapped only to come up against a wall. I shine my phone's flashlight over it and reveal a tiny image of a sickle in the corner. Yanking off my necklace, I press it to the symbol and let it glow.

Nothing happens for a moment, and then there's a crumbling sound as the drywall gives and the wall begins sliding, tearing through the single drywall layer made to hide it. Shit. Someone is going to notice that for sure. If my parents have to foot a bill for campus repairs, I will never hear the end of it. The weapon had better be here.

The hallway beyond the opening has no light and is roughly made with only compacted dirt for walls, and barely large enough for two people to stand side by side.

I walk through the passage, going at a faster clip. I have no idea

if someone is going to notice the ripping sound the passage entrance made or what. Better to go through as soon as possible.

At the end, there's another door. I search to find the symbol and swallow when I see the five up close. I'd suspected this would be the case but had hoped I was wrong. The artifacts depicted are the sickle, the shield, the staff, the saber, and the chain—or as it was known originally, the shackles. Some members felt that this name was less than empowering, given enslavement, and changed its name to "the chain." Later, the chain fell out of use among the council entirely and was replaced by the spear until Grandma brought the chain back into rotation. She'd always scoffed at the renaming of the artifact, as it was meant to represent the breaking of shackles, hence why the links separate.

But, of course, Inaya still made a stink about not getting to use the chain because it was "lost," even though without my family's influence, she would have used the spear anyway.

I drag my hands over my face. I could ask the student council to help because this is what the elders want, but they could easily refuse just to see me fail.

No.

I shouldn't need them.

I'm Riley Townsend. A Historic. The president of QBSS. I can do this on my own.

My pendant glows within my closed fist, growing into its sickle form, and I dig into the wood of the door, ripping away splinters of it, and then dig into it again. I can see a hole starting to appear. It's working! The floor lurches beneath me, and I stumble. I look up, and a piece of cracked earth falls on my face. I turn to the door I was hacking and see the white shine of bone in the wood.

Shit. This must be happening because I don't have all the artifacts. The reaction of the sickle connecting with the bone in the wood isn't right. Another rumble shakes me, and I fall. I stare down the tunnel, which is starting to narrow.

It's caving in and compressing.

I whip back toward the door and pull away more splinters, more desperate than ever to break through—until I see the metal. I press my palm to it. There's a metal door behind the section of bone and wood. There's no way I can break through that. Maybe with a third-stage scythe, but not a sickle. I grip the weapon, willing it to just fucking work!

Nothing happens.

It remains a sickle.

I turn around and run through the narrowing tunnel back the way I came, gritting my teeth and trying to focus.

I cough as more dirt crumbles down on me and makes it harder to see, the passage entrance becoming a smaller and smaller pinprick in the distance. I fall, only registering when I'm on the ground that I tripped on a hunk of rock or dirt. My purse dropped somewhere, and I can't bother grabbing it.

The passage is so narrow that it squeezes my shoulders, and I scramble up, hacking. I trip again, and the sickle goes flying out of my hands. The golden glow dulls as it returns to its miniature form, and now I'm crawling around in the dirt trying to find it. That is *not* something that can be left behind.

I close my fingers around the sickle, but it doesn't matter.

It's too late.

The walls have compressed so much that I can barely move.

I'm not going to make it.

I'm going to die here.

Alone.

A failure.

What did Sammie think about when those claws raked across her back and she was lying on the pavement bleeding out? Maybe it's selfish, but I can't help but hope she thought about me. At least a little bit. I wish that I had been braver. That it didn't take her dying for me to realize how much she meant to me.

Something tugs on my arm, dragging me forward. I blink through the dirt, and it's Corey, her dark hair caked in dust. "You can do it!" she screams. "You're almost there!"

We're squished into the space. She shouldn't have come here. Now we'll both be crushed.

No. I can't let that happen.

I grip the sickle in my hand, and it grows—the *scythe.* I ram the hilt into the ground, and the space explodes with golden light.

Everything goes still.

The walls stop shaking.

My chest stills as I hold my breath.

Finally, Corey tugs me again, and slowly we're able to squeeze through the tunnel and break out on the other end of the passage.

We both fall to our knees, panting and covered with dirt. I crawl to Corey, holding her face between my palms. "What were you thinking?!"

"Came . . . to help you," she pants, still trying to catch her breath. She reaches for her left leg, pushing her pants up to adjust her prosthesis. I'm positive that it's her everyday leg. Not even a specialized one. Like she was so desperate to get here she couldn't even take time to change it. "Figured out . . . the clue."

I lay my forehead against hers, and we stay that way, kneeling on the ground, breathing too hard.

Have you ever thought about kissing a girl?

Yes. I thought about it when Corey and I were crammed into that closet last year, and she was giggling at August and Virgil arguing under the bed. I thought about it when we were in the back seat of my car, and I held her hand as she waited to see if her friends would make it out alive. I thought about it when I traced her palm in the library. I thought about it when she grinned, holding the Squishmallow I'd gotten her. I thought about it when she hugged me close, and it was supposed to be platonic. I thought about it when she said we could just be friends.

Because I have never wanted to just be friends with Corey Yang.

I lean forward and press my lips to hers. She gasps against me, and that just makes me pull her closer. She tastes like dirt and clay, and there's too much spit between us. And none of that matters. Because I'm kissing the girl I like, and she's kissing me back.

CHAPTER FORTY-FIVE

I narrow my eyes at Virgil and Nolan whispering to each other in the corner of the greenroom. We're here to check in as usual, but the second Nolan entered, Virgil dragged him aside for a "private" conversation. Meaning, not involving me. They keep their voices low enough that even tapping into second-evolution skills, I can't pick up what they're saying.

Virgil turns to look at me for a moment, Nolan following his eyeline. I wiggle my fingers in a wave, which makes Nolan scowl.

I shove a croissant in my mouth. The greenroom is pretty much empty now. At this point, it's only repechage participants. Barbie and Ellis have advanced to the finals, which won't happen for another month. The winner of our match today against Melani and Shay will determine who goes on to fight them.

In the MiT league, Margot and Isaac have advanced to the finals, and Jules and Natalie have their match today in the repechage to determine if they'll go forward.

The doors open, and Melani and Shay enter the room. The croissant turns to mush in my mouth. Melani tosses her braids over her shoulder and throws me a grin, waving at me in the same condescending manner that I did Virgil and Nolan.

Fuck, am I like that?

I haven't seen Shay in her human form before. She's a slight Black girl who hunches her shoulders as she walks, her dark eyes hidden behind thick glasses. Given that Monsters have heightened senses, it's an interesting move to choose those sort of lenses for an aesthetic. She's not at all like the Monster we met in the arena.

Virgil and Nolan break their huddle to walk to the woman at the check-in counter before making their way to me. Virgil straightens. "I want to do this match. There's no rule against switching the order that Nolan and I compete, as long as we both fight roughly half the time. But you have final say as the Bachelor."

I look at Nolan. "You're cool with this?"

"It's your choice," he says crossing his arms.

Virgil wants to make this a grudge match. I get it. I can't help but want to wipe that smug smile off Melani's face. We weren't just defeated. We were slaughtered. Even their healing was faster than ours. Now, things are different. The last match showed that.

"Let's do it," I say to Virgil, and he beams. It's like a ray of sunshine shot straight into my veins. My lips peel into their own smile. Nolan, on the other hand, is like a storm cloud.

"I'll go tell the check-in lady," Virgil says, turning and heading over to her.

Nolan stares me down. "You think you're being yourself with him, but you're holding back. You could be the most powerful woman in that arena, but you're too afraid of what he

might think of you. We decimated the competition."

"We hurt my friend," I say, meeting his gaze head-on.

Nolan curls his lip. "You can't suppress who you are. It doesn't work." He steps closer, his chest inches from mine. "And don't act like you don't like giving in." I swallow hard enough to hurt. "Who do you want to be, August? Someone who lives by the whims of others or someone who lives for herself?"

"That's not what I'm doing," I say, but my voice is small. I hate hearing Jules's words echoed.

"Isn't it? You don't want to upset your friends, so you won't fight in the way you know wins. You don't want Virgil to think badly of you, even while he continues to deny what's between you. You want to kill the man who murdered your mother, but you don't want them to look at you like a monster. Wake up. We're *all* monsters. The only difference between us is that some want to deny what they are and others embrace it." Nolan steps away just as Virgil is walking back to us. "I'll be in the stands."

"You all right?" Virgil asks me.

"Peachy."

We head to the antechamber, where we do our stretches, and I pull on my holsters, check the leather straps, and secure the bracers on my forearms. Even with the indicator still red, I know it's almost time.

Virgil reaches out his arm to me. "We're a team, right?"

I clasp his hand, tugging close, our forearms pressed together and our breath mingling. "We are."

Virgil's unwilling to cross the lines that Nolan will, and because of that, this partnership is all we can have. This is how it *should* be. Boundaries set and defined, the way they were before Nolan interrupted that careful equilibrium.

And still, Nolan's voice is in my head.

I used to let the expectations of other people run my life. But I stopped doing that. I did, didn't I?

I squeeze my eyes shut. Last semester, I hadn't liked Dr. Weiss's words about how we all swap shadows with the monster sometimes, but what mattered was being able to control it. I thought that maybe they shouldn't be controlled. I forgot that in the face of seeing what it means to let the monster run wild.

With me and Virgil, we're striking a balance. He may be more restrained, but I never have to worry about the fallout of anything other than losing. Who I am with Nolan is freeing, but it also reminds me of the version of myself who would drink doubles in the club and not care who she hurt in the process.

The light turns green, the doors open, and I walk out with Virgil at my back.

I've seen her form before, but Shay is still impressive with those raccoon-like features. The mask across her eyes reminds me of the glasses she wore. I examine her bulging muscles with protruding veins. The foam at her lips draws my attention, acidic and deadly.

Melani grins as she steps out, hyping up the crowd into cheering louder. I have to give it to the girl. To be in the repechage, Barbie must have handed her ass to her. She's a loser, like me, but she doesn't act like it. She presents herself like she ended up here by chance, and it's just a stepping stone to getting back into the ring with the real threat.

I let out a slow breath through my mouth. This is the way it should be. Me and Virgil. We weren't prepared last time, but we are now.

The monster sets its paws on my shoulders, and for the first time, it doesn't dig its claws in. It's just there. Present. But no longer overwhelming.

Yes, I'm not the August from the Bachelor candidacy. I was never going to be. Bonding to Virgil changed something. And I'm going to keep changing. And no one, *fucking no one,* is going to make me think there's something wrong with that. If they don't like the current iteration, too bad.

The horn blows.

I make my move as Melani does, leaping toward her. We meet in the air, her larger blade clanging against two of my smaller ones. But I've learned a thing or two. As I fall and she rears back for another hit, I throw the blades, one catching her in the thigh.

By the time she lands, it's already been pulled out and the wound healed. She bares her teeth at me in another grin.

I sprint around the arena, throwing blades to try to catch her off guard. She cackles as she evades them and occasionally swipes them aside with her blade. This time, I can keep up with her speed.

Somewhere, in the back of my mind, I'm aware that we're moving ridiculously fast, my arms pumping at a speed that my mind can barely comprehend. But all that matters is that she keeps following my lead. Keeps underestimating me.

Unaware of how close we've gotten to the Monsters.

Unaware until Virgil's tail slams into her side.

Her scream sends a delicious shiver down my spine. I dash forward, driving a blade into her thigh. She's trying to wrench herself off Virgil's tail, but the spikes have gone in deep. I know intimately that it's not that easy to get away from.

Shay spits, and I jump back to avoid it. Virgil is forced to whip Melani off his tail to avoid getting any on it. Shay keeps going, driving him away from her partner now that she's realized what's going on. But I won't let her separate us.

I send a blade at her eye, messing up her spitting concentration, and use the pause to get closer to Melani, who's landed near her partner's legs.

The girl rips my knife out of her thigh and tosses it aside, ducking under Shay's feet and hiding behind her.

Fuck. She's going to use the time to heal.

Virgil rushes Shay and flings his side toward her. The black metal spikes extend, stabbing Shay, who roars. I shake off the shock. Henry told us my extending the metal from my body was just part of a skill Virgil had already mastered. And he's finally decided to use it.

Shay tries to keep her footing as Virgil retracts the spikes and they tear from her flesh. She starts to fall back, and Melani has the sense to move out from her partner's shadow.

I open my mouth and roar.

Melani swears, doubling over, though she keeps her eyes open and still attempts to move out of the way. But it's not enough.

I spear her through the stomach with five blades, each one a claw that's shredded through my nails. It hurts like a son of a bitch, but it's worth it. She coughs out blood.

"Come on," I say to her. "You gotta put up more of a fight."

She chuckles, blood on her lips. "You're such a bitch."

"Takes one to know one."

She grins and spits in my face.

I manage to move just in time, so it gets my cheek instead of my eye, but that doesn't mean that it doesn't burn. I scream and wrench away, tearing my claws out of her at the same time.

Even with healing, the sheer amount of pain I feel as the acid eats through my cheek and goes onto my teeth is very, very good motivation to avoid getting spit on again. When I lost myself in the

monster, I didn't notice when I was in pain. I guess this is the downside of keeping my facilities intact. My taking time to recover has given Melani time too. Virgil's wound created more of a mess, so it's still oozing, but my cuts were clean.

Melani shouts, "What's wrong?! I thought you wanted a challenge!"

I should have known she could spit like that too. Just because I hadn't seen her use that skill doesn't mean she can't.

I reach for my holster and find nothing. Not on the left or right thigh. I used them all to drive her toward Virgil. I have four more under my arms. I don't want to be wasting time collecting blades right now.

Fine. Knife fight it is.

I storm forward with two blades in my hand, and Melani counters with her own much longer blade. She stabs me in the side and leg, but I get her in the gut and shoulder.

It's a waste of time for both of us. This is why close quarters knife fights are useless. You both end up stabbed a bunch and nobody wins.

Only . . . Melani is bleeding more. I squint at her, and she fights harder, her movements more feverish, leaving holes everywhere.

I dart back and blow smoke. She swears as she loses me in the fog. Meanwhile, across the way, Shay is . . . yes, she's slower. She's still spitting at Virgil, but the period between them is getting longer.

Five-minute fights.

It sounded like a badge of honor, but what if it was a necessity?

Go out hard in the beginning and end it. Don't give your opponents time to wear you out. That was likely the strategy. And I let myself get drawn into it. I wanted to end it fast too. Who wouldn't?

Melani breaks through the fog, leaping at me with a scream, openings everywhere. I kick her in the stomach, sending her barreling across the arena, right into Virgil, impaling her in several different places.

Shay roars and spits in his direction, but it's too late.

When Virgil retracts his spikes, Melani falls to her knees. She's still healing, but it's too slow. She's losing blood faster.

Looking into her eyes, I know that she'll never yield.

So I make the decision for her, sprinting forward and punching her in the face.

She slumps onto her front.

The horn blows.

Virgil looks at me with a grin, black lips spread wide, fangs gnashing together. The monster in my mind and the one in front of me meld into a single image. I smile back.

Virgil wrings his hands as we stand in front of a white condo door with the number 417 written in gold font. I glance at Corey, who looks back at me. It took several minutes just for Virgil to enter this building, and another five for us to buzz, then several more to get into the elevator. I'm sure this entire process has taken half an hour already.

We're meant to be meeting the former partners of his parents. According to Corey, Virgil hasn't spoken to them since the attack. Both Masters were stripped of their titles and forbidden from ever holding anything more than "student." But given everything we found in Virgil's childhood home, they're needed to fill in gaps. Which is why Virgil finally reached out to them to set up this meeting.

I knock on the door.

Virgil whips his head to me, mouth hanging open.

"August," Corey groans.

"I couldn't take it anymore," I say.

The door opens to reveal a guy who looks more like he's showing this place to clients than living here. He's a white man around Dad's age with brown hair flecked with gray, wearing a lavender dress shirt tucked into a pair of tan chinos.

He answered so fast that I wonder if he was standing behind the door, waiting for us to knock.

"Declan," he says, sticking out his hand.

"August," I say, shaking. Corey introduces herself next. When Declan reaches Virgil, who holds out his hand, the man instead flings himself at my partner, tugging him in for a hug.

"I'm so sorry," Declan says. "I should have been the one to reach out. And sooner. I just . . . sorry."

Virgil's eyes fill with tears, and I turn away to see an East Asian–looking woman hovering in the doorway. I give her a little space, and she darts forward, past me, clinging onto Virgil and Declan.

I look at Corey, who's also teary-eyed.

Once everyone has recovered, we actually enter the condo, filling up the small living room. The couch can only really fit two people, but Declan and the woman, Jackie, squish right in there with Virgil. Me and Corey perch on the barstools at the kitchen island.

"We watched the match today," Jackie says, looking from Virgil to me. "Congratulations on making it to the finals. Faith and Martin—" She chokes up for a moment. "They would have been so proud."

"Thank you," I say on behalf of myself and Virgil, who just nods and swallows. "Can I ask why you didn't reach out?"

Virgil throws me an alarmed look, but he must want to know too.

Declan sighs. "I suppose we thought it would make things more difficult for him. But I guess to be honest, we were dealing with our own stuff too." He runs a hand through his hair. "My wife left when I lost my title. I struggled to find work. And, I mean, I had a time of resenting Faith. And then hating myself for it, and then being ashamed to see Virgil after having those thoughts. He was doing well with Henry, so I just thought, well, I guess Henry was the better friend. I didn't deserve to be in Virgil's life."

"But didn't *he* deserve it?" I ask.

"He did," Jackie says.

"I avoided you too," Virgil says. "I thought that, maybe if you'd been better, you could have stopped them, or known, or something."

Declan shakes his head. "You're the child. You're allowed to do that. We shouldn't have."

"Which is to say, we're happy to help however we can," Jackie says. "Forgiveness is a journey, not a destination. Don't feel like you owe us anything, okay?"

Corey makes a small choking noise in the back of her throat. I look at her, but she only blushes and shakes her head. "Um, Virgil, you had questions, right?" she says.

Virgil hesitates for a moment before saying, "Can you run through what happened that day? Anything at all that you remember?"

Declan says, "Faith and Martin asked us to meet at their house for coffee, which I remember thinking was weird? They were foodies. They always preferred to meet at restaurants or cafes. Also, it was nighttime. But we went."

"Do you remember the specific time?" Corey asks.

"Uh, we got there around eight, I think?"

Jackie nods. "Yes, I remember because they would usually put

Virgil down at seven, but they hadn't yet, which was strange. He was just there with Doctorate Shaw."

"What?" Virgil blurts out. "Wait, you mean Adam Shaw?"

Jackie looks a bit taken aback but recovers. "Yes, well, he was more Henry's friend than our friend, but Martin and Faith were close to Henry. I guess they'd needed a sitter, and the Doctorate volunteered?"

Eight p.m. would have been shortly after the time that Virgil's parents were supposed to meet with "A," so there's no doubt anymore who that was.

Declan says, "I thought it was weird because if they'd invited us over already, we could have looked after Virgil? He didn't really know the Doctorate. But now I understand that they needed someone to stay home with Virgil while they did . . . well, and I guess it worked in their favor to have the Doctorate do it."

"But Doctorate Shaw was at Summerhill during the attack," Virgil says.

"Yes. So, basically, they sent the Doctorate to put Virgil to bed and then drugged our coffees and put us in their bedroom. When the Doctorate came down, they weren't in the room, so he looked around for them and found us in the bedroom. That's when he chased after them. I assume he contacted Henry to make sure someone was around to watch Virgil, because Henry was in the house when we finally came to. Though by that time . . . the attack had already happened."

"How were they?" Virgil asks. "Like, while serving you coffee?"

Jackie says, "Faith was tearing up. I remember that. Because I asked her what was wrong, and she insisted it was nothing. She started saying how much she and Martin cared for and appreciated

us. How she hoped we would . . . that we would look after Virgil."

Something they had failed to do. Adam must have been using Virgil as insurance to make sure Virgil's parents would one, drug their partners, and two, transform. He couldn't control them unless they were in Monster form, and threatening their son would have been enough to make them do it. He'd probably left with Virgil's parents. Though why send Henry to look after Virgil? Was he worried that his friend might catch on to what he was doing and wanted to keep him occupied?

I meet Virgil's eyes across the room, watching as they fill with tears again.

His parents didn't die trying to kill a Doctorate. They died trying to protect him.

"Is there anything else you remember from that day? Anything odd?" I ask.

"Yes," Jackie said. "After we woke up, Henry left to deal with things, and we stayed with Virgil. Then this woman came to the door. She was asking if Martin and Faith had taken a journal to show to Adam. That she couldn't find it. Said something like they shouldn't have shown it to him or he couldn't have it. That she needed it."

"She did say a name, who the journal belonged to," Declan says, screwing up his face. "Polly? No. Sorry, this was a while ago. We reported on it to the society because it was odd."

"Pattie?" I try.

Declan snaps his fingers. "Yes! Yes, I remember because Virgil started singing 'Patty-Cake,' and I was so stressed, I couldn't play it with him. But we'd never seen her before. We thought it was suspicious, but nothing ever came of it. Any journal they had, I assume

Henry would have packed away and given to Virgil." I open my phone and show them a picture. Declan's jaw drops. "That's her. Who is she?"

The picture is from the album Bailey gave me. One from just before we moved, of Mom holding onto me and Jules.

Pattie hadn't given Virgil's parents the journal before she died—she had hidden it in the QBSS cache—but they knew about it. They knew about it, and Mom had thought they showed it to Adam. Was worried that they had. Because she had known. Virgil's parents may not have had the journal, but they must have talked to Adam about it. Why else would they meet with him? And he had sought to eliminate them like he had Pattie because of what they knew. That was why Mom ran. Why Carrigan went underground.

It all came back to Adam.

CHAPTER FORTY-SIX

Virgil is going to crack. I can see it in the disheveled look of his clothes, the weary droop of his eyes, and the way he shuffles from place to place. Yesterday, after meeting his parents' partners, he went to his childhood home again because he wanted to be alone.

Now, as we walk through the ARC toward the gym for training, there's something absent in his eyes. Nolan has noticed, I'm sure, but isn't saying anything. Usually, we'd have training next week, but Henry's moved it up, for whatever reason.

The space seems more packed than usual, and the students more tense. I'm sure Stauffer and Douglas are both crowded too. Final exams are coming up fast alongside the finals of the Monster's Ball. Because it wouldn't be a society competition if the finale didn't coincide with the most stressful period of the academic calendar. I wish my only concern could be exams.

"Henry's partner," Nolan says.

I flick my eyes to the right, where Laira walks from the Booster Juice with a clear cup of something green. She sees us and heads over, and we wait by the gym entrance for her. I have to force a smile once I get a good look at her face to cover my real reaction. She looks . . . well, *rough*. There are even flakes of dry skin on her usually moisturized face. Her bag doesn't seem heavy, but it's like she's sagging under the weight of it.

Her and Virgil are twinning.

"Hey, girl . . . ," I say.

She rolls her eyes. "I know I look like shit. It's worse watching you try to pretend otherwise." She takes a big gulp of her green juice and leads the way to the elevators. "Henry wants to do something of an assessment today." She stabs the button for the third floor and slumps against the elevator wall.

"An assessment?" Nolan asks, hands tucked into his jeans pocket.

"Is there an echo in here?"

Nolan's demeanor, already very much a dark cloud, grows darker. Virgil hunches his shoulders.

We reach the combat room, where Henry is already waiting for us. In lieu of a greeting, he turns to me and says, "Try to land a blow on me. One slice, and you're do—"

I whip off the blade I usually keep on me before he can finish the sentence, which he evades almost lazily. I shrug off my backpack and get suited up properly while Henry waits.

I blow out smoke, coating the room in fog. I toss knives through and only hear the odd, muffled thud of them hitting the mats on the wall and cushioned floor. I'm sure some are sticking in the mats. I wonder how Henry is explaining that to the ARC staff.

"Do you know why the fog is ineffective?" Henry asks.

"Because you know my scent?"

"Because you aren't using it correctly." Before I can do anything, Henry sucker punches me in the gut. *Hard.* I gasp and crumple to the ground. The monster wakes, eyes snapping open and narrowing.

"What the fuck?!" I growl.

Henry sighs. "Mr. Murphy, what does your ability do?"

"Extends the scent of the user." It sounds like Nolan is speaking through gritted teeth.

"Exactly. Ms. Black, what do you think it does?"

"I get it. I messed up. I thought it made the field smell like Nolan. So when I used it, I guess that's what I made it do. But then people just pick my scent out of it. If I made it smell like me, they wouldn't be able to."

"And how do you think you could have learned that?"

Now I'm the one gritting my teeth. "By asking Nolan."

"Amazing! A simple solution. Now, go again."

I blow out more smoke, this time understanding that I can make the fog smell like me, apparently just by thinking of it. Or I hope that's what I'm doing. This isn't an exact science. But this time when I move, it's clear that Henry is shifting around, trying to figure out where I am.

I throw blades at what feels like my higher speed, and yet all I hear is the thud of them landing on the ground. Which is confusing because Henry's not even using a weapon.

This time, I catch Henry as he zeros in on me, and metallic claws shoot out of my fingers to form a makeshift shield that Henry's fist hits instead of my stomach. He jumps back and conceals himself in *my* fog.

The claws retract, and I wince as my fingers crack and crunch in the process.

"Why are you using the spikes in one specific way?" Henry reappears out of the smoke and kicks out my legs from under me. I slam onto the ground, groaning. "If you'd grown a spike out of the back of your leg, you could have gotten your cut instead of lying there."

I make a truly pathetic attempt to grow a spike out of my ankle, but it feels like growing a spike out of my ankle. Meaning I scream, and it goes back in right away.

Henry looks over his shoulder at Virgil. "This is your flaw, by the way. It shouldn't hurt to use your abilities."

Virgil hunches his shoulders.

"It hurts you, too?" I gasp, rolling onto my side.

He nods. "When they come out, yeah. I figured it was a side effect or something."

Henry says, "You are reluctant to do it, and so you've made it painful." He shakes his head. "You waste so much time clinging to humanity. You were never human, Virgil."

Virgil stands ramrod still. Never human and possibly an experiment. We may have had something of a breakthrough during the fight with Violet—maybe Virgil now acknowledges that he and the Monster are one and the same—but that doesn't mean there isn't still a part of him clinging to the desire to just be human.

The professor says, "Stop assigning moral superiority to humans. People destroy as well as they build. They made the name 'monster' for animals they feared."

"You talk like you're not one of those humans," I say.

"I'm not. I'm a Master. And so shall you be. You are a bridge between species. And you, in particular, have more advantages than most, given that you have two partners. I have allowed you growing

pains, but you should not be going into the finals with anything less than a clear win."

"I'll get the title. That was the point."

Henry laughs. "That was the point? No, the point was that you establish yourself as someone not to be fucked with in this society in order to give yourself and Virgil the necessary insulation to thrive. Where do you think this is all leading?"

"Leading . . ." I falter, looking to Virgil and Laira. "I dunno, defending the title . . ."

Henry snaps his head toward Virgil again, the boy shrinking under his gaze. "This is on you. You said she could be counted on. But you have done nothing to impress upon her the seriousness of our situation. You have bent to her will and coddled her. You have let her master *you* instead of the monster."

"I beg your finest fucking pardon," I say. But I can't help looking to Virgil. "What is he talking about?"

Virgil swallows. "Adam is struggling. Other Masters are talking. I mean . . . once we were concerned about the other Doctorates maybe unseating him, but it's not like that's a concern anymore."

"Not a concern?" Henry says, his voice pitching. "Have you missed the part where someone is trying to murder him? This is *exactly* what we were meant to be preparing for."

"What does that mean?!" I shout.

"*It means war!*" Henry roars. "We are building to *war*, and we need our strongest to stand at Adam's side. The election was a farce. And now we see just how much. Carrigan has been making his moves, and it is building."

"I didn't volunteer to fight for Adam in a war."

"Didn't you?"

I reel on Virgil, whose hands are balled into fists. Adam is the one doing this, and now Henry's getting worked up about fighting for his friend in a war against Carrigan? Nolan was right. This was what Henry was arranging his game pieces for, and Virgil knew and didn't say shit to me about it.

Virgil avoids my gaze and says to Henry, "What if Adam isn't who you think he is?" I give him a warning look that he doesn't see because he won't look at me. "How much do you really know about your friend?"

Henry's voice turns deadly. "I don't know that I like your tone. The Doctorate was instrumental in my bid to save your life succeeding. Without his and his father's support, you would have been killed."

Virgil's voice gets louder. "You're worried about a war, but as far as I can see, everything is coming out in Adam's favor. The only other brother who wanted his title is dead, and the other one, who never wanted it, is hiding. Meanwhile, Adam is demonstrating powers you didn't even know he had. You prize critical thinking so much, and yet you can't apply it to him—why?"

Henry's hand flies up in the air, and before I can comprehend moving, me and Nolan are in front of Virgil. But the professor wasn't preparing to hit his ward; he was just throwing his hands up.

Henry pauses and laughs, staring at us. "Look at the three of you. A triumvirate, for sure. I don't know how or why you have developed this ridiculous theory, but I suggest you drop it. You're biting the hand that feeds you. Are you Monsters and Master or just a group of savage dogs?"

"And the Wilds?" Nolan asks. "You expect them to fight in your war?"

"Who else would they fight for? The man using them?"

"Seems to me that we're being used either way."

Henry grins. "You know what I like about you, Mr. Murphy? You act high and mighty, but at the end of the day, you expose exactly why your kind struggles so hard to keep a foothold in this society. You lack *control.*" Henry reaches into his jacket and tosses an envelope at Nolan's feet.

Nothing happens for a moment until finally Nolan picks it up and opens it. He stares at the contents, then looks at Henry. "Is this a threat?"

"Oh, it is a threat. But it's not mine. I got that lovely package in the mail."

"What?" I ask. "What is it?"

"It is the reason why none of you may even get to fight in the finals," Henry sneers. "Why you have now put our Doctorate in the precarious position of having to justify why you should even be allowed to *live,* given that he cannot break your bond. So I hope it was worth it. And you'd better fix it and fix it soon. Because if this goes public, I don't know that we can protect you. Until then, don't bother showing up to Mastery group." Henry turns and walks out of the room. Laira sighs and follows him, giving us a lingering look as she does.

"What is it?" I ask Nolan.

He hands the envelope to me. I pull out the photos, my eyes widening. It's . . . it's my room. There's me sitting on top of Virgil, my lips pressed to his. Several of those. And in another, Nolan on top of me, shirtless. I still have my clothes on, but it's clear enough where this is going, because his hands are pushing the hem of my dress up.

And just behind the photos is a note:

Ready to find out what happens when you break the rules?

I drop the envelope, and Virgil picks it up, looks through the contents, then swears and shreds the photos, though I'm sure they have copies.

How did they even get inside my bedroom? I've never lost my key, and they don't let you make duplicates. The room key itself has DO NOT COPY written in bold on it.

"Why did you hint about Adam?" Nolan snipes at Virgil.

Virgil whips around with a laugh. "I'm sorry, you're getting mad at me for *my* choices?"

"That's funny," Nolan says. "You acting like you weren't involved in this. Like you're not in those pictures too. Like you didn't know what was happening after you left. You could have stopped it if you'd really wanted to. But I don't think that's what you did. I think you went home, got into bed, stuck your hand in your pants, and—"

"*Stop,*" I say, and Nolan goes quiet.

"You signed me up for a war?" I ask Virgil.

He swallows. "It's not on a volunteer basis. It's conscription because of who we rely on."

"So you plan to fight for the man who killed your parents?"

Virgil shakes his head and turns away from me. "Obviously not."

Adam won't kill us. He needs me, and if he hurts Virgil or Nolan, he must know he won't get what he wants. But at the very least, he would have to disqualify us. Without that win, we can't get to him.

It's over.

I turn and walk out of the combat room, fighting tears, leaving the boys behind me.

CHAPTER FORTY-SEVEN

Riley

In some ways, I'm less surprised at the situation in which I've found myself, and more surprised that it didn't happen sooner.

There's no council today. Just Dr. Michaels and me in one of the study rooms in the clubhouse. Like everything else, it's impeccably furnished, dark lacquered wood surfaces and textured wallpaper that cost more than most people would find decent for an accent wall. I sit in the leather armchair on the other side of the desk.

Dr. Michaels gazes at me. "I hope this will be the last time I sacrifice a weekend with my family to be here."

I say nothing, as I expect I'm not meant to. I caused significant damage to a historic building and have nothing to show for it. The time for apologies has long passed.

"I'll need the sickle," he says.

"Malachi's a senior. He'll be gone in a few months."

"Inaya will take over after as she's been promoted to VP. We'll

take applications among the artifact-wielding members to fill the vacant positions."

Ah. I see. This isn't a demotion. It's an expulsion. "Will I still be a member?"

"Of course. But you won't carry bones. Next year, perhaps the new elder council can reconsider." Dr. Michaels folds his hands on the desk surface. "Adam Shaw has reached out to the council personally. He understands the mistakes of his ancestor. And we can acknowledge some of the flaws of ours. He will be drawing up a treaty that will be agreed upon by himself and the elder council. So we no longer need that weapon."

Malachi doesn't have the guts to draw blood, and apparently neither do the elders.

Ultimately, this is what I want too. Peace and harmony between our groups. My being a disappointment doesn't matter.

I unlatch the sickle from my neck and place it on the desk before standing.

Dr. Michaels clears his throat, reaching into a drawer and placing a small leather bag on the table. "We were able to retrieve your purse for you." I was too flustered between the tunnel collapsing and kissing Corey to think of it until the next day. I went back to get it in the evening, but by then Douglas was crawling with security. "And, to our pleasant surprise, we were also able to recover the chain, which it seems you had in your possession."

"Yes," I say. "I'd found it that day. I'd planned to bring it in, but a cave collapsing around you is rather distracting."

"I'm sure," Dr. Michaels says. "Well, there's always next year."

Yeah. There's always next year.

. . .

I lean against the bus stop shelter in front of the Metro grocery store, scrolling through the socials of the QBSS student council members. Only Inaya has the gall to write *God's timing is always right* over a selfie. I don't blame her. Since freshman year, I didn't even consider her to be competition despite the fact that she was a year older. She was a seat warmer to me, holding a position I had no doubt I'd take. And then I'd skipped the line, hopping over her and killing any chance she had at the presidency. Now that's all gone.

Downtown is buzzing tonight. It's that transition period between winter and spring when nobody quite knows how to dress, so some people are wearing jackets and others are trying out shorts. Well, white guys are trying out shorts.

When August strolls out of the Burger King parking lot in a tight black long-sleeve shirt tucked into a pleather skirt and fishnet tights, I nod to her. Part of me expected her to ditch. We haven't spoken since the first Douglas attempt. But I did make her certain promises to get her here.

"Lemme see it," she says by way of greeting. I dig in my purse and pull out the ID. She takes it, squinting at the picture. "Yeah, that'll do. Let's get fucked."

With that grand proclamation, she stands in the line for Stages, and I join her. She holds out her hand.

I grab the vape I picked up for her, preloaded with cannabis oil. The second promise. In a couple of minutes, she's figured out how to work it and is taking hits off it. She offers it to me.

Automatically, I wave it off.

She furrows her brow. "You're the one who texted me saying you wanted to party. So do you want to party or not?"

"Are you seriously peer pressuring me?"

She sighs and pulls it away, taking another hit.

I lick my lips and say, "Okay, whatever, give it to me."

"Do you know how to use it?"

"Yeah." It's a lie that becomes obvious when I inhale too much and choke, coughing. A few people in line look over at us, and I duck my head.

August is cackling openly. I try again and manage this time to not choke, expelling vapor out of my mouth. Sammie used to regularly offer me hits off her vape, but I'd always said no. Even when I was of age. It didn't fit. The president of QBSS had one, perhaps two, alcoholic beverages at any function and did not consume recreational drugs of any kind. She was an example of proper and dignified behavior, and a pillar of strength.

She didn't destroy school property or fraternize with Learners, and she certainly did not lose her position.

"Don't you want to know why I asked you to come out?" I say to August.

The girl shrugs. "Not really."

When we get to the front of the line, I hand my ID to the bouncer first, and he shines a flashlight on it, the holographic on the card shimmering. He hands it back to me, then tells August she can't vape inside as he checks hers, handing it back after barely a glance.

Wow. That easy. I mean, I know people do it. Trade IDs. I just hadn't expected it to work.

August saunters inside like she comes here all the time. I guess she must. She was the one who suggested Stages. After coat check, we head to the bar. I hover behind her as she orders doubles of vodka cran. Four drinks.

When it comes time to pay, she nods to me. "She's gonna open a tab."

Classic. I pull out my credit card and slide it across the counter. Mom checks my statements like it's her job. She won't believe a lie that I came out with QBSS members. Not now. From the multiple missed calls, I know she's already heard about my expulsion.

The drinks come up, and August grabs two, nodding at me to grab the other couple. There's only standing space, but she's unbothered, slamming back one of the drinks in seconds. She gestures to me. "Keep up, or I'm going home."

I follow her lead, and then she heads back to the bar, getting us another two doubles. Then she pushes her way through the crowd out the side door to hit the vape again. By the time we get back inside, I already feel slightly ill, my stomach churning and cranberry juice sticking to my tongue.

"I think you're ready to dance now," she says, pulling me onto the dance floor. I don't know the song, but I guess August does, because she immediately starts moving to the music. Excusing the fact that she can truly be absolutely insufferable, August has a magnetism that's hard to ignore. But she's not the girl on my mind. I gnaw my lip. I thought about inviting Corey. And now, in this crowd of bodies, I can't help but wonder what it might be like to dance with her. Her body pressed against mine, moving with the music.

But the last thing I would want Corey to see is me attempting to party my shit away. Besides, I don't even know how I would broach something like that. So far, Corey and I have just . . . been acting like normal. Which is maybe my fault, since I didn't address the kiss or anything.

I kissed a girl I like, and everything is different, but it's also the same.

"More drinks!" August shouts.

I follow her to bar even though I feel like drinking more is the last thing I should be doing. Once we've downed them and returned to the dance floor, the edges of everything are soft and almost seem to ripple in the strobe lights.

August grabs my hands and physically forces me to move more, interrupting my side-to-side shuffle that Sammie used to make fun of. I giggle without meaning to and let her. August twirls me around and dips me, and I can't stop laughing because it's so funny, and then I return the favor.

My phone keeps buzzing intermittently, and after a while, I don't even notice it.

Then suddenly, I'm not moving as much, and we're winding our way to the bathroom. I'm staring at myself in the mirror, my makeup still intact thanks to a very good setting spray and powder. It's like looking at someone new. This version of myself in a crop top and tight skirt.

August presses against my side and holds out her phone, and for some inane reason, I make a peace sign, and she laughs while taking the picture.

My stomach lurches. "I . . . don't feel so good."

August's eyes widen, and she practically shoves me into the toilet stall just in time for an explosion of red to project into the bowl. She holds my hair back while other girls in the bathroom offer sympathetic coos. Several minutes later, I tug a wad of toilet paper out of the dispenser and wipe my mouth after spitting into the bowl.

"All done?" August asks.

"Yeah." I stand, swaying a bit before righting myself and then going to the sink to wash out my mouth. "I feel dizzy," I mumble.

"Let's go eat something. And drink water."

I follow August out of the bathroom. We close the tab, get my jacket, and leave. The cold night breeze hits hard, and suddenly I feel a lot more sober, though the dizziness remains. August seems unaffected by the temperature. I try not to be jealous. Without thinking about it, I walk toward the Bubba's across the street. August has to jerk me back so I don't get hit by a car I didn't see, and then we cross the street properly.

She lets me order a large poutine, double gravy, double curds, and two Cokes.

"And a bottle of water," August adds, and I allow it.

We find an open table and sit. The hard metal seats aren't comfortable, but they feel nostalgic. Like the framed photos of the Monopoly man and famous athletes on the walls.

August cracks open her Coke and my bottle of water, ordering me to drink. I do while we eat. A quarter of the way through, I hiccup, tears sliding down my face.

August sighs. "I can't believe you're a sad drunk. I may come to regret this, but what happened?"

"I used to do this with Sammie. Come here."

"Fuck," August mutters. "I'm sorry."

"I lost her because I was so obsessed with being the perfect QBSS member. I had to do everything by the book. And then I went off the rails last semester, and I tried to fix everything and get it all back. Because I *could* get it all back. I avenged her or whatever, and now I could move on and be perfect again. But there's just more avenging, isn't there? And more to do and prove." I toss my plastic fork into the poutine box and press my palms against my eyes. "I just keep screwing up."

"When were you happy?" August asks.

"What?"

"When, during that whole time, were you happy?"

I stare at her, open-mouthed. *When was I happy?* "When I was with Sammie," I say.

"Why would you think being a perfect QBSS member could replace that?" She leans forward. "Is there anything that could replace that?"

I try to fight the sob, but it tears its way out of my throat anyway, and I hunch over the table, shoulders shaking. Crying in a goddamn poutine shop.

There is nothing.

Nothing is ever going to replace the way I felt with Sammie. Because Sammie is who made those moments. Nothing is ever going to feel the way it felt to be with her.

I don't know how long it takes me to stop crying. Just that once I'm done, the poutine is cold. But August is still here. I'm sure she knows too that nothing is going to replace the feeling of having her mom around. I can't blame her for wanting to make her mom's killer pay. That's what I want too. Adam owes us both a life.

August glances at my neck. "You aren't wearing the sickle."

"They took it."

"Is it that easy to take what's yours?"

I stare at her, and she stares back. "Why did you agree to come out?"

She heaves a sigh. "Remember when I told you that I hooked up with Nolan?"

"Yeah."

"Someone took pictures, apparently. From inside my room." She

wrings her hands. "I went to sniff out the cameras, and they're gone. If they go public with the information, we'll at the very least be disqualified from the Monster's Ball. I don't think Adam will kill us—he needs us—but I also don't know how long that will last. And now we've lost our shot at him."

"But they haven't taken the pictures public yet?"

She pauses. "No . . . but—"

"If they haven't yet, they must want something."

Her brow furrows. "What would they want?"

"That's for you to figure out. Count me in for roughing them up if you need me."

She grins, then it falls off. "I'm sorry for freaking out at Douglas. You're, like, still my girl or whatever."

"Yeah," I say with a laugh. "You're still my girl or whatever too."

CHAPTER FORTY-EIGHT

I know things are dire when I take my textbook with me to meet Margot, Virgil, and Nolan. We've decided to gather in the mostly abandoned atrium of the Biosciences Complex. The massive space is broken up by several real trees in planters set into the floor, and scattered seating.

Tomorrow is the final official day of classes before the exam period starts, but my last class was yesterday. I still have two essays to finish, one for Gender Studies and another for Film, both of which I feel confident I can BS my way through and then get Corey to read them over for me. Then I can use the rest of the exam period to focus on studying for the Astronomy, Health Studies, and Psychology exams—the last one in particular because I need to get a 75 percent minimum to declare Psychology as my major.

I'm so focused on my notes that I don't notice Violet until she's taking a seat at my table. "Didn't want to cram in the library with everyone else?" she asks. Her hair is in a messy bun, but she's done

her makeup. Even without the eyeliner and lipstick, it would be the best she's looked all semester.

I say, "I'm supposed to be having a mentee meeting with Margot and the guys."

"You weren't at the last Mastery group."

"Henry told us not to come. We've . . . pissed him off."

"Classic."

"Yeah. Hey . . . I'm sorry about Bryce. I lost control, and he paid for it."

Violet leans back in her chair. "I can't accept your apology for him."

"I'll tell him myself when I see him next."

She plays with her hands, the black polish on her nails chipped at the tops where she's bitten them down. "You were right about me. Since Bryce and I were kids, I was the one who excelled, and he was my shadow. His mom was well loved, but she was never more than a student. And after she passed, his dad never bothered to try to rise in rank. But both my parents are senior Masters. Even with our partners, I got Frankie, from a legacy family, and he ended up with Mitch, who was spontaneously born."

"I didn't know that." Mitch is so strong that I figured he was from a Monster family.

"They knew they were underdogs and so they worked harder." She smiles. "Frankie and I didn't do shit. I assumed we would be good. Then the week before winter semester, my dad booked us space in the ARC so we could warm up, and it was pathetic. Then Bryce and Mitch kept getting better, while we lost in our first match, and you showed up with two partners. And of course *I* couldn't be the problem, and so it must be Frankie. She was faulty. I kept thinking it, and she felt it."

It's shitty behavior, and Violet knows it. She says, "I get what it's like to be cruel to a friend and come to regret it. I was lucky Frankie forgave me. So there's no bad blood between you and me. There wasn't any the instant you saved me at the cost of an easy win." She stands and nods to the door, where Margot and Virgil are entering. "Spoiler, Bryce isn't even mad, so you don't have a lot of work to do there. Mitch, on the other hand . . . Yeah, that'll take some time."

"I'll work on it. And Frankie?"

Violet laughs. "Frankie doesn't like most people. You were lucky to get indifference from her for as long as you did." She waves at Virgil and Margot as they come over but leaves without saying anything to them.

Virgil gives me a searching look. "Everything okay?"

"Yup. Violet is no longer mad at me, Bryce was apparently never mad at me, Frankie doesn't like me but she doesn't like most people, so I only have to win over Mitch after apologizing to his partner."

Virgil says, "Start using his team names for everyone."

"Glad to see that being blackmailed hasn't made you lose your sense of humor," Margot grumbles.

I say, "Typically, people make a request when blackmailing you." I've been thinking about it since Riley said it. It's been over a week now. Whoever sent the threat should have turned us in or at the very least made clear what they want from us.

"Where's Nolan?" Margot asks.

Virgil says, "He's not coming. He's got two finals just before the Monster's Ball and said that he didn't want to 'come to another bullshit lecture' when he could be studying."

"Fine," Margot says. "I hear that Virgil spilled the beans about

Adam to Henry?" A fact that she heard from me because I texted her about it.

"Yes," I say, and Virgil hunches. Good. I know I'm no saint, but he hid that war shit from me, and I want him to feel bad about something. I'm not the only one who messes up.

"Thankfully, he's not going to tell Adam."

"And what about you?" I ask. "Are you on board to fight in his war for Adam?"

Margot levels me with a stare cold enough to sting. "I won't have my brother in a war. I've been trying to get involved to prevent that, which Henry knows. And I especially won't have Isaac fighting for a man who isn't even who he says he is. We made a plan, and we need to execute it."

"We can't do that if we get disqualified."

"No," she says. "But I'm sure the blackmail is coming. You've done nothing but mope and study for days. We still need the Osseous. Get on that shit."

Easy for her to say. Riley's not even a part of the QBSS artifact branch anymore. I have no idea how we're supposed to make this happen. I take a good look at Margot, from her darting eyes to her hands once again covered in gloves. "You good?"

"Sure," she says with a laugh. "The man I've relied on for the past three years is trying to prep for war on behalf of a man who's manipulating him. I have no other support, and no backup plan, and definitely don't have enough money to manage on my own. And I have to fight a Master with decades of experience who only lost because she's been letting Jules take the lead with every fight so he gets the practice in. I'm fine."

I balk. "Natalie's been doing what?"

Margot sighs. "Issac and I have caught a couple of their matches. She was just standing around and letting Jules do everything. But since they've landed in the repechage, she's been active, I assume not wanting them to lose again. If I want Isaac and me to have a soft place to land if Henry's shit blows up in his face, we need that money."

"Henry will—" But Virgil stops as Margot throws him a sharp look.

"Don't act like this stuff with Adam doesn't change everything," she hisses. "Henry isn't winning anymore. He never was. And as long as he's being duped, he can't keep us safe. If I were you, I would start figuring out *your* backup plan." Margot slings her backpack over her shoulders and strides out of the building.

Virgil slumps on the table, resting his head on his forearms. I brush my fingers over the curls on his head, and when he doesn't stop me, I continue, looping the strands around my nails. I pull my hand away, and he reaches out and catches it.

"I really thought he would listen to me," Virgil says. "My parents were his friends. And that was a big deal back then, for a Bachelor to be friends with Monsters outside of their partnerships."

"His life revolves around Adam and his family. Believing Adam is the villain would upend his carefully arranged chess pieces. He doesn't want to believe it, so he won't."

"I spent my whole life thinking of my parents that way," he mumbles. "Adam didn't just kill them. He destroyed their memories." A couple tears leak out of Virgil's eye, and I catch them on my finger. He stares at me. "My mom would have liked you."

"Of course she would have," I say. "I'm the bird in the fable. Her favorite character."

He quirks a smile, and just like that, I can't stay mad at him. Henry is the closest thing Virgil has to a parent. He sought him out because he thought he would get the support he'd always been given. But Virgil forgot that the second he aligned himself with me, he stopped being the obedient boy Henry raised. I tainted everything that Virgil had forged just by being myself.

Virgil befriended the bird, but Henry would have abandoned it at the first errant peck.

Henry stops in front of his office in Humphrey Hall, where I stand leaning against the door. The man has dodged me for almost a week now. Yesterday I even stood outside his classroom, waiting for his lecture to finish, and he still brushed me off.

"Are we going to keep doing this dance?" I ask. "Or are you going to just talk to me?"

Henry grinds his teeth together. "Fine. Come inside." I move so he can open the door and follow him into the room. He goes behind his desk, taking a seat in the leather chair while I sit across from him. I wish I could cross my legs, because it seems like it would be intimidating, but I have big thighs now so it doesn't feel comfortable anymore. I manspread instead, which has the same effect, I think.

"What can I do for you, Ms. Black?" Henry asks.

"I want you to forgive Virgil. Take him out to dinner, pat him on the head, whatever. This silent treatment has gone on long enough. You're going to mess him up for finals on Saturday. You still want us to win, don't you? We haven't been disqualified yet."

Henry gives me a flat look. "I planned to invite him for dinner on Good Friday. But I'll put out the invite today if that pleases you."

"It pleases me," I say with a grin. Classic Henry. He was going to

make up with Virgil but intended to keep him feeling bad for upsetting Daddy for as long as possible.

I move to stand, and Henry speaks again. "I understand needing a vessel for your anger. Someone to blame for your misfortune. But you should take care to choose the correct target."

"Will do," I say, turning for the door.

"Sit down."

I sigh and return to my seat, slouching in the chair.

"Do you know that there's both an official and unofficial story of what happened to my family?"

"No . . ."

Henry laces his fingers together. "The official story is that Cyrus, led by Adam, came to our rescue and saved me just in time. That Cyrus led that Monster to the Pen, where they have lived out their days. An uncontrolled spontaneous Monster." He rests his chin on his hands. "Unofficially, that Monster escaped. It's true what Adam told you. Wilds are more difficult to control for Doctorates. It's always been this way. That's why the rebellion was so feared by Cyrus. Because this fact is a weakness. And the last thing a Doctorate wants is for his students to know he is not as close to God as he acts."

The Monster who killed Henry's family was a Wild. Well, look at that. A pattern of behavior. "Wait . . . the Monster got away?"

"Yes. Cyrus searched, of course, but he was eluded. And so he pretended it had been caught and jailed. Much like when Bernie's son was missing, and the official story was that he had been killed despite the lack of a body. Under Cyrus's rule, the writing of history was always more important than the actual events." Henry plays with a paperweight on his desk, rocking it under his fingers. "That Monster stayed hidden for a long time."

"But not forever."

"No. Like you, I dedicated myself to finding the cause of my misfortune. Pursued them relentlessly until one day, I found them. He worked construction. He had the gall to feign ignorance. To act like he had no idea what happened and wasn't involved. I assume someone hired him to unseat the power my family had amassed. Though he denied it. Had a wife and two small children. A family like my own had been." He leans toward me. "Do you know what I did?"

I see where this conversation is going. Like knowing the end of a game before the moves have been played. I fight not to roll my eyes. "You realized revenge wouldn't change anything, so you spared him, and became a better man for it."

Henry looks me in the eyes when he says, "I stabbed him in the back exactly one hundred and eleven times. Forty-one for my father's age when he was murdered, thirty-nine for my mother, thirteen for my sister, and fifteen for me, because I'd died the same day." Henry pulls his hand away from the paperweight. "Lewis, my partner at the time, discovered me. He was horrified. He ate the body to hide the evidence of what I'd done. He never forgave me for that. He insisted that my revenge hadn't fixed the wrong committed against me. But do you know what?"

"What?" I breathe. I'm shaking. This isn't how I thought this conversation would go.

"It *did* fix me. Until that point, I felt that my entire life was spent in powerlessness. I couldn't save my family. I had to rely on the goodwill of the Shaws. And no matter what I achieved in the Bachelor candidacy or the Monster's Ball, whenever people looked upon me they did so with pity. But that moment undid it all. I *was* powerful. I believed in myself in a way I never had, and I used that

power to protect the people I loved so they could never be taken from me. Not ever again. I have protected Margot and Isaac. I have protected Adam. I have protected Laira. And I couldn't protect Virgil's parents, but I have done everything in my power to keep that boy safe. Can you say the same of yourself?"

I swallow. My breaths are too short. This is why Henry has been helping me. Why he keeps trying to show me how I could have saved my mom. Because he understands. He understands in a way that no one else does, because he's done what I want desperately to do. As long as Adam is still alive, none of the people I care about are safe. It isn't just about revenge, about being powerful. It's about never suffering like that ever again.

For the first time since meeting him, I understand the devotion that Margot and Virgil have when it comes to Henry. He isn't kind. His life has been too hard for that. But he knows his charges. Even me.

"Do not be misguided, Ms. Black. You cannot take back what's lost. You can only hold onto what is already within your grasp. Hit the bullseye or don't even bother aiming. Do you understand me?"

"Eye on the prize," I say.

He nods. "Dismissed."

For once, I don't have any witty comeback to spout. I just rise and leave the room.

CHAPTER FORTY-NINE

I slouch against the wall in the greenroom. The first day of finals, and we're still in the Monster's Ball. Virgil has been tapping his foot nonstop for the last ten minutes. Nolan is across the room because he said either he physically moved or he would tear Virgil's foot off. I keep my eyes on the door.

Check-in time is almost over.

"If they don't come in time, they'll forfeit," Virgil says.

I shake my head. "Like hell they'll forfeit."

Margot and Isaac will be facing Jules and Natalie right after us this afternoon. Both matches have the potential to be the last ones in each respective league. Because of the way the double elimination bracket is set up, we need to win twice to win it all, but Barbie and Ellis only need to win once. If they beat us today, it's over.

Assuming we get to compete.

Two minutes before check-in time closes, Barbie saunters through the door with Ellis on her heels. She's chosen a black leotard for the

match, and it covers her from neck to ankle, following the contours of her body. She leaves Ellis and walks over to me, blond ponytail swinging. Virgil stiffens.

"Can I help you?" I ask her.

She smiles. "Do you mind if we have a private conversation?"

"Now, why would I want to do that?"

She stares with her head tilted, her hair shiny even in the dim light.

"What?" I say, breaking first.

"I'm waiting for the two brain cells in your head to rub together and manage an appropriate thought. Why would I, today of all days, be coming over to you to ask for a private chat?"

I narrow my eyes, and then it hits me. Barbie and Ellis have the ability to disappear and reappear in smoke. She wouldn't need a key to get into my room. All she had to do was wait until I was gone and then figure out what room I was in. Like the day that girl on my floor said an Asian girl was looking for me. I knew it couldn't be Corey but had brushed it off.

Barbie grins. "There they are. Look at those little guys, working overtime."

"Let's go," I snap at her, walking out of the room. I know Virgil is staring at me, but I ignore him.

Though I was in the lead, Barbie overtakes me easily, choosing a side room and peeking in. "Looks private to me."

I follow her inside and shut the door.

"What do you want?" I say, getting straight to the point.

"How was it, by the way?" she asks, twirling her hair around her finger. "I really thought you'd sleep with Virgil. That was the vibe I got. But the Wild was unexpected. Then again, seeing you two come

out of that side room looking hot and bothered after your match was what tipped me off to the possibility that you might be up to something . . . extracurricular, shall we say?"

"You saw how it was," I grind out between my teeth.

She rolls her eyes. "Come on, I'm not a monster. Once it got to nudity, I cut the feed. That sex tape doesn't exist." Something between my shoulders unwinds, and they drop. Barbie says, "You really think so little of me."

"It's hard not to when you put cameras in the place where I sleep. So, again, what do you want?"

"Did you or did you not promise to help Ellis reconnect with Corey?"

I reel back. "That's what this is about?! You're the one who shat on that bed in the first place!"

"I'm aware," she snaps. "We all make mistakes sometimes. I'm rectifying it now."

"With blackmail?!"

Barbie throws her head back in a dramatic sigh. "Yes, with blackmail. It's effective." She holds up her phone. "The footage only exists on my phone. Those photos were stills that I printed. You can watch me delete everything."

"And I'm supposed to believe that?"

"Yes, because I truly do not care who you sleep with. It's honestly an arcane rule, and more people than you think break it."

"You'd win automatically."

She laughs. "Oh, honey, we could wipe the floor with your ass any day of the week. All I need you to do is FaceTime Corey right now and arrange a meetup and we're good."

"Now?"

"Yes, because you've proven that your word is worth shit." She claps her hands. "We have to get to the antechambers soon, and if you don't do it now, I'll report you."

I dial Corey's number and she appears on the screen, already in the stands next to Margot, who moves into the frame, I assume because she saw my face. "What's up?" Corey asks.

"Can you go somewhere more private?"

Margot's eyebrows shoot up.

But Corey nods and moves into the hallway. "What's going on? Is Virgil—" She stops as I turn the phone toward Barbie, who waves. ". . . Hi."

"Hi," Barbie chimes.

I turn the phone back to me. "Barbie is the one who sent the photos. She . . . she would like you to set up a meeting with Ellis, and then she promises to delete them and not report us."

Corey heaves a sigh. "Okay, I'll do it."

"Is that good?" I ask Barbie.

"Tonight," she says.

Corey nods. "Tonight."

"Good. I'll delete the footage after the meeting."

I scowl, which Barbie ignores. "Fine," I say and end the call.

Once again, someone else is paying for my fuckup. And I wish it weren't Corey.

The only thing that I can think as the antechamber doors open is that I'm glad I didn't have to hear whatever the announcer said. I assume some bullshit about how Barbie is the favorite to win, conveniently not mentioning Ellis, while somehow managing to bring up something about Virgil's parents.

I walk into the arena to the screams and cheers of the crowd, scanning this time to see Nolan, Corey, Margot, Jules, and even Henry and Natalie in the stands. Henry is seated beside Adam. I can't reconcile the man who waited to make sure I was safely inside Vic Hall before driving away as being the same man who killed Mom. It doesn't mesh, but the evidence keeps stacking up.

I'm going to end him. Not just for me. But for the people I need to protect.

Barbie grins at me from across the arena, the sheng biao gripped in her hands almost lazily. When the horn blows, instead of rushing in like she did with Bryce, she raises her right hand and twitches it toward herself, inviting me to come at her.

The monster flexes its claws and clamps its jaw.

"Like hell," I say.

She shrugs. "Have it your way."

In what feels like a blink, she's in front of me. Instinct is the only thing that makes me manage to get a knife up to defend. She hops back with a bounce like a bunny. I fling a knife, aiming for the rope. It hits and ricochets off. I grit my teeth. Not ordinary rope, then. It does have a sort of plastic look to it, which I thought could be cut, but apparently not. Not that easily, anyway.

"Good try!" Barbie coos.

The crowd laughs, and my brow furrows. This is a game to her. She has no real skin in this.

Virgil growls on my left, playing whack-a-mole with Ellis, attempting to rush the panther only to land on nothing but air as Ellis shifts from place to place in shadow.

Also drawing laughs from the crowd.

We're one big joke to them, apparently.

The monster prowls behind my eyes. Let them laugh.

I spin, fast, whipping out knives as I go. Barbie hops around to evade them. Which is fine. She's not the target anyway.

I get Ellis in one of the eyes on his body just as he appears in my periphery, relishing in the screech of pain that gives Virgil enough time to hit the boy with his spiked tail.

No one is laughing now.

Barbie whips her sheng biao out, and I grasp the dagger, ignoring the pain of the blade ripping through the skin of my palm. It doesn't hurt much more than extending spikes. She attempts to pull it back, but I hold firm, and her eyes narrow, the mirth gone from her face. With my other hand, I grip the rope, tugging her toward me.

I expect her to pull back. I don't expect her to let go. As I flail, adjusting to the change in balance, she rushes forward to sucker punch me. But I'm ready, placing her own blade against my stomach, where it spears her between her knuckles. She hisses but manages to rip her dagger out of my hand.

I don't let her retreat. I follow, throwing knives as I go. One slices through the skin above her eyebrow, sending blood into the eye below it. She closes the eye, and now she's flailing to keep her balance. I thrust out my arm, metal blades shooting toward her stomach.

I have her!

Or I thought I did. Barbie disappears in a puff of smoke and reappears behind me, kicking me in the back. I fly toward the concrete, slamming into the floor. I gasp, attempting to scramble to my feet, working through the pain. I force myself to stand and spot Barbie pressing her palm against the cut above her eye, trying to stop

the bleeding, but it's no good—it keeps dripping down, narrowing her field of vision to one eye.

I sprint toward her, but I'm too late. Once again, she disappears in a puff of smoke. And now I'm playing the same game that Virgil is with Ellis. Or . . . was. Across the arena, Virgil seems to be predicting where Ellis is going.

But how? Fuck, if only we could manage the sort of connection we had in the initiation. Then I would just know. Is there a pattern to the movements? Or is it something else?

"Pay attention," Barbie chides as her dagger slices across my eye in the same spot where I got her.

Except, of course, I can heal and she can't.

She curls her lip. "I can't stand regeneration."

"Too bad, so sad."

I chase her around the arena, tossing knives and trying to figure out what this pattern is.

Barbie smiles. "Time for a countdown, I think. Ten."

What's she talking about? I follow her throughout the arena, at one point having to jump over both Virgil and Ellis. But there doesn't seem to be any sort of pattern emerging. What is it? And why does she keep counting?"

"One . . . and . . ."

I reach for my next blade and grasp air. My knives. Once again, I've failed to realize how many I'm using. She rushes in. I thrust out my hands, spikes growing, but she evades them. *Shit, shit, shit.* The monster is howling, slamming against the sides of my mind, as frustrated as I am.

But the fact remains that even with the monster, I'm struggling to keep up with her.

I leap into the air, and Barbie follows me, her dagger poised to strike. From the corner of my eye, I catch Margot in the crowd, standing on her feet and screaming alongside Corey.

I think back to that training session with Henry. How I used Virgil's spikes, not just the way he does, but in my own way. Manipulating his ability to work for me.

Something in Barbie's expression changes as I shift my body in the air, remembering the stance Margot taught me, making sure I get enough torque in my hips to throw a solid right hook. Barbie's eyes shift to the fist.

It coats with black iridescent metal before slamming into her gut. She crashes to the ground.

I land with a thud, and the arena is silent.

I stand, wobbling on my feet, staring at her.

She doesn't get up.

The horn blares, and the crowd goes wild.

I'm breathing hard and can't catch my breath until me and Virgil are once again in the antechamber. In the dim room, I turn away as Virgil transforms back and dresses hurriedly.

He rushes over to me, lifting me off my feet and swinging me around. He holds me there, and I tilt my head down, our foreheads pressed together. "You were amazing," he breathes just before he kisses me. Our lips move against each other, me gripping his shoulders while he keeps his arms sealed around my back.

We break away, and he stares into my eyes. "I don't know what to do with how I feel about you," he says. "I know you said to stop toeing the line, and I should stop, but . . . you make me want to do things I *want* instead of what I *should*. All I want to do is give in again and again."

There was never a line between me and Virgil to cross in the first place. I pretended it existed, but it doesn't. It hasn't since the moment I decided to risk my life to save his.

I want to concentrate on what he's saying to me. I want to be in this moment. But I can't.

"She threw it," I say, voice hollow.

Virgil falters. "What?"

"She threw the match," I repeat. "She saw that the hit was going to connect. I was going to get her right in the face. And she moved enough so that I hit her in the stomach instead. Do you understand?! If she had time to move, she could have moved *away*. She *wanted* me to hit her."

"Why would she do that?"

I grit my teeth. "To make sure we keep our promise." Virgil's brow furrows, but it makes perfect sense to me. Barbie refused to delete the video until after the meeting happens tonight. She wants to make sure we hold up our end of the bargain. If we don't, she'll blow the whistle. And now that we're so close to winning it all, there's no way we won't follow through.

Barbara Hu, you are one crafty bitch.

CHAPTER FIFTY

Jules's eyes widen as I step into the antechamber. He's crouched on the ground, knees tucked up to his chest, head down. Literally thirty minutes ago, me and Virgil had been in this spot.

"You aren't supposed to be in here," Jules says.

I shrug. "Natalie texted me." She said he needed me, and that was enough.

Jules shakes his head and sits fully on the ground, stretching his legs out. I sit beside him and lean against him. As usual, he bears my weight.

Jules says, "I said that winning was what Natalie wanted. And I mean, she cares, but only insofar as we place within the cutoff. Winning it all was never something that mattered to her."

"Then why did you say it did?"

He hunches. "If I win, if I can do better on my own, you can be less involved."

I groan.

"You're my little sister. Mom specifically instructed me to take care of you. Instead, I got manipulated by Bernie, and you had to save me. Now, you're here getting involved in this Adam stuff. So if I win, maybe you'll see me as more capable and stop doing all this dangerous shit. I owe—"

"No!" I pull away from him and shake my head, braids flying. "I'm so tired of people saying they owe things to me. Since when did our relationship become transactional? We were supposed to work on this *together*. Instead, you spend the whole semester excluding me out of some deluded sense of duty or whatever, and I'm so tired of it. Mom is dead, and you're still trying to be the perfect son for her."

"Isn't that what you're doing?"

"No. I'm doing what I'm doing for me." *I* want someone to pay. Henry understood that. Understands it better than my own flesh and blood. "If you want to win, Jules, fine, win. But don't do it for me, or Mom, or Natalie. For once, do it for yourself."

I spin on my heel and stomp out of the room. Natalie is leaning on the wall and throws me a lazy grin. "I hope that was helpful," she says.

"What's your game?" I snap at her.

"I don't much care for games."

"Whatever," I mutter, moving past her.

"There's nothing more deadly than a taste of power. Once it touches your lips, you lick, and lick, and lick until they're dry and chapped and cracking, if only to get a bit more of the flavor. And you're a fool if you choose to pretend that you're immune to the temptation."

"This is relevant to me, how?"

Natalie smiles. "Just a thought I had."

. . .

I'm aware of every bit of Adam Shaw as me and Virgil arrive at Henry's section. While Virgil heads to the right of Henry, where Nolan and Corey are already waiting, the Doctorate has saved a seat for me on the other side, next to him. He's dressed in a soft cream sweater, his leather cord necklaces resting against the collar, his hair shorn close to his scalp. A normal man, by all appearances. I settle into my seat.

"Great match," he says, grinning. "I hope you don't mind sitting next to me."

I force something resembling a smile onto my face. "Not at all."

Henry grumbles, "You'd be safer in the box."

"I like being close to the action," Adam says. Serene, because he knows he won't be attacked unless he wills it.

This man took a train to Toronto, sent Laira of all people after Mom, and forced Mom to kill herself. He manipulated a man who tortured my brother and was almost the reason the society killed him. And of course, Bernie and Davy *did* die. He made a Wild slaughter his brother and sister-in-law and nieces in broad daylight. He destroyed Virgil's family using his parents to try to take out his father early. He's the worst kind of monster. The sort that hides behind a facade of kindness.

The lights strobe and flash, indicating the start of the match. I face the front, peering into the arena.

"I suppose you'll be avoiding choosing sides," Adam whispers, leaning toward me.

I stiffen and make myself relax. "Yeah, best not to."

"Either way, they're both within the cutoff. Jules has secured his partnership with Natalie, and we can celebrate Margot and Isaac's graduation to the title."

"Do you not worry about Natalie getting too much power?"

Adam says, "Natalie Soer is no enemy of mine. Not a fan of my dad, no, but he's gone now, and she doesn't seem to have transferred the grudge to me, thankfully. I'm hopeful that we can cultivate a better relationship."

"Even though what you want is fundamentally opposed? She wants to see the society end, and you want to see it improved."

"Why do you say those goals are in opposition?" he asks. "Sometimes broken systems have to be destroyed before they can be remade."

He turns back to the arena before I can prod on that particular point, and the booming voice of the announcer fills the room. "Welcome to the Master-in-training league finals! This is going to be one for the history books, folks! We have Natalie Soer and her partner, July Black. And what a pair they are. I cannot think of a duo more shrouded in mystery and controversy, but we won't get into that."

I cannot stand these announcers. Natalie walks into the arena in a loose pair of cargo pants and a tight black T-shirt without any weapon that I can see. Jules looms behind her. For a moment, I freeze, looking at the bear with its ridges of white bone around its neck and the coral-like bone formations on the rest of its body. It's hard to think that that's my brother. Like seeing him emerge in a new outfit. Foreign yet familiar.

"Natalie is, of course, a senior Master here at this competition for the purposes of qualifying with her new partner, July. We expected nothing but wins from them, but they had a stunning upset landing them in the repechage, and they clawed their way back. If they win this match, they'll have to fight once more to secure the prize." The

doors on the other side of the arena open. "And the challenger is Margot Bouchard and her partner, Isaac Bouchard. This sibling duo have been absolutely tearing apart the competition—though is it any surprise with the stellar mentorship of senior Master Henry Scott, who we see is seated next to our Doctorate? Give us a wave, Henry!"

Henry does not wave. In fact, he glowers, which is projected on the jumbo screens. Meanwhile, Adam stifles a laugh, putting a hand over his mouth and trying to play it off as a sneeze. Henry turns his glower on his friend.

It's amazing, really. How normal Adam can act. How well he can fit into the role.

I focus on Margot as she steps into the arena, slamming her brass knuckles together. Isaac bounces on his toes behind her, tail wagging, eager. Jules wants the win for me, and Margot wants it for her brother. Twenty-five thousand dollars could help them out a lot. Henry's generosity is nice, but it comes with accepting complete dependence on the professor.

The horn blows, and Margot and Isaac wind around each other, bobbing and weaving. Jules ambles forward, head down, going for Isaac just to have the boy leap over him, teeth bared at Natalie.

Natalie hops out of the way of Isaac's teeth right into the path of Margot, who's sliding between Jules's legs and leaping up, slamming down her fist, only to be stopped by Natalie holding up a single palm, catching Margot's fist in hers. She lifts Margot, flinging her toward Isaac, who was changing course to head toward the senior Master.

Margot recovers in the air, flipping and landing on Isaac's back, where she stands and peers at Natalie.

"That should have burned her," I say.

"Look closer," Adam replies, pointing. "Natalie's palm."

That's when I see it. The coating of white where skin should be. Of bone. The same hard bone that litters my brother's body.

Margot and Isaac both shoot back toward Natalie, leaping over and under each other. They treat Jules like more of a nuisance than anything. Launching only enough attacks to get him out of the way so they can coordinate on attacking Natalie. I've gotten used to Masters and Monsters fighting separately, but you can get great results when you work together. Mine and Virgil's match with Melani and Shay proved that much. We should have done that more with Barbie and Ellis. Had she not thrown it, we probably would have lost.

"Come on now," Adam says, eyes glued to the arena. "Don't let them underestimate you, Jules."

Natalie is doing well, but they're backing her into a corner. She won't have anywhere to go soon. I catch the grin on Margot's face as they get her up against the wall. But then Natalie has her own smile.

Jules teeters on two legs and tugs a hunk of bone from his body, flinging it toward the three of them at the wall. I recognize the technique. Remember the way Mom positioned us with knives in front of a target.

The piece of bone is massive and hurtling toward them. As I would expect, they move toward the opening on the right, where Natalie has sprinted and greets them, a hunk of sharpened bone protruding from her forearm. Margot manages to squeeze through, but Isaac is too big and howls as Natalie slices through the tendons of his left front leg.

Margot gets the woman back, turning on her heel and slamming a fist into Natalie's side, only to find that it's coated in bone.

Jules is still throwing more of his bone chunks like massive

knives, which Isaac is being forced to evade with a bleeding leg. They were working together, but now the sibling duo are forced into fighting apart—Margot handling Natalie and Isaac with Jules.

Jules has the bipedal advantage, looming over Isaac, but he's shakier that way. It's clear that he's more comfortable on all fours.

Henry is tapping his foot and has his arms crossed over his chest so tightly that it's wrinkling his sweater. "If they can't break through, they're going to tire out."

"Did you suggest she use those things? The knuckles?" Adam asks his friend. "I would have thought you'd make her throw them away by now."

"Why?" I ask.

"Senior Masters like Henry or Natalie, you'll find that they don't use physical weapons. Dad always said that the weapon is rather like training wheels. It's there to help the Master until they reach the third evolution. Once you get to that state, abandoning them is the more old-school method. Because it's easy to start using the weapon as a crutch." He gestures to me. "Take you, for example. You throw those knives, but it's limited. You run out of them, and they have a certain size and dimension and level of control. However, if you threw those spikes that Virgil can grow instead, then you'd have an unlimited supply and no need for collection after. But it's hard to turn your mind to that when you have the blades in your hands. You rely on them and only use the spikes when you're in a dire situation, even though they're actually the better weapon."

I blink at him. He's right; I only use the spikes as a last resort.

Henry sighs. "We tried without the knuckles earlier this year, but she burns herself. And unlike Ms. Black, Margot doesn't have access to regeneration abilities."

That's why Margot's been wearing those gloves! She's been burning herself and putting them on to hide the wounds. But if they tried and failed earlier in the year, she should have stopped. I saw her with those gloves just last week. She's been pushing herself because she's losing faith in Henry.

Adam gazes at his friend. "You have such a soft spot for her. I've known you to have students reporting pains using third-evolution skills who you told to suck it up."

Which is exactly what he told me and Virgil. That it shouldn't hurt and only did because of how Virgil feels about his monstrosity. If Margot is being burned, it must say something about how Isaac is dealing with his power. Considering the way he flinched in those earlier fights, the memory of burning Davy has left a lasting impression on him.

Henry says, "Pain is one thing. Permanent burns that would inhibit her ability to take impact to her fists are another."

Adam hums, turning back to the match.

It becomes almost grueling to watch both sides continue to fight without making any real headway. Natalie is no longer looking composed. Some of her hair is singed. Margot has a bruise forming on her cheek. Isaac is limping, and Jules winces as more bones grow in to replace the ones he threw.

A timer appears on the screen, counting down from a minute.

Adam says, "If they can't end the match in a minute, then it'll be sudden death. Margot and Natalie will be made to fight one-on-one."

Right. Our matches go so fast that I keep forgetting about the time limit.

Margot shouts for Isaac, and they attempt another team-up, but it's not quite working. You can feel the desperation pouring off them in waves. Margot's brow is furrowed.

"Wouldn't sudden death be better?" I ask. "Margot could focus." Though as soon as the words are out of my mouth, I realize the issue. "You can't use weapons in sudden death."

"Precisely," Henry mutters.

The time runs out, and the horn blows.

Henry sighs and slouches. The announcer lets us know the rules of sudden death, and Isaac and Jules are forced to exit the arena. A volunteer comes out and collects Margot's brass knuckles. Down the row, Virgil is leaning forward, leg jiggling, and even Nolan looks nervous.

Natalie rolls her neck, pleased about the turn of events. The horn blows, and she flies at Margot, who's forced to evade while taking blows to the face and stomach. She's getting slaughtered.

"I can't watch this," Corey says from down the aisle, burying her face in her hands.

Henry is grinding his teeth so loud it's as if he's doing it right next to my ear.

It's brutal, but I know that Margot won't yield. Even as a tooth flies from her mouth. She said herself that they need the money. I wasn't going to cheer her on against Jules, but he's not on the field right now.

"Come on, come on, come on," I chant.

Natalie kicks Margot hard enough to send her flying into the wall. Margot slumps, her head down. The announcer calls for a check of vitals, but it's unnecessary. Margot coughs, showing she's still conscious. Natalie strolls over to her, crouching in front of the girl.

The camera zooms in.

Natalie tips Margot's head up. Margot's brown irises go molten, turning from a chestnut into a churning swirl of orange and red.

"No!" Henry shouts, leaping to his feet.

Natalie lifts her arm in the air, her fist closed. The horn sounds.

Margot's eyes melt back to brown.

Henry practically sobs, slamming his hands onto the glass barrier, breathing heavily.

I make fun of Henry for playing Daddy, but it's different with Margot. He chose her as his protégé. More than that, he cares about her as if she were his child in a way that's different from how he cares for Virgil.

While Virgil and Corey hug and dance around celebrating, there's chatter behind me about why Natalie would yield.

But I know.

Henry said that Margot burned herself when she used fire without a conduit. Whatever was churning behind her eyes, it would have been all consuming. Every bit of that desperation I only glimpsed the other day came pouring out in the match. The need to win, to give her and Isaac independence, some place to land now that Henry no longer feels like the safe bet, it all came out.

Natalie saved Margot from herself.

I watch the senior Master walk out of the arena. I've spent so much time questioning Natalie's motives when it comes to Jules, but this is what finally makes me believe that she wouldn't put him in real danger.

It's the first time I realize that Natalie Soer has a heart.

CHAPTER FIFTY-ONE

Riley

When I enter Mekong in the evening, Corey is sitting at a table in the corner, grasping her hands so hard that her knuckles are white, her dark hair falling over one shoulder. Even nervous, she's beautiful. I try to look natural as I walk over.

She spots me and moves her purse off the booth beside her, and so I sit there instead of across.

I lick my lips and swear I can taste dirt.

"Thanks for coming," Corey says, attempting a smile that falls flat. "I just . . . I didn't want to bother August and Virgil with the final match happening tomorrow, and I . . . well, I wanted you here, so thank you."

"It's cool. Uh—" I start to think better of what I was going to

say. To smother it. But I can't do that anymore. "I'm happy to be here to support you. If you ever need me, just call and I'll be there."

Her cheeks redden. "Thank you. Uh, same, if you ever . . . you know."

I ask, "What made you decide to finally meet with him?"

"Barbie's blackmailing August, Virgil, and Nolan, and her condition was that I meet with him."

"Ah." I guess that solves the mystery.

Corey rhythmically flexes her left hand and massages the shorter nubs with her thumb.

The door to the restaurant opens again, and Ellis enters. I at least know who he is this time when I see him. Corey grips her hands into fists. I hesitate for a moment before reaching out and grasping one. She lets her fingers loosen, joining her right hand with mine instead.

I swallow. Ellis glances at our clasped hands as he comes over and sits. I think about letting go so he doesn't get the wrong idea. But then again . . . anything he thinks would be the right idea, wouldn't it?

"I've always liked this place," Ellis says. "Do you still like Viet food or . . . ?"

"I like it," Corey mumbles.

The server comes over, and Ellis orders a round of potstickers. I don't know if we'll actually eat them. I think it's just something to do. He asks, "Did you get the book I sent? I know we always talked about traveling to Korea."

She nods. "I've been reading it."

Ellis beams as if she's given him a huge compliment instead of a begrudging acknowledgment. He drags his hand through his hair. "Good. I'm glad." He looks at me again. "Uh, I guess we haven't formally met? I'm Ellis."

"Riley," I say.

"You're the QBSS president, aren't you?"

"No."

He falters for a moment, glancing at Corey like she'll fill in the blank, but she looks just as surprised. "What happened?" she asks.

"Doesn't matter." I gesture to Ellis. "You don't go to Queen's . . . ?"

"Uh, no, I technically don't go anywhere. I have to do some course catch-up for high school, but I should be able to start at Ottawa U next year." He quirks a smile and runs his hand through his hair again. Every single time it flops back perfectly in place. To Corey, he asks, "What are you majoring in?"

"History," she says.

"Makes sense." When Corey doesn't ask any follow-up questions, he adds, "I want to do biology. I know, not super practical, right?" This with a grin at Corey that has her lip twitching up a bit. "But the Scientist faction always needs more people."

The potstickers come, and I help myself so that I'll have something to do with my free hand while they talk. Corey's grip on my other hand keeps compressing and releasing intermittently.

Ellis runs his fingers through his hair again. I heave a sigh and say, "Do you really think small talk is the way to go here?" The siblings both jerk their heads toward me. "I'm just saying. This meeting is literally only happening because of blackmail—"

Ellis cringes. "I didn't tell Barbie to—"

"Regardless of how it came about, it's happening now. Really, the issue here is whether you, Corey, want to have a relationship with him. He wants to have one with you, obviously."

Corey grips my hand tighter. "How can I have a relationship

with someone I'm afraid of?" she whispers. Ellis shrinks in his seat. "How is that fair to you? None of this was ever fair for either of us. Doesn't sitting here with me just make you think about the fact that I couldn't save you? That our parents set us up so that all we could ever be to each other is an obligation?"

"I never saw you as an obligation!" he blurts out, then looks at me, his face going red.

I raise my hands. "Just pretend I'm not here."

Ellis swallows, refocusing on Corey. "I wanted to pair with Barbie so you wouldn't have to do it."

Corey reels back in her seat. "What?"

"I tried to get Barbie nominated instead but by that time, everything was already in motion for you, and it couldn't be stopped. I told Mom and Dad that I didn't want you to be the one. Barbie and I . . . we wanted to save you; we just . . . couldn't."

"You never told me that."

Ellis shrugs. "Didn't seem to be a point in telling you what we wanted when it's not what happened."

"You went behind my back!" Corey snaps. "I am so tired of people acting like I'm too fragile to know things. I'm afraid, yes, I was always afraid, but that doesn't make me weak. It doesn't . . ." She trails off again as if she'd only made the realization once she'd said the words.

"I'm sorry," Ellis croaks. "I'm sorry for so many things. For your leg and fingers—"

"It wasn't your fault," Corey says. "I . . . I wanted you to stay that monster in the dark so I wouldn't have to think about everything we could have been. Properly. Without all this shit attached."

"Would you like us to be something?"

Corey bites her lip for a moment. "Forgiveness is a journey. I heard someone say that the other day, and it just hit for me. Do you get what I mean? I can't do it all at once. I feel like you and Mom and Dad just want me to be okay right now, but that's not fair. You don't get to rush me."

Ellis ducks his head. "I guess our parents spoiled me. They were so relieved I was back that everything just fell into place again. And you're right. I wanted that from you, too, but it's more complicated than that, isn't it?"

"It is."

He raises his head. "If it's a journey, can I be on it with you?"

"Yeah but . . ." Corey straightens. "Barbie backs off. She can hate me if she wants, but she's not interfering in our relationship anymore. You have to set that boundary."

"I will."

"Otherwise . . . uh, I guess, what's your number?"

Ellis laughs and accepts Corey's phone to input his number, and she sends a text with hers.

To the possible relief of the waiter, we order a proper lunch, and the atmosphere improves. Ellis shares more about what he wants to do in the Scientist faction while Corey chats about some of the book rebinding techniques she's learned—including a critique on her brother's binding skills—and even about some of the research she was doing for Henry.

"Henry isn't interested in the spontaneous births anymore?" Ellis asks.

Corey shrugs. "Apparently not. I admit that I did get busy with everything else. I would love to write a paper about Meredith one day."

Ellis says, "It's interesting, though—Carrigan was also doing

quite a bit of research into spontaneous births. Though he'd renamed it recently as 'induced monstrosity.'"

"Induced?" Corey narrows her eyes. "He thought something was causing it?"

"Yes. It's something he was looking into before his sabbatical."

I roll my eyes. "Are you seriously still calling it that?"

Ellis clears his throat. "Yes, well . . ."

"If the births are induced . . . then it stands to reason that the apocalypse would be the same, right?" Corey asks. "Caused by something and therefore preventable, not inevitable."

"That's the thought," Ellis says.

Corey still seems to be mulling that information over as we finish the meal. Ellis insists on paying, citing an internship as his source of income. The three of us leave the restaurant and stand outside.

Ellis initiates an awkward hug between him and Corey, made more awkward by the fact that she won't let go of my hand.

"Will you cheer for me at least a little bit tomorrow?" he asks.

"Just a little bit," she says.

He laughs, then sobers. "I hope . . ." He shakes his head.

"I hope we'll make it to the end one day," Corey says. "Of the journey."

The corner of his lip quirks up. "Yeah. Me too." He nods to me. "Nice to meet you, Riley. I guess I'll be seeing more of you, too."

I swallow but don't comment on the remark, and he leaves, cutting through the Burger King parking lot and heading back to campus.

"Now," Corey says. "What's this about you not being president anymore?"

I heave a sigh and explain the whole situation to her.

"But we can still get the Osseous," she argues.

"Uh, no, we can't, because like I said, we need the whole student council to help."

She wrinkles her nose. "So get them to help."

I bark out a laugh. "They don't want to help me!"

"No, but they'll help themselves." She stares at me. "The Doctorate could easily turn on QBSS. If you have the Osseous, you have a certain amount of security. And it's still your artifact. Get them to understand. Show them that you always deserved the title. Then next semester, when Malachi is gone, take it back."

"You'll really have to explain to me how people keep mistaking you for fragile."

She laughs. Both of us are looking at our linked fingers now. "This means something to me," she says. "And I . . . It can mean something to you, too, without needing to label it. Do you know?"

Instead of replying, I pull Corey into a hug, burying my nose in her neck and winding my arms around her back. I lean away just enough to press my lips to hers, my hands on her cheeks and hers around my waist.

We break for a breath, and I ask, "Will you come with me? To talk to them?"

"They won't like that," she says, her cheeks still flushed.

"I don't care."

"Okay."

I stand behind the kitchen island, gazing out at the group gathered in my living room. I have to admit that I didn't expect them all to come. But here they are, the four people who could make or break this plan. Jackson throws me an encouraging smile while Inaya

crosses her arms, Malachi stares without blinking, and Darius scrolls through his phone.

I pull myself up to my full height. "I've asked—"

"What's she doing here?" Inaya says, jerking her head at Corey.

"She's a society representative. I've asked—"

"An official representative or just one that you've decided on?"

I grit my teeth. "I've asked—"

"You're going to ignore me?"

Malachi says, "You need us for something. So just say what it is."

"I was trying to!" I snap. "The weapon—I can get it if the four of you help me. I need you to use your artifacts to unlock a door. We also need the chain, which I assume Malachi has access to."

Inaya says, "I thought we didn't need the weapon anymore since the society is cooperating." She throws a significant look at Corey.

"You really think that's the right move?" Malachi asks her. "Putting our trust in a leader who has only just come to power? With no guarantees?"

Jackson adds, "You don't think acquiring a powerful weapon will be perceived as a threat?"

"How would he know?" Malachi jerks his head toward Corey. "Unless she's planning to tell."

"I'm not," Corey says.

"Golden." Malachi stands. "We'll do it tomorrow night. I'll get the chain." Inaya tries to protest, and Malachi silences her with a raised hand.

I balk at him. "That easy?"

He rolls his eyes. "Advice for you, Townsend: don't question when you've won." He gives Corey a look. "And QBSS members only, sorry not sorry."

Fair enough. I thought this was going to be a much longer shot. I never expected that Malachi of all people would be my ally in this. "What's your angle?"

"My angle has always been the protection of QBSS. There's a reason Joseph Lawrence broke from the Learners. I don't care if their new Doctorate is playing nice. The past informs the present. I want to know that my legacy includes making sure we have some insurance." He stares at me, and I can't help but think that Malachi also wants his legacy to be something more than being unseated by a Townsend. He wants to achieve something, and he's got less than a week left before this school year ends, and with it, his time as president.

He needs this just as much as I do.

CHAPTER FIFTY-TWO

The crowd is loud enough to be heard even within the antechamber's thick stone walls. A vibration, sending chills through my skin straight to my bones. They're this hyped, and we still have at least five minutes before it starts. But I get it. This is the final match of the Monster's Ball. Margot and Isaac won, robbing them of an additional round from the MiT league, and so all eyes are on us. They even pushed our match to the evening to make it more of an event.

"Do you have a plan?" Virgil asks, coming to stand next to me and Nolan. Since visiting Jules, I noted that the rules about who can and can't be in the antechamber seem to be lax, and so Virgil came along, even though this is mine and Nolan's fight.

Nolan slides his eyes to me. "Do we?"

I say, "Win." Virgil sighs. "Do you have any better suggestions?"

He stays quiet because there is no plan. Barbie and Ellis have

decimated in every match, and the only reason we won last time was because she let us.

"If there was ever a time for brutality, it's now," Nolan says to me.

Virgil scoffs. "Or maybe not, considering that Corey is repairing her relationship with her brother? You can't just go in for the kill."

Nolan rolls his eyes. "No one wants to win the finals with a kill; it's sloppy."

"Right, that's why we don't want to murder people, because it's sloppy."

Nolan turns to Virgil, getting right into his personal space bubble. "Don't act so sanctimonious. Like I've never been in your head."

"Don't act so callous," Virgil says. "Like I've never been in yours."

I ask, "You gonna kiss, or . . . ?"

Virgil sighs while Nolan makes an actual retching sound. And people say I'm childish.

"Ellis will appear wherever you're failing to guard," Virgil says. "You can trick him sometimes that way too, pretending to leave an opening and turning at the last moment."

"I know," Nolan says.

"But I didn't. Thanks, Virgil." I hold out my arm and then falter. "We should probably adjust this now that there's three of us. Is there a three-person version?"

Virgil says, "Not that I know of. I guess we'll have to create it."

I hold out both arms, one for Nolan, one or Virgil. Virgil grasps my right, and we both turn to Nolan. For a moment, I think this is going to be something he's too cool for, but he grabs my left. I stare at the boys, and then their loose arms.

Virgil holds his arm out, and after an exasperated sigh, Nolan grasps it. When Virgil pulls me in, Nolan comes along, and I tug them both toward me. Forearms pressed, the three of us inches apart. No one signals it, but we lean our heads together until they're touching, locked in a triangle.

Triumvirate. We could be that.

The room is bathed in amber light.

We step back, releasing our hands. Virgil mutters something about luck and leaves the room while Nolan undresses and transforms.

The monster paces back and forth. We need to win this. Riley's on her way to get the Osseous tonight. I know she's going to succeed with her end of the plan and so I have to with mine. I squeeze my eyes shut, and I'm in the Scarborough Bluffs, fighting the shadow, Mom being flung over the cliff.

I open my eyes at the same time that the doors are sliding apart and walk out to screams and shouts. Violet, Frankie, Bryce, and Mitch are in the stands alongside Adam, Henry, and Corey. Corey waves from her spot, having made a new sign to cheer on the three of us.

I meet Barbie's eyes across the arena.

The final match of the Monster's Ball.

Thankfully, I do my best dancing just before last call.

Compared to Adam, fighting Barbie and Ellis is a warm-up. If we can't win here, we can't win there.

The horn blares.

Barbie and Ellis disappear in puffs of black smoke. I whip around and get my guard up just in time for her dagger to ping off my raised knife. Barbie smiles and disappears again. Flashing in

and out at a rapid speed, pushing me onto the defensive.

Fog floats over us, and I grin. I may not have had time to lay the cover, but Nolan did. I blow out my own fog, mingling our scents together, giving us time to get on the offensive.

And yet, even in the fog, I still feel like I'm defending.

Barbie's voice floats from another part of the arena. "You've done better. Doesn't only smell like Nolan anymore, but you can't keep using the same trick. Maybe you haven't been to all our matches, but we've been to all yours."

I freeze. *Had they?* I never noticed them in the stands, but I only ever look at Henry's Mastery group section. I shift, and the toe of my boot scuffs the floor.

I don't notice the dagger until it's slicing into my side. I swear and hop back, flipping, but Barbie is on me already. And now that she's found me in the fog, there's nowhere to go. There's no rhyme or reason to how she wields the sheng biao. It feels impossible to predict, especially when we're moving at these speeds.

I'm so preoccupied with Barbie that I don't notice Ellis until his shadow is over me, jaw wide open, teeth gleaming.

Nolan slams into him from the side, and Ellis disappears, reappearing closer to me. My leg, inches from his lips. I think of Corey. How she lost her leg in one snap of his teeth. He must remember too, because he hesitates, and I use the moment to fling a knife into one of his eyes. He hisses and disappears. The knife falls, clattering to the ground.

Barbie reappears only to be kicked in the stomach by Nolan. Or it seemed like she was, but when she reappears a few feet away fine, I know he just missed her.

Nolan pants beside me as Barbie and Ellis stalk around us. The

monster snaps its jaws, gnashing its teeth. The only thing I can be sure of now is that Ellis won't be as brutal as Barbie, not with Corey in the back of his mind.

Barbie narrows her eyes at my side, where the wound has already healed. I don't have more time to think as her and Ellis begin to move again. But every time I manage to avoid Barbie, Ellis is there, and Nolan is running himself ragged trying to keep up.

Enough of this shit.

The next time Barbie appears, I grab the sheng biao just like last time. "Nolan!" I cry, and he rushes forward, snapping his jaws around the rope and tugging. My knives couldn't cut it fast enough, but his teeth can. The rope snaps, and the dagger stays in my grip.

I run toward Barbie. One good hit and I can take her down. I throw my fist at her face, and a dagger materializes in her hands and she stabs me between the knuckles. I scream and roll to the side, moving to rip the thing out of my hand, but the dagger has disappeared into shadow. *What the fuck?*

Barbie stands, swinging her sheng biao. I stare at the remaining dagger clutched in my hand. I have no idea where she got that second weapon until I look at it properly. At the swirls of black. This sheng biao seems to be formed from shadow. Somehow, Barbie can solidify it. I ruined her physical weapon, but that doesn't matter since she can wield shadows as one.

I swallow. Just like Melani, my healing is getting less effective as the match goes on. Barbie and Ellis have already fought and beaten that pair. She may not like my regeneration abilities, but she also knows they're not infinite.

I open my mouth to roar but shut it as the sheng biao flies toward my face. I sprint away, darting around the arena as Barbie pursues me.

I just need a moment! I huff, trying to get breath in, and I can feel the same struggle in Nolan. We're suffocating out here. And we're taking too long. I don't know if I can manage being pushed to sudden death.

I grip my fists hard enough to hurt, digging into my own metal blades. We need to do something. We're going to lose.

In my periphery, I spot Nolan, the pools of fog in his sides almost fluttering. He stomps his feet and widens his green eyes at me, like he's wanting me to understand something. He flares his nostrils, then widens his eyes and bats his paw through the fog over and over.

Nostril flare must mean smell, and I mean, I can smell us in the fog. Eyes . . . I can't see through it like Nolan does. I stare around at the space, not sure what else I could see. And the paw movement through the fog . . . Feel? Touch?

I take a leap of faith and close my eyes, concentrating.

I assumed that Nolan could see through the fog, but that's not right. Henry wasn't wrong. I really should have had more of a discussion with Nolan about his ability. But I feel the sensation now, the movement of bodies through the space. The way they brush against the fog and flow through it.

And then I feel the part that doesn't fit. The odd ripple that's *wrong*.

Barbie and Ellis aren't disappearing and reappearing, they're moving. Riding a current of air from one point to another. Transforming into smoke, moving, and then rebuilding.

I can't see the movement with my eyes, but I can feel it. I wait, following the sensation, and then I rip through it with metal spikes.

Barbie screams, reappearing with blood on her lips and my claws in her stomach.

"There you are," I say.

She twists her lips, stained with dark red. "And there you are." She spins on her heel and kicks me into the opposite wall with a form that would impress any taekwondo instructor. I'm vaguely aware of slumping to the ground, ringing in my ears.

I roar. Across from me, Barbie swears, dropping to the ground clutching both her ears and stomach. I'm still on my knees. Fuck, I might have hit my head.

Nolan and Ellis lock paws in the middle of the arena, ripping and clawing at each other. Dark blood spilling as they grapple.

Barbie is clutching her stomach, face pale. I throw a knife at her from my position on the ground, and it falls short. My temple is throbbing. But we're so close. We're so fucking close.

I try to roar again, but all that comes out is a croak.

Barbie disappears in a wisp of black smoke. I can only manage to prepare myself as she reappears with a blade clutched in her hands. *My* blade. She must have scooped it up on her way over. She straddles me, pushing the knife down while I shove against her, arms shaking. The tip of the blade drives ever closer to my heart. She's seriously trying to kill me right now!

I buck her off me.

She falls to the side. Giggling to herself.

I shake my head. "You're such an unhinged bit—" Something slams into me, and the last thing I see is Barbie grinning as I fly off my feet.

I'm conscious before I open my eyes. I give myself several minutes before I bother. And when I do, I stare at the concrete ceiling. Fists gripped in the sheets, tears slipping down my face. I could stay

conscious after a kick from Barbie, but not Ellis smashing into me.

I turn to my right, where Virgil sits, and then to my left, empty.

"Don't look for him when I'm right here," Virgil says.

I bite my lip. I don't want to care. Don't want it to matter that I'm such a loser that Nolan couldn't even bring himself to stick around until I woke up.

Virgil licks his lips. "Maybe Ellis could be convinced to—"

"To what?" I snap, my voice cracking. "Question the Doctorate? Invite us on the exclusive tour? You think Barbie is going to agree to that?"

We lost. *I* lost.

It's over.

CHAPTER FIFTY-THREE

Riley

Not for the first time this evening, I wish Corey were here. I lead the way through the halls of Douglas, down the stairs, and past the UNDER CONSTRUCTION signs. Malachi keeps in step with me, and Inaya is so close on my heels that she's literally stepped on them multiple times. Not all accidents either, I'm sure. Meanwhile, Jackson and Darius follow at a more leisurely pace, the latter seeming like he would rather be anywhere else.

When Malachi gets a view of the dirt tunnel and associated carnage, he whistles. "No wonder you got demoted."

"Fired, technically," Inaya adds.

"Commentary is unnecessary," I say, striding forward. It feels wrong somehow, bringing them here when I've designated it in my mind as the spot of Corey's and my first kiss. I push through the tunnel, and faster than expected, we reach the door with its five symbols. The narrow space felt longer when I was running for my life.

Malachi eyes the gouges in the wood. "Your first attempt, I presume?"

"Just stick your necklace in the right spot and activate it," I say, and hold my hand out. "The chain."

He digs in his pocket and sets the black chain in my hand. The others come forward, pulling their own necklaces off and pressing the charms to the appropriate spots in the wood. I can't believe I really tried to make it work by myself. God, it feels more like something August would do. I shudder. Jackson furrows his brow at me, which I ignore.

We stare at the door and for a moment, nothing happens; then there's a grinding of metal on metal as it slides open. I turn the knob, which gives easily now, and walk into the space.

It's a large circular chamber with stone walls. There are sconces lining the stone, but the torches are unlit. Darius pulls out a lighter and goes around to each one, setting them ablaze.

"That's it?" Darius asks, pocketing his lighter. "There's nothing here." He runs his tongue over his gold teeth. He capped not one, not two, but four teeth in the front of his mouth. If he has that much pride in wielding an artifact, he should show it more with his actions.

There's a crunching sound as the metal door we came through slides shut. I swallow.

"Good sign," Jackson mumbles.

Metal vents on the walls open, releasing a hiss as a faint mist seeps from them. Automatically, I cover my nose and mouth with the hem of my shirt, but it doesn't seem to matter. My eyes water, and my vision swims. The others are groaning, and Inaya is saying something I can't decipher.

The mist is thick now, swimming around me. "Is everyone okay?"

I ask, though I don't hear any answer. There's a low whistle. I squint into the fog. As I lean in to peer closer, metal links shoot toward me, and I duck to dodge them.

Out from the mist comes a figure holding a chain like mine.

"Grandma?" I whisper.

It *is* her, several decades younger. Thick curls surrounding her head in a halo, picked and shaped into a perfect circle. Her form is muted as if made of shadow—grayscale. I know the artifacts can hold memories but thought that was more metaphorical than literal.

Grandma grins and sends the rings at me.

I jerk up my chain, letting my own links fly to counter hers.

"Watch out!" Jackson shouts, and I only just manage to avoid him as he leaps, his shield held high as he throws it at something I can't see. He looks at me, incredulous. "He could have gotten you!"

"Who—" A link slices me across the cheek, and I bring up the rings to block. "What are you doing?" I ask Jackson.

He gapes at me. "What are *you* doing?"

"It's the bones!" Inaya shouts from somewhere in the fog. "I think the mist is reacting to the bones in the artifacts. Making us see things!"

I touch my cheek. There's even a cut there. Grandma doesn't let up, slamming her chain links into mine hard enough that my teeth rattle. I would bet money that we can't get out of this room, much less get the Osseous, unless we defeat them.

I can't see who Jackson is fighting and he can't see who I'm fighting because my bones aren't in his artifact and vice versa. I assume, anyway.

I grit my teeth. It feels especially unfair to make me fight my own grandma. She wasn't even the last treasurer on record. Though many

people did say she was excellent with the chain even if she never ascended from that title.

Grandma flips over my head and spins, whipping the chain behind her and catching me around the legs. I fall, gasping, and dodge the links as she slams them down. I spin on the floor, using the momentum to get back to standing, and knock into Inaya.

"Do you mind?" she grunts, lifting her staff to block her invisible foe.

Ignoring her, I shove my hands forward, sending my links to try to pin Grandma to the wall. But she jumps and twists out of the way. Grandma really used to move like that?! We are going to have several conversations about this the next time we talk.

"Enough!" I roar, and jerk my hands up. I pull at the rings—not just mine, but Grandma's, too. The shadowy version of the weapon strains as she fights for control and I pull harder. I may have only had the chain for a year, but it was a year when I had to fight several Monsters. I'm not going to be beaten by a hallucination of my own grandma.

Power floods through my arms as I wrestle the chain away and thrust the rings forward. Sending them toward the younger version of my grandma.

I swear she smiles as she disappears in a wisp of smoke.

"Darius!" Jackson shouts. He's on the ground with his shield held in place by one arm, panting, pointing across the room with his free hand.

I jerk my head to where Darius is thrashing on the floor, his eyes rolling in his head, pawing at the air.

"For fuck's sake." I rush over to his side, trying to drag Darius away and kick the air in front of him, but it's no use. There's no one for me to fight.

Shit, shit, shit.

Darius is the secretary, and before him . . . "Inaya!" I whip toward her.

"Kind of busy!" she says, brushing her twists out of her eyes.

"You have to help Darius! You were the last secretary, so the artifact has your bones. You're the only one who can do anything."

"What about me?!" Her neck snaps to the side and she swears. "I'm barely hanging on here!"

The mist is thin enough now for me to see Malachi across the way, struggling. His weapon hasn't changed form—it's still a sickle. He can't manage the scythe release, not even now with a lot of motivation. He's definitely not in any position to help Inaya.

Darius's breathing is slowing.

"He's dying!" I shout to her.

"Urgh! Fine!" Inaya leaps back and darts toward Darius. A well-aimed kick frees our secretary, who gasps, scrambling backward. I haul him to his feet by the armpits. Inaya says, "There! Happy no—" Something slams her into the wall. "Motherfucker," she hisses.

She leaps back across the room, I assume dealing with her original enemy while Darius struggles to get his bearings. I grab the saber from the ground and press it into his hands. "You need to end this."

"Easy for you to say," he croaks but brings up his blade in time to fend off a blow.

Inaya screams and jumps up and down, grinning, I assume signaling that she's dealt with her attacker. Jackson gets to his feet slowly, wiping sweat off his brow. I follow his eyes to where Malachi is getting his ass handed to him.

Still wielding the sickle.

He's fighting Cece. The way she moves is ethereal. Smooth dips

and turns and angles. It feels more like she's playing with Malachi than anything. I thought it was hard to reconcile the woman cooing at her baby as being the president before, but it's completely different to watch her in action like this. She practically floats in the air, like she's working with different laws of gravity.

Like how August jumped the Fort Henry wall.

Our artifacts are made of bone. But not just *our* bones. Francis McLaughlin's bones too. If the artifacts are our Monsters, then we should technically have the ability to ascend to higher evolutions. And we do—or whoever uses the sickle does, at least.

Malachi crashes into the wall, gasping.

"She'll slaughter him," I say to Jackson, shaking my head. "If you can't release the scythe, the sickle is one of the weakest weapons. He's not equipped for this."

"Fucking finally!" Darius screams, collapsing onto the ground. His face is split in the biggest grin I've ever seen on him, until he catches Malachi in his sights.

We wince as the president is thrown against the wall again.

Cece actually laughs, spinning the scythe around like it's made of air instead of metal and bone.

"If he loses . . . ," Inaya says, licking her lips, "how do we get out of this room?"

"We don't," I reply.

"You can do it, Malachi!" Jackson shouts.

Malachi is gripping the sickle so hard, I almost wonder if he'll crack the handle.

"You're not worthy of the sickle."

It takes me a moment to realize that Cece spoke. *It* spoke. Malachi jerks back as if slapped.

"Time to end this."

The ghostly scythe glows, and the others gasp. They can see it now. Malachi stands in place, gaping. Cece whips the scythe around and around, so fast that it's humming. It crackles and sparks like it's electric. And then that current rushes straight toward Malachi.

I move before I can think better of it, snatching the sickle from his limp fingers and whipping it in front of me.

"The sickle knows you. When you unleash it, you'd better have a damn good reason, and you'd better be willing to die for it."

I scream as the blast hits the metal, digging my heels in, the impact shaking me from my toes to the tips of my ears, but I don't let go. A stray bit of current whips across my cheek in a hot flash of pain, but I don't move. I push forward, jumping into the air—

I bring the scythe up and land, spinning on my heel, and slice through Cece.

The mist disappears.

I stand there, panting, the scythe gripped in my trembling hands.

The floor rumbles and opens, and a stone pedestal rises from its depths. On it is a wooden box. I let the scythe go, clattering to the ground, where it reverts back to a sickle.

I tip open the box to reveal a dagger, the stark white of bone from handle to sharpened tip. The Osseous.

"Well done," a voice says, and I jerk my head up. Standing at the now open steel door in the tunnel are the elder council. Ms. Howard grins. "You found it. Good for you. We'll be taking that now."

Dr. Michaels strides forward, closing the box and lifting it into his arms. "This was not what we told you to do, but you did succeed."

"How?" I croak, looking around the room. I spot Inaya, hiking her shoulders up to her ears.

"They had a right to be informed," she mutters.

Ms. Howard jerks her head at Malachi. "Pick up the sickle."

"You can't be serious," Jackson barks. "Riley found the weapon. She did what she said she would!"

Ms. Nelson sighs. "Ms. Townsend broke the rules several times over. She should be grateful that we still allow her to retain her role as a member. But she cannot be on the student council."

Jackson's jaw drops, and he looks around at the others. As if they'll help. Inaya won't meet my eyes, Darius drops his gaze to the ground, and Malachi stares at the discarded sickle.

These are supposed to be my people. My community. I did everything right for so long. And none of that matters. I wasted so much time being their perfect girl.

I meet Ms. Howard's eyes. "You can keep your membership. I resign."

The legacy of my family in this society stretches back to the very beginning.

I will be the first not to be a part of it.

CHAPTER FIFTY-FOUR

"We're fucked," I say, leaning into the cushions of one of the settees at McIntosh Castle. Say what you want about mass-produced furniture, at least it's made for lounging. Everything in this place feels like it was made for sitting upright hunched over a book. Which it likely was. It feels especially uncomfortable now at nearly two in the morning after our loss in the Monster's Ball.

Riley sighs. There's a discoloration across her right cheek from her chin to just under her eye, a couple of shades lighter than her usual sepia skin tone. She refuses to talk about it. "It's not that dire." I also notice that she and Corey are sitting awfully close together on a couch that's already small for two people. "I can still get the Osseous."

"Can you get it before tomorrow night?" Nolan asks. I'm shocked that he showed up at all. He's decided to perch on the edge of where I'm sitting next to Virgil.

Margot narrows her eyes. She's sitting next to Isaac, who's so excited to be involved he's acting like he downed a liter of coffee—alert and jittery. "We don't necessarily need the knife to threaten him. It may be enough that he knows we have access to it. In fact, that might be better. If it's on your person, he could take it."

"That's not a bad point," Corey says. "If Riley gives you the details of what the weapon looks like, that should suffice."

"We don't know for sure, though," I say.

Margot says, "We don't know *anything* for sure."

"And if he sends a bunch of Wilds after QBSS?" Riley asks.

"We don't have to be honest about that," Virgil says, leaning his elbows on his knees and threading his fingers together. "We can say we have it in a hidden location."

I'm trying to think of a counter when Riley says, "And if he kills you on the spot?" She looks around the room. "I'm sorry, but I have to say it. You're talking like this is a rational man, not like he's the one who slaughtered his own brother and his children to secure his position. We don't know why he's kept Jules and August alive to this point. There's no guarantee of immunity. Even then, that only protects August in this operation. Say he makes Virgil and Nolan fight to the death? What then? They both die, and August's powerless anyway." I twitch at that and bite my lip. Corey hunches in on herself. Riley swallows, glancing at her. "I'm not trying to be a bitch. I just don't want us to go into this situation underprepared. I can get the weapon. I have to go for it at night, so it'll be tight, but I can do it."

Bless Riley for staying the course. Though if I couldn't even beat Barbie, I have no idea how I'm supposed to manage Adam. I say,

"Okay, but we lost. Meaning no tour, meaning no way to get him to the vault."

Virgil says, "If Barbie forfeits her tour for some reason—feigns sick, for example—it'll go to the next winner."

Nolan snorts. "Good luck with that."

Corey bites her lip. "She would . . . for the right price."

"We already did what she wanted," I say. "You and Ellis met up. What else could she want?"

"You'll have to ask her."

I groan and drop my head against the cushions. "This plan is shit."

"But . . . we can't exactly wait for another chance, right?" Isaac asks.

"Exactly," Margot says. She's wearing her gloves again, her fingers gripping into fists and then loosening. "The celebration ball at the Doctorate's island is exclusive to people gaining a title in each league. No senior Masters will be present except for whoever is guarding Adam. We can't guarantee another chance like this. Find out what Barbie wants and give it to her. Riley collects the Osseous and brings it to us. August gets the tour and confronts Adam in the vault. Myself, Isaac, Nolan, and Virgil will be nearby in case things go sideways. Inside the vault, he's just a man. Same with whatever senior Master comes in with you."

Even if it's not the best plan, we won't get another chance. This has to be where we win.

This time, he'll be the one without power, and I'll be the one holding the knife.

The yacht that waits to transport us from the Kingston dock to the Doctorate's private island is moderately sized, not much bigger than the Thousand Islands tour boats, but it's still a yacht, sleek white and

climbing up two stories with large panoramic windows.

Virgil and Nolan go on first, the former in a three-piece black suit I've never seen before with a subtle print of vines on the jacket you can only see if you stand close—tailored, of course. Nolan's gone for a pair of slacks and a black shirt, tucked in, but no tie, the top buttons as loose as the hair settled on his shoulders.

Both of them reach out a hand to help me onto the vessel, though I could have managed fine on my own. I've noticed the separate times their eyes have roved over my outfit. Another black dress, but this one is sheer all over. Sheer bodice with intricate lace and boning. Long flowing sleeves, sheer. And finally, the sheer skirt that falls to my feet. It's meant to be worn with high-waisted underwear, and while I've gotten more comfortable with showing off my body, I don't know that I'm "flashing the bottom of my ass" comfortable, so I went with a pair of high-waisted shorts instead.

When I looked in the mirror, there was that voice in the back of my head that whispered it would look better if I were smaller. If there weren't rolls on my back or if my arms were slimmer. I had to remind myself that I looked good exactly as I was. Great, even. I couldn't hinge my self-esteem on Virgil choking on his spit when I stepped out of Victoria Hall or Nolan's eyes trailing down my body. It had to be me, in that mirror, seeing and believing it first.

A buff white man pats us down, checking to be sure that we didn't bring any weapons. This year especially they want to be sure of the Doctorate's safety.

We're given flutes of champagne without showing IDs. Margot enters with Isaac in tow and narrows her eyes as he accepts a glass of champagne but doesn't stop him. She's gone the power suit

route, wearing a maroon suit jacket and pants paired with a corset top in black. I'm jealous that she can manage in heels. I went with Docs, because I'm not about to make a fool of myself stumbling around being uncomfortable. Besides, given that I plan to fight, it's more practical.

Isaac grins and comes over, holding up his glass. "They didn't even ask how old I was," he whispers. Monsters have only been allowed to attend this celebration this year due to Adam changing the rules, so it's new for Isaac, too. Mia also told me her and Isaac have been tentatively talking again after he apologized for not being up-front with her, which is likely also helping his mood. I wish I could be that happy too. Instead, the champagne bubbles churn in my stomach.

"Any sign of Barbie?" Margot asks.

I jerk my head across the boat to where the girl in question stands, leaning against Ellis. She's gone for a pastel pink dress in a sleeveless style, with a row of embroidered flowers across her chest; the waist of the A-line is adorned with silk ribbon and flowing out in a soft puff with more flowers on the hem. I down my drink and set it on a nearby table. "I'll go over now."

I didn't invite them along, but Virgil and Nolan fall into step behind me as we approach the pair. Closer up, it's easier to see that Barbie isn't casually leaning against Ellis; she's using him for support. She should be resting and recovering. But this is her night, and she's determined not to miss it. Ellis doesn't look in great shape either, favoring his right side. I did wonder if poking eyes on his body would affect his actual eyes in human form, but other than looking a little red, they seem fine.

"Look who it is," Barbie says, grinning. "The losers."

Ellis sighs. "Barbie."

"What?" she says, pressing a hand to her chest. "I'm being nice! I could have called them worse. She did stab me in the stomach."

"I won't mince words," I say. "I want you to pretend to be sick when it comes time for the tour so that we get it instead."

She blinks, well and truly shocked for a brief moment, and then chokes out a laugh. "Why in *hell* would I do that?"

"Name your price."

"You can't be serious."

Ellis nudges her shoulder. "On the way here, you said you wished you could skip the tour because it's probably boring. If they want it that badly, why not give it to them?"

"I don't care if it's boring," she says, crossing her arms. "It's *my* prize."

"Barbie."

She scowls at her partner before turning to us, looking from Virgil to Nolan and then back to me. "I'll think about it."

"There's not a lot of time," I say.

"Don't rush me!" She shoos us away as Melani and Shay approach. They definitely earned their title, though unfortunately, so did Hudson and Remy. The former glares at me across the room. My God, that boy holds onto a grudge like a life raft.

We head back to Margot and Isaac, who have now been joined by Violet, Frankie, Bryce, and Mitch.

"Do we want to know?" Violet asks, looking over my shoulder at Barbie.

"No," Virgil says.

I square my shoulders and turn to Bryce. He's looking good, still

limping some, but his leg is healing. "I'm sorry," I say. "I shouldn't have—"

He waves me off. "It's a competition. If you'd gone easier on us, you might have lost."

"You *would* have lost," Mitch grumbles.

Bryce laughs. "I'm fine. We're fine."

"Good," I glance at Mitch. "How about the other half of team Brytch?"

Mitch's cheek twitches, and he holds an annoyed expression for a total of two seconds before his lips quirk up. "It's a really good team name, isn't it?"

"The *best* team name."

Frankie rolls her eyes, but Mitch pulls me to his side with a grin. "I guess we can be okay, if Bryce is cool."

"I still don't care for you," Frankie says to me.

"Most people don't."

Margot snorts, and despite herself, I get a chuckle out of Frankie.

I can almost forget that we're heading into the most dangerous situation of a year spent fighting deadly humans and deadlier Monsters.

The yacht docks at an island that houses a giant mansion a few feet away from its shore. It looks like a resort that you'd find in Banff: Sleek wood accents with massive windows. Too many balconies and patio spaces to count. Lit up beautifully.

"Welcome to the Doctorate's cottage," Nolan mutters.

"Fuck off," I say. "They don't actually call that thing a cottage."

"They do," Margot says, stepping past me with Isaac, who's openly gaping.

We're led inside to the ballroom. Every space we walk through

has a towering ceiling and windows, with so many chandeliers you'd think the things were on sale. The ballroom itself has been done up to the nines like some million-dollar wedding. Everything sparkles, even the linens.

My phone vibrates, and I dig it out, scanning a text from Mia. *We have evidence that Carrigan has a boat. Grandad thinks he's headed to the island. I have a bad feeling about this. . . .*

Is Garrett sending Wilds here? I ask.

No. It'll just give A more fodder against them. Be careful. Especially with Nolan. He's the only Wild on the island.

Nolan peers over my shoulder, and I let him and Virgil read the texts.

"Why is Carrigan coming here?" Nolan asks. "Does he *want* to get murdered?"

"Heads up," Virgil says as Jules appears in front of us.

"Too cool to say hi to your brother?" he says. I saw him earlier with Natalie, who is a vision in a trailing black ball gown.

I roll my eyes. "You were schmoozing. Didn't want to interrupt."

"Nat likes to make connections." He eyes me. "You aren't planning anything, are you?"

"Wouldn't dream of it."

He shakes his head and has to leave as Natalie summons him to meet yet another group of people. I keep my eyes on Barbie, and when she jerks a single finger my way, I sigh and go over. Virgil and Nolan fall into step with me. We reach the girl, and Ellis is nowhere to be found, which is not great. He's the only one who keeps her in check. And she's grinning. Great.

"I know what I want," she sings.

"What is it?" *Be polite, August. Don't be a bitch, August. You need her.*

"You just have to answer a question for me." She lowers her voice. "And don't you dare lie. If I think you're lying, you won't get shit."

I blow out a breath. Just a question. That's fine. Easy. "Okay, ask."

She points at Virgil. "Between him"—and then a point at Nolan—"and him"—she looks back at me—"which one are you in love with?"

"Grow up," Nolan snaps.

Barbie only smiles. "Let me rephrase that. Love is such a . . ." She waves her hand around. "Too dramatic a word. Ohh!!" She actually claps. "Let's do this. Fuck, marry, kill. But not that first one, you've already done that. Marry or kill, which is which?"

I grind my teeth, gnashing them so hard it hurts.

"Just answer," Virgil says, his jaw stiff. "We need the tour."

"Yeah," Barbie chimes. "Just answer. Should be easy. Here, I'll start it for you, 'I'd marry . . .'"

Across the room, someone screams. We turn our heads as one of the MiT league boys bursts into fur and claws, baring his teeth and standing eight feet tall.

Barbie scoffs. "Some people just can't manage their liqu—"

He turns and rips the head off his partner.

For a moment, nothing happens. We stare as blood gushes from their neck and their body slumps to the ground. Then the next person drops to their knees, screaming as claws grow and their form expands. I swivel as across the room, Monsters transform.

"Ellis," Barbie gasps. Then louder, "ELLIS!!"

Ellis stumbles out of the bathroom, already on all fours, becoming the panther. And his eyes . . . I can't see him behind them. He catches us in his sights and bares his teeth. He disappears in a curl of smoke and reappears above us, his mouth wide open, teeth gleaming.

CHAPTER FIFTY-FIVE

Riley

I wince at the click of the lock as I open the back door to the QBSS clubhouse. I tiptoe into the space and wave Corey in behind me. Dinner would have started about half an hour ago, so most members will probably still be in the dining room, or else hanging out in the common areas. It's Easter Monday too, though lots of them have decided to stay on campus since the year-end banquet is this Saturday.

"This is a lot of breaking and entering," Corey whispers.

"It's not breaking and entering if I have an entrance code." I don't mention that I didn't use my personal code, instead choosing the one belonging to Darius. As president, I was once privy to every code and Darius's was the easiest to remember. The last thing I want is the security information showing that I came in the back door when I have no reason to be here.

Ideally, I'll get the Osseous before anyone notices. Right after I bring the man who orchestrated Sammie's murder and the attack on

QBSS to justice. However that happens. The bottom line is that Adam can't be trusted. Maybe he's playing nice with QBSS now, but it won't last.

I don't know what I'll do if August doesn't kill Adam. Let the society punish him, I guess. It worked for Bernie. Though that's only if we assume there will be consequences for his actions. He's still the Doctorate, after all.

I make my way down the hall toward the study rooms. There are placards beside each door with sign-in sheets. I grin at the paper. Perfect.

Inside, the room is compact with a large wooden table and chairs. There's also a couch and armchairs in the corner. I tug the couch away from the wall and motion for Corey to get behind it. There are so many ways this can backfire on us. But this is the best I could manage within the limited time frame.

I sit down at the table and wait.

Five minutes later, the door opens, and Malachi starts in the doorway. "I've booked this room."

"I know. Why do you think I'm here?"

With a sigh, he sits down opposite me, his back to the couch. Exactly the way I hoped. I make sure my hands stay on the table in plain view.

"Are you happy with yourself?" I ask him. "I saved your life, and in return you didn't say shit in my defense."

"What do you want me to say?"

I lean across the table, getting in his face. Never one to back down, he leans forward too. "I should be on the council," I tell him. "I should be president. You and Howard made this big show of saying I couldn't handle the sickle, and there you were, unable to use it."

"There's more to being president than mastery of the sickle."

I laugh, sitting back and shaking my head. "You're so full of shit."

"Once upon a time, you would have been a perfect president, but you're not that girl anymore. Not since Sammie died," he says. My eyes are steel as they stare back at him. "You're impulsive, careless, and worst of all, bloodthirsty. We're trying to live in peace, and you're acting like we're at war."

"Fuck you," I snarl and get to my feet. I move toward the door, but he stays seated.

Shit. Get up. *Get up, get up!*

I look back at him. "Maybe I am all those things, but at least I'm not a coward." I walk out of the room, slamming the door and stalking down the hall, sweat beading on the back of my neck.

"Riley!" Malachi shouts from behind me. I fight to keep the relief off my face. He always wants to have the last word. "You had everything! The pedigree, the money, the smarts, and you threw it all away for what? For a girl?!"

"Let me tell you something about having everything." I walk to him, getting in his face. "It's not worth shit if you can only use it for what other people want. I'm not some shadow of my parents, or grandparents, or even Joseph Lawrence. I'm Riley fucking Townsend. I am what my ancestors fought for. I am free to be whoever and whatever I want. So yes, I wanted to avenge a girl I loved. A girl who never compromised herself for someone else. I wish I could have been this version of myself when she was still alive to see it. So fine, I'm impulsive, and careless, and bloodthirsty. I may not be able to say I was the best president QBSS had ever seen, but at least I'll be able to look myself in the eye."

Malachi gapes at me, not able to find a comeback this time.

I turn on my heel and stride out the front door, letting it slam shut. I stand there for a moment, breathing out, and then disappear around the corner, still shaking.

I get into my car parked a block away and sit there, head in my hands.

The door opens, and I jolt to the side as Corey slips in. I pull her close, burying my face in the crook of her neck. She winds her arms around me. With a sigh, I move back, and she lifts Malachi's phone. "I got it."

I grin. "You're amazing."

Her face lights up, and her cheeks go pink. I lean forward again, pressing our lips together. It's awkward with the angle of the seats, but we manage. We break for a breath but stay close. "I like you," I say. "You're smart, and you're a good friend, and you're gorgeous, and you're so yourself, exactly who you are, always. And I like you, and I don't want to pretend that I don't. I don't want to . . . I don't know, make a grand announcement. But I also don't want it to be a secret. I just want to be with you, that's all."

Corey doesn't pretend to be anything else but who she is. Even when she's scared, or embarrassed, or self-conscious. She doesn't make herself into something she's not. It's not just about being attracted to her. I admire her too.

"I like you too," she says. "And I like calling myself a lesbian. It works for me. You do what works for you."

I nod before setting my face. "Okay, let's do this." We leave the car and come around the back of the house again, the way we originally entered. Malachi should assume that I've gone. This time when we go in, we head down the stairs to the basement.

We step into a long corridor, which has a door on the left that leads to the chamber where the elder council sits, which doubles as a ballroom, and one on the right that goes to storage. At the far end is the vault. The one that was specifically built to house the artifacts not currently in use.

From the outside, it's a normal-looking door with a combination lock. Corey steps forward. But I hold out a hand, keeping her back. It's difficult to notice, but some ceiling tiles have little pinpricks in them that show the cameras.

I drop my backpack and take out the jammer I ordered with a gift card and had delivered to McIntosh Castle so it wouldn't be traced back to me. Rush order. It promises to disrupt the camera signals so they can't transmit footage. I set it up and wait for it to do its thing.

The problem is that there's no way to be sure it's working. These cameras don't have indicator lights of any kind, so I'll just have to trust that it does. I did a test at home that worked, so I'm hopeful.

The screen lights up green, and I nod to Corey.

This lock, unlike the entry doors, uses a rotating series of codes through an authenticator app. Every few minutes, the code changes. I pull out Malachi's phone and enter his password.

"You know his passcode?" Corey asks.

"He used to live in my house, and we had a code for the front door. Everyone gets their own login, and I had to set it up. I assumed he uses the same code everywhere because people usually do." He also keeps his passwords stored on his phone, making it easy to log in to the authenticator app. I plug in the code, and the door light goes green. I grin at Corey, who grins back.

I swing open the door and freeze.

Malachi stands inside the vault holding the Osseous. "Looking for this?" he asks.

I swallow.

He flips the handle to face me and holds it out. "Take it."

My jaw drops. "What?"

"Don't make me regret doing this." I take the knife, reaching around to put it in my backpack using the spare holster August gave me. He pulls the sickle necklace off and hands that over too. "I assume you'll also need this."

"What are you doing?"

"Trusting you," he says. "If I'd done that last semester, we wouldn't have lost any lives, and I wouldn't have lost the presidency. I stand by what I said. You're not fit to be president . . . but you're more than capable of wielding the sickle. I'm trusting you to be the blade of QBSS."

"The elders won't like it."

"The elder council has never had authority over the artifacts. They're supposed to be here for guidance. The student council was always meant to make these decisions. Joseph Lawrence wanted new generations to lead. So I'm leading."

I stand tall and meet Malachi's eyes. "Thank you."

"Like I said. Don't make me regret it."

I stop the boat at the edge of the Doctorate's island and drop the anchor. Tensing, I look around the space, but no one is there. Instead, we're alone down here, the massive cottage looming above us. I turn to Corey, who drops next to me, tilting slightly to adjust for the height of the running leg she's put on. We left her other prothesis in the boat. Thankfully, my parents have one docked at the marina that

they like to use in the summer. Cheaper than docking in Toronto. A fact which, once I mentioned it, sent Corey into a fit of giggles, followed by her saying that she couldn't wait to tell August about this.

"Aren't there supposed to be guards or something?" I ask.

Corey purses her lips. "There should be at least one senior Master-Monster pair guarding Adam. Maybe they're sticking close to him?"

I double-check my hip, where I've holstered the Osseous, before unlocking my phone. The party just started. We even saw the yacht docked on our way over here.

Corey stares at her phone. "August's not answering my texts. Virgil isn't either."

"Margot? Isaac?"

"No and no. I even tried Violet."

I shake my head and start up the grassy hill. Corey groans behind me. "Shit," I say. "Are you going to be able to make it up?"

"Not ideal terrain since it rained yesterday so it's slippery, but I'll manage. I still want to use this leg. We're more likely to be running than fighting."

I squat on the ground. "Get on."

Corey flushes. "You don't have to do that!"

"Just to get up the hill. It's fine. I can squat two hundred."

"Wow, humblebrag."

"Just get on!"

She scrambles onto my back, and I hook my hands under her legs, heading up the hill. She winds her arms around my neck, and I shiver. "Cold?" she asks, but from the teasing in her tone, I know she knows that's not it.

We get up the hill, and I set her down. I say, "There's no one here

eith—" Corey shoves me to the ground, and I land hard. "What—" I whip around to see what looks like a giant hyena, but with too many humps and bumps on its skin, its mouth slathered in dark red.

That's when I hear the screams.

I tug off my necklace, the metal warming in my hands. I bypass the sickle and go straight to the scythe, stepping beside Corey, swinging the blade with ease. It feels light in my hands now.

"I think the plan is out the window," I say.

Corey lifts her fists, spreading out her legs. "Should have worn the taekwondo leg," she says with a sigh.

"I think you made the right choice. We can't beat a Monster. Just fight our way through enough to run."

"True. Good plan." She tilts her head, blinking. "Oh my God, this is our first couple fight!"

I snort.

Fuck. I really, really like her.

CHAPTER FIFTY-SIX

I stare open-mouthed at Ellis looming above us, his jaws open wide before instincts kick in and I dodge along with Virgil, Nolan, and Barbie. Barbie seems to have regained her wits because she peels out of the room with Ellis hot on her heels. I guess she's his priority, not us.

Meanwhile, the impeccably arranged ballroom has descended into chaos. Bachelors and Masters scream as they dodge their own partners. Tables are upended, and flimsy kitchenware meant for serving has become makeshift weapons that are largely useless against Monsters. There are multiple dead bodies on the ground, people with glassy eyes and missing limbs.

This isn't the Monster apocalypse, but it sure feels like it.

"Why haven't we turned?" Virgil gasps, staring at his trembling fingers and then at Nolan.

Nolan shakes his head. "I don't know, but we need to go. We have to get to Adam. This is obviously his doing."

"He can't control this many Monsters at once," I say. Even for the Doctorate, this can't be possible. Besides that, it's not like the Monsters are moving in a coordinated way. It truly feels like they're out of control, their connection to their partners just *gone*. . . . "I think it's a partial break."

Virgil's eyes widen, and he nods. "That has to be it."

"Is that what we should be discussing right now?" Nolan snaps.

"Yes, because that explains why we haven't been affected. Adam already told us that he can't break our bond. I guess now we know that's the truth." I almost want to cheer for Virgil finally stopping use of Adam's proper title. He frowns. "But he should know that too, so why isn't he controlling us?"

"Maybe he's too far?" I try. Unease settles on my shoulders. What's Adam's plan here? Why create this carnage?

Nolan crosses his arms over his chest. "I don't know. But what I do know is that now that there's a threat, the senior Masters with him will take Adam to the vault for safety. They close those doors, and we lose our shot at him."

"We can't go with her," Virgil says. "Adam could make us do anything once we're in range of him. Remember that Wild who was in human form that he somehow forced into partial transformation? We're not safe."

"If we don't go, she'll have to manage all these Monsters alone. I'm harder to control, so I'll take the lead. When we're close enough, we let August go ahead."

Virgil nods. "Okay. Let's do that. August?"

Across the room, I spot Margot with her hands up, walking backward as Isaac looms over her. Violet is dodging Frankie's quills, and Bryce is locked in a one-sided fistfight with Mitch.

"August," Virgil says. "We need to leave."

"I know!"

Nolan adds, "We can't get caught up in staying here and helping them. We have to catch Adam before he can make it into the vault."

I look over at my friends, fighting losing battles with their own partners. Margot isn't fighting at all. She's yelling at her brother like she can talk him down.

Brother . . .

I swivel my neck around the room. Jules. *Where is Jules?!*

"Focus!" Nolan shouts, putting his hands on my cheeks, pulling me close. "If we take Adam down, all of this will stop. If we don't make it in time, this will keep going. The senior Masters here would have already sent out a distress signal for backup. When the backup arrives, they'll slaughter the out-of-control Monsters. You're worried about them now, but it's only going to get worse."

The plan has to change. Not for me, but for Virgil. I meet his eyes. "The stakes are too high for just a confession," I say.

"I know," Virgil says.

"Then let's go." I run ahead, forcing myself not to look back at the carnage and fighting in the ballroom, focusing on inhaling and picking apart Adam's scent—expensive cologne and shampoo, and the leather of the cords he wears around his neck. The ground rumbles behind me as Nolan and Virgil shift into their Monster forms.

I squeeze my eyes shut.

Live. All of you had better fucking live. Jules. Margot. Isaac. Violet. Frankie. Bryce. Mitch. Ellis, for Corey. I have to believe that my friends can manage on their own.

I slow to check my texts and almost sob at the one from Riley.

They're on the island. She has the Osseous. We need to stop Adam from getting to the vault, but we won't have a chance at killing him without the weapon. I send a message to Riley about where we're going, hoping she can bring it to us.

A Monster explodes from a side room and heads straight for me. I've seen him before when he fought against Isaac and Margot. His body is scaled like a lizard, and he moves low to the ground, his tongue long and barbed. I manage to leap over him, but Virgil and Nolan went to help me at the same time, almost colliding, avoiding each other just in time.

I feel for the monster inside, the press of its fur and flash of its teeth, trying to focus on that power.

The lizard reappears in front of me, and I try and fail to block its tongue with a metal spike sprouting from my wrist. I wince—it still hurts to produce the weapon from my body. The Monster gets a grip around my leg, barbs digging into my skin. I stifle a cry, scrambling to get away as the tongue drags me toward its waiting mouth with all those sharp teeth.

Virgil snaps his jaws around the tongue and rips it back. I relax as the barb drops limp and tear it from my skin, the wound patching itself up.

Only, the lizard is unaffected. I watch on in horror as the tongue Virgil severed splits into two barbed tongues.

"Amazing," I mutter. "I'm sure you're loads of fun at parties."

Adam's scent is getting farther away. We don't have time for this.

Nolan leaps and smashes the lizard into the ground, pressing his full weight on the Monster, whose eyes bug out of its skull. The Monster whips at Nolan with the barbed tongues, but Nolan holds fast, digging his nails into its leathery hide.

At least until Virgil slams into him from the side. Nolan growls at him, and Virgil growls back. But Virgil's right. We can't kill these Monsters. It's not their fault that they're attacking like this.

I'm jerked off my feet by a wet tongue and am flying toward a mouth full of teeth faster than I can process. *Fuck! Not again!* Just as its teeth graze my skin, light explodes in front of us. I drop to the ground, gasping.

The lizard rolls around on the tile, its tongue not just severed but burned. The cauterizing has stopped it from being able to grow new tongues. I turn around to see Riley catching her scythe in her hand, eyes glowing gold, blood splattered on her face and clothes. Behind her Corey pants, hands on her knees, her running leg on.

Riley settles her weapon on her hip. "How is it that there are three of you, and one of them, and I still had to save your asses?"

"Unnecessary commentary," I grumble. I run over to her and hold out my hand.

Riley rolls her eyes and unlatches the holster on her belt, handing the Osseous to me. "You sure you can do this if you could barely handle that lizard?"

"Yes," I snap. ". . . and thank you."

"Oh my God, someone taught you manners?"

"Fuck off."

Nolan stomps his feet and jerks his head down the hall. I say to Riley and Corey, "We're trying to get to Adam before he reaches the vault. All this will stop if we get to him."

"If you kill him, you mean," Corey says, her eyes downcast.

I lick my lips. "He's pushed us to this."

"I know. . . ." She gazes past me to Virgil, and they share a look. That nonverbal language that exists between the two of them. Even

though me and him are bonded, it seems at times like this she can still understand him better than I can. "Don't get too close. Stay out of range. And you know that this is different than it was with your parents, right?"

Virgil nods.

"We have to go," I say, and dash forward, only to have Ellis appear in a puff of black smoke, teeth bared.

Nolan attempts to evade him, but everywhere we go, he reappears. Nolan growls, and when he makes his second attempt to pass, and Ellis reappears, Corey is between the two of them. Ellis falters, pivoting toward her instead, a new focus.

"Go!" Corey screams.

I shake my head. "We can't leave you with him!"

"Go!" she says again, teeth bared. "My brother and I are going to have a heart-to-heart. You have to stop Adam. So go. It's okay. Riley's here." Virgil whimpers, staring at his friend. Corey smiles. "I'm stronger than you think. I always have been." With that, he rushes after Nolan, and I follow them, sprinting as fast as we can toward Adam. Leaving our friend with her Monster.

We're closing in on Adam much faster than I expected. Inside my head, the monster is working itself into a frenzy. Like it, too, knows how close I am to getting what I've wanted all year. Virgil might be the reason it exists in me, but the monster and I have our own bond forged by simmering rage. It's my claws. My teeth. My viciousness.

This man took my mom.

And finally, *finally*, I'm going to make him regret it.

We turn the corner and freeze, sliding to a halt. Adam is in front of the vault. The giant, shiny chrome wheel staring at us. At his feet is Carrigan, covered in blood. Not moving.

Worse still, we overshot it. We're in range.

Adam's eyes blow wide, his shirt stained with his brother's blood. "August?" His head swivels to Virgil and Nolan. "And you boys. I—I don't know what's happening."

"Go!" I snap at them. Nolan moves to back up, but it's Virgil of all people who stands in his way. Fuck, is Adam already controlling him?

I move toward Adam. If I can distract him, maybe they can get away. "You don't know what's happening? Really?" I say to him, striding forward. "Because I do. You've taken out your last bit of competition."

"What— No! I didn't do this."

"Just like you didn't go to Toronto on November twenty-fifth when you told me you'd been at the Doctorate's Ball?"

I glance at Virgil and Nolan out of the corner of my eye. They still aren't leaving. Instead, they keep trading glances in silent communication.

Adam swallows. "I— Look, yes, I lied. It's complicated, and . . ."

"Try to explain," I snarl. "I'd love to hear the lie you come up with. Because you need me for something, right? That's why me and Jules are still alive?"

Something shifts in his face. He blows out a breath. "So you've decided, then? I'm the villain. I can see that nothing I say is going to change that." He shakes his head. "She was exactly the same." He meets my eyes then. "Your mom."

Those words. Each one snaps something inside me.

In that instant, there is no monster. Nothing prowling in my mind.

There is only me, the power, and the fury.

A scream tears out of my throat as I leap toward him, ripping the Osseous from its holster and driving it toward his heart. He meets my blow with a shard of metal from his wrist. Virgil's metal. Virgil's ability. I jump back, whipping around, expecting him to use Virgil himself against me, but my partner is standing still. *What's going on right now?*

Adam's gaze zeroes in on the blade. "What's that?" he asks.

"You don't recognize it?" I ask. "You sent Bernie after it."

Nolan roars behind me and races toward us. I dodge but . . . Nolan doesn't come at me; he goes for Adam, who jumps away with a speed so fast it looks like he teleports. My jaw drops when Virgil takes a shot at the Doctorate, who kicks him in the stomach, sending Virgil flying into a wall.

Adam's forehead is screwed up, veins popping on the surface of his skin, eyes narrowed. When Nolan goes for him again, the Doctorate can't hide the befuddled look on his face.

He . . . he can't control them. Just like he couldn't break our bond or affect it. The Doctorate ability keeps coming back to bond manipulation. Forging and breaking them or temporarily taking advantage of them.

What if that's really what Adam does when he uses Virgil's ability? He temporarily adds himself to our bond. Meaning that to control the bond, he would have to not only add himself but also supersede both my and Nolan's control. Not only is that two against one, but our bonds are so tangled together that it's probably impossible for him to wrest control from either of us, allowing Virgil to keep a hold of himself.

Something that clearly both Virgil and Nolan have realized, at least to some extent.

It isn't just me in this fight. It's the three of us.

Adam turns and punches Nolan on his maw, sending him flailing to the left where he crashes into Virgil. I move to strike, blade poised, and Adam stops me with one hand on my wrist. His grip is iron, rooting me in place.

"Listen to me," he says. "Everything I have done has been to protect you and Jules. Has been to right my dad's wrongs."

"The dad who you had Virgil's parents try to kill?"

He balks. "I had nothing to do with that!"

"They met with you in secret the day it all went down. You were there when they drugged their partners, holding Virgil for ransom!"

"That's not what happened!" he shouts back. "I'm sorry to say it, but they'd gone insane. The things they were saying . . ."

Virgil roars, and the walls and floors shake. Adam tosses me away to slam his hands over his ears. Wait, he can use our abilities, but he isn't immune to them like we are. Of course, because our bond is what makes us immune, and according to my theory, he's only temporarily tapping into it from moment to moment.

"August, please!" Adam says, pulling his hands away. "You need to believe me. I'm trying to help you!"

"Tell me one thing to change my mind. One thing!"

Adam clutches at his shirt like he's in physical pain. He shakes his head. "Not like this. Not while you're thinking the worst of me. I made that mistake once already with Annie."

"Fine," I say, raising the Osseous again. "Then take it to your grave."

CHAPTER FIFTY-SEVEN

Riley

Howls and screams are the music of the halls. Sweat slips down my back, and I roll my shoulders, tightening my grip on the scythe. Beside me, Corey flexes her own shaking fingers. I stare down the hall at her brother. The version of himself that snapped off and ate her left leg. The same leg that trembles now, from the knee up, while the metal is rooted to the ground from the knee down.

Corey was right after all. We should have gone back to the boat and swapped for her taekwondo leg. But I wasn't expecting us to be fighting a Monster to keep it away from August. I thought we would deliver the Osseous and get out of here.

Ellis snarls, baring the rows of razor-sharp teeth, the eyes on his body whirling in a way that eyeballs shouldn't, claws digging into the hardwood. When he leaps at us, he disappears in a puff of black smoke, and only Corey shoving me to the side saves me from his teeth.

We tumble and skid on the floor, and I have to help tug Corey

up from the ground as her bladed leg slips beneath her. "How did you know?" I gasp.

She says, "He usually appears wherever you might be vulnerable. Behind or— *Move!*" I dive left while Corey goes right, just missing Ellis again. Corey is breathing hard, and I know it's not only the physical exertion. "Your left!"

I rear back and flip the scythe, swinging up. Ellis howls and disappears again, materializing this time behind Corey, but she's ready, already turning, and kicks him with her prosthetic leg, landing with a bounce.

But Ellis is apparently prepared for the landing, reappearing too fast, jaws open around Corey's right leg. I whip the scythe through the air, hurtling it toward him, but it's taking too long. *It's not going to make it in time!*

Corey tucks her leg up and flips backward, and Ellis's jaw closes around nothing but air.

Ellis bares his teeth and makes a second attempt at Corey, who is wincing, reaching for her left leg. I raise my arm, calling the scythe, making sure Ellis is in its path back to me, forcing him to disappear to get out of the way. "What's wrong?" I shout to Corey.

"Landed weird, it's fine." But it's clearly not fine, because she's still wincing. "Behind you!"

I was too busy worrying about Corey to pay attention. I swing around, and Ellis appears, only to disappear again as a dagger comes toward him. I follow the trajectory to see Barbie in a torn pink party dress, blood on her temple. Not to mention the crimson soaking through her stomach. Swaying on the spot, the girl looks like she's two seconds away from collapsing. She grips the rope connected to the dagger, both weapons seemingly made out of smoke.

"Your wounds . . . ," Corey says, staring at the girl's torso.

Barbie shrugs. "Yeah, thank you very much, August." She turns on her heel and swings her dagger, stabbing one of the eyes in Ellis's side. He hisses again and disappears. "You know, when you're on the other side, I can appreciate how annoying this ability is."

"We can't keep going like this," I say. "We need a plan to incapacitate him." I grit my teeth. If I had the chain, I could bind him with the links and force him to revert.

"Better think of something quick," Barbie says, jerking her head down the hall. "'Cause we've got company."

A massive dog bursts through the wall of a nearby room, and from the wreckage, Margot steps, her hands shaking, bloody and raw, flames leaping off the skin.

"I have a plan," Corey shouts. "If Ellis and Isaac collide with enough force, they'll knock each other out." Margot turns toward Corey from down the hall. She must have heard her. "We can bait—"

A roar rips through the mansion, shaking the walls and floors.

Ellis reappears but doesn't attack, shaking his head from side to side instead. I stare down the hallway, and Isaac is doing the same thing.

"What's happening?" I ask.

Corey blinks at me. "I . . . I don't know. That must have been August and Virgil. Only they roar like that, but . . ." Her eyes widen. "August said when Adam staged that attack on himself, the control he had slipped for a bit. She thought it was because the roar distracted him, but what if the roar itself affected his control?"

"Move!" Barbie screams.

Everything happens as if in slow motion. I watch Ellis reappear, claws out, and Corey turns, but she's going too slow. I remember

what she said when she told August and Virgil to go. That she would be okay. "Riley is here," she said.

Gold flashes behind my eyes, and my body moves in a way that it shouldn't. Faster than anything should move. I'm shaking and gasping by the time I've realized what's happened, Corey cradled in my arms, the scythe still gripped in my right hand.

Corey stares at me, wide-eyed, but we don't have time, because Ellis is recovering. She gets to her feet with a wince but sprints down the hall. "We need to make them collide! Now!"

I rush to follow her, and after a moment of hesitation, Barbie comes along. From the other side of the hall, Margot sprints toward us, all of us running as fast as we can at each other.

"Don't stop!" Corey screams, as we close in on each other.

The Monster I now know is Isaac is bounding behind his sister, teeth bared like a hell hound. He leaps into the air, determined to crush Margot beneath his paws.

At the same time, a bit of black smoke appears in the air.

Margot ducks as I roll off to the side, while Barbie and Corey run off the edges. In the middle of us, there's a massive *thunk* as Isaac and Ellis smash into each other in midair. The two of them fall onto the ground. Isaac is out, but Ellis is still moving.

Corey leaps into action, swinging her left leg with a scream and kicking Ellis's muzzle so hard that his entire head snaps to the side. Every eye on his body finally slides shut. She drops to her knees, gasping. I go to her, falling beside her and tugging her close to my body. "You did it," I whisper against her neck. "You did it."

"Well, that was horrible," Barbie says, leaning against a nearby wall and sliding down it.

Margot jerks her head up. "It's about to get worse."

“What?” I ask. I don’t have the sort of hearing they do.

“I hear boats and helicopters,” Margot says. “The senior Masters are here.”

“Isn’t that a good thing?”

Corey shakes her head. “No. They won’t let uncontrolled Monsters roam free. They’ll kill them.”

“But Adam’s the one controlling them!”

“They don’t know that, and they’re not likely to believe us.” Corey bites her lip. “Unless August, Virgil, and Nolan can stop him.”

Margot’s hands spark with flame again, and she grits her teeth. Her hands are raw, burned and pink in spots. “They’re not killing my brother,” she snarls. “We won their games. Again, and again, they made him earn the right to live, and he has. So if I have to burn myself alive to protect him, I will.”

Corey peels herself away from me, standing next to Margot, in front of Isaac and Ellis. Even Barbie forces herself to her feet to plant herself beside them.

I swallow and stand with them.

In no universe would I ever have expected to be here, with a bunch of Learners, prepared to protect Monsters.

I can picture Sammie grinning at the sight.

I flex my hands around the scythe. August is a lot of things—a bit of a mess, rude as hell, impulsive, bloodthirsty. All the things Malachi called me and then some. Which is how I know she’s a girl who gets shit done. She understands the consequences of failing to stop Adam in time more than anyone.

She’ll do it. I have to believe that.

CHAPTER FIFTY-EIGHT

I don't need the perking of both Nolan's and Virgil's ears to know the senior Masters are closing in. I lick my lips and wipe sweat from my brow. Right now, my friends are fighting. Some of them are Monsters, murdering people they love because a man wants power. I could stop it right here and now if I were strong enough.

My chest heaves, and tears prick at my eyes. Every time I think I'm stronger, I find myself here, on the edge of a loss. It's like staring at the door, waiting for Mom to come home, but she doesn't. She never will.

I squeeze my eyes shut, seeing her flying off the cliff while I kneel. Failing again.

I open my eyes and rush at Adam, and he blows fog in my face, throwing me off-balance before grabbing my arm and flinging me against the wall. I slide down and try to get my bearings as Virgil and Nolan attack him in combo, only to be evaded time and time again. But he can't control them. The single weakness every Monster

has against the Doctorate, but we don't. And it still doesn't matter.

When the senior Masters get here, they'll protect Adam and slaughter the out-of-control Monsters. Jules, and Isaac, and Ellis, and Frankie, and Mitch. I can't let that happen.

"Stop this," Adam says. "You aren't a killer." He holds out his hand. "Give me the knife." His eyes aren't on me, but the blade. "If you give me the weapon, I'll make an excuse for the others. None of you will be punished."

"Before, you acted like you didn't know what it was," I say. "If you're so innocent, why would you want a weapon specifically designed to kill Doctorates?"

Adam laughs. "Do I need an excuse to want to secure something that could kill me?"

"You do when it's what Bernie and his son died for."

He shakes his head. "That wasn't me."

"Sure. Made James look like the bad guy. I thought it was interesting that Carrigan seemed pissed when you won, but it makes sense now. He knew it was you. That was why he went into hiding the instant James was murdered." I jerk my head toward Carrigan's body. "I see that you found him." Or rather, Carrigan had found Adam. I have no idea why he risked coming out here.

"I didn't want to do that to Carrigan! He was trying to kill me! I don't know how I ended up enemy number one—but wait, I do." He laughs again, on the edge of hysterical. "I became the Doctorate. August, please, just give me the knife." I grip it tighter, and his smile fades. "Don't make me take it from you."

Virgil snarls, and my lip curls. I say, "You think you can? Come and get it."

Adam's face contorts for a moment before he wrestles it back

under control. Yes, he's always had that rage simmering under the surface. I felt it when he talked about Henry and his dad. Henry was the son Cyrus wanted, but Adam was the one he got. "Fine."

He moves fast enough that only Nolan snapping his jaws at the space in front of me saves me. I flip backward, jumping out of the way, and rip a spike from my wrist, flinging it at Adam. His cheek heals as the blade is slicing through skin.

I'm starting to understand why Barbie hates regeneration so much.

Adam grips my arm, and I duck my head and sink my teeth into his hand. The monster snarls in triumph in my mind. He shouts and backhands me, sending me flying across the room. I skid on the floor and lick the blood off my lips.

Shaking his hand, Adam swears as the wound heals. This is a man who has never had to fight. Not really. He's the puppet master, moving people and Monsters as he likes while he remains in the shadows. Pain is new to him. I don't think he likes it very much.

"Fine, you want the villain? I'll give you the villain," Adam snarls. "At the end, you'll wish you'd just had a nice chat with the other guy."

In an instant, fog descends. I brace for the attack, turning, expecting him to come from behind me—instead, spikes rain down from above. Virgil and Nolan howl and I scream as metal shards rip into my arms and legs. I finally get the wherewithal to use spikes on my arms to block them. But I'm too busy defending my head to keep from being slammed in the stomach.

I'm gasping, sliding down a wall, bleeding. Trying to heal.

I squint and spot Nolan on his side. Not moving. Not healing, either. Virgil is still on his feet but swaying and struggling. Which is likely why healing isn't working as well.

The fog dissipates, and the shadow Monster walks toward me. Only it's Adam. It's a man, splashed in my blood. I croak, trying to make my body move, but I'm in so much pain.

Adam crouches in front of me, and I do everything in my power to hold onto the Osseous, keeping my eyes over his shoulder on Virgil. Virgil can't read me like he can with Corey—but I will him to try. To understand what I'm communicating.

Adam begins to pry my fingers from the blade, but I'm not making it easy for him.

I widen my eyes.

Please.

Please understand.

Virgil shakes his head.

I widen my eyes more.

Do it. Fucking do it!

Spikes fly in our direction, faster than Adam can prepare for, given that he's fighting to get the dagger from me. They rip through both our bodies, pinning Adam to me and me to the wall. He chokes, blood spurting from his lips and onto me. I smile at him.

He looks down at his chest, where the Osseous has plunged in. The blade pulses in my hands, rhythmic, like a heart.

Adam looks at me with a weary smile. "I was trying to save Annie that night. But I was too late." He gazes at the blade in his chest. "I stopped looking for that a long time ago. I didn't recognize it at first. Didn't know it would be a knife." He stops to take several breaths. "I gave those journals to Pattie because I believed in her. She couldn't . . . she couldn't tell anyone without revealing how she knew me. Dad . . . he would have killed her if he knew she was a spy." His eyes start to get glassy. "I . . . forgive you," he chokes out. "And . . .

I'm sorry. So . . . sorry." He tries to reach for something, and I tense. "Right . . . pocket."

Adam is torn away from me, and I gasp. It's Virgil, standing on shaky legs. He comes over and gathers me in his arms, pulling me close. "You have to heal, August," he says, eyes watery. "You can do it."

My vision is blurry, and I'm struggling to take in everything that Adam said to me. His chest is moving slower now. I look at my stomach, where the wound is closing, but not for Adam. Even his hand—the wound that was healing before has halted now.

The Osseous.

That's the power of it.

A God killer, because it has the power to make a God mortal.

"What's in his right pocket?" I wheeze.

Virgil sets me down and reaches into Adam's pocket. It's a paper. He flips it over and goes perfectly still.

"Virgil?" I ask.

He turns back to me. With shaking hands, he gives me the picture. It's the one of Pattie and that baby. I flip it over. On the back, Adam has written, *Me and Mom.*

No. That's not right. "You weren't born in 1981," I say.

Adam smiles, his lips coated in blood. "Dad . . . kept secret . . . changed birth date . . . I . . . just wanted . . . to . . . know . . . you . . . protect you . . . from . . . all this . . . just . . ." His mouth goes slack, and his already cloudy eyes fade.

Adam Shaw, the seventh Doctorate, dies.

By my hand.

A wisp of black smoke explodes, enveloping Carrigan. Familiar black smoke. By the time another plume of it appears around Adam, I already know I'm too late. "No!" I cry, moving to grasp Adam, but

my body isn't cooperating. I'm full of holes, still healing, and I'm so tired.

Then the smoke is gone, and so are they.

Adam, Carrigan, and the Osseous are gone.

Virgil says, "That was Ellis—"

"I know," I say. "I fucking know."

Adam was dead, but I never checked to see if Carrigan was. But Ellis . . . Ellis is part of the Scientist faction. This entire time, he could have used any opportunity while in Kingston to spy on us. To exploit Corey's connection to us. All that evidence we kept finding that made Adam look guilty—Ellis could have gotten into locked rooms and planted it. I was right the first time! Carrigan set us up, and I fell for it.

I killed his brother for him.

Adam.

My *uncle.*

I hunch over and scream. Glass shatters, walls shake, the floor rumbles, and none of it matters.

I've ruined everything.

Henry doesn't look at us as he speaks. He keeps his back to me, Nolan, and Virgil. The senior Masters arrived, but it's too late. The Monsters once again have their faculties and aren't running around killing people. I don't know how the partial breaks in their bonds were fixed—if Adam somehow managed to do it before he died, or if Carrigan repaired them. Though I have no idea why Carrigan would do that.

Henry found us right away and brought us into a room to hear the whole story. Laira must be here too, but we haven't seen her.

After I finished explaining what happened, Henry turned his back on us, and that's how he stays now.

"You're certain he was dead?" Henry says, his voice little more than a whisper.

"Yes," I reply.

He blows out a shaky breath. "I cannot trust you."

"Henry—" Virgil says, stepping forward.

Henry rounds on him, tears in his eyes. "I have done everything for you! EVERYTHING! I stopped them from killing you. I found you a place to live. I supported you. I BELIEVED IN YOU. Believed you could be more than a mindless killing machine, and now here you have proven me wrong."

Virgil falls to his knees.

I come forward and touch his shoulder, but he shrugs me off.

I pull my hand back and swallow.

Henry shakes his head. "You have done the exact same thing as your parents, except worse, because you have succeeded."

Virgil hunches over on himself, shaking.

Nolan, meanwhile, looks empty, like a husk. Staring at nothing and no one. Like he's not here at all.

"Did you know?" I ask Henry. "Did you know he was my uncle?"

The man glares at me. "No. He kept that to himself. I assume to protect you from becoming a target. You and your brother. Not to mention that exposing your familial connection would have been a clear show of nepotism. It would have created issues for you. He must have gone to Toronto to try to contact your mother, and in the process, unfortunately, gave away her whereabouts to whomever Carrigan had following her."

No. That was wrong, wasn't it? Adam said he went to protect Mom. As if he already knew she was in danger.

The spit is thick sliding down my throat. "What now?"

"Now the three of you can get out of my sight. Consider your membership to the Mastery group rescinded. Just keep quiet and out of the way until I can fix this."

"Fix it?" Virgil croaks.

"Yes," Henry snarls. "I'm going to craft a story about what happened here. One in which Carrigan found a weapon that he stole from QBSS and used it to murder his brother. Where the three of you attacked him and tried to protect the Doctorate. You failed. Carrigan escaped, injured. Until then, you will say nothing of what happened to anyone."

"You're . . . you're saving us?" Virgil asks, peering up at his mentor, his face wet with tears.

"I'm not doing it for you. I'm doing it because you're useful. You and Nolan are the only Monsters on record to have ever been unaffected by the Doctorate. So yes, I am saving you, and you will repay me for this."

I step forward. "It's not his fault—"

"*It is!*" Henry roars. "It is his fault for tying himself to you. You're a poison that tastes sweet. Perhaps Carrigan deceived you, but you deceived Virgil. I have done everything to help you, and you spit on my offerings again and again." He jerks his head to the door. "Dismissed."

Virgil peels himself off the ground and leaves first, and I rush out after him. "Virgil!"

"Don't," he says, spinning around. "Stay away from me. Just . . . stay the fuck away from me."

I stand there while Virgil leaves.

Nolan wraps his arms around me from behind, pulling me to his chest, setting his chin on the top of my head. "It was never going to work with you two. You're like me. We break things. We destroy.

We mess up even when we don't mean to. That's all we can do."

He's right, of course. I knew that. I let Virgil trick me into thinking I could be better.

I slouch into Nolan's embrace.

After all, this is where I belong.

I think of that bird. That bird with its ugly songs and its injury. The one who Virgil wanted to get to know. Who he felt deserved to be loved as it was. And so the bird never changed. She pecked and pecked and pecked, digging up pieces of his flesh. Eventually, he realized that all the bird could ever do was sing ugly songs and ruin things.

Something the bird had known all along.

CHAPTER FIFTY-NINE

Riley

The ballroom is especially beautiful when it's on full display like this. The sleek floors are now crowded with people dancing to the music pumping through the speakers. There are various tables set up with fresh linens and perfect centerpieces, filled not only with alumni but also artifact-wielding members of QBSS and their families.

This is a celebration of the continued success of our organization and a special occasion meant to usher in the new student council. I shouldn't be here. But Malachi insisted that I come, and I owe him that, at the very least.

Grandma nudges me in the shoulder. We've been sitting at one of the tables, watching my parents cut it up on the dance floor. Both of them are drinking too much. I assume because the instant we walked in the door, everyone had something to say about me.

"Fix your face," Grandma says. I present a serene smile for her,

which she beams at, then let it drop. "Riley Jane," she chides with a smile.

I wind my arm around hers and press my head to her shoulder. I swallow, the saliva thick in my mouth. "What would you think if I said I had a girlfriend?" My hand trembles on hers, and I try to make it still.

She smooths her fingers over mine. "Is she Black?"

"No."

"Is she pretty?"

"Yes."

Grandma shrugs. "Good enough for me." She presses a kiss to the top of my head. "You have always been good enough for me, Riley Jane. I only hoped that one day you'd be good enough for yourself, too."

"I am," I say.

The music cuts out, and the elder council assembles themselves on the dais. "Here we go," Grandma mutters.

Dr. Michaels leans against the microphone. "If everyone could please take their seats. I would like to invite the student council to come up to the front of the room. We're ready to announce the new student council for the 2025 to 2026 school year."

My parents return to their seats beside me. Mom rearranges my twists like they were out of place. I know she can't stand the look. She would prefer braids with perfect parts, not my free parted passion twists with gold accessories. I'm tempted to do a short cut. I always wanted to.

Malachi, Jackson, Darius, and Inaya go to the front of the room, where Malachi is given a microphone.

He says, "Thank you all for being here with us tonight. To start

things off, I would like to announce the new secretary. Please join me in applauding Mr. Victor Morby."

We clap as a slim freshman boy with a clean-shaven head and light brown skin comes to the front of the room. He stands in front of Darius, who unclips his necklace and attaches it to the boy's neck.

From there, Darius is announced as being promoted to social chair while Jackson continues on to the role of treasurer. Jackson should be VP. I mean, I wouldn't want Darius to handle money either, but then they should have found someone who would be a better fit.

Malachi says, "Inaya Williams will be continuing as the vice president." I stiffen in my seat. What is he talking about? "I would like to invite Riley Townsend to the front."

All heads in the room turn to me.

"Riley," Dad hisses, and I shoot to my feet.

As I approach the dais, Ms. Howard throws me the most stank-eyed look I've ever seen, before directing the same ire at her nephew.

Dr. Michaels clears his throat. "Mr. Jones, can you please explain what exactly you are doing?"

Malachi puts his hand on my shoulder. "Riley is an asset that our society cannot stand to lose. While some may not agree with her presence on the Doctorate's island, I admire that she took it upon herself to chase down the thief and try to reacquire our artifact, even if she failed to do so. I believed in this mission, which is why I gave her the sickle. She is one of the few members of this entire organization who has fought Monsters, and she has a positive relationship with the Learners."

"Positive relationship?" Ms. Howard drawls. "With the girl who was kicked out of Henry Scott's Mastery group?"

Grandma looks like she's about to throw hands, only kept in place by Dad begging her to stay out of it.

I say, "August is taking a brief hiatus from the group to focus on her studies. I will also note that she came in second in the Monster's Ball, has not one but two Monster partners, and also defended the Doctorate against Carrigan Shaw." August is sticking to this story despite how easily I could call bullshit on it. Though it suits me too, to push the narrative that Carrigan stole the Osseous, and technically, he did. He disappeared with it, ensuring that no one could steal his ability the way his brother's was.

Disappeared with Ellis, of all people, which Corey isn't taking well. I refuse to believe that all his interactions with her were manipulation. I'm not that bad a judge of character, and neither is she. Still, it doesn't look good. They can't find Barbie, either.

Meanwhile August has thrown herself into her studies with a fervor she's never shown before. Finished all her exams and is even getting a head start on next semester. As far as I know, she hasn't spoken to Virgil, who's spent most of his time in McIntosh Castle with Corey, pretending that August doesn't exist. And Nolan has sequestered himself on the Murphy compound. The three of them forming their own little islands away from one another.

It's a shit show that I'm more than happy to conceal from QBSS.

Malachi says, "Considering this, I will be naming Riley as my successor."

I almost choke on my spit but somehow manage to keep it together.

Ms. Howard laughs. "Come on, boy, be serious."

"Did he stutter?!" Grandma hollers from across the room, standing finally. My parents cringe, trying to make her sit.

"I *am* serious," Malachi says. "She can wield the sickle better than I can, and she can call on the scythe. We cannot afford to go forward without a president fit for what may very well become war times. The Learners will hold their competition to name a Master for their new Doctorate, but whoever they choose will not have the bloodline power. Carrigan will no doubt rise to claim it eventually. There will be a power struggle, and our people will need protection. I'm graduating. Riley will still be here."

Ms. Howard scoffs and looks around, but the other elder council members are staring at Malachi.

"He's right," Ms. Nelson says. "We need a student council with combat experience. If anything, we need to be able to recruit and train more artifact-wielding members. Carrigan has already stolen an important artifact from us. He may come for the rest to wage his war."

Dr. Michaels nods. "Then let's hold a vote—"

"With all due respect, sir," Malachi says, "this isn't for you to decide. According to the handbook, it was one thing to remove Riley when you felt she was not fit, but the appointment of the president title has always been the privilege of the active students. The elders have been overstepping, and it stops now. The decision will be made by the student council."

"I beg your pardon?"

"It is in the handbook. Section six, article seven. Decisions regarding the appointment of titles to the student council are made by the active students and their council. The elder council may advise, but they cannot enforce."

Dr. Michaels looks at Ms. Nelson, who's flipping through the handbook. She bites her lip and nods. "He's right."

"When I was a student—" Dr. Michaels starts.

"It was wrong when they did it too," Ms. Nelson says, closing the book. She nods to Malachi. "Take your vote, then."

"It must be unanimous," Malachi says, turning to the four people behind him. Inaya, Darius, Jackson, and Victor. I swallow. "Raise your hands if you agree to make Riley Townsend the president."

Jackson raises his hand immediately. Darius follows right after. Victor does too, looking nervous, I assume afraid to rock the boat. I look at Inaya. She's supposed to be president. This is her only chance. She'll be graduating next year. She won't get another shot at the title. I know Malachi must have told them he was going to do this, but is she seriously going along with it?

She stares at me for a long moment.

Then she raises her hand.

Grandma is the first person to start clapping, and the entire room follows suit. Mom is actually crying. I can't believe her. But then, I can. Neither Dad nor Grandma managed to be chosen as president. And here I am, doing it twice.

Malachi removes the sickle from his neck and settles it on mine.

Dr. Michaels motions for the music to come back on, and everyone returns to the celebration.

"Don't fuck it up," Inaya says, turning on her heel. "If you do, I'll take the title and the sickle." She leaves without waiting for a response, and Darius gives me a smile before he follows after her. Victor mumbles something about it being nice to meet me formally and scurries off too.

I reach for Jackson, pulling him into a hug. "Thank you," I whisper.

He laughs. "I was always going to vote for you."

"No . . . for . . . You were right. About Sammie. About Corey."

Jackson holds me tighter. "You were right about me. I never believed I was good enough for you, and it became a self-fulfilling prophecy." He steps back and smiles. "This is a Riley who I never got to know. I'm excited to meet her."

He nods to Malachi and goes over to his parents, who no doubt will be asking if we're getting back together.

Malachi says, "I meant what I said. I trust you to make this society better than what it was before. I said you weren't fit to be president, and I believe that's exactly why we need you. Because you don't fit. You're a leader, Riley. An innovator. I look forward to seeing the change you bring to QBSS."

I grip the sickle, holding it tight.

Being president this time around feels different. Instead of trying to be what they want, I'm finally ready to be who I am.

It's perfect timing, because Malachi is right. There's something brewing on the horizon, and I need to be ready to meet it.

EPILOGUE

Her prison cell is perhaps the most comfortable one that has ever existed. She has a wall-mounted flat-screen TV with all the streaming services, a king-sized bed with Egyptian cotton sheets, a sectional couch big enough to take naps on, a kitchenette, and dozens of books to keep her busy. Though none of that takes away from the reality that it is, in fact, a prison cell.

Or she supposes, more specifically, it's a vault. It's *the* vault, actually.

Impenetrable steel lined with the dust and bones of countless people who bear the moniker of Patient Zero. After all, Dr. Weiss could never settle for just one. Not once he knew what the body of Francis McLaughlin could do. He needed more. And with them, he built himself this fortress that no Monster can penetrate. The perfect panic room.

Assuming you make it there in time.

She heard the growls and the shaking of the walls and floors. Everything was too thick to make out any words, but something happened earlier this week. Something significant.

The clicking sound outside of the room makes her whip around, dropping the book she was reading on the table.

The vault is a two-room operation. There's the outer room that the entry door leads into with all the historical documents and objects, and then there's this inner room, where she resides. A panic room within a panic room.

The TV screen flashes to life, and Carrigan's face appears. She rears back from it. He looks like shit. His eyes are swollen and his face bloodied. She walks to the microphone on the coffee table, lifting it to her lips. "What happened?"

"Adam is dead," he says, voice deadpan.

She's still for a moment before a smile slides across her lips. "Who did it?"

"August."

She hadn't wanted that for her. She had hoped that Jules would take care of it, though she hadn't wanted that for him, either. Hadn't wanted this for either of her children. She would have done it herself, but Adam would have killed her on sight. It was already a miracle that she survived. And it cost them. She brushes the spot on her arm. The place where Carrigan had a Monster bite her to save her life. She couldn't have survived her wounds as a human, but as a Monster, she could make it. And she had.

But in exchange, Carrigan's abilities had waned. Doctorates weren't meant to be permanently bonded. Now, more than ever, Annie was in danger. Any Doctorate could control her in her Monster form. She learned firsthand how well Monsters could be

used when Martin and Faith were manipulated. She had to stay hidden.

Annie supposes she shouldn't be surprised that August was the one in the end. She's a winner. Annie knew that from the first day she put a blade in August's hand. "Then it's over. We won. We're safe." She can leave and be with her family again. She doesn't have to keep hiding. Carrigan will be the Doctorate. Everything will be fine now.

"They're suspending the Bachelor candidacy to hold the Doctorate's Challenge in the fall and choose a senior Master to lead. I've been branded a traitor. People are assembling teams as we speak. One of them . . . It has to be one of them."

Traitor? No. This was the moment to expose Adam. They had even made sure Ellis planted the evidence August and Virgil needed to discover the truth about their leader. It should have been enough to back Carrigan up when he finally appeared and confronted his brother. *Their* brother, really, though Carrigan hated when she said that. Implied that they were related when they shared no blood. "What are you talking about?!" she asked.

"Annie," Carrigan chokes out. "We were wrong."

"What does that mean? Did you get the weapon? Where is it?"

"Listen to me!" he cries. "Someone else took the Osseous. Ellis got me out, but they—they used his ability, and they took Adam's body and the weapon before we could. Do you understand? There's another Doctorate! It has to be one of the senior Masters, and if they win the Doctorate's Challenge, we're fucked. We were wrong about Adam. Even Bernie didn't think it was him. I could tell from our communications that—"

"Shut up," she says, her voice cold. She doesn't want to hear about the man who made her child suffer. Bernie was supposed to be

their pawn. He wasn't supposed to get Jules mixed up in his shit. He was just supposed to find the weapon for them. Instead, he'd done all this unnecessary crap, and it'd blown up in their faces. Adam became the Doctorate anyway, but finally her half brother was dead, and now Carrigan had not only fumbled taking his title, but he also wanted to say they were wrong?

No. They couldn't be wrong.

Otherwise . . .

No.

"Carrigan," she says. "Let me out."

He stills. "It's not over."

"Let me out."

"I can't. . . . Not until I know it's over. You're still not safe."

"Let me out!" she screams. "This was supposed to be temporary. Let me out of this fucking cage! I want to see my daughter! My son! I want to see my family!"

"I'm sorry . . . ," he says, and the feed cuts out.

Once again, Annie Black is left in her chrome prison. When she screams, no one hears her.

ACKNOWLEDGMENTS

I remember thinking that the middle book of a trilogy would be the most scary and difficult, but *Clash* was the most fun to write. Like enjoying the playground of a world that I already built, and I'm so glad you could join me in it. The second book in three feels so much like a transition—a waypoint that marks the shift between the character you met in the beginning to the one you'll leave at the end. Similarly, I feel like it's been like that for me during the time I spent working on the novel to the moment of writing these acknowledgments. I look forward to the author I'll be able to show you for the finale.

Thank you to my agent, Kristy Hunter, who I can always count on to be in my corner and fight for my work. And thanks to my editor, Sarah McCabe, whose amazing vision and feedback helped make this book such a stellar addition to the series.

I would also love to thank my amazing friends and support system who cheer on my work, comfort me during the lows, and celebrate

with me during the highs: Cassie Spires, Laura Fussell, Kevin Savoie, Lindsay Puckett, Lainey Kress, and Ashley Shuttleworth.

Thank you to Lune Dubé, Kendra Herber, and Dani Moran for their expertise and continued invaluable feedback.

Another thank-you to Tom Roberts, who once again absolutely killed it with the cover illustration, and Greg Stadnyk, whose incredible design has blown me away. I couldn't think of a better companion to the *Mastery* cover.

Thank you as well to the Simon & Schuster US and Canada teams, who do such absolutely amazing work: Anum Shafqat, Maryam Ahmad, Cayley Brightside, Justin Chanda, Karen Wojtyla, Anne Zafian, Jen Strada, Elizabeth Blake-Linn, Chrissy Noh, Caitlin Sweeny, Bezi Yohannes, Perla Gil, Remi Moon, Amelia Johnson, James Akinaka, Saleena Nival, Elizabeth Huang, Trey Glickman, Shannon Pender, Amy Lavigne, Julia Ashley Romero, Lisa Moraleda, Nicole Russo, Christina Pecorale and her sales team, and Michelle Leo and her education/library team.

Last but not least, a huge thank-you to my partner and my favorite beagle co-worker, who are always there to support my art and career.

LISELLE SAMBURY

is a Trinidadian Canadian author and Governor General's Literary Awards finalist. She has a love for stories with dark themes, complicated families, and edges of hope. In her free time, she shares helpful tips for upcoming writers and details of her publishing journey through a YouTube channel dedicated to demystifying the business of being an author.